I0599760

This Side of the Moon

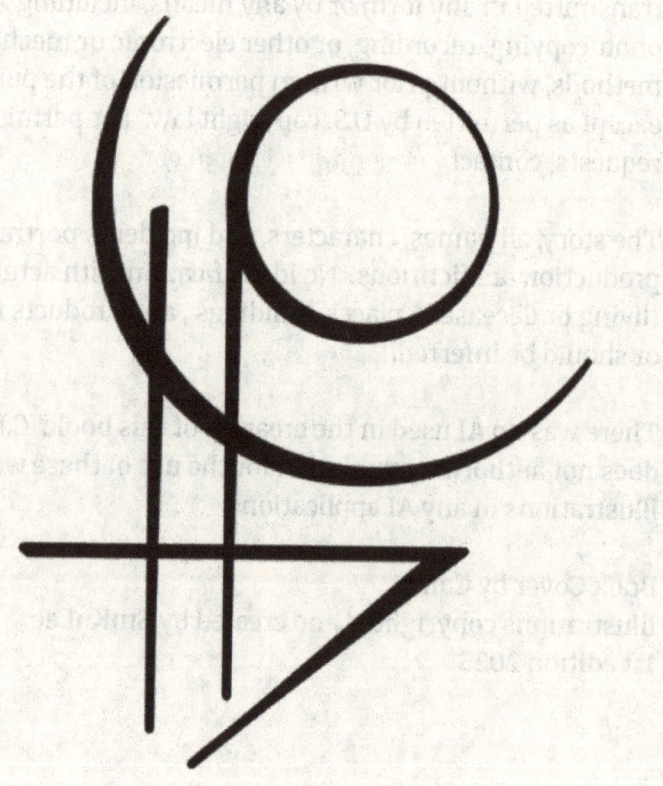

The Gods Series #3

C.J. Phillips

Trigger Warning

Extreme Language
Body Dysmorphia
Childhood Illness
Retelling of Parental Death
So...Much...Girl Drama
Extreme Sexual Situations
BDSM Topics
Light Bondage
Leashes
Men making stupid f**king decisions
Cancer
Light Edging
Orgasm Denial
Sex in Public Locations
Elvis Impersanation
Sibling Rivalries
Light Choking
Masochism
Drug Use
Alcohol use
Anal Sex
Self-loathing
Emotional Damage

If you have ever wanted a whirlwind romance to turn into infatuation....
This one is for you.

Playlist

Contortionist - Arankai
Look To Windward - Sleep Token
You Put a Spell on Me - Austin Giorgio
Provider - Sleep Token
Higher - Sleep Token
Trouble - Camylio
THE GREATEST - Billie Eilish
Say That You Will - Sleep Token
I Told You Things - Gracie Abrams
Everything Changes - Staind
touchin' me - Chandler Leighton
OMENS - The Pretty Wild
Do or Die - Natalie Jane
Euclid - Sleep Token
Past Lives - Borns
The Summoning - Sleep Token
Specter - Bad Omens
Like A God - Lia Marie Johnson
Crazy in Love - Sofia Karlberg
Take Me Back To Eden - Sleep Token
Only Love Can Hurt Like This - Paloma Faith
Missing Limbs - Sleep Token
Pray To Me - DeathbyRomy, Palaye Royale
Damocles - Sleep Token

1

Apollo

Contortionist - Arankai

I guess I just need to learn to accept that I am going to be alone forever. Well, that's not entirely true. I can have my fill of just about anyone that I want, but I am not getting any younger. Everyone around me is getting married and having babies then here I am, 29 years old with nothing or no one to call my own.

I thought for a minute that Simone and I would have something.

Something more than just a fuck about.

But I should have known better. Simone is not going to settle down. At least not anytime soon and definitely not with me. She made that abundantly clear when she blew me off yet again.

Even when I kissed her in the rage room, I knew that it was useless. I just saw her standing there, sweating and panting. There was something in her eyes, something I mistook for want.

But I was wrong, again. There is no point waiting for someone who doesn't want all of you. If they have to sort through the parts they want and the parts they can do without, they aren't for you.

And that is what she does to me, every fucking time. I think things are going well and she slowly starts to remind me of all the parts of myself that she doesn't like.

I am not a risk taker.

I'm not a golden retriever.

1

I don't follow her around, swooning over her every breath. I get it to an extent. She wants somebody that loves every little bit of her to the point of obsession.

But that is not me.

I don't feel comfortable stalking my woman like she is prey on the Serengeti. I don't think I could be like that with anyone actually. Sure, I would accept her for her. But I don't think I could ever fully be what she wants.

She will never accept me for me. Or what I am actually offering her.

And that is fine.

I'll be fine.

I am fine.

I never really allowed myself to truly fall for her. There was always some voice in my head telling me to hold back. Not to let her in fully. But I became infatuated with her so quickly. Or maybe it was with the convenience of her.

Possibly there is some romantic part of me that believed that we were meant to be. Because of the band, because we had known each other for so long.

But very quickly, I learned she only cared about herself, never me, never my pain. I just got caught up in the person I was trying to turn into for her.

But that is not love, that is settling.

Settling for someone who doesn't deserve you or your attention. That is not healthy for either person involved.

I thought that we were growing but I apparently had a blindfold on. Until it disintegrated and I saw her for what she truly is.

Not mine.

Luckily, we have a week in between shows so I can take some time to decompress and just be. That is something I have been seriously lacking. Just some me time. No women, no band, no tour, just me.

I stretch out on the oversized couch in Lily's sitting room at the beach house. I love this fucking house. I love how no one bothers us here. I love that no one knows who we are.

It doesn't hurt that this place is big enough for us all to have our own space but close enough that if we want to rehearse we can. Though right now, no one is thinking about music.

Lily and Gideon are still in full parental mode. Picking out furniture and names to coordinate with colors. Even though they haven't even closed on a house yet. Also, they refuse to even find out if it is a boy or a girl. But they are trying to keep their excitement to themselves for now. Considering what Edge and Susie just went through.

That was fucking rough. Finding out you are pregnant one day then the next being told it wouldn't be viable. I can't imagine the loss that they both feel.

But in a selfish way, I am kinda glad it happened the way it did. They weren't ready for a kid yet.

Edge still has a lot of shit to work out. He has a lot of demons he needs to get a firm grip on before they are in a spot to start a family.

But who am I to judge?

I have never even been in a real relationship. Secondaries don't count.

That was a lifetime ago.

I don't even think I want kids. I mean kids are great but I just can't see myself as a father. I don't think I want to see myself as a father. I am completely content just being Uncle Matthew to all the little brats everyone around me are going to spawn.

I let out another yawn around the quiet room around me before I decide I need a drink.

Yeah, it's 10 in the morning but I don't give a shit.

We have been touring for months already, with 2 more months still to go.

If I don't enjoy the time off, is it even really considered relaxing?

I move to the bar in the living room and pour myself a glass of Dalmore. I take in the rich earthy scents of it, smiling at the bottle in my hand. The fact that Lily can't consume it like water right now means I get to have as much as I want.

Of course, I will have to slip her some cash if I drink too much. Even though I know she wouldn't accept it, I would still try to find a way.

I take a deep drink as I turn and look around the room. Everyone is off doing their own things this morning apparently. I guess lonely day drinking is all that is on my schedule for today. I smile to myself as I take another drink. The doorbell rings loudly through the house and I nervously look around the room.

I turn my body and try to see out the back window in case Lily is on the deck. Seeing no one though, I turn and sit my glass down on the bar then make my way towards the front door. I look out the window to see Lucy standing there rocking back and forth on the balls of her feet.

Smiling, I open the door wide for her, "Lucy! What are you doing here?"

She smiles back at me, small laugh lines coming off her eyes and mouth, "Matthew. Hey! I am sorry to just show up unannounced but I am staying in town between shows. I

4

thought I would just pop by and see how Susie is doing after everything."

I nod my head back at her as I open the door, swinging it wide for her, "Certainly, come on in. I think her and Edge are still upstairs. I can go get them if you want."

She nods her head back to me as she steps into the doorway, bracing her hand on the jam of the door before pointing back towards her rental in the driveway, "That would be great. Hey, my daughter is with me. Is it okay if she comes in too?"

I look around her seeing no one, but this is Lucy. I trust her just as much as I trust the rest of the band. Lucy has been with us since the beginning.

She is family. Blood means nothing.

I have heard her talk about her daughters' many times but I have never actually met them. All I really know is that they are twins, around 22 or 23.

I am actually kinda surprised that they are vacationing together but then I would probably be doing the same thing if my family were close by.

I smile back at her, "Of course it's fine. I will go get them. Just have a seat in the sitting room. I will be back in just a minute." I point towards the living room so she knows where to go.

She grins widely at me as she turns around and starts waving at someone in the car parked in the driveway. I quickly turn and run up the two flights of stairs to the third floor.

I put an ear to the door, just to make sure I am not about to see a lot more of Edge than I want to. I smile to myself when I hear him strumming his acoustic. I gently rap on the door with my knuckles. Not 10 seconds later, I see a smiling Susie opening the door.

I raise a hand and give her a quick chin nod, "Hey Susie. I don't know if this is a good time or not but Lucy is here."

She looks a bit surprised as she pulls the door open a bit further, turning just a bit so Edge can see us from the chair he is sitting in.

Edge looks just as confused, "What is Lucy doing here? Is something wrong? Did something happen?"

I shake my head at them both as I stuff my hands into my jeans pockets. I have never been the best with words. That is 100% Gideon's department.

I shrug my shoulders just a bit, "I think she is here to talk with Susie as well. I think she wants to basically give her condolences about the situation."

I see Susie's eyes get a bit misty before she smiles and nods her head, "Yeah. That is fine. She is so sweet. Give me just a few minutes and we will be down."

I give her another small smile, "We will be in the sitting room. Oh and I think she said her daughter is with her. Not sure which one though."

Edge smiles as he stands up and puts the guitar in its stand. He walks slowly towards the door, placing his hand low on Susie's back, "So we don't know if it's the rebel or the angel? This could get interesting."

I laugh my agreement, "Yeah, I know. I will see you down there."

I turn and start making my way back down the stairs. I round the bottom of the stairs to see Lucy sitting on the couch. There is another person sitting in the arm chair with her back to me. All I can really see is long curly blonde hair.

I smile at Lucy as I make my way back over to the bar, "Would you ladies like a drink? We have the best whisky you could ever dream of drinking. Or I am sure there is some sweet tea or something."

I pick my glass up and take a sip as I hear Lucy, "I will take some sweet tea. I am driving so I really shouldn't drink any whiskey right now."

I nod towards the bar as I sit my glass back down. I turn to move towards the kitchen when I hear another soft spoken voice, "I would like to try the whisky. If it's not too much trouble."

Her voice is almost a whisper. With a hint of rough gravel to it. Nothing like Lucy at all. It is not like any voice I have ever heard before actually.

I continue to smile as I move forward to reach into the cabinet for a tall drinking glass, "Sure thing. Let me just get Lucy her tea." I quickly turn to the refrigerator and open the door to pour some tea into the glass.

I look around the door but the girl has turned and is now looking towards the fireplace. Probably looking at all the artwork Lily has leaned up against the walls.

I shut the refrigerator door and move back towards the couch, "Here you are Miss Lucy." I turn towards her daughter, "I'm sorry, I didn't catch your name."

The girl turns to me, pinning me with big beautiful hazel eyes and a wide smile. She is fucking gorgeous. Lucy has been holding out on me.

I smile back towards Lucy then at her daughter. She stands and reaches a hand out towards me, "I am so sorry. I have forgotten my manners. My name is Hope."

I smile back at her and I take her outstretched hand in both of mine. From just the one touch of her skin, I can feel tremors running through my veins.

I feel my chest start to get tight as thoughts overwhelm my brain. I let my hand linger on hers probably longer than it should, "It is nice to meet you Hope. My name is Matthew."

She nods back at me then her gaze goes to her mother. Her eyes dance from her mother back to me and I can feel an astonished smile creeping up my face. I could listen to this girl talk all day.

7

She has the softest voice I think I have ever heard. It is a far cry from the females that usually surround me. Lily would be the next closest in line for that honor. I let go of Hope's hand reluctantly then move back towards the bar. I grab another glass then pour both of us some Dalmore.

As I hand her a glass, Edge and Susie appear from around the bottom of the stairs. Lucy immediately sits her glass down on the coffee table then moves around the table to hug Susie. I can see a slow tear roll down Susie's face.

I glance at Hope and see she looks almost as uncomfortable as me. Her eyes keep going from her glass to the floor then past me towards the kitchen.

I give her a quick nudge with my elbow and nod towards the kitchen, "Let's step out back. Give them a little bit of privacy."

Hope looks at me gratefully, eyes sparkling as she smiles and nods her head. I turn and move towards the back door. I graciously open it for Hope then give one last look towards the living room before stepping out onto the back porch.

I shut the door behind me, squinting in the sunlight then point towards the patio furniture, "Let's go sit under the umbrella. That sun is scorching today."

Hope follows my hand with her eyes before smiling and moving towards the chairs by the pool. She sits down, smiling out over the property then turning her head towards the ocean.

She takes in a deep breath as if breathing in the sea itself. She lets out a small breath, "Is this your house?"

I shake my head as I sip my whisky, "No. I wish but no. This is Lily's house. She is Gideon's wife."

Hope turns back towards me, bright eyes shining gold in the sun, "I don't think I have met them yet. But they have a beautiful home."

I watch her as she takes the first sip of her drink. Her eyes go wide as she turns towards me pulling the glass from her lips, "Holy crap, I was not expecting that at all! This is so fricken good!"

I laugh back at her and her little southern twang when she speaks, "It really is. And it should be. You wouldn't believe what Lily pays for it."

She looks nervously from me to the glass then back again. I put up one hand, stopping her thoughts right there, "Don't worry about that. I know what you are thinking. Not only will Lily be offended if we don't drink it, she would be even more angry if we offer to pay for what we consume. Trust me, I have tried."

She lets out another small giggle, "Well, if you insist then." She takes another generous drink and I realize I cannot take my eyes off of her.

Hope seriously could be a fucking model or an actress. Every single detail of her face is gorgeous. From her high cheekbones to her button nose. Her complexion is a warm tan like she spends all her time out in the sun.

I watch her pouty lips as the glass is raised back to them again. I clear my throat and quickly look away. I have to look like a fucking creeper right now.

I take a quick drink of my own whiskey as I try to take my mind off of the track it is currently headed down, "So, Hope. What do you do for a living?"

She smiles and turns slightly towards me, "In all honesty, nothing right now. I had thought about going to college but I just couldn't see myself being happy spending any more time in a classroom than I already have.

"My sister and I went to a boarding school in England until we were 18. Then we stayed with some family over there for a few years after. We have only been back in the states for a little over a year now."

I smile widely back at her, turning in my chair a bit, "I am from London. All of us are actually. Except for Lily and Susie.

9

They are from New York. Where abouts in England did you go to school?

Hope grins again as she takes another drink, this one a bit larger than the last. She sits the almost empty glass down on the table in front of us as she shoots me a timid smile, "Small world then. We went to Queenswood in London. That's ironic isn't it?"

I nod back at her as I lean forward and sit my now empty glass on the table beside hers, "That is. That is. So since school is out of the question, what is it you want to be when you grow up?"

Hope tilts her head to the side just a bit before turning and looking out towards the ocean, "I'm not really sure. I mean I would like to maybe, someday, do what my mom does. I absolutely love music. Basically, any type that I can listen to. I have yet to find a genre that I can't connect with. Also, I am jealous of all the travel she gets to do. But I will admit, it makes it hard to have any type of a normal life."

She turns to me, giving me a soft smile, "Which I am sure you know all about."

I nod back at her and give her a sympathetic look, "I guess that is partially my fault. Your mom has been our manager since the very beginning. We would be lost without her though. She is the only one that can seem to keep us all in line."

Hope nods as she smiles back at me. Her eyes connect with mine and I feel my insides start to boil again, "Yeah, that sounds about right. We were 14 when we went to Queenswood. Luckily, we were only there for 4 years.

"Don't get me wrong, it was a wonderful school. It was just hard being away from everything and everyone I had ever known. It was easier for Dai, that is my sister, because she wasn't really attached to anyone in Georgia before we left.

"She has always been more of a free spirit than me. I had tons of friends that I missed like crazy. Still do sometimes."

I nod at her, "Yeah, I get that. I miss my family like mad when we are touring."

A thought instantly flies into my head, "Do you know who we are? The band I mean?"

She shakes her head back towards me, "No. I just know that my mom is your manager. She has always told us she had to sign an NDA or something. She always said it wasn't her business to talk about."

I let out a slow breath and nod back at her.

She leans towards me just a bit, "Is it really that big of a secret though? I mean, I don't really pay attention to social media and I also don't watch a lot of tv.

"Music I know, bands I know but not really by sight. So I have no idea who anyone really is, or what they look like. But I mean if she has to keep it hush hush then it must be a big deal right?"

I smile at her awkwardly, not really knowing what to say. It is not really my place to just word vomit our life story as a band.

But at the same time, I feel like I have taken a decade of this girl's life away. She deserves some type of answer for that. Some reason to understand why her mom had to do what she did.

As I argue with myself internally, Hope smiles and takes her glass back in her hand. She takes another large drink finishing it off.

She waves her hand at me as she sits the glass back down, "Don't worry about it. You don't have to tell me. It is a secret for a reason right?"

I let out a small exhale of relief, "It's not that I don't want to. Truly. But it's kind of a whole band decision kind of thing. We don't really let anyone know who we are. Not voluntarily at least."

She laughs, small and breathy, "I mean are you guys like really well known though? How would people not recognize you out on the streets? It's not like you are Carnal Decay or something right?"

She continues to laugh as I feel the color draining from my face.

Well shit.

I try to laugh along with her but she can apparently read me better than I think. Her eyes go wide, "Shut up! You are not!"

I smile and lean back in the chair, "Well hell. Cat's out of the bag I guess. I trust you will keep our secret though. Your mom will be out of a job if not."

I laugh at her reaction, the way her face lights up and eyes go wide. I watch her mouth as her lips start going a million miles a minute in excitement.

Hope leans forward in her chair and turns to me completely, "Dai is going to lose her mind if she ever finds out! I won't tell her but seriously she loves you guys. I mean I love you guys too but she is 'posters on the wall' kind of loves you guys.

"I swear our dorm was half covered in nothing but Carnal Decay pictures and albums. She even has a stuffed doll of Ares. She slept with it every night for 3 years. Which is just fucking weird considering she is a lesbian. But she did and then she also had this tapestry that..."

Her eyes come back to mine before going wide then she looks down towards the table, "I am so sorry. I ramble when I get nervous or excited. You have to tell me to shut up, I swear."

I smile as I turn my face towards her again, "I am not going to tell you to shut up. I think it's pretty awesome actually. That she was such a fan before we were even really that well known. But what about you? You didn't have any of our posters up?"

I see a streak of crimson fall across both of her cheeks at the same time. I lean forward in my chair again, "You did, didn't you?"

She shakes her head back and forth, "No. No, I didn't have any posters or anything. But I....nevermind. I can't say it."

Fully fucking intrigued now, I scoot literally to the edge of my chair, "Oh, you have to tell me now. I am dying to know!"

She puts her face in her hands while giggling. I reach out and gently take her wrist moving it down towards her legs.

Her eyes lock onto my hand wrapped around her wrist and I swear I hear her breath shudder in her chest. She smiles back towards me as I release her wrist and move my hand back. I feel that weird zap of electricity roll through my veins again.

She watches my arm as I move it back over into my own space, "You can't say anything to him. To anyone in the band, I would be mortified. Seriously, but I kind of had a huge crush on someone in the band. But I never really told anyone.

"I would sit and listen to you guys with her and she would just veg out. Usually she was high, but me, I just always tried to imagine what he looked like. What he was really like. Behind the mask ya know. Like as a normal person."

I can feel my heart trying to pound out of my chest.

Please god, I have never asked you for anything before.

Please let it be me.

To think that this beautiful woman has been dreaming of me, I could die a happy man. I can see her cheeks starting to turn pink again but I just have to know.

I give her a smoldering smile, the one that gets me out of and also into almost anything, "Who was it? Which member?"

She smiles back and parts her lips to answer when the back door opens. We both turn and look to see Lucy standing there waving at us, "Thank you Matthew for keeping Hope company while we talked. That was really great of you."

I see Hope stand so I stand up next to her, still smiling towards Lucy, "Your welcome. You are both welcome to stay for a bit if you want. I am sure Gideon and Lily will be down soon. Simone and Mona are in town but should be back soon as well."

Lucy shakes her head at me while motioning Hope back towards her.

I watch Hope step around the table and start walking towards her mother, "No, we have dinner plans but thank you. But there is a street festival going on in town tomorrow. If anyone wants to go, I think we are going after we switch over to our other hotel. We had to change our stay a bit and the hotel I booked couldn't accommodate us."

I don't even think before the words are flying from my mouth, "Why don't you both stay here then? There is plenty of room and I know Lily wouldn't mind at all!"

Hope turns towards me smiling brightly before turning back towards her mother, "That sounds like fun mom. Then you wouldn't be stuck with just me. You would have other people to talk to."

Lucy makes a sarcastic face at her, before turning back to me and smiling, "Ask Lily. If it really is okay, just shoot me a text and we will come back after dinner."

I feel excitement rising up in my chest as the two women start to walk back inside.

I take a step out into the sun, "Hope, you didn't answer my question. Which member?"

She smiles again shyly as she tucks a strand of hair behind her ear, "Apollo. He is the reason I learned how to play the drums."

And with that she is gone and I am left thrumming with emotions and fascination under the hot North Carolina sun.

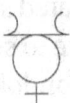

Lily doesn't know it yet but if she doesn't let them stay here I am prepared to go into full toddler mode, flailing arms and screaming. I don't even care that I am a grown ass man. I *will* get my way on this one.

I told myself that I was going to be patient.

I was going to let Lily and Gideon come downstairs and get comfortable before asking them. But with each ticking minute on the clock, my nerves are becoming more and more frayed.

20 minutes later, I am banging on their bedroom door. Gideon answers the door, eyes half open and hair going everywhere.

I smile at him, "Sexy."

He flips me off before turning around, leaving the door open and moving back to the bed to curl back up behind Lily.

Lily opens her eyes and glances at me, "What's up Matthew? Is everything okay?"

I shove my hands back down into my jeans pocket. I know it is my tell that I am nervous but right now I don't care. I have to make this happen. Getting to spend 4 or 5 days with Hope is all I can think about now.

I glance nervously towards Gideon, seeing that he can sense that I am on edge. He leans up onto an elbow, "Seriously. What's going on? Did something happen?"

I shake my head, feeling a blush come over my cheeks.

Fuck, I feel like a damn teenager asking my parents for permission to have a party or something.

This is fucking painful.

I let out another frustrated sigh, here goes nothing, "So, Lucy just stopped by. She came to see Susie, after losing the baby. She wanted to give them her condolences. But I also found out that she is staying in town.

"Apparently, there is something going on with her hotel and she is going to have to switch to another one. I told her she could stay here but she said she would only do it if it was okay with you, Lily."

Lily sits up and leans back into her pillows. She looks to Gideon who shrugs his shoulders and gives her a smile back.

She turns back to me, smiling widely, "Yeah, I am okay with it. I love Lucy. She is always welcome."

I let out a heavy sigh of relief before I grin back at her, "Oh and her daughter Hope is with her so she will need a room too. I will go make sure there are two open rooms. Thanks Lily, you're the best!"

I immediately turn and run for the door.

Right as my hand reaches the handle I hear Lily, "What do you mean her daughter? I didn't even know she had a kid. I don't know Matthew. The house isn't really kid friendly right now. Maybe we shouldn't give her the green light."

I feel my head fall towards my chest. I knew it wasn't going to be that easy.

I give Lily my most charming smile as I turn back around.

I can feel Gideon's eyes boring into the side of my head as I continue to walk back towards Lily with my hands splayed out before me, "She has two daughters, twins actually. Hope is the only one with her right now. And you don't have to worry about child proofing the house, Hope is like in her early to mid 20's."

I look towards Gideon in time to see a devil's grin fall over his face.

Seriously, he looks like a clown about to crawl out of the sewers. He belts out a laugh as he falls onto his back on the mattress.

I roll my eyes at his antics before looking back at Lily who is also smiling widely.

She swings her legs around then slides off the bed, "Well in that case then. Let's go see what rooms are clean."

I let out another held breath as I put my hands in a praying motion, "Thank you so fucking much Lily. Seriously. You have no idea."

She chuckles as she steps around me before turning back towards Gideon, smiling, "Hope must be something. I have never seen Matthew trip over himself before."

Gideon slides off his side of the bed as he makes his way towards us at the door, "Me neither. It's hilarious."

I flip him off quickly, "You know I can hear you right? Just fuck off with that shit, the both of you."

Lily is laughing as she steps out into the hall, "I think we just have two rooms open. The one next to you and the one Susie stayed in last time. I will go check them, make sure they are still clean. Gideon, you wanna come help?"

He continues to grin at me like a jackal again as he steps around me, "Sure thing babe. Matthew, you wanna call Lucy? Let her know she and Hope are both welcome."

I give him a quick salute and a smile as I run back down the stairs and step out onto the porch. I walk over and sit down in one of the white rocking chairs and pull out my phone. I quickly send Lucy a text letting her know that Lily said they are both more than welcome.

I sit my phone down on the table and pull my smokes out of my pocket. I light one and sit back in the chair, slowly rocking as the sun starts to set on the horizon.

When my phone dings a few moments later, I reach for it quickly. Lucy and Hope will be back here in about an hour. I smile to myself again as a car stops in front of the house.

Mona and Simone climb out with a few bags from what looks like a mall trip. Mona stomps up on the porch steps before noticing me sitting at the far end, "Hey. What are you doing out here?"

I smile back at her as I take another drag off my cigarette, "Just chilling. Lucy and her daughter Hope are going to stay with

17

us here for a few days. I am just out here waiting for them in case they need help with their bags or anything."

Mona's eyes light up.

I know how much she loves Lucy.

Simone gives me a touch of a side eye though, "I don't think I have ever met her daughters. You said it's just the one though, Hope?"

I nod back at her as I take another drag, "Yeah, not sure where the other one is. They were here earlier and I offered up this place cause they were having hotel issues. Lily said it was fine so they are coming over after dinner."

Mona squeals obviously excited before running into the house.

Simone gives me another quizzical stare, "What has you acting all chivalrous?"

I know she is probing for information.

She doesn't get to play this game though.

She is the one that called everything off with us. We wanted different things. Yeah the sex was fucking phenomenal but I have a feeling alot of people feel that way about sex with Simone. I never really felt a deeper, more intimate connection with her though.

No matter how hard I tried.

I smile back at her, "Nothing wrong with being a gentleman every now and again. Right?"

She nods her head at me as she looks around and back down the road, like she is expecting Lucy and Hope to just be standing there or something.

She turns back to me, giving me another half smile, "Just be careful. Don't ruin shit with Lucy because you fuck around with her kid."

I instantly get pissed off.

What right does she have to fucking lecture me?

I give her a sarcastic smile back, "Nothing to worry about. Hope is a really nice girl, with a conscience. It's a breath of fresh air compared to my last relationship."

I know it is too much as soon as I say it.

I instantly regret it when I see the look that falls over her face.

She growls back at me, "Fuck you Matthew."

I give her another sarcastic grin, unable to control my own mouth, "You already did that love. Remember? It wasn't enough for you."

She turns from me and stomps inside slamming the door behind her.

I hate that this is where we are now. But I will be damned if she is going to think she can just sit back and talk to me like I am the problem.

Because I am not.

And she fucking knows it.

2
Apollo
Look to Windward - Sleep Token

I don't even bother going back inside. Those walls could not contain the excitement radiating off of me right now anyways.

Not only has this beautiful creature been dreaming about me for years now, I am the reason she learned to play the drums. That is the hottest fucking compliment I think I have ever received in my life.

It doesn't hurt that the only thing she really knows about me is my playing.

I don't sing.

I am not up front.

I mean yeah, sometimes I am up and moving around but that is very rarely. Fuck, most times I am in fucking sweatpants and people don't even realize it.

I smile to myself as I start to realize it was the music, the drums that pulled her towards me. I have never had that one thrown at me before. And the best part is that she doesn't even know she has thrown it at me.

She has no idea who I am.

I could be Ares to her for all she knows.

Two more cigarettes later, I see a little blue Prius pull into the driveway. I smile at them as I pocket my smokes and move to head towards the driveway.

Hope slides out of the passenger seat and gives me another heart melting grin.

I move across the yard quickly, smiling back at her, "Hey! Glad you guys were able to make it back. Pop the boot! I will help you with your bags."

Lucy smiles over at me as she hits a button on her key fob, "Thank you Matthew. Are you sure Lily is fine with us staying here? I don't want to be an imposition."

I wave my hand at her, shrugging her off, "Lucy, you know Lily. If she found out you were in town and *not* staying here, she would have been offended."

She laughs back at me nodding her head as I reach in and start grabbing suitcases. Hope steps up beside me and reaches in for a small carry on bag.

She shoots me a quick smile as she stands back up and looks at her mom, "We will bring this stuff in mom. Go on in, we'll be right behind you."

Lucy nods her head back at her and turns to make her way across the lawn and up the steps. She doesn't even shoot us another look as she makes her way inside.

I reach up and pull the hatch down, noticing a new expression on Hope's face. I pick up the bags and start to take a step, "What is that face about?"

She lets out a laugh and juts one hip out the side, placing her hand on it, "You could have told me you were Apollo."

I smile widely back at her, "Where would be the fun in that?"

Hope smiles at me again as she starts shaking her head. She turns walking ahead of me so I can get a good look at the extremely tight jeans she is wearing. I try to keep my gaze north of the equator but it is fucking rough.

She turns her head over her shoulder, "Ya know, it is just a little bit embarrassing for me. I just rattled on about my daydreaming and stuff. And the whole time it was you."

I laugh out loud as I follow her up the stairs, "There is absolutely nothing to be embarrassed about. I am flattered if anything. I am glad you spent so much time thinking about me."

She turns, smirking at me as I reach the top step beside her. I smile as I lean in close to her ear, "Since I am going to spend so much time thinking about you."

She lets out a shuddered breath as I pull back and look at her rosy cheeks again. I give her another smile as I reach forward and pull the door open for her. She seems to still be nervous but continues through into the foyer of the house.

Lily is standing at the bottom of the stairs with Lucy. When she sees us enter she steps up to Hope, wrapping her in a warm hug, "Welcome Hope! I am so happy that you are both gonna be here with us this week. Your mom is amazing so I know you must be as well!"

I watch the reservation melt off of Hopes' shoulders as she hugs Lily back, "Thank you so much Lily. You have a beautiful home."

Lily pulls back smiling, "Thank you. We like it. This is kinda our hideaway here. No one really knows who we are so it helps. We can just tuck away from the world in here."

Lily turns to me, noticing the luggage in my hands, "There is a bedroom open on the second floor and another on the third floor. You are welcome to both."

I turn to Lucy, as she catches my gaze, "Which one is the quietest? I am kind of a light sleeper."

Nodding back at her, "We can put you on the third floor. Away from the most foot traffic."

She gives me a thumbs up and turns to walk up the stairs. I turn to Hope, smiling again, "That means you are going to be my neighbor."

She gives me a titillating smile back, "Lucky me."

I laugh back at her as I start up the stairs. I sit her suitcase in front of her door then follow Lucy up to the third floor.

I move her towards Susie's old room, "Susie and Edge are right across the hall from you and the bathroom is right down there. You should be comfortable up here."

She nods as she opens the door and rolls her suitcase in. She smiles around the room before turning back towards me. I give her another soft smile as I turn to head back downstairs. She steps closer to the doorway, "Matthew?"

I turn back to her, bracing a hand on either side of the door frame, "Yeah Lucy, what's up?"

Her eyes laser in on me and her gaze turns a bit more feral, "If you hurt my daughter, I swear to god, the police will never find your dick. Because I will cut it off and puree it before I feed it to my huskies."

I feel my eyes go wide with surprise and a small amount of fear.

I don't think she would actually do it but then again judging by the look on her face, maybe she would, "I uh. I mean, yeah, no I won't. Ma'am."

She laughs loudly at me, "Don't you pull that ma'am bull shit with me. I am serious. She likes you. Don't fuck her up. And don't fuck her over."

I nod back at her, giving her a reassuring smile, "I won't. I promise."

She nods back at me before patting me on the shoulder, "Good. Now go away. I am exhausted and you have some flirting to do when you think no one is looking."

I laugh at her as I turn and make my way back down the stairs.

That was unexpected.

I have never heard Lucy talk like that before.

If anything, it is a fucking nice change of pace.

23

Mona nearly runs me over as she races up the stairs to tackle Lucy. I don't know what Mona's infatuation is with her but she has always clung to her like she was her own mother.

I can see that Hope's door is cracked slightly as I walk by. I smile as I gently rap my knuckles on the door and hear her say come in. I slowly push the door open and lean into the door frame.

Hope is rummaging through her open suitcase, looking for god knows what. Her golden hair falling down her back in soft tendrils.

She is not the type of girl I am usually drawn towards. Normally they are a bit darker, sharper, edgier.

But something about Hope has caught my attention, making it extremely hard to write her off.

I smile in her direction, "Getting settled in alright?"

Her head turns towards me, smiling brighter than the sun, "I am. I am just setting out something to wear tomorrow and trying to find my bathing suit, just in case the waves call to me. Do you know if Lily has a board I can borrow?"

I can feel my face fly into a shocked expression, "You know how to surf?"

She laughs back at me, "Don't look so surprised. I *have* been living in California for the last year and a half."

I shake my head at her, "No, that is awesome. I have never tried it myself. And honestly, I have no idea if Lily has a board or not. If I have to guess, I would say no but we can always find you one, maybe at a rental or something."

She nods her head back at me as she pulls a few more garments from her bag, "Yeah, we will see if I even get the time to."

I watch her for a few more moments before I start to feel like a creeper again. I finally go to turn out into the hallway, "Well, I will leave you to it then. I will just see you in a bit, yeah?"

She smiles back at me then shuts her suitcase lid, "I am good for now. Wanna go downstairs and steal some more of Lily's fancy whisky?"

I grin widely back at her, "That is the best idea I have heard all day."

Hope walks over to me quickly, then touches my bicep as she pushes beside me, "Let's do this then."

I smile down at her hand grazing my arm then quickly follow her out into the hall while trying to calm down my racing heart.

This girl is just sweet.

I am not used to that.

I am used to basically women that are firecrackers with short fuses. But there is just something about Hope. It is intoxicating.

Addictive.

I follow closely behind her, taking her scent deep into me. I have no idea what the smell is but it is enchanting all the same. It is sweet and crisp, making me think of fresh pressed linens dipped in orange juice.

She rounds the corner and walks straight over to the bar. I step up beside her smiling, "So how long have you been playing drums?"

She eyes me the entire time I am pouring her a drink, with a devious grin on her face, "For about 4 or 5 years. Trust me I am not great but I think I am okay. Ish."

I laugh back at her as I pour myself another glass as well. I turn to face her as I point towards the couch for us to take a seat, "Well, it takes time. I didn't just wake up one day and start jamming out. I have my setup in the other room, maybe you can play me something while you are here."

Hope gives me a small giggle back, "I don't know about that. And well, I kinda assumed that you have been playing for a long time. I *have* listened to all your songs ya know. How long have you been playing?"

I watch her as she takes a seat closer to the middle of the couch than the arm on the other side of her.

I slide comfortably onto the cushion, realizing now that our thighs are going to be touching, "I have been playing probably close to 20 years actually."

I see the surprise in her eyes before she narrows them at me, "How old are you?"

I pretend to be offended, throwing my hand splayed out on my chest before smiling and leaning back in the seat, "I just turned 29. How about you?"

She grins a bit, before turning back to her drink seemingly shy again, "I will be 23 in a few weeks. I must seem like a toddler to you huh?"

I shake my head back at her, "Not at all. Age is just a number. I don't care if you are 22 or 102. As long as I am not catching charges, then I am cool with it."

She barks out a loud laugh followed quickly by a snort.

I turn my head towards her completely, the grin on my face widening as her cheeks turn a deep crimson and she covers her mouth with her palm. I lean forward, pulling her hand down, "Did you just snort?"

She shakes her head no at me, "Definitely not, you need to get your old man ears checked. You have been listening to your music too loud. I definitely did not snort."

2 hours and 3 more drinks later we decide to make our way down to the beach. The sun has set hours before but neither of us are

ready to call it a night. We haven't left each other's side all night actually.

Hope was able to meet the rest of the crew, which was interesting. Simone seemed to be a bit pissed at me but I don't really care.

She doesn't get to play that game with me.

She didn't want me, so it is not cool for her to be all butt hurt because I moved on.

Mona on the other hand seemed to fall into instant infatuation with Hope. I would say I was worried if Hope hadn't been clinging to my side the entire time.

And also, Mona is already head over heels for the groupie's best friend. I don't think I have anything to really worry about on that front.

I just smiled as she met everyone, letting me lead her from person to person with my hand on her lower back.

Now, we are standing shoulder to shoulder staring out across an endless ocean that is twinkling under the full moon. It feels like the hands on the clock are spinning by way to fucking fast. I want to spend as much time as I can with her.

I smile and turn to her, "So, Hope. Are you dating anyone right now?"

She laughs as she tilts her head to the side, still staring out over the water, "You would think you would have led with that instead of flirting for hours *then* asking."

I laugh back at her as I turn and look back out over the water, "Fair but that wasn't an answer ma'am."

She chuckles again then turns to me, smiling shyly yet again, "I am not seeing anyone right now. My last relationship ended when I came back to the states."

I smile and as I turn back to face the ocean again, "So, what you are telling me is that you like guys from London, eh? Well, isn't that just convenient for me?"

Hope smiles back at me before turning and looking out over the ocean as well, "It really is beautiful out there isn't it?"

I look over at her profile shining in the moonlight and it takes every fiber of my being not to say something fucking corny like 'yes it is' while staring directly at her. I let out a hesitant sigh and turn to look across the waves again.

I can almost hear Simone's voice in my head telling me that this girl is vanilla as fuck.

But I don't care.

I like her, she is a refreshing change.

There aren't any games being played. She has the same interests and she just seems to be real and honest. She hasn't treated me any different since finding out who I am either. That means a hell of a lot to me.

I hear an intake of her breath before she speaks again, "Have you ever wondered just how many dead bodies there are out there under the surface? I mean between ships sinking, downed planes, natural or forced drownings. That number has to be in the 10's of thousands right? If not higher?"

I can feel my face contort as I try to process the question she just asked me.

I turn my head slowly towards her, probably with an insane expression on my face as she looks over and gives a soft laugh, "I'm sorry. My brain sometimes just kicks into overdrive. My ADHD started that whole conversation off with how many boats could we fit into the ocean at the same time? Then 18 questions later it ended on that. I know that probably sounded morbid as fuck."

I laugh out loud at the insanity of what is actually happening.

I cross my arms over my chest, turning to her fully, "So what you are saying is your brain just played a game of telephone and how many dead bodies are in the ocean is what came out?'

28

Hope eyes me quickly then puts her face in her palms, obviously completely mortified. She is laughing but shaking her head back and forth at the same time.

I step up a bit closer, "Are you one of those women that beg for no one to check their google search history?"

Her eyes fly wide as she turns and grips my biceps, "Please god don't do that. I would never be able to face anyone ever again!"

I laugh at her again, realizing just how close we actually are now. I can feel her warmth as I stare down into the ever shifting watercolors in her eyes.

I give her a soft smile as I take one arm and slip it over her shoulders as I turn her back towards the ocean then pull her in close to my side, "Don't worry. Your morbid curiosity is safe with me. As long as you swear you are not a serial killer."

She slaps me in the abdomen as she laughs and puts an arm around my back to lean into me further, "Well, considering I am always trying to nurse some animal or hell even a person back to health I think that means I am not a crazed murderer."

I let out a heavy sigh, "Thank god. It would have sucked trying to cover up your tracks for you. Be an alibi at the drop of a hat."

She turns her face up towards me as she looks me over, "You would do that for me? Try to help me fake my innocence."

I turn my face down to hers, as I watch her lips moving a sudden realization comes crashing down onto me, "Hope, I have a feeling there isn't much of anything I wouldn't do for you. And not gonna lie that kinda scares the shit out of me."

She blinks hard as she leans in further, putting her head on my chest. Not 2 minutes later she moves in front of me, pulling me in close for a hug, "You are not how I thought you would be."

I smile out towards the ocean as I put my cheek on the top of her head, "And how did you think I would be?"

She smiles into my chest before pulling back, "You know, like a rock star. All temper tantrums and alcohol abuse. One night stands and drug paraphernalia."

I laugh loudly as I pull back to look down into her face, "Well, alcohol yes. Cigarettes, yes. Pot, definitely yes. Temper tantrums, I would have to say no. I am probably the calmest one in the band, besides Gideon. That man is chill 98% of the time."

She turns to face me and I feel her hands tighten around my back, "And the one night stands? What about them?"

I look down into her beautiful hazel eyes, "Not recently no. Even before, I was never really a one night stand kind of guy. Don't get me wrong, I greatly enjoy the company of women.

"But I am also a bit of a hermit. I am not big on change either. So if I ever find somebody that can stomach my particular brand of crazy, I will probably lock that down pretty quickly."

Hope smiles up at me deviously while tilting her head a bit to the right, "So in that case then, we probably shouldn't just destroy each other right here on the beach for god and everyone to see. We don't want to break your streak right?"

I see her eyes flare with a heat that instantly starts to make me hard. I feel my eyes grow wider as I try to exhale slowly and calm my racing heart, "Yeah, I think your mom might frown on that."

She nods and looks at my lips before licking her own, "How about a kiss then? Nothing crazy, just one single little solitary kiss."

I slowly slide my hands up from her sides and place one on each cheek. I smile as I lean forward and gently press my lips into hers.

She smells fucking divine.

I still can't put a finger on what the scent is but it rolls off of her like a cool autumn breeze. It is tart but still with a hint of sweetness behind it. I feel her moan into my lips as her hands start to press me closer to her as they roam up my back.

I tilt my head to the side just a bit and part her lips with my tongue, letting it dance across her teeth. I feel her smile into my mouth and I step closer as she wraps her tongue around mine.

I feel her hand bunch into fists on my back, pulling my shirt into her clenched fingers. I continue to explore her mouth as I feel a moan coming out of my own.

I try to gather some self control as I pull back slowly. I look down at her and she is still smiling with her eyes closed. I rub my thumb across her cheek then down across her pouty bottom lip.

She continues smiling with this mesmerized look on her face, "If you are that good of a kisser, I can only imagine how you fuck."

I pull back again, surprised by her candor.

She slowly opens her eyes before blinking back at me, not even beginning to blush, "I bet you are like a feral ass demon in bed aren't you?"

I start blinking repeatedly.

This just went from sweet to triple xxx really fucking fast. I try to compose the shock on my face, "It just depends on the partner I suppose. What about you? Are you just as insane as your thought process?"

She laughs as her hands move under the back of my shirt, her nails running down the now taut skin on my lower back, "You better fucking believe it."

Oh yeah. She is going to destroy me.

I let out another laugh as I pull her closer to me. We stand under the stars for just a bit longer before deciding to call it an evening.

I hold her hand as I walk her to her room, leaning in to give her one more slow kiss before calling it a night.

I pull back from her slowly, reluctantly, "I am right next door if you need anything. Just come on in. You don't even have to knock."

Hope smiles again as she reaches behind her and slowly twists the door knob to open the door, "Ditto."

I watch her door slowly close as I let out another held breath.

This girl is something else.

I think she might actually be crazy.

But I also think I fucking love that about her.

I shake my head slowly as I step down the hallway and open the door to my room. I sneak one last peak at her doorway, hoping to see her there before I turn the knob and head into my own bedroom.

I slowly undress and slide into bed in nothing but my boxer briefs and try to calm my raging thoughts. They are scattered everywhere.

I have to be careful with this girl. Her mom basically runs my entire life. I don't want to fuck up my relationship with my manager by fucking up my relationship with her.

Hope is literally unlike anyone I have ever met before. She has this look of pure innocence but when she is comfortable this whole other side to her comes out.

I completely believe that she could be feral. And the thought of what she would do with all that feralness lights up something deep inside me.

I smile when I hear my door slowly opening a few minutes later. I roll onto my back and sit up, resting my weight on my elbows. I try to let my eyes focus onto the soft light flooding in from the hallway.

I see her approach me then realize quickly, it is not Hope.

I know that smell.

The smell of vanilla and weed.

I lay back down flat as I roll onto my side, putting my back to her, "What do you want, Simone?"

I feel her sit down on the side of the bed as she runs her hand up my arm and then through my hair, "I was just coming in here to see if maybe you wanted to keep each other company tonight."

I sit up quickly, knocking her hand away from me, "I know what you're doing."

She sits back, pretending to look offended, "What do you mean? I am not doing anything."

I shake my head at her, "You said you didn't want me. You didn't want this. Whatever it was. Now that you see that I am interested in someone else, you suddenly find worth in me. I'm sorry Simone but it is too late.

"I gave up on us already. I am not holding out for someone who only wants me when it is convenient for them. You need to go back to your room now. And know that this, us, it won't be happening again. Ever."

I can sense her anger though she doesn't say a word. She instantly gets up and walks out the door, slamming it behind her.

Most likely waking up the entire god damn house.

3

Hope
You Put a Spell on Me - Austin Giorgio

I can feel my heart about to jump out of my chest as I shut the door behind me. I gently run my fingers across my lips, still feeling Matthew there. I can still smell the musk of the earthy scent of his skin in the air around me.

Letting out a soft giggle, I make my way towards my suitcase and pull out a silky short pajama set. I quickly strip down and pull on my shorts then top.

I take a quick glimpse in the mirror, not necessarily liking what I see. I run a hand through my hair, probably my best feature.

My eyes are too wide, too far apart. My nose, though small, has always leaned just a bit to the left. That was a little present Dai left me with when we were 12.

I scan my body, seeing my collarbone jutting out. No matter how much I work out, I cannot seem to put on weight.

I know, I know, first world problems but still.

I wish I could at least fill out a bit. I hate that you can count my ribs just looking at my sides. I glance back up into my eyes, trying to figure out what Matthew even sees in me.

I hear a door slam somewhere close by and I jump unexpectedly.

Loud noises always do that to me.

Growing up in my house, Dai always tried new torture tactics with me. Locking me in the closets and cupboards.

Removing all the light bulbs from my bedroom. Slamming things on the ground close to me, just to watch me jump in fear.

I quickly make my way to the door still breathing heavily and peek out into the hallway. Not seeing anyone there brings out a whole new level of fear.

What in the hell could have made such a loud noise that it would shake the house? Then a new series of dark thoughts start to roll through me.

What if the house is haunted?

What if in the middle of the night some ghost tries to possess me or stand over my bed breathing their sickly death breath on me?

I swear to god, if I feel the breeze of ghostly fingers on my skin I will lose my shit.

I look up and down the hall again as I think about running straight up to my mothers room.

No, Hope.

You are a fucking adult.

You can't run to mommy every single time you get spooked. I look to my left and smile towards Matthews door.

Maybe he would let me cuddle with him so I could actually get some sleep tonight.

Before I lose my nerve, I step over towards his door and raise my hand to knock, quickly remembering he told me to just walk right in. I take a deep breath then turn the knob and slowly start to step into the room.

I can see Matthew laid out on his bed with his back to me. I smile as the light softly rolls over him and I can see all of the tattoos almost covering his entire back.

I take a step in, slowly starting to push the door shut behind me when I hear him, "Simone, I meant it. Leave me alone. I am trying to sleep."

I smile out into the room again, "It's not Simone."

35

He whips around, instantly smiling at me. He sits up quickly, the sheet falling down so I can see his entire abdomen now.

Sweet baby Jesus, I could do laundry on those abs.

I quickly try to avert my eyes so he doesn't think I am perving on him. The heat that instantly rolls over my body is almost embarrassing. But thankfully it is dark so he can't see my skin as it turns red.

I am suddenly more nervous than when I was thinking a ghost was going to try to grope me in my sleep. I look towards the floor awkwardly, "Sorry, I just heard a noise. I wanted to check on you. I will go back to my room now."

I turn to leave but see movement out of the corner of my eye. Matthew quickly stands up and makes his way over to me. God damn this man.

I have never seen so much ink and muscles in my life. I mean he didn't look that built earlier, but Jesus. I don't think he has an ounce of body fat on him. His shoulders are tan and taut. The skin pulling over the muscles I didn't know were hiding under that shirt earlier.

He looks like he works out all the fucking time or something. I mean I know playing the drums non stop has to keep him in shape as well but Jesus this is a bit next level if I am being honest.

He moves with grace, not making a sound. As soon as he stops in front of me, one hand wraps around the back of my neck while the other pushes the door the rest of the way shut.

He smiles down into my eyes as the room falls dark again. I gently place my hands on his chest then look up into his eyes again.

I go up on my tip toes and kiss him. Gently, though I am wanting to do a lot more than that.

Both of his hands wrap around my neck as he pulls me in closer to him. I continue to kiss him with a ferocity that I haven't felt before.

I mean I am not a virgin by any means.

Far from it.

But very rarely have I been this attracted to someone I am touching. Usually, I am just looking for a release. Any dick will do in that situation.

I feel myself pant into his mouth as I try to pull back slowly. My breathing becoming more laboured by the second.

This is a lot.

I don't want him to think I only want him for his body. He is actually a really sweet guy. I honestly assumed all musicians were assholes. That is what you see in the movies and on tv.

I smile up at him, "What was that for?"

He smiles back down at me as he runs his thumbs down my jawline, "Because you made my wish come true. You came in here."

I smile back at him as I lean forward and push my lips into his again. He is completely irresistible. I let my hands roam his muscular sides then up his lean back.

I can feel his muscles tensing under my touch. I can also feel him starting to get hard as he is pushed up fully against me.

I pull away smiling and then raise one eyebrow as I turn my gaze downward, "Seems like someone is trying to say hello."

Matthew chuckles at me, "You have that effect on me. Just feeling you running your fingers down my back is driving me insane."

I bite my lower lip, seeing the action causing his eyes to move down to my mouth. I take a deep sigh and step back just a bit, "I actually, I heard that noise and then my brain went into survival mode again. Do you know what that loud bang was? Is the house haunted by any chance?

"I mean the last thing I want is to be comfortably asleep and then get groped by Bernie the creepy ghost. Or maybe it is a female ghost which could be..."

His lips slam back down into mine. I can feel his grin spread across his face as he lifts me up by the back of my thighs.

I squeak and wrap my arms around his neck so I don't fall on my ass but continue to kiss him fiercely as he walks us back over towards the bed.

I continue to straddle him as he lays me down on my back and then presses himself into me. He is no longer smiling but instead I feel the need and heat rolling off of him.

As if being electrocuted, he pulls away from me quickly. His eyes searching my face for something. Matthew smiles at me then shifts over to lay beside me.

I roll myself towards him, "Okay, then what was that about?"

He laughs as he pushes a strand of hair away from my face then pulls me in closer to him, so that I can now place my cheek on his chest.

I can hear the deep rumble of his voice through his chest, "Your mouth was getting the zoomies again. I thought I would give your brain something else to fixate on for a minute."

I let out a low sigh as I smile and start running my hand up and down his stomach. I turn my head to look up at him, but his eyes are closed though he is still smiling towards the ceiling.

As if he can feel my eyes on him he looks down at me, "Don't worry. I will protect you from the ghosts. And the mouth zoomies."

I let out another laugh as I lay my head back on his chest, "My hero."

I hear him chuckle then his hand is rubbing up and down my back. I know he can feel my spine, my shoulder blades. I immediately start to get self conscious again.

I push off him a bit and try to roll out of bed, "I am good. I will just go back to my room."

He pulls me back closer to him, "Why? You are welcome to stay here with me. We can fight off the ghosties together."

I smile as I bring my arm down and wrap it around my middle. I would love nothing more than to sleep in here with him tonight but I don't want him to see me in the light of day.

Not with so little on.

He will be able to see every single bone in my body. I shake my head at him, feeling my hair fall into my face, "I don't want my mother to get the wrong idea. I don't want her thinking anything bad of you either."

He nods his head at me as I turn to make my way across the room. I give him one last look back, "Good night Matthew. I will see you tomorrow."

He gives me a sad smile as I quickly leave his room and head back to my own. As I open my door, I hear another close further down the hall.

The ghosts must be out again because when I turn to see who is coming towards me, nobody is there.

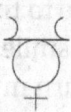

I slept like complete and utter shit all night long. Every time I thought I was actually falling asleep, it turns out my brain was just rebooting.

My eyes crack open to barely see light coming in through the window. I decide I might as well get up. There is no reason pretending like I am actually going to get any sleep.

I move across the room and slide on some yoga pants then an oversized shirt before throwing my hair into a messy bun. Quickly I scan the room for my running shoes then quietly sneak downstairs.

I round the corner and quickly notice that I am the only one awake. Letting out a sigh of relief, I slide my sneakers on then step out the back door.

I look up and down the beach as I slide my air pods into my ears. I turn up the volume on my phone as Spotify lands on Kami Kehoe singing Dopamine.

Ironically, what my brain produced all night, not allowing me to sleep or the ability to focus on anything.

A small laugh leaves my lips as I stretch out my shoulders and legs before lightly jogging down the steps and onto the open beach in front of me.

It looks less populated to the right so I turn and start jogging. A few moments later, the jog has become a full fledged run.

My body takes over for a solid half hour before turning around and making my way back. I don't even realize how far I have ran until I check my watch and see a missed message from mom asking where I am.

I send a quick message back letting her know I am out for a run and will be back soon. I slow my pace and then start just walking as the house comes into view.

My tongue feels like sandpaper. Not realizing it would be this humid already, I didn't even think to bring water with me.

I check my watch again before looking up and seeing Matthew sitting on the steps of the house.

I smile as I step up towards him. He grins back, raising his coffee mug at me, "I didn't know you were a runner."

I shrug back at him before looking around to make sure no one else can hear, "I am trying to build some more muscle mass. Not be so scrawny."

He lets out a laugh then shakes his head at me, "Yeah, okay."

I wrap my arms around myself again. He doesn't have to mock me. I know I look like Skeletor. Something inside me dies a little bit with his words.

I thought he was different.

He had acted like he was at least a little bit attracted to me. I really thought he liked me.

A heavy breath leaves my chest, giving him a sharp look, "Nevermind."

I run past him up the stairs and wave quickly to Lily in the kitchen. I sprint to my room and grab a change of clothes before moving out into the hall towards the bathroom.

I hear Matthew call my name as I step inside. I turn to look in his general direction, trying not to let him see me hurting, "Just leave me alone."

I shut the door and lock it quickly. Thinking about him right now will bring nothing but more heartache. More frustration.

I get it.

I will apologize when I get out.

Make sure he understands that I am okay with him but that nothing between us will work out. I don't need someone putting me down at every turn.

I put myself down enough to fill my own arenas.

Slowly, I peel out of my sweaty clothes as I turn the shower on. My reflection is staring back at me in the mirror.

All I can see is skin and bones.

I try to cave my shoulders forward so you can't see my collarbone protruding but then it just feels like my spine is about to break through the skin on my back.

I stand back up letting out an exhausted sigh.

It's useless.

It's not like I want to be huge. I just want to feel healthy. I don't want to see someone so fragile when I look in the mirror. I want to see someone who can hold her own.

41

I drink protein shakes every single day. I work out, monitor my carbs, and eat plenty of red meat.

But still nothing.

I can't seem to break over the 130 lb mark.

Mom keeps telling me that is a healthy weight for my height since I am only 5'4" but when I look at myself, I feel like I look like a terminally ill patient that escaped the chemo ward.

I feel a tear roll down my face as I step into the shower and under the lukewarm water. If I stand here long enough maybe the tears will turn into resolve. Maybe I will find the guts to face him later.

Slowly, I clean my body and my hair before stepping out and drying off. I realize quickly the clothes I had grabbed and brought with me were actually just two shirts.

I let out a frustrated growl towards the ceiling. Why can things not just go right?

Just one time.

Is that too fucking much to ask for? I look back at my reflection...why Hope? Use your fucking brain!

I peek my head out the door and don't see anyone so I quickly step out and try to dash across the hall wrapped in nothing but a towel.

That is when I realize there is someone behind the door.

That someone being Matthew.

Had he really stood out in the hall the entire time I was in the bathroom? Why the hell would he do that?

I can feel him step up behind me as I grab the doorknob in front of me, "Hope, can we talk? After you are dressed of course?"

I turn around giving him another exhausted stare, "Why? Is there really any reason too?"

He looks at me confused as he raises his hands in defense, "What did I do? Why are you mad at me right now?"

I shake my head at him as I lean back into the door, wrapping my hand around the doorknob. Smiling, I give him what I hope is a soft and understanding smile.

This is not the first time I have tasted rejection, "I am not mad. I promise. I am just tired of meeting someone and realizing too late that they are not what they appear. It just, it gets exhausting is all."

He shakes his head at me then steps closer, "So what, you want me to be the spoiled rock star with paraphernalia and one night stands lined up down the hallway?"

Letting out a small laugh I answer, "No, that is not what I am saying at all."

He moves even closer, so close now that I can feel his breath on my exposed skin. His presence is starting to overwhelm me. Making my blood start to churn faster in my veins.

The towel starts to tighten around my chest as my breathing becomes heavier, "Then what are you saying?"

I place my hand holding my sweaty clothes on his chest, trying to keep a bit of distance between us. I bring my eyes back up to his and they seem to be pleading with me.

For some type, any type of answer.

I tilt my head to the side just a bit, "I just, I know that you see me as just skin and bones. I know I have a weight issue. It is not something I like to talk about. So when I told you I was trying to bulk up and you mocked me, it hurt. Okay?

"I get it though. No one wants to be with someone who looks like a fucking meth addict. It's fine Matthew, truly. It's fine."

I turn the doorknob and start stepping backwards into my room. His hand flies out and pushes on the door I am trying to close, forcing it open.

Shocked, I stumble back just a bit as he steps into the room fully, shutting the door aimlessly behind him.

Matthew steps closer to me as I drop my dirty clothes and cling to the towel that is my only lifeline right now. I don't think he will hurt me but I don't understand the look on his face.

I don't know him well enough to read him yet. My eyes scan him as he steps up closer and then he kisses me fiercely.

I feel his arms wrap around me, his hands gripping onto my bare back. I resist for only a half a second before I feel myself melting into him again.

I grip his shirt in both fists pulling him closer to me, keeping his mouth locked onto mine. His lips smile into mine just a bit before he is devouring me again.

My heart is racing and all I can really focus on is his hands on my body. His lips on mine. My brain has completely turned off as desire starts to sweep through me.

I feel myself losing control, which is something I have never done before.

Not with anyone.

Anytime I have allowed anyone to touch me, it was only because I wanted the white noise in my brain to stop. Not because I actually wanted them as a person. I only wanted part of them.

But with Matthew, it's different.

I want to consume him entirely.

I want to devour his every breath and leave him panting for more. But I don't know how to do that. I don't know what to say that will satisfy him. Or myself.

I don't know what to do that will convey what I want from him. That I want everything from him.

He slowly pulls back from our kiss and his eyes go instantly to my lips. I slowly bring my eyes back to meet his gaze and he is shaking his head at me.

I don't know why, it just doesn't feel right. It feels like he is pitying me. And I don't fucking like it.

At all.

I take a step back and reach up to secure the towel around me tighter. His hands come out gripping my own, though his eyes never leave mine. I start blinking at him rapidly, not knowing what he is going to do next.

I feel his grip tighten as he starts to part the towel. My eyes close tight as I feel his hands grip the ends of the towel.

I don't want to see the horrified expression on his face.

I don't want to see the disgust.

And I really don't want to watch him walk out the door and away from me. I feel the towel as it falls into a heap on the floor.

A single solitary tear starts to slide down my cheek as I feel him step up closer to me, "You are fucking stunning Hope."

My eyes fly open, filled to the brim with tears and rejection. I shake my head at him, "Don't fucking mock me Matthew. I know I am fucking hideous. I know that you can count every rib. I know that my fucking hip bones could cut glass. Do not make fun of me. I can't take that from you. Anyone but you."

I feel the tears roll off my jaw and land on my chest.

Matthew shakes his head at me as his hands come up and wrap around the sides of my face, "Are you fucking delusional? How can you not see what I see?"

I shake my head but then start to wonder. What does he see? Is it worse than what I see?

Is it better?

At this point, any type of different would be alright with me. I slowly bring my eyes back to his, giving into the temptation, "What do you see?"

He gives me a crooked smile, his dark eyes hooded as he pulls back and looks me from head to toe, "You are fucking beautiful. I can't count your ribs baby. I can barely see your hip bones. I see a lean, toned beautiful woman standing in front of me. How can you not see that?"

45

I look down at myself, seeing the exact opposite of everything he just described. I bring my arms around to cover my small breasts.

Matthew steps back up to me, grabbing my hands and bringing them down, "Can I touch you?"

I shake my head at him, "This isn't real. You aren't real. It's some sort of trick. You are just waiting for me to say yes so you can run back and tell everyone the skinny bitch is easy."

I see the anger flash across his face as his neck starts to turn crimson. He reaches out and grabs my hand from my side and pushes my palm hard onto his dick.

He is hard as steel.

My eyes immediately fly back up to his.

God damn it, he is huge. I can feel my eyes bugging out of my head as I try to understand what is happening.

He closes his eyes for just a second before letting out a shattered breath, "Would you be able to do that to me if this was all a joke? Would I be wanting to take you up against this wall and shove my dick so far into you that we wouldn't know where I ended and you began? You are fucking beautiful Hope. Your body. Your mind. Your soul. You are fucking breath taking."

I stare at him waiting for the other shoe to drop. Expecting the door to slam open and someone to be standing there pointing and laughing at me.

But it never comes.

The door is still shut.

Matthew is still standing before me.

My hand is still on his dick.

I give him a small squeeze. My hand reacting before my brain has time to tell it not to.

Matthew lets out a moan around the room as his eyes roll up in his head. I can feel a small breath escape my own chest as I watch him trying to hold himself back.

I close my eyes, "Touch me."

46

His stare is burning a hole into me but I am too afraid to open my eyes to see his expression. I just keep listening for the door to shut behind him as he takes off.

I feel him move closer and my eyes open back up to him. He is smiling at me, "Only if you promise to keep your eyes on me."

Slowly, I allow my eyes to settle on his chest before I look his face over.

He means it.

He is actually attracted to me.

I allow a small smile to come over my lips, "I promise."

Matthew wraps one hand around my neck, gripping my hair at the base of my neck and the other hand wraps around grabbing my bare ass as he pulls me closer to him.

I let out a gasp at the force of it then his mouth is on me again. I continue to let him destroy me with his lips as his hands start to wander my body.

Reaching up I grip his hair with my closed fists as I shove my tongue into his mouth. He tastes like tobacco and some type of deep dark roasted coffee.

I press myself closer to him as my hands start to lower. I pull back just long enough to grab the hem of his shirt, "Take this off. Now. I want to feel your skin on me."

Matthew lets out a low growl as he pulls the shirt over his head, throwing it to the other side of the room. I watch him as he kicks his boots off as I run my fingers down his abdomen.

His lips slam back into mine as I unbutton his jeans then reach my hand inside to grip his hard dick.

It feels like velvet.

Hard, pulsating, velvet.

He hisses back at me like I have hurt him and my eyes fly open. He nods his head at me, "Keep going baby. Don't stop."

47

Smiling again, I begin to kiss him harder. I squeeze my hand around his length and I can feel him trying to hold back. I can tell he is trying not to thrust into my hand.

I smile around our kisses before removing my hand and tugging his jeans down his hips.

Our lips never part as he continues to remove his clothing then steps up close to me. I can feel him hard against my stomach and the need to have him inside me starts to thrum.

I take a few steps back and sit down on the edge of the bed. Looking him up and down then smiling slightly before I scoot back and part my knees as I lay back onto the mattress.

I hear his breathing heavy again, "Fuck you are gorgeous. You are fucking dripping for me baby."

I smile towards the ceiling as I bring my hand to my center and run a finger across my slit, feeling the truth of his words on my finger.

I let out a low moan when my finger skims my clit. I hear him shuffling around and I look up to see him grabbing his jeans.

Immediately, I tense up. He is running. He doesn't want me. He doesn't want this.

Why would he take it this far?

Why would he be so cruel?

Then I see his hand slide up with his wallet. He quickly opens it and pulls out a condom.

I smile as I sit up and lean forward. I grab the condom from his hand and frisbee it across the room.

His eyes come back to mine, practically begging to be allowed to go back and grab it off the floor. I smile widely at him again, "We don't need that. I won't get pregnant."

He shakes his head at me before looking back towards the condom on the floor then back at me, "I uh. I have never taken someone bare before."

Goosebumps roll through my entire body. I feel myself panting as I lay back down and spread my knees again, "I am clean. I haven't been with anyone in almost 2 years."

His eyes continue to bore into mine, "I have been tested, a few months ago. I haven't been with anyone really since then."

I smile wickedly back at him, "Then it looks like it is time to make another wish come true."

He is on me within a second. He is holding himself up with one arm so as not to put all of his weight down on me. He leans down and takes a nipple into his mouth.

I let out another hard moan as he flicks his tongue across my peak. I start tearing at the bare skin on his back with my short fingernails, "God dammit Matthew. I want you. I want you so fucking bad."

I feel his face lift up and I glance down at him, "Are you sure this is okay?"

I smile as I reach down and grab his dick again, pulling him and pointing him towards my entrance, "Fuck me Matthew. Please."

I move my hand as I feel his wrap around his dick then he is sliding inside of me. I take in a heavy breath as my chest arches towards him.

He is stretching me to my limits and I don't even fucking care. He feels too fucking good to complain. Just the weight of him inside of me is making my body beg for more.

I raise my hands up and wrap them around his sides as he continues to slide in and out of me. I look up at him and see his eyes are shut.

Smiling wildly at his intrusions, "Look at me."

His eyes fly open as he starts to speed up his movements. I let out another deep moan, "Fuck Matthew. You feel so fucking good."

His mouth is on mine seconds later. His rhythm is steady, pounding into me relentlessly. I can already feel my release growing deep within me.

4
Apollo
Provider - Sleep Token

Hope has to be out of her ever loving mind. I am shaking my head at her, trying to understand where exactly her head is at.

I take a step closer to her, "So what, you want me to be the spoiled rock star with paraphernalia and one night stands lined up down the hallway?"

She lets out a small sarcastic laugh as she rolls her eyes at me, "No, that is not what I am saying at all."

I move closer to her. Close enough that I can feel her heart beat against my own.

Close enough that I can smell that scent rolling off of her again. Citrus and innocence.

Being this close to her, with her hair wet and her skin still damp from the shower, I can finally place her smell.

It is like an orchard of mandarins.

It just rolls off her naturally, earlier I had thought it was maybe a perfume but no, that is just pure Hope.

I lean in breathing her in deep, "Then what are you saying?"

She places a handful of dirty clothes on my chest like that would somehow make me move away. Those clothes are covered in her. I would wear them as a second skin if given the chance.

I look at her, trying to convince her with my presence to just open up to me. Just talk to me.

Hope tilts her head to the side just a bit, seemingly upset that she has to explain herself, "I just, I know that you see me as just skin and bones. I know I have a weight issue. It is not something I like to talk about. So when I told you I was trying to bulk up and you mocked me, it hurt.

"Okay? I get it though. No one wants to be with someone who looks like a fucking meth addict. It's fine Matthew, truly. It's fine."

Is she fucking insane?

She is not that fucking thin.

I can barely even see her collarbone.

The door starts to slowly open as she takes a step backwards. As I watch the door closing between us, I reach my hand out and push it open.

There is not a chance in hell that I am letting this conversation die like this. I watch Hope as she takes a few steps back, almost stumbling as I sling the door shut behind me.

Her dirty clothes fall to the floor and she grabs the towel like I am going to pull it from her body. I pull her in close to me and kiss her, hopefully with enough fire that she knows that this is real.

I don't see what she sees.

But I do see the most beautiful girl I could ever imagine.

I see a kind soul, a crazy brain, a kindred spirit.

She starts to put her hands up but then instantly starts to mold herself into me and my kiss.

I feel her grab my shirt with both hands as she pulls me in closer to her. I run my hands all over her bare back and shoulders.

I am just grateful that she is letting me touch her instead of kicking me out. I fully believed she was going to punch me instead of letting me kiss her.

Reluctantly, I pull away from her, watching her pant into the air around us. I can not believe that she thinks that I am not

52

attracted to her. I was pretty sure I had made it very fucking obvious that I want her.

She takes a few steps back and tries to hold her arms close to her middle like she is holding herself together somehow. I guess I am just going to have to make it even more clear.

I slowly reach up and start to pull her arms from her chest. Her towel parting with her arms.

I watch her face as her eyes close almost as if she is in pain. The towel finally falls from her body and I take her in.

I still don't see what she is saying about herself.

She is fucking stunning.

I can see the muscles in her stomach as they form that tight v. Sure her tits aren't huge but they are not tiny either. They are perfect for her size, for her build. The muscles around her sides hug the curve of her hips, inviting me forward.

I let out a slow breath, "You are fucking stunning Hope."

Her eyes fly open and I see pain and tears running down her face. I go to move towards her when she starts shaking her head at me, "Don't fucking mock me Matthew. I know I am fucking hideous. I know that you can count every rib. I know that my fucking hip bones could cut glass. Do not make fun of me. I can't take that from you. Anyone but you."

I shake my head at her, moving closer as I watch the tears roll of her jaw, "Are you fucking delusional? How can you not see what I see?"

Hope shakes her head towards me again before wiping the tears from her face and looking towards the floor. A moment later I see something take over. Something apparently more powerful than the denial she has been throwing at me.

She slowly brings her eyes back to mine, "What do you see?"

I give her an honest smile.

She has no idea how fucking sexy she is. She does not know what she does to men, what she is doing to me. How has no one told her this before?

I want to find every man that has ever paid any attention to her and punch them in the fucking throat.

I scan her body again before landing back on her eyes, "You are fucking beautiful. I can't count your ribs baby. I can barely see your hip bones. I see a lean toned beautiful woman standing in front of me. How can you not see that?"

She looks down at herself and I can see the expression that comes over her face.

She still doesn't believe me.

She still thinks I am just trying to make her feel better.

I watch her as she tries to hide her body with her arms. I continue to grin at her as I step up close, "Can I touch you?"

Pleading to her with my eyes. I just want to feel her skin against mine. I want to show her exactly what I am seeing, what I am feeling.

She shakes her head back at me again, like she is getting angry or something, "This isn't real. You aren't real. It's some sort of trick. You are just waiting for me to say yes so you can run back and tell everyone that the skinny bitch is easy."

I am not going to allow her to talk about herself this way.

I can feel the anger start to roll through me.

Fine, if she doesn't want me to touch her then I will just have to prove myself another way. I grab her hand and take her palm, planting it right on top of my extremely hard dick.

I have been busting at the zipper of my jeans since I shut the door behind me earlier. I watch her eyes go wide as she looks from her hand to my eyes then back down again.

I press her hand harder onto my throbbing cock, "Would you be able to do that to me if this was all a joke? Would I be wanting to take you up against the wall and shove my dick so far into you that we wouldn't know where I ended and you began?

You are fucking beautiful Hope. Your body. Your mind. Your soul. You are fucking breath taking."

Hope continues to stare at me for a long moment.

Like she is expecting me to yell 'Just Kidding' and run away. I let my hand fall but she keeps her palm pressed against me.

My breathing is only getting heavier with each moment of silence that passes between us.

She has to say something, do something.

Anything.

Then I feel her squeeze my dick. My eyes instantly roll up into my head as I let a growl out into the room. Goosebumps explode down my spine almost instantly. I have never had anyone do this to me. Not from just a touch.

I am trying to keep my composure but all I want to do is fucking own her.

To hear her screaming my name.

I want to break all these delusions she has about herself and prove to her that she is all I want. That she is all I need. Then I hear her small voice float up to me, "Touch me."

I open my eyes and drop them back to her face. She has her eyes closed but is still holding onto my dick. I smile as I step forward, sad to feel her hand fall away from me.

I am towering over her now, "Only if you promise to keep your eyes on me."

Her eyes open and she smiles up into my face. I can feel her walls crumbling around us. The weight in the air around us starts to lift. Her smile is melting me right in front of her.

She might actually be starting to understand that none of this is a joke.

This is 100% real.

I want her.

I need her.

Just like I need air to breathe. I watch her lick her lips , smiling at me again, "I promise."

I can't hold back any longer. Hearing her let those walls fall around us. I feel her insecurities melt away as I take her in my arms.

I wrap one hand around her neck, gripping her hair tight at the base of her neck, allowing me to tilt her head up. The other hand goes straight to her ass. I grip her roughly as I pull her body closer to mine.

Slamming her mouth into mine, I force her lips open with my tongue and push inside of her mouth. Tasting her is like capsules of sin exploding in all my senses at the same time.

I feel her hands move across my shoulders then wrap into my hair, yanking me hard back down into her mouth.

I let go of her hair and start exploring her body. Running both hands across her back then bringing my right arm between us and grip her tit, rubbing my thumb over her nipple as she moans into my mouth.

Hope starts to pull away from me but then grabs the bottom of my shirt and starts to lift it off my body, "Take this off. Now. I want to feel your skin on me."

I reach behind my shoulders and pull the shirt straight off my body. I smile as I watch her reach out and run her fingers down my stomach, letting them run through the lines in my abs.

I kick my shoes off to the side and I watch her fingers as they start to unbutton my jeans.

Leaning back down, I kiss her forcefully again. Then I feel her soft little hand wrap about my bare dick.

I can feel myself almost pass out.

Her skin is so soft. Her fingers foxtrot on my skin and I let out a hiss into the air around us.

I feel her instantly stop moving, nodding my head in her direction I whisper, "Keep going baby. Don't stop."

56

Hope slams her mouth into mine again as she starts to run her hand gently up and down my dick. I am trying so hard not to cum all over her hand right now.

I have never felt like this before.

With anyone.

Usually I am the one working myself up. Or if I am drunk enough, my dick just has a mind of its own.

But with Hope it is different.

One tiny little touch from her and I am about to fall over the edge. One look from her and I am harder than I have ever been in my life. I feel her pull her hand from my jeans and I am almost upset until I feel her hands tugging on the waist of my jeans to pull them down.

I quickly remove my pants while keeping my mouth pressed to her the entire time. I step up close to her again. Close enough that she can feel me hard against her abdomen.

She starts to take a few steps back and I feel empty without her consuming my perimeter. She slowly sits down then slides up on the bed.

I am trying so hard to not grab ahold of my own dick right now. It is throbbing and begging for some kind of friction.

She is so fucking sexy.

Hope lays back onto the bed beneath her, slowly parting her knees. I let out a loud sigh as I see those perfectly toned legs part and spread open, exposing herself to me.

Her glistening cunt is practically thrumming with need. The desire to slam myself inside of her is a stronger pull than I have ever felt before. With anyone.

I can feel my own breathing getting heavier, "Fuck you are gorgeous. You are fucking dripping for me baby."

I watch her hand as it slowly moves down her abdomen to her center. She takes her pointer finger and runs it straight up her center from her entrance to her clit.

I can see her smiling and when she lets out a low moan I instantly start rushing around to find my wallet. I have to be inside her.

Now!

I finally rip it from my pants pocket and pull out the condom inside.

I look up at her as I take a step towards the bed. She smiles at me as she reaches out and grabs the condom from my hand.

I swear to Christ if she puts it on me, I may not last two minutes.

Then, I watch her for just a second before she sends the condom skidding across the floor to the other side of the room.

I look at her completely fucking broken, thinking she has changed her mind. I won't force myself on her but this is going to be a hard moment to move past.

But when I look back at her face, she is smiling at me, "We don't need that. I won't get pregnant."

I feel myself shaking my head at her. I have never not used protection. Not even when I was too drunk to stand. Not even when Simone begged me.

I have always used protection.

I look from the condom back to Hope on the bed. I take a hesitant step closer, "I uh. I have never taken someone bare before."

She smiles at me as she leans back on her elbows, parting her knees further, "I am clean. I haven't been with anyone in almost 2 years."

Her eyes stay connected to mine as she lays back flat on the bed, running her fingertips up the inside of both thighs. I let out a feathered breath, "I have been tested, a few months ago. I haven't been with anyone really since then."

I watch the wicked grin that rolls back over her mouth, "Then it looks like it is time to make another wish come true."

58

This woman has me changing my entire way of life.

I instantly don't care about the condom anymore. If she isn't worried then I won't be worried.

I crawl up her body and lean in close to her. She smiles into my face as I lean forward and pull her nipple into my mouth. I gently circle the peak with my tongue before sucking it deep into my mouth then flicking it with the tip of my tongue.

I can hear her moaning beneath me and it is the best fucking moment of my life.

I can feel her short nails raking down my back, digging in deeper with each second, "God dammit Matthew. I want you. I want you so fucking bad."

I lift my mouth from her tit and look into her eyes. Giving her one last chance to walk away from this, to change her mind, "Are you sure this is okay?"

Then I feel her wrap her hand around my dick again, pointing it towards her entrance, "Fuck me Matthew. Please."

Jesus fuck this woman.

I grab my dick at the base and push myself inside of her. Hope takes in a deep breath as her back arches, pushing her breasts into the air below me.

She is so fucking tight.

I can feel her pussy gripping me, pulling me in deeper. I have never imagined what heaven might actually feel like until this moment.

I close my eyes, trying to make the moment last as long as possible as I start to push myself in and out of her. Going just a little bit deeper with each thrust.

I hear her breathy voice below me, "Look at me."

My eyes slam wide staring into her own. She is just as wrapped up in me as I am in her. I start to speed up, still going a bit deeper each time.

I still haven't seated myself inside her entirely. I don't want to hurt her. I don't know truly how long it has been since she has done this.

And not bragging but I know my dick isn't average, and it sure as fuck isn't small.

I hear her let out another deep moan below me, "Fuck Matthew. You feel so fucking good."

I lean down slamming my lips into hers again. I roll my body against hers over and over again. Feeling myself falling deeper into whatever this is that we are creating with each thrust.

I want to slam myself into her but I am holding back.

I want her to control that the first time. I would not be able to live with myself if I hurt her.

I feel her panting below me as I roll to the side, bringing her with me and seating her on top of me as my back hits the comforter.

She opens her eyes and smiles at me as she starts to rise up on my dick. I smile back at her as she slams down onto me hard.

I let out a growl as I feel myself fill her to the brim, "Jesus, Hope."

Hope lets out a soft scream as she raises up and does it again. She leans forward, bracing herself on my chest as she starts to slam herself down on me quicker, harder.

Wrapping my hands around her waist, I help her slam her entire body into mine. I let out another growl into the room as I feel myself about to lose control.

I don't want this to be over already but she had me so worked up from the jump that I am surprised I have even lasted this long.

I put some weight on her hips when she slams down on me again, "Baby, if you keep doing that I am going to cum a lot sooner than either of us want."

Hope smiles at me as she leans forward and starts to kiss my chest, slowly sliding up and down my dick. Her mouth goes to my nipple and she flicks my nipple bar with her tongue.

I let out another moan into the room.

I don't even fucking care who hears us at this point. We can wake the fucking neighbors for all I care.

Her mouth starts to climb across my collar bone then up my neck. She moves back to my lips and kisses me hard as she starts to speed up her movements.

I open my eyes and watch her as she sits back up and starts slamming herself back down on me. There is something in her movements, something just under the surface.

This woman is owning me right now and I am not entirely sure when it started.

I just know I don't want it to ever stop.

She lowers herself back down just enough that our breath is mingling and I feel my release crashing towards me. I put my hands on her hips to try to slow her down again when her eyes fly wide and her cunt squeezes my dick so tight that I feel like she is trying to break it off inside of her.

She screams into the room around us at her release. Her hips start slamming erratically into mine.

I bite my bottom lip then look into her face as I feel myself start to pulsate inside of her, "Fuck Hope. God damn it baby I'm cumming."

She smiles down at me as she continues to slam down into me, "Yes.. Yes.. Matthew. Fuck me!"

She screams again as I feel another orgasm rip through her body. I sit up quickly, still seated deeply inside of her as I slam her hips harder into mine.

Hope obviously has no control over her body at this point. I roll her back underneath of me as I continue to ride out my release, thrusting harder and deeper into her than before.

66

I growl before another scream rips from my own throat, "Fuck Hope. You are so fucking tight baby."

I feel my release finally starting to slow down but she is still gripping me tight. I continue to push into her until I feel her legs fall out flat around us and her pussy finally releases its hold on me.

Even then I continue to push into her.

She opens her eyes and smiles at me, "I knew you could fuck. This is why you go by a gods' name isn't it?"

I laugh back at her as I finally stop throwing myself into her. We are both covered in sweat and I don't even fucking care.

This is by far the best workout I have ever had.

I lean forward and kiss her hard before pulling back and placing my forehead to hers, "That was honestly the best I have ever had."

I open my eyes just enough to see her smile and whisper, "Ditto."

I smile wider as I kiss her again.

I slowly pull myself from her then roll onto my back beside her. I turn my head to look at her and she is beaming back at me.

I roll to face her and place one hand on the side of her face until her eyes meet mine, "What are you doing to me Hope?"

She smiles back at me as she leans down and kisses my fingers, "Whatever you will let me."

She doesn't know this.

I may never have the balls to even tell her, but she can do whatever the fuck she wants to me.

She can break me, bend me, destroy me and my heart.

I don't fucking care.

She is mine.

I am hers.

I never want to fucking touch another woman for the rest of my life. She has swallowed me whole.

I watch her for a long moment. Her chest heaving into the air around us. She is glowing. She is radiant. She is mind numbingly breathtaking.

After a bit, I roll towards her and let my fingertips trace the curves of her body. I still don't know what she meant about being able to see all of her bones. Even laying on her back, sure I can see her ribs but not nearly enough to count them.

Hope turns to me smiling, "Well, fucking a rock star was definately not on my 2024 bingo card."

I chuckle back at her as I let my fingers slide up her breast and circle her pert nipple, "Yeah, you're not complaining though."

She smiles a moment before she brings her hands up to her face, "Definately not but the whole fucking house probably heard us."

I laugh at her again, "Do you know how many times I have heard Gideon and Lily? This is called payback."

She laughs out loud again, a quick snort following.

I move closer to her face, laughing along with her, "Seriously. You gonna tell me it was my hearing again or are you going to admit that was a snort?"

Hope giggles as she slaps my hand. She turns her face back towards the ceiling and lets out a heavy sigh, "I don't want to go out there and face them."

I smile at her as I continue to trace her shadows with my fingers, slowly moving them lower, "We don't have to go out there right now."

She looks back at me, one eyebrow raised, "Calm thyself sire. My mother is out there. I can't just hide away for the next 3 days."

I laugh back at her as I bring my hand back up, wrapping it around the back of her neck, pulling her mouth to mine, "At least give me 5 minutes. I just want to hold you before we open that door."

Hope nudges my chin with her nose before bringing her mouth to mine and giving me a deep slow kiss.

I pull her body closer to mine and hold her tight against me as our tongues dance in rhythm with each other.

We finally part, gulping in air as our foreheads meet. I close my eyes smiling into the in between, "Where have you been all my life, Hope? You are seriously everything I have ever dreamed about."

I feel her hands tracing my chest as I open my eyes and see her staring into mine, "I have been looking for you. I just didn't know it. I have always felt like there was something missing. Before, being with other people. I have never felt complete, until now. With you."

I can feel my breath stilling in my chest as I let her admission sink in.

I feel the exact same way.

I open my mouth to tell her as much when we hear a quick knock on the door. Hope instantly glues her body to mine as she leans her giggling face into my chest.

I grab a pillow and cover her ass with it, "Yeah?"

The door cracks open, not enough for me to see them or vice versa.

I hear a voice clearly as Lucy speaks up, "I get it is play time right now but we have plans today Hope. So cover your ass and get out here."

Hope is giggling relentlessly into my chest as I feel a smile covering my entire face. I see Lucy's hand shoot through the opening with all her fingers splayed out, "You both have 5 minutes to wrap it up and get downstairs. And don't even think about bailing on us Matthew. By the sound of things, you have been initiated into the family. Mazel Tov."

The door closes and we both start laughing loudly about the room. I bring Hope's mouth back up to mine and give her another kiss before sitting up and looking around the room. I turn and look back down at her and she quickly tries to hide her body with her arm.

I smile as I pull her arm down, "Don't. Don't hide yourself from me. You are perfect just the way you are, Hope."

I see the small streak of crimson start to color her cheeks as she gives me another shy smile, "So. What is this then? What are we?"

I smile at her as I stand and retrieve my underwear and jeans from the floor. I quickly slide them both on, hopping bare feet, "Well that depends. What do you want it to be?"

I watch her intently as she sits up on the bed and smiles quickly before standing and moving towards her suitcase. Her back is towards me now and I can see the muscles in her back move as she roots around looking for clothes. I let my eyes go to her ass.

It is perfect, just like the rest of her.

I can see the toned lines of her glutes as they mold into the muscles along her hips. It takes every ounce of will power not to walk to her and take her again. I watch her grab a tank top and slide it over her body before turning around and sliding on a pair of tiny lace panties.

Hope smiles at me, "I mean, it can be whatever you are comfortable with I guess. I am only here for a few more days so I don't want you to think it has to be anything serious. Maybe we just enjoy each other's company? Take it day by day? See what happens?"

I nod back at her as I step up to her pulling her close to me, "That is fine baby. But you are going to have to pack up your stuff. You are moving to my room.

"There is no way in hell I am going to get any sleep knowing you are on the other side of this fucking wall and I can't touch you. I will talk to Lucy about it if I have to, but it is happening. Non negotiable."

Hope grins widely at me again, nodding her head, "I would like that. You can keep me safe from the ghosts."

Laughing loudly, I give her a quick kiss and look for the rest of my clothing. Just a few minutes later we are fully dressed and heading out into the hallway.

Thankfully, there is no one standing there. And when I say no one, I mean Lucy. Or worse, Simone.

I wrap her hand tightly in mine as we make our way downstairs. I can feel the eyes on us but I ignore them and just continue to hold her tight to me.

Literally everyone from the house is sitting in the living room just grinning at us. We definitely made too much noise.

I glance around the room, at all the smiles until my face lands on Simone. She is glaring at Hope. The smile on my face instantly falls as I stare her back down.

I swear to god, she does not want to fuck with me.

Not when it comes to Hope.

If she fucking ruins this for me, I don't know what I will do. And I can't be held accountable for what I might say either.

Lucy steps forward, looking at her watch, "The street fair doesn't open for a few more hours. I was thinking about walking downtown though, maybe do some window shopping. Anyone wanna join?"

Hope smiles around the room then looks at me with her eyebrows raised. I smile back down at her and give her a soft kiss, "Wherever you go, I go."

She grins back at me before turning back to Lucy, "Count us in!"

5
Hope
Higher - Sleep Token

I can't believe I am in a situationship with Apollo.

Mother fucking Apollo!

I may have the body of a 22 year old but the teenager inside of me is losing her fucking mind right now. I smile over at him as he glances around the room.

Following the path of his eyes with mine I see that mostly everyone is smiling back at us.

Mostly everyone.

I see the daggers coming out of Simone's eyes and I look back over my shoulder at Matthew, seeing him throwing shade right back at her.

What the hell is that about?

Before I can even get a chance to ask the question, mom is shooing us all around the house to get our things so we can go shopping. There are only a few of us going this morning, though everyone said we would meet up this afternoon at the street fair.

I squeeze Matthew's hand as he opens the front door for Mom, Mona and I. One last glance over my shoulder confirms Simone is still fuming, though I still can't figure out why.

Maybe she just doesn't like new people. I give her a soft smile before turning back towards the door.

We all make our way towards the rental car and pile in to head into town to hopefully find a decent parking spot.

Matthew sits beside me, rubbing my bare thigh gently while talking to Mona and Mom about the last leg of the tour. His eyes never leave the front of the car as his fingers run up the inside of my thigh in a repetitive motion under my skirt.

Not in a sexual way, but more in a comforting way. Like he knows I am not comfortable in my own skin. Like he is trying to show me that he actually does like every single part of me.

I already don't want him to leave.

I have known him less than 48 hours but everything about him is already so familiar, so constant. Once I actually got it through my head that he is attracted to me.

I still don't see what he does but I guess that doesn't matter, as long as he doesn't get his eyes checked we should be solid.

15 minutes later we are pulling into a parking spot and stepping out into the hot, humid North Carolina air. The street they have closed off is super cool though.

It looks like a proper southern small town main street, cobblestone and all. All the stores seem to be open but there are little booths and tables set up in the road for what looks like almost a mile.

There is a stage as well so they must be thinking about live music at some point.

I squeeze Matthew's hand again as he smiles back at me. There are all kinds of little stores open. Mostly clothes, books, a few specialty shops. We step into a coffee house and smile at each other as we hear a Carnal Decay song playing softly overhead.

This is still just weird as hell. No one knows who he is. They can all just walk around without anyone bothering them even though they are quickly becoming one of the largest bands in the country.

There are a couple of teenagers sitting over in a both aimlessly singing along to the song overhead. Not even realizing that Apollo is standing 6 feet away from them.

We order our coffee and step back out onto the street, walking past vendors selling everything from candles to cookies. I grin towards Matthew, "What is your favorite cookie?"

He grins back as he takes a sip of his coffee, "Well that depends, are we talking American or British? Because our impression of cookies is a bit different from yours."

I nod my head back at him, "Both then."

He looks over the vendor's table in front of us, pointing to a classic chocolate chunk chip cookie, "Definitely chocolate chip then. I have yet to find one that I don't enjoy. Back home though, I could devour like a viennese type cookie. I have to have some chocolate in there somewhere. How about you?"

I smile back at him, "I am a little different. I like a good sugar cookie but if you add some kind of fruit or even a fruit compote on there, I become a cookie slut. I will devour them all."

I will.

I once ate 18 cookies in one sitting. And they were huge.

Matthew laughs out loud at me, causing Mom to turn around and give us a grin. I smile back at him, taking his hand again and moving towards the next booth.

I step up looking over all the jewelry. I quickly glance over the selection before landing on a beautiful moss agate necklace. It is set in a square setting, uniquely bent and molded by the craftsman. The style is rustically vintage but still holding a simplistic beauty to it. I pick up the piece, turning it over in my fingers a bit before sitting it down and moving onto the next booth.

While turning to look at some handbound leather journals I hear my mother, "Hope, look over there."

I look up to see her pointing towards the stage. There is a sandwich board sign set up next to a drumset that reads, "Try me, $10 for 5 minutes."

I instantly laugh and shake my head, "Nope, not for me."

My mother just shakes her head back at me before turning around to face us, "Why did you even learn to play if you never actually want to play in front of anybody?"

I feel Matthew squeeze my hand a bit harder and I grin back at her, "You know it was just a hyperfixation that I couldn't walk away from. I am not good enough to play in front of people."

Mom shakes her head at me, "You are a lot better than you let on. I wish you could come out of your shell a bit. Live a little."

Her words cut through me.

Like I don't want to live a little.

I do.

I really do.

There is just always something inside of me, telling me that I am not going to be good enough so why even try. I feel the frown as it crosses over my face. I don't even know if she realizes how much her words deflate me sometimes

Matthew raises my hand to his lips. I look up at him as he kisses my knuckles, "Not even for me. You won't let me hear you play?"

I give him a glance that screams 'Not Fucking Fair'.

He grins against my knuckles, knowing exactly what the fuck he is doing. I shake my head back at him as Mona comes walking back up to us, "Too bad. I already paid and they have your name."

My eyes go as wide as half dollars, "What?"

Mona giggles back at me, "Now you have to play. We won't laugh, I promise. You don't even have to play something

7l

we would know. Just let loose for a few minutes. You do realize we know what it feels like to get lost in it right? Go get lost."

I smile up at her and her insightfulness. Turning towards Matthew I see him smiling coyly back at me.

I look towards the stage and feel the pull to walk up on it. Taking in a deep rattled breath, I nervously drop his hand then point at his chest, "You laugh, I leave."

I can feel my heart trying to beat out of my chest as I walk towards the stage. I have never played in front of this many people before and I can feel my palms starting to sweat in anticipation. Hopefully, I don't fuck it all up.

Cautiously, I step up to a man behind what looks like some sort of karaoke set up. He smiles up at me, "Your friend already paid for you. Your name is Hope right?"

I nod back at him, my eyes roaming all the equipment on the table before him. He smiles back at me, "Okay, so you can just play on your own or I have some tracks here you can play along too. The drums have been removed so they will only hear the singers and other instruments. You would supply the drums."

I let out another shaky breath, regretting that I agreed to do this. Nodding my head, still in shock that I am even doing this to begin with.

But I can't back out now.

I look over my shoulder quickly and I see that Matthew has moved to the center of the stage so he will have a clear and clean shot of me while I play. I turn back around nodding at him, "Do you have anything by Carnal Decay?"

The man's eyes fly wide before he smiles widely, "My kind of girl. Yeah, I have some of their stuff here. Just pick one and jump up on the stage. Just count me in when you're ready to begin."

I nod at him again as I roll my finger down through the list, immediately seeing one of their older songs that I know by heart. I point it out to see the man smiling at me again.

72

I can feel the nerves running through my veins. It feels like waves of crashing heaviness making my fingers stiff, muscles tight. I quickly shake out of my hands before launching myself up onto the stage and stepping towards the drumset.

There is a headset sitting on the stool. I sigh, reaching out towards them before glancing back at Matthew again.

God, I hope I don't fuck this up.

This is alot of fucking pressure on me. I mean...it is his fucking song.

This is something he created.

I quickly slide the headphones over my head and get settled into the stool. I roll my neck over my shoulders before testing out the set, making sure the stool is in the perfect position for me to reach everything. I pull the stool forward about an inch before readjusting and looking out over the crowd.

Thankfully, the only people paying any attention to me are Mom, Mona and Matthew. Everyone else is just glancing as they continue to shop and walk the festival.

Hesitantly letting out another heavy sigh, I turn towards the man behind the table then nodding and counting him in with a 4 count of the drumsticks.

I hear the music start in my headphones. There are just a few strikes of the cymbals and snare in the first minute and a half of the song.

But I chose this song for a reason.

There are few runs that really test your skills. I figured if I am going to show him what I can do, I might as well go for it.

I look up again to see the questioning in Matthew's face. But I can't tell if he is just worried about how I am doing or if he is questioning whether or not I can actually play the song.

I close my eyes as I feel the first drop about to hit.

Ares' voice sets deep inside my chest.

I can feel the reverberation of the guitar and bass in the song as it starts to imbed itself into my bones.

73

Before I can even think twice about it, my hands are flying across the drums. From snare to crash. My body just feeling the beat as my brain screams at me, 'floor, ride, hi-tom, floor' all while hitting the kick pedal to the beat rolling down my spine. I smile as I continue to blast across the crash then snare back around to floor.

My eyes close in the licks, just letting my hands use the muscle memory of playing this song a million times in private.

Repeating them every few moments.

When the fill hits, leaving nothing but the guitar and drums, I feel myself come up off of the stool with every burst of a roll across the set. I can feel the electricity shooting through my veins as the song comes to an abrupt end.

Nervously, I pant into the air around me. Letting the moment really sink in. Hesitantly admitting to myself that I just play Resist the Violence to the creator of the fucking song.

But I have yet to find the nerve to open my eyes. I sit the sticks down on the snare before sliding the headphones off and standing up.

I look towards the man at the music table and he is staring at me wide eyed with a large smile across his face. Relief begins to pour out of me as I smile back down at him. I must not have been butchered too badly after all.

I sit the headphones down on the stool before turning towards the front of the stage. When I get to the edge, I sit one hand down flat on the stage before propelling my feet down towards the ground.

As soon as I land, I feel Matthews' hands on both sides of my face. I raise my eyes just in time to see his mouth crashing into mine.

I smile into the force of the kiss he is slamming into my mouth. He pulls away and looks around us quickly.

I smile over at my mom as Matthew grabs my hand pulling me out of the flow of the crowd that is now standing in front of the stage.

Matthew yells over his shoulder, "We'll be right back."

I laugh over my shoulder at my mom waving at her as Matthew drags me down in between two buildings towards the alley.

Laughing loudly now, "Where are you taking me?"

Matthew doesn't even turn around to acknowledge my question. He looks both ways at the end of the alley before turning towards the back of a building that has an old set of wooden stairs going up to the second floor.

I see him eyeing the building closely before he pulls me quickly under the stairs then backing me into the shadows. I can feel the air rushing from my chest as he pushes me up into the wall, feeling the bricks rough through my t-shirt.

His mouth is back on mine within seconds. Matthew pushes his body into mine, pining me to the wall. His hands are everywhere all at once. The rough slide of his fingertips on my skin is making my body flush with anticipation.

I smile back into his mouth, my eyes closed as I wrap my arms around his neck and just enjoy him destroying me.

Matthew pulls back just long enough to lift my right leg up over his hip. I hear him unzipping his pants and my eyes go wide, looking behind him over his shoulder to make sure no one is there. My eyes move back to his as I feel him reach under my skirt and yank my underwear to the side.

I go up on my tip toe trying to settle into the height difference. I have never done anything like this before. Anyone could see us, though his body is completely covering mine.

He is like a starving man.

He seems frantic as he reaches his right arm around me and picks me up then pins us both to the wall. He pulls his other arm down and uses his hand to help guide him as he slams into me.

I try to stifle the scream in my throat as I feel him sinking deep into me. My eyes roll back in my head as he sinks all the way into me, harder than he was even this morning.

He doesn't say a word. His eyes are on me the entire time but his mouth is perched like he is just trying to keep his thoughts to himself.

He just grunts as he slams his cock into me relentlessly.

Something about being here, in this alley, hidden under these creaky old stairs is doing something to me. Maybe it's the thought of someone seeing us. Maybe the thrill of being caught, but I don't care. He is filling me so full all I can focus on is the climax that is about to take over me.

I look at his face and his eyes meet mine, narrowing on me as he continues to force his dick into me, "You are in so much fucking trouble."

Confused, I continue to stare at him as I feel myself becoming slicker. A heavy breath leaves my lips, "What did I do?"

His eyes come back to mine again as he slams deep into me again, "You knew exactly what you were doing, didn't you?"

He shoves himself deep into me and I feel the air as it leaves my chest. I try not to moan but it is taking all of my restraint.

Matthew moves his mouth to my ear as he continues to slide in and out of me, "You want me to fuck that brattiness right out of you, don't you?"

I can feel myself start to pulsate around him and he leans back to look into my eyes. I can hear myself panting back at him as my eyes connect with his, nodding my head convulsively, "Yes. Fuck me."

He starts grunting louder, throwing himself into me roughly, "God you are fucking perfect baby. Cum on me. Cum on my cock."

76

I feel myself starting to flutter deep inside before ecstasy starts to course through me. I let out a small scream as I put my mouth on his neck, biting hard so that I don't get us caught.

He lets out a loud moan into the alley around us as he rams into me relentlessly before I feel his body start to shake as he releases himself into me.

Matthew is choking out a groan into my neck, "God dammit Hope. Your cunt is strangling my dick."

I can feel myself still pulsating around his dick as he continues to fucking pummel me. I let out another small moan as he pounds into me deep again.

I lock my eyes shut as my fingernails dig into his shoulders, bringing my mouth to his ear, "You fuck me so good baby."

He slams deep into me again as we moan around each other. I can feel the tension as it rolls out of both of us on our release.

I am panting with my eyes still closed tight, just feeling him slowly moving in and out of me, riding out the last of his tremors. I finally feel my pussy start to release its grasp on his dick and I smile as I lay my head back onto the brick behind my head.

I laugh into the open space between our faces before opening my eyes and seeing his boring down into mine. I am trying to read his expression but I don't know how. I have never seen anyone look at me like this before.

I let my right leg fall off his hip before grinning at him again as I try to straighten my skirt and underwear.

Matthew quickly tucks himself back into his jeans before he starts wiping little debris pieces of brick and rock from the sides and back of my shirt.

I move my hands to his chest and smile back up at him, "What was that about?"

Matthew shakes his head back at me, "I have never been so turned on in my life. Why didn't you tell me you could play like that?"

I shake my head back at him, "I told you I could play. Ish."

He shakes his head back at me, as his hands start to run up and down my sides, "You never said you could fucking destroy the drums like that. I know the feeling it gives me when I am on stage.

"I just watched you with your eyes closed, running through those drums like a second skin. Playing my rhythms, my song. You are fucking perfect. Do you know that?"

I feel his hand as it grazes my cheek. I move my eyes towards his and I can feel the intensity in them. Something snaps to attention within me. He truly does think that I am perfect. Perfect for him. There is a nagging voice in the back of my head telling me that he is my other half as well. I heard it earlier but now, it is like a fog horn being released into a foggy night, signaling me home.

I feel my smile going wider, "Well if this is my reward for a job well done, I should play for you more often."

Matthew tilts his head back and laughs into the stairs above us, "I will happily reward you anytime you want baby. You are amazing."

I smile back at him as he grasps my hand again and starts to lead me back towards the festival. I look myself over quickly before we make it back to mom and Mona.

My mother immediately runs up to me and wraps her arms around me, "That was amazing Hope. You have gotten so much better since the last time I heard you play."

I smile as I hug her back, "Thanks mom."

She smiles as I pull away and Mona reaches out and grabs my hand. She gives a sly smile over my shoulder at Matthew, "We are going to go find a bathroom. We need some girl time."

She quickly starts to pull me through the crowd. I look over my shoulder to see Matthew and my mother smiling at us. Mona points to the other side of the road towards a little shop that looks like a book store with a cat room.

We enter through the front door quickly as I look around us completely baffled, "This isn't a bathroom. This is a cat house with a book store? And coffee?"

Mona nods around us before stepping up and ordering two shots of espresso. I find us a little table to sit near a big glass window allowing us to see into the cat room.

This is actually a pretty cool place. You can drink coffee, buy a book, and play with a cat. It is winning at every turn. I watch two kittens wrestling on the other side of the window while Mona waits for our order.

I watch a little orange demon of a kitten tackle a calico and giggle at the feistiness of both of them. I barely notice Mona as she approaches the table.

Mona sits down across from me then hands me one of the espressos. She puts her elbows up on the table and rests her chin on her folded hands, smiling devilishly at me, "I hope you know what you are doing."

I sip my espresso then look at her with a confused stare, "What do you mean?"

She lowers her hands to the table, looking out the window front behind me before bringing her eyes back to mine, "You have Matthew eating out of the palm of your hand. You do realize that right?"

I feel my cheeks starting to heat up as I look down at the table, fidgeting with my cup, "I can tell he likes me if that is what you mean."

Mona starts shaking her head, laughing out loud, "No, he more than likes you. I can tell. I have known him for 15 years. He doesn't get infatuated. But with you it is different. I have never seen him look at someone like he looks at you. Not even with Simone."

My head whips to hers quickly as it feels like my heart jumps to my throat, "What do you mean *with* Simone?"

What the fuck is she talking about? She can't be saying they are together right now. I feel my pulse starting to go crazy in my chest.

Her eyes go wide, apparently realizing she has misspoken, "Nevermind. Nothing. It's nothing. I have just never seen him like this before."

I feel my palms getting sweaty. My stomach starts to roll, "Tell me Mona. What do you mean *with* Simone? Is there something I need to know? Are they together or something?"

I can feel my walls quickly building back up around me, brick by brick. I am going to lose my shit. I am going to throw up all over these poor cats and be banned from the property.

I watch my hands as they begin to shake.

I see her eyes as they notice my shaking as well. Mona reaches out, putting her steady hand overtop of mine, "No, they were never really together. They just had some on again off again thing going on for a while."

I nod my head towards the table.

Maybe it's not as bad as I am imagining.

I try to breathe steadily, "Okay. How long is a while?"

Mona lets out another reluctant breath, "I mean, in total, on and off over the last 6 or 7 years."

I feel my eyes go wide as the room starts to spin around me. I grip the edge of the table tight, like I am expecting to fall out of my chair at any moment.

Holy fuck!

What am I supposed to do with that?

He has been with Simone in some capacity for the last 7 fucking years? How can he have something so casual going on with her yet he just told me that I am perfect?

I thought they were just friends, just band mates. I clear my throat as I feel my eyes darting around the room, "Is there anyone else I need to know about? Are you fucking him too?"

Mona pulls her hand back from mine, seeing obviously that I am now on edge, "No. I am not into guys. And as far as I know it has been awhile since they actually hooked up. Like almost a month or longer."

Why am I just now finding out about this?

It doesn't feel like he is trying to hide me. So what is going on with Simone that he feels the need to hide her from me?

Why did he just fuck me in an alley if he is in another situationship with her? So much truth is being thrown at me right now, I don't know whether to believe my ears or my heart.

I nod back at the table as I feel a tear roll down my cheek, "Why didn't he tell me this?"

I watch Mona as she sits her now empty cup down. I don't even have the guts to look her in the eye right now.

Her voice is low, almost a whisper, "Did you ask him about any relationships?"

I shake my head back at the table, "No. I didn't."

My thoughts are everywhere at once.

It is 100% my fault.

I didn't ask him if he was in a relationship. No wonder Simone was staring at us like that. Those daggers she was throwing were not at him, they were at me. She literally saw me taking him from her.

He belongs to her.

That is obvious now.

I pick up my espresso and take a slow drink. I look through the window at the cats before looking back towards Mona, "Give me a little bit of a head start. As much time as you can. I just need to be alone. I need to get out of here."

Mona shakes her head at me, her eyes wide. She knows she has said too much, it is written all over her face, "Don't take off. Don't do anything stupid. He really cares about you. Don't ruin that."

I shake my head back at her, trying to hold back a flood of tears, "I can't. I don't share. And by the look that Simone was giving me earlier, she obviously still believes he is hers. I am not going to break up the band over a crush.

"I just, I am gonna go grab my stuff then go back to California. Or maybe go find Daija. She will know what to do."

Mona's eyes whip to mine quickly, "Who is Daija?"

I give her a bogus smile before picking up my cup and finishing my espresso quickly, "My sister. I just need to not be here. It's too much. It's too loud."

I stand before she can say anything else and I take off through the front door. I quickly order an uber and move one street over through the alleys to be picked up.

I know I am running away like a coward but I am not going to be the one to break them up. No matter what I feel for Matthew.

He is taken.

And my heart is broken.

15 minutes later, my ride is dropping me off at the front of the house. I turn back towards the driver as I step out of the car, "Can you wait here for like 10 minutes? I need to go to an airport or bus station or somewhere."

The woman must sense the urgency in my voice. She looks down at her steering wheel before looking back at me, "Yeah. Hurry though."

Nodding my head quickly, I turn towards the house, running up the front steps. I don't even say anything to anyone as I barrel past them all and up into my room.

I quickly throw everything into my suitcase then grab my carry on. I scan the room quickly, grabbing my phone charger and purse at the last second.

I turn towards the door to see Simone is standing there with a smug grin on her face and her arms crossed over her chest.

Like she knows she has won.

I shake my head at her not really knowing what to say or do. I run past her and back down the stairs.

But I come to an abrupt stop at the bottom of the stairs. Lily is standing in front of the door with her hands out in front of her, eyes blown wide, "Slow down Hope! What happened? What are you doing? Where are you going?"

I know I have to look like a crazy person right now, tearing through her house like it is on fire. The gravity of everything that is happening right now hits me like a brick wall.

I instantly feel myself starting to crumble as the tears roll down my cheeks. Her eyes instantly soften in compassion.

I shake my head at Lily, "I didn't know. I didn't know and I don't want to be in the way. I don't want me to be the reason that anything comes between the band. I just want to leave."

Lily lowers her hands and steps in closer to me. She wraps her arms around my trembling body and pulls me close, "Didn't know what Hope? What are you afraid of?"

I sniffle loudly, trying to find the nerve to actually speak the words.

Letting out an exhausted sigh, "I didn't know about Matthew and Simone. I don't want to be in the way. I just want to leave. I just want to forget."

I feel her grip on me tighten as she pulls me as close to her as humanly possible. She turns her head past me and tells someone, "Call Lucy. Let her know she is here and she is safe. We are gonna go have some girl time in our room, okay?"

I can hear Gideon behind her, "Sure thing babe. Just let me know if she needs anything."

I pull back from Lily looking in between the two of them. Lily grabs my hand and my suitcase then starts to lead me back up the stairs.

I don't want to be here.

I want to leave.

Hide...run away. Get as far away from this embarrassment as possible.

I open my mouth to say as much when Lily says, "There is a lot you need to know. And honestly shame on fucking Matthew for not telling you all this himself. But trust me, once you hear me out, you will understand. And if you still want to leave at that point, I won't stop you."

She rounds the top of the stairs and pushes her bedroom door open. I drag my feet following behind her. She sits my suitcase down then shuts the door behind us.

I look up at her and she motions towards the bed for me to have a seat. Throwing my carry on and purse beside my suitcase, I nod back at her and make my way to sit down.

She sits beside me, pulling my hands into hers, "First thing you need to understand is I totally get where you are coming from. I have had my own experiences with Simone so I completely get where the apprehension is coming from. She is fucking gorgeous and quite frankly it can be intimidating."

I nod back at her, letting out a small chuckle, "That's putting it fucking mildly."

She sighs back at me, squeezing my hand, "Whatever was going with Matthew and Simone is over. He ended it. I am not going to pretend to understand what all went down between them and I haven't been around from the beginning.

84

"But from what I understand, they were never really together. Just kinda fucking around. Never anything truly serious."

Lily lets out another sigh as her eyes roll from me to the dresser, "I think maybe at one point Matthew may have wanted more but then the next thing I knew they were over-over. Like completely over."

I nod back at her, letting out a heavy breath, "Why wouldn't he just tell me that? Why would he leave me to find out on my own? That is just fucking cruel. I didn't think he was like that."

Lily shakes her head at me as she reaches up a hand and wipes a stray tear away from my cheek, "He's not Hope. I promise you. He is not a cruel person. Furthest thing from it honestly. He is the one you call when your world is falling apart. If he cannot help, he will at least give you a shoulder to cry on.

"And if I am being completely truthful with you, I don't think he told you because I don't think he is proud of whatever it was they had going on. I don't think he is ashamed of it, but instead maybe he feels like he was putting more into it than she was. Maybe it is some level of embarrassment? I think he thought it was one thing, when the whole time she saw it as something different."

I pull my hands from hers and smooth my hair down the back of my head before standing up and start pacing in front of her, "That still doesn't tell me why he didn't just tell me about her. This is a huge deal, they are together every single day.

"I feel like what you just said, maybe I am thinking there is more here than he is. Maybe he is just seeing this as a good time. Which if he is, then that is on me, I never really declared my feelings on it.

"He just...he made me feel so fucking special, Lily. I really believed that he cared. Now I just feel like he has made a fucking fool out of me. I feel like he was just stringing me along the whole time. Like I have just been filling in for her. I just feel so fucking stupid."

I know I look just as defeated as I feel. I can tell by the pity look she is giving me. I just don't understand why he was so forthcoming with me if he wasn't all in like me. Why did he tell me I was perfect for him if I obviously am not? Because I am not Simone and never will be.

The weight of the afternoon is starting to catch up with me. My shoulders feel just as tense as my nerves. My brain feels like it has run a marathon. My heart as well feels drained and just echoing with emptiness.

Leaning into the wall behind me, I slide down onto my ass. I am just lost, confused.

I don't know what to believe. My heart or everyone else around me. My brain obviously doesn't know what to think so it's opinion doesn't matter right now.

Lily sits up straighter, but seems to be fidgeting with her fingers a bit, like she is afraid to say what she is thinking.

She finally rolls her eyes, throwing her hands down to her sides, "So, full transparency here. I was in a similar ish situation. With Simone and Gideon."

My eyes fly to hers immediately.

I do the only thing I can honestly think of and that is to laugh loudly. You have got to be fucking kidding me?!?! Who is she not fucking in this house?

She raises her hands, "Wait, let me finish. So, Gideon and Simone had a thing but it was literally just sex. No feelings involved. Gideon was using...coke. He has quit, but when he was using, Simone would help him from time to time. To kind of alleviate the pressure if you know what I mean.

"But when I found out I kinda lost my shit over it. Gideon and I were finished before we even had a chance to start. But after some time, I figured out that I felt more for him than I was letting myself realize. I should have given him the chance to explain to me what the whole situation actually was.

"That is what I am afraid of for you. I am afraid that you are going to just walk away from something that has the potential to be great. Only because you don't know every side of the story.

"I just, I really hope that you decide to at least talk to him about all of this before you just leave. Matthew seems to really care about you. I don't want to see either of you hurt. He truly is a nice guy."

I nod at her, as I stand again.

I cross my arms over my chest and let out another sigh as I look to the ceiling, "Yeah. A really nice guy that apparently has a thing for easy women. I feel really fucking special now. Also, he seems to not mind letting his partner be passed around. That is a bit of a red fucking flag if you ask me."

I look at Lily but she can't disagree with what I am saying. She just shakes her head, "I was afraid of what Simone was capable of in the beginning. I was afraid that he would choose her over me, that she meant more to him than I did. But he didn't. He chose me. And once I got to know Simone, I realized what they had was literally just a friend helping a friend out.

"Sure it was with sex. And still in my head, that doesn't really sit well. But I have talked with her, what they had was literally nothing like what we have.

"Gideon is my soul mate. The way he is with me is nothing like what he was with her. She was just a means to an end. With us there is more there. We complete each other in every way, not just with the sex."

I shake my head at her, "But I am not afraid of what Simone is capable of. My only concern is what Matthew is capable of, what he can so easily keep from me.

"And Gideon's situation, that doesn't make it any easier for me. Because Matthew isn't addicted to anything. Other than

87

her apparently. I mean, does it bother me that he was so easy with letting her jump from bed to bed? Sure, but at the same time I have had casual sex too so I can't really be too upset over that. I guess I am just upset that he was able to fool me so easily. I thought I was smarter than that."

I watch as Lily's shoulders sag in defeat.

She can't fight me on this one either.

She can't argue back because there is nothing to argue.

Matthew going back to Simone time and time again just proves my point. Quickly, I retreat back into myself again. I wish we had never come here. But when I hear the knock on the bedroom door I tense up, knowing exactly who is waiting for me on the other side.

Smiling towards Lucy I chuckle, "Apparently, they really needed some girl time."

Lucy smiles back at me as we walk back down the booths, checking out everything again. I stop when we make it to the jewelry booth that Hope had been looking at before.

I reach down and pick up the necklace Hope had been admiring earlier.

It really is beautiful.

I smile as I nod to the guy behind the table, "Do you take cash?"

He grins back at me as he reaches out his hand for the necklace, "Yeah. This one is $250. Want me to box it for you?"

I nod back as I pull my money out of my wallet and hand it over to the woman next to him. I pay for the gift quickly then take the small bag. Reaching down, I grab one of their business cards and tuck it into the paper bag as well, "Have a good one."

I turn back around to see Lucy smiling at me, "What?"

She shakes her head at me, "I have never seen you smitten before. It is cute."

I roll my eyes at her and let out a laugh, "Funny. But for real, does this mean I can call you Mom now?"

Lucy lashes out and slaps me in the chest with the back of her hand as I start laughing at her. I turn to see Mona approaching us, with a solemn look in her eyes.

I look over her shoulder and scan the crowd but can't find Hope, "Where is Hope? Did you guys get lost looking for a bathroom?"

Mona shakes her head at me then looks to Lucy for some kind of help. Lucy lets out a heavy breath, "How long has it been?"

Mona looks down at her watch then back to me quickly, "About 15 minutes."

I shake my head back at them both, confused as to what the hell is actually happening, "15 minutes since what?"

Mona lets out another heavy breath turning to me, "I didn't know that Hope didn't know about Simone. I told her that I had never seen you like this. Not even with Simone. I didn't expect her to just take off. I thought you would have told her. I'm sorry."

I look over her shoulder again expecting Hope to be standing there but there is nothing but strangers passing by.

I look from Mona back to Lucy as panic starts to set in.

Lucy pulls her phone out and looks down at it shaking her head, "Fuck."

Stepping closer to her, I am still unsure what the hell is actually happening, "What? Where is she?"

Lucy shakes her head at me then looks back to Mona, "She is gone. She texted me about 5 minutes ago. She said she is going home."

The ground starts to shift under me.

She is gone?

Home?

Why?

I turn to Mona, "What did you do?"

Mona throws her hands up in defense, "I didn't know you didn't tell her about you and Simone. I assumed you guys had already had the ex's talk."

I shake my head at her, feeling the panic and fear rising quickly from deep within, "Simone isn't an ex. We were never really anything. You know that."

She nods her head back at me, "I know. I told her that you guys were just kind of an on again off again thing. She didn't care. She says she doesn't share.

"That she wasn't going to break up the band over a crush. She said she was going to go find her sister. She asked me to give her a head start, so I did."

I turn to Lucy, who is just nodding her head at Mona. She turns and looks at me with pity in her eyes, "She doesn't handle confrontation well. She always just kinda closes up, closes off. We need to just give her some time, some space. I will call her later. Try to explain it all to her."

I am completely dumbfounded right now.

How does she not realize that I want her?

Only her.

I thought we were on the same page. Why would she think that I wanted Simone?

Confusion continues to wrack my brain. Emotions start to cloud my judgement along with my vision. Mona steps up to Lucy, "Is Daija your other daughter?"

Lucy nods her head as she looks around the crowd of people moving past us. There is easily triple the amount of people here than earlier, "Yeah. Daija is her twin."

Mona nods at her, "That's a pretty name. What made you come up with it?"

Lucy looks back to Mona, "Hope was for the future. Daija was for the past. It means 'remembrance'. Their dad died before they were born. Daija looks just like him. Black hair, bright blue eyes. Hope looks more like me. They are fraternal twins."

Turning abruptly, I start walking back towards the car, "Fuck this. Come on Lucy. Take me to her. I am not letting her leave, not like this."

Lucy shakes her head at me, "I don't know Matthew. Maybe she just needs some time to think. To process."

I turn back to her, nailing her down with my stare, "You can either drive me back to the house now or you can give me the keys and I will drive my fucking self. Either way, I am not letting her go."

Lucy takes a step towards me just as her phone starts to ring.

She pulls it out of her pocket, letting out a heavy sigh as she looks at me while putting the phone to her ear, "Yeah Gideon. What's up?"

She looks down at the ground as she walks past me, heading towards the car, "Yeah okay. We are heading back now. Don't let her leave. We will be there in like 10 minutes."

I stride past her, quickly reaching the car before her or Mona. After climbing in I sit the necklace on the seat next to me. I don't want to imagine how much she must hate me right now.

But she has to know there is nothing there.

Not anymore.

Hope is the only person I want in my life.

I feel my stomach roll and my heart rate skyrocket the closer we get to the house. Mona has told me at least a dozen times how sorry she is.

But it's not her fault.

She has nothing to apologize for. I should have been honest with Hope. She should have known upfront what she was walking into.

As soon as the car stops in the drive, I am barrelling down the walkway. I notice there is a car parked out front but I don't really give it much attention.

92

Instead, I take the porch steps two at a time. Gideon is waiting for me just inside the front door. He points towards the stairs, "Her and Lily are up in our room, talking."

I nod at him as I run past him and up the stairs to the landing. Attempting to take in a solid breath, I try to calm my nerves a bit before knocking loudly on the door. I stare at it for a few moments before raising my hand to knock again.

But the door opens before I even have the chance to knock again. Lily is standing in front of me, her face completely somber.

This can't be good.

I look around her, "Is Hope in here?"

Lily looks to her right, behind the door then back to me, "Yeah, but I don't know that she wants to talk to you."

I shake my head back at her, "I don't care. I have to talk to her. I have to see her."

Before Lily can argue with me, I am pushing the door open and stepping around her. Hope is leaned up against the wall with her arms wrapped around her center.

I have seen her closed off before but this is somehow different. She just seems defeated somehow.

I step up to her, reaching a hand out, "Come on. Let's go talk, privately."

She shakes her head towards the floor before bringing her red rimmed eyes up to meet mine.

I am instantly crushed.

I did this.

I broke her.

Just like everyone else that has ever been in her life. I fucking broke her. I reach out and snatch her wrist in my hand, "Yes. We are talking. Now."

She tries to pull away from me but I basically drag her down the hallway and into my room. I can hear Lily behind me, begging me to just let her go but I can't.

93

I have to make this right.

As soon as she is in the room, I shut the door behind me and lock it. I turn and see her looking around the room while she slowly backs away from me.

She looks terrified.

I run my hand down my face, throwing the gift bag on the bed. I let out another slow breath, "I am not going to hurt you Hope. I just want to talk. I will stay on this side of the room. You can stay on that side."

I see her visibly loosen up a bit to this. She takes another step back before leaning against the wall on the far side of the room.

She wraps her arms back around herself, "Just say what you have to say so I can leave. Please."

I take a step towards her, before making myself stop in my tracks. No matter how much I want to hold her right now, I am not going to force myself on her.

I close my eyes, turning my face to the ceiling, "I should have told you about me and Simone. It is 100% my fault. And I am sorry."

I look back towards her but her face is completely blank.

She stands a bit taller, "Thank you. I am leaving now."

She moves to walk widely around me and I take a step closer to her, "Why? I told you I was sorry. Why are you still going to leave?"

Hope turns her glare back towards me, but something has changed in her eyes.

She laughs at me, "You really fucking think I want to be here? In the middle of all of this? Do you honestly think that because you apologized that everything is fine now?

"You don't fucking shatter someone then say your sorry and everything is magically okay again. That is not how life works Matthew."

94

I nod my head back at her, "No. I get that. But why don't you want to even try? Why is it so easy for you to walk away?"

She turns her steely gaze back towards me, "Because it was so easy for you to lie to me. This whole fucking time Matthew. You could have told me you have been fucking her for years.

"YEARS Matthew! Or do I not deserve to know that? Because I am just some fucking side piece you are playing with until she decides she wants you again?"

I take another step towards her, my own anger rising from deep within, "That is not how it fucking is. Her and I, we are done. We have been done for a while now. I don't fucking want her. I want you!"

She shakes her head at me, "I don't believe you. I don't know that I can ever believe you. Everything has been a fucking lie Matthew. I don't fucking need this in my life. I have enough shit going through my god damn head on the daily. I don't need anything else to be fucking insecure about."

I try to take a step towards her but she takes a step back. I stop, just staring at her, "So none of it was fucking real to you then. Nothing that we have shared meant anything?"

She takes a step towards me, tears falling from her face.

She points a finger at me and I hear her louder than I ever imagined her voice could ever go, "Obviously it fucking did or I wouldn't be the one who is upset right now. I truly fucking believed you. Like the idiot I fucking am. I trusted you. I thought you actually fucking wanted me.

"That you actually fucking liked me. But I am just your next fucking conquest. But that's okay. It's my fault. I should have asked how many people you are currently fucking. I did this to myself."

I scrunch my face up at her in anger, "That is fucking bullshit and you know it. You are fucking running away because something got tough. Something happened that you are not

95

happy with and you are running the fuck away like a god damned coward!"

She takes another step towards me poking her finger into my chest, "You don't know what I am doing Matthew because you don't fucking know me. You just fucking met me. How dare you stand here and judge my reaction to you treating me like a piece of fucking garbage! You have no right! None!"

I can feel myself shaking, but I don't know if it is from anger or the realization that she is right.

I have treated her like shit.

I should have just been honest with her from the beginning. But I wasn't and nothing can change that now.

"If I fucking wanted her, I would have her. But I don't. I fucking want you okay? I am choosing you! But if that is not fucking enough for you then fine. Just fucking leave. And take all your fucking childish insecurities the fuck with you because I don't fucking need them okay?"

As soon as the words leave my mouth, I know that I have lost her. I don't even know why the fuck I said what I did.

Hope takes another step towards me and slaps me hard across the face. I bring my eyes back to hers, watching her shatter in front of me. Tears start to roll down her face as her chin starts to quiver. I want to reach out to her but it is very obvious that she wants nothing to do with me now.

She takes in a rattled breath, "I fucking hate you Matthew. I wish I had never fucking met you."

She steps around me and walks through the door, slamming it loudly behind me. I flinch at the impact of her walking out of my life.

No, not walking, running.

And I fucking deserve it.

I deserve everything that she is doing to me right now.

I turn and run after her. Opening the door my eyes quickly tell my brain that she is not here. There is nothing but an empty hallway in front of me. I make my way down the hall then barrel down the stairs.

I round the bottom and see her standing at the bar with a bottle of Dalmore at her lips. Edge comes out of nowhere and grabs me by the arms, keeping me back from her.

Hope slams the bottle down on the counter and points to me, "Stay the fuck away from me Matthew. I mean it. I am done with your bullshit."

I try to pull myself away from Edge when Simone comes around the corner from the stairs. She smiles at me then at Hope.

She turns back to me, placing a hand on my bicep, "What's wrong, baby?"

Before I can tell her to get her hand off of me, Hope is crossing the room towards us. Simone looks up just in time to see a fist flying at her face. She screams as she grabs the side of her face before turning back towards Hope.

I never in a million years would have imagined that Hope would have this side to her. I knew she was crazy but I thought it was the harmless kind of crazy. Like owning a pet raccoon and putting it in dresses kind of crazy.

She leans into Simones face, screaming at her, "You are such a fucking whore Simone. All you do is fucking run around here jumping from dick to dick. With absolutely zero regard about who you fucking hurt in the process."

Then she turns to me, laughing wildly as she points between me and Simone, "You two fucking deserve each other. You're both heartless pieces of shit."

I watch her as she walks back over to the bar and grabs the bottle of whisky before turning and walking towards the back door. I look at Simone who is still holding the side of her face.

She turns to me, "What the fuck was that about?"

97

I rip my arms away from Edge, "You getting what the fuck you deserve. Why the fuck did you even come in here? And why the fuck did you call me baby? I am not fucking yours Simone. I never was and I never fucking will be.

"You need to get your fucking shit together. Or changes are going to have to be made. I am not going to live my entire life walking on eggshells because you might decide to give a fuck about me that day. You have no fucking right to try to lay any type of claim on me. We are over Simone. For good."

Simone steps up close to me, "Matthew no. We are not done. We are never going to be done. We are meant for each other and you know it. I am yours. I want you okay. Only you. I am sorry that it took me seeing you with someone else before I could realize it."

She leans up closer and before I can even react her hands are around my neck and she is kissing me. I put my hands up and push her away but the damage is already done.

I look over her shoulder and see Hope still standing in the doorway, staring at us. Her eyes are wild and wide as I watch her entire face turning crimson.

She turns and throws a 10 thousand dollar bottle of whisky towards the ocean as she screams into the air around her.

I push Simone to the side and run towards the back door. But before I can get to Hope she is running. She is down the stairs before I can even get to the door. She turns and continues to run down the beach.

I take the back steps two at a time. I quickly turn in the direction she has taken but she is so far ahead of me I don't know that I will be able to catch up.

This is a woman who runs for fucking fun every morning. I watch her veer in between two houses so I cut through as well, trying to meet her back at the road. I finally come out at street level and I turn to see her running full speed before coming to a stop at a taxi. She gets in and the car drives away.

I scream into the sky, knowing no one fucking cares.

No one gives a fuck that I am completely falling apart.

I turn and start marching back towards the house. Gideon is standing at the end of the walkway that leads to the front door.

Pointing my finger towards the front porch, my voice is loud and prevalent, "If I just fucking lost her forever because of that bitch inside, know that I am fucking done. Fuck this band. Fuck Simone. I am fucking done. She either fixes this shit or I am walking Gideon. I am fucking serious."

I turn and stomp towards the porch.

Simone is standing there crying with the start of a black eye forming on her face. Good, I hope it fucking hurts.

I give her a quick side eye before stopping and pointing at her, "You are a fucking disease. Never fucking touch me again. Do you hear me? Never!" I continue past her and slam the front door open before running up the stairs.

I round the corner towards my room to see Lucy standing there with her arms crossed, just glaring at me. I come to a stop and stare back at her.

I hurt Hope.

I fucking promised Lucy that I wouldn't hurt her and I did. Everything is catching up to me all at once. The fight, my feelings, this persistent pounding in my head to make things right. All of it.

I move past her, forcing my way into my room. Lucy follows right behind me. I turn and sit down on the edge of the bed, putting my head in my hands as I lean down onto my thighs.

Lucy moves to the other side of the room and leans against the dresser. I let out a heavy sigh as I look up at her, unable to even put a sentence together. Her phone dings and my heart jumps into my throat. Leaping up from the bed, "Is it her? Is she okay?"

Lucy looks from the phone to me then hits a button and puts the phone to her ear. I watch her, just praying that it is Hope on the other end of the line.

Lucy looks away, "Hey sweetie. Yeah some shit has seriously gone down. How soon do you think you could be in Nag's Head? Yeah, North Carolina. Your sister needs us."

I feel my heart deflate knowing it is not Hope on the other end of the phone. I turn around seeing the necklace laying on the bed. I snatch it up and walk over to my bag, throwing it inside.

I can't fucking do this.

I can't fucking be here.

I shake my head as I grab my bag off the floor and throw it onto the bed. I am going to just load up and meet them in Orlando. Silence is what I need. And to be someplace that Simone is not.

I can hear Lucy behind me, "As soon as you hear from her you call me. I need to know she is alright. I don't care if it's two minutes or two hours from now."

I turn back around and stare at her, trying not to lose my shit. She turns and looks at me again, this time with empathy, "Thanks Daija. I love you baby."

Lucy brings the phone down and slides it back into her pocket. She shakes her head at me as she walks towards me. I am fully ready to embrace the anger that I deserve to have thrown at me. I am just too tired to give a shit.

Lucy takes another step closer then I feel her arms wrapping around me. She pulls me in close and squeezes me tightly to her.

Tears start to roll down my face before I even realize I am crying. I hug her back, putting my cheek on top of her head, "I lost her."

Lucy pulls back and gives me a sympathetic smile, "We will find her. She just needs time to cool down. To process. Like I said earlier."

I nod back at her, snickering at her 'I told you so'. I let out another huff as I sit down on the side of the bed, "I told Gideon that if I lose Hope over this bullshit that I am done. I am done with the band."

I turn my eyes back to Lucy who looks like she is in complete shock. She doesn't realize that her daughter could very well be the love of my life. Sure I have only known her for like a day but when it is right, you just fucking know. And I know. I also know that I have eternally fucked everything up.

I shake my head at her, "I can't lose her, Lucy. And not because of Carnal Decay. I fucking love her. I love her insane brain. I love her heart, her smile. I love her even when she is letting her intrusive thoughts get the best of her. I know it is quick. I know it is crazy. It doesn't follow any of the rules of logic. Doesn't make any sense but I just...I can't help it. She made me fall in love with her."

Lucy smiles at me and wipes a stray tear from her face as well. She nods her head at me with a soft smile. I know she can feel the truth in my words.

I lean forward again, "You should have seen her fucking clock Simone. She was so fucking mad. I didn't know she had it in her."

Lucy laughs as she walks up to me, sitting down next to me on the bed. I watch her hand as it comes out and pats my leg, "I have never seen her get violent before. Ever. She has been to the point of breaking a million different times but she always shoulders the responsibility of the situation. She always puts it on herself. But with you, it seems she felt she had something to fight for. I have never seen that side of her."

I look at Lucy in amazement.

Hope has never lost her shit over anyone before.

That, for some reason, makes me feel better. It makes me think there might be a chance after all for me and Hope to come back from this.

Lucy leans in and lays her head on my shoulder, "I truly pray that you two are able to work this out. And not just for job security. I have never seen her as happy as she was with you. She has smiled more in the last 24 hours that she has in the last 10 years. She has been through so much already. I just want to see her happy."

Smiling, I lay my head down on Lucy's, "I want to be the one to make her happy. Truly. I don't want anyone else. I don't think I ever will. No one will ever compare to her. And now I have fucking lost her Lucy. I don't know what to do."

Lucy sits up and turns to me but before she can say anything her phone goes off again. She pulls it out of her pocket before standing abruptly, "Where are you Hope?"

I stand up beside her, praying to god that Hope is okay. She paces the floor before turning back and looking at me wide eyed, "Yeah no. Hold on."

She walks towards me and hands me her phone. I stare at it like it is a bomb waiting to go off. I take the phone from her hand and clear my throat before putting it up to my ear, "Hope?"

I hear her sigh on the other end of the line, "I will be coming back to get my things. I do not want to see you or Simone. I do not want to talk to either of you. Understand?"

My heart shatters into a thousand pieces.

I can feel the tears rolling down my face again. Taking in a shuttered breath I whisper, "Yeah. I understand."

I look at Lucy and feel myself starting to break, "I will give the phone back to your mom. I am sorry Hope. I truly am. I promise I won't bother you again."

I hand the phone back to Lucy. She puts the phone back to her ear, "Yeah baby. I am here."

She reaches up and wipes a tear from my cheek before she turns and leaves the room, slowly shutting the door behind her.

7
Hope
THE GREATEST - Billie Eilish

I try to calm myself as much as I can when I hear him breathing on the other end of the phone. Matthew's voice is low, almost a whisper, "Hope?"

I let out a sigh, looking around my surroundings. I am standing on the corner of some street in town, no fucking clue where I really am. I just had to not be there.

My eyes close hard as I try to muster up the strength to speak, "I will be coming back to get my things. I do not want to see you or Simone. I do not want to talk to either of you. Understand?"

I hear Matthew take in a ragged breath, then I hear his voice cracking, "Yeah. I understand. I will give the phone back to your mom. I am sorry Hope. I truly am. I promise I won't bother you again."

I am crying harder than I ever have before.

To hear him so broken, hear him give in.

I half expected him to yell at me some more but instead he just gave up. I hear my mom on the other end again, "Yeah baby. I am here."

I let out another shuddered cry, "I am sorry mom. I didn't mean to cause so much shit between everyone. I completely understand if you hate me right now."

My mother sighs into the other end of the phone, "Hope, I do not hate you. You never intended for any of this to happen. I

103

know that. And if something does happen and Matthew does leave the band, I don't want you wearing that weight on your shoulders. This most likely would have happened with or without you."

I wipe the tears from my face as I stand up a bit straighter, the air stilling all around me, "What do you mean if Matthew leaves the band?"

I hear her shut a door, "Matthew told Gideon that if he lost you because of Simone that he was done. Forever. That he was going to leave the band."

I start sobbing even harder.

I am now pacing back and forth on this abandoned street corner. God only knows how far away from my family. Every step leaves bent footprints in the dust of the sidewalk before me.

The bite of the scent of grime mixed with the salty air leaves a harsh taste in my mouth as I try to gulp in air.

I am left standing, a lonely silhouette in the shattered ruins of this life...this band. My tears become a raging river down my face, unstoppable and wild.

I can feel my shoulders shaking, "Why? Why would he do that mom? I am just some random girl he hooked up with. I don't fucking want him to do that."

I can hear the sternness in my mothers tone, "You are not some random girl, Hope Elizabeth. I believe him when he says he will leave. I also believed him when he told me he loves you."

I stop pacing and stare down the road in front of me.

The sun is starting to set as the salty ocean breeze sweeps around me. My heart now pounding as loud as his bass drum, "He said that?"

I hear my mother chuckle, "Yes, Hope. He told me that he loves you. And I believe him. I have never seen him happier than when he is with you. I don't think I have ever seen him happy at all actually until now.

"Just promise me one thing, okay baby. Promise me that you will think about all of this. Before you just run away and hide yourself away from him. Don't make a decision that you might regret. If you feel anything for him at all, don't just run away. You both deserve better than that."

I let out another anxious sigh as I watch my feet, kicking random gravel around again, "I don't know that I can be with him mom. Regardless of how I feel about him. She is always going to be there. She is always going to be a part of his life."

She knows I am right.

She has too.

I hear her moving around, doing something probably in her bedroom, "Yeah. She will. She will always be a part of his life. But you have the chance to be all of his life. You have the opportunity to be what he comes home to every single day. Think about that before you just walk away from him okay? Will you promise me that?"

I roll my eyes, knowing she can probably feel it through the phone, "Yeah. I will think about it. I uh, I told him I am coming back to get my stuff. I don't really want to see him or her. I just want to get my stuff and go. I will text you when I am there. I will just go hang out on the back porch until you tell me the coast is clear. Is that okay?"

I hear my mother chuckle into the phone, "Yeah. That is okay. I love you Hope. I will see you soon. Also, your sister said she is on her way. She should be here in the next few hours. She is driving up from Augusta."

I let out an angry breath, of course she is on her way. The attention isn't on her so she must show up and make it all about her somehow.

I turn and squint towards the setting sun again, "Yeah. Okay. I love you too mom. I will talk to you soon. I am going to take a cab back there in just a minute."

I look at my phone as I hit the end call button then glance back up at the setting sun again. Why would he tell my mom that he loves me if he doesn't?

Why would he apparently pour his heart out to her if it isn't how he actually feels? Confusion is setting in even deeper than earlier and I don't fucking know what to do with it all.

I roll my shoulders as I reach up with my arm to hail down another cab. When it finally stops and I am seated inside the realization of everything finally hits me.

He is willing to leave the band because of me.

I mean, I don't want him too but he actually would. He wouldn't just do that for any random girl.

At least, I don't think he would.

The taxi pulls up to the house about 15 minutes later. The sun is almost completely down now. It is dark enough that the porch lights are on.

I can see people moving around in the sitting area so I pay the cabbie then start to make my way down the side of the house towards the beach.

My plan is to just hide in the shadows until mom lets me know the path is clear to come in and get my stuff. Figure out my next move.

I have to figure something out before Daija gets here. I love my sister but I just don't have the energy to deal with her right now.

I round the back of the house and come to a halt when I see Matthew standing at the edge of the water. He doesn't seem to realize I am here, not 20 feet away from him. Quickly I look to the house then back towards him.

He seems solemn.

I watch him for a moment then I see his hand go to his face. He wiped a tear away.

He is standing out here crying.

My heart starts to hammer in my chest as my arms beg me to reach out to him. I take a few small steps towards him, "Matthew?"

He turns on me quickly and I see that his eyes are completely red rimmed. His cheeks have tear stained trails running down them.

He lifts his hands and wipes his face on both sides before shoving his hands down in his jeans pockets, "I'm sorry. I didn't know you would come back here. Your mom said you were on your way to get your stuff so I came back here to stay out of your way. I will just walk down the beach until you leave."

I nod back to him as I lower my eyes to sand between us. He walks past me, not fast but not hesitantly either.

I close my eyes and take a deep breath before jumping off the metaphorical bridge I have been presented with. I turn towards him as he is walking away from me, "Did you mean what you told my mother?"

He turns back towards me before tilting his head, "Which part?"

Scared, I look down at the ground between us. It feels like a mile though I know it isn't even 5 feet, "That you love me."

I can see his bare feet fidgeting in the sand. His toes curl as if they are trying to hold him back from stepping towards me, "Yeah. I meant it. I didn't know she told you that. I mean, I don't care that she did but I don't expect it to change anything."

I let out a heavy sigh as I look back up towards him. His hands are still shoved into his jeans pockets. His hair flying in every direction from the breeze off the ocean. He gives me a small smile before he starts to turn and continues to walk away from me.

I take a small step forward, "I love you too."

Matthew stops and turns back towards me. He looks at me like I have grown two heads.

I give him a soft smile, shaking my head at him, "I know it isn't smart. I know that it will cause nothing but pain. But I love you. I have loved you from the first moment I saw you. Before I even knew who you were. I feel like I have loved you since long before that even.

"Like I was just waiting to find you. Then I thought that you were playing with me and I...I don't know. I just closed up. I should have listened to you earlier."

He is taking small steps towards me again. I wipe the tears from my own face before heaving a sigh back out towards the ocean, "But this probably won't work. Regardless of whether we love each other or not.

"There is always going to be a little part of me that thinks you want her. That you will leave me for her. And like you said, you don't have any room for my childishness in your life."

I see him stop in the sand at my words.

He is now close enough I can feel the heat rolling off his body towards my own, "I should have never said that. I was just angry. I am not bothered by your insecurities. I should have never tried to use them against you. I was just pissed that you were throwing us away so effortlessly. It hurt. I'm sorry."

I turn and look at him.

Really look at him.

The moonlight is bouncing off the water beside us, causing little beams to bounce around us. I see in his eyes that he means every word that he is saying.

I let out another sigh as I turn back towards the ocean, "I don't know where to go from here."

Matthew steps up close enough that I can feel his breath on my neck. I naturally lean my head in towards him, like the pull from his body is wrapping me up in him.

He shifts a bit, bringing my eyes up to his, "I love you Hope. I want you. Only you. No one else. I never loved her. I have never loved anyone. Not like this. I don't want any of this if you are not with me to share it."

I watch his hand as it comes up and wipes a tear from my face. Closing my eyes hard, "I love you too Matthew. I just don't know how to make this work. I don't know how we can..."

His lips crash into mine as he wraps his arms around me tightly. His warmth embraces me as I feel myself fall into him. Mind, body and soul.

I feel the waves of anxiety run through my veins from my fingertips all the way to my heart. His hand wraps up in my hair as he starts to walk me backwards, under the cover of the back porch. I wrap my arms around him as well, gripping his shirt in my fists as our tongues explore each other.

I feel my back come across something solid and then he is pushing himself into me. I let a moan leave my throat as I bring my hands up and wrap them around his neck, up into the back of his head. I grip his hair tight in both hands as I force his lips into mine harder than before.

He finally pulls away a moment later as we are both panting for air. Matthew puts his forehead to mine as we feel each other pulsing through each other's veins. He smiles and with his eyes still closed he whispers, "Marry me."

I pull back, like I have been judo chopped right in the throat. I look up into his dark eyes now staring down at me, "What?"

He smiles again as he rubs his hands up my back, "Marry me. We can leave right now. We can go to Vegas and get married. By the time we get back for the show, I promise you that I will have proven to you that you are all I want.

"I want to spend forever with you, Hope. You make me feel alive again. I have been dead for so long and you are the fire that has woke me up. I can't lose you. You mean everything to me."

I stare at him, shaking my head at his insanity. Letting out a small laugh, "And they said I was the crazy one."

He laughs again but looks hopefully into my eyes. I shake my head at him before looking past him into the vast ocean.

Can I handle walking away from him knowing that he loves me enough to want to marry me?

Obviously, he cares about me more than he ever cared about Simone, or else he wouldn't be asking me to run away with him.

I feel my heart start drumming in my chest hard again as the hairs on my arms start to stand up.

My mothers words from earlier are still rolling through my head, 'You have the chance to be all of his life'.

A nervous energy runs down my spine. I was never one to step away from a challenge. Never one to not hesitate to go after what I wanted. It's not hesitation though, it's excitement.

I love him.

I smile back at him coyly, "Okay, yes. Let's do it. Let's get married."

His eyes go wide with surprise and shock. His smile covers his entire face as he leans in and kisses me again.

Hungrier this time.

I laugh into his mouth as I try to pull away, "But if we are going to do this though, there is no going back. There is no walking away. Nothing left for interpretation, nothing left unsaid. I accept your crazy, you accept mine. Deal?"

Matthew leans down and picks me up by the back of my thighs before pinning me to the shed door behind us. He smiles as he looks at me, now at eye level, "Deal."

He kisses me again, harder this time as I wrap my arms around his neck holding him close to me.

We lose ourselves in each other for a long moment before he pulls back smiling at me again, "Go back around front and meet me at the end of the drive. I am going to go get our stuff.

We can book a flight on the way to the airport. I will tell your mom we are just sneaking off for some alone time, away from Simone and the rest of the band."

I smile widely at him before nodding a yes and giving him another small kiss. I can not believe we are doing this.

He sits me down gently and kisses me again before turning and running through the sand to go up the back steps.

Watching him leave, I try to calm my racing heart.

I am certifiable.

I am literally going to marry the guy that earlier today crushed my heart into powder.

Shaking my head, I look towards the moon. I close my eyes and whisper into the night sky, "Dad? Please watch over us. Make sure we don't completely destroy each other."

I smile as I feel the breeze pick up and dance around my body. I never met my father but somehow it feels like he is here with me right now.

That he heard me and he approves.

I open my eyes and stare back out into the ocean for another moment before making my way around to the front of the house.

I stand in the shadow of the garage, where no one can see me even if they were to look out the window. Not 3 minutes later, Matthew is running out the front door with a smile on his face and our luggage in his hands. He stops at the end of the walkway, looking both directions before his face falls.

He thinks I am not here.

I smile widely as I step out of the shadows and his eyes turn towards me. He lets out a relieved sigh as I run towards him. Looking down the road, I see a car heading our way, "Uber?"

Matthew nods at me before leaning down and kissing me again. The car pulls up to the curb and he loads our luggage into the back.

∎

I turn and look up towards the house, noting a light on in one of the third floor bedrooms. I know my mom is watching me right now. I smile then blow a kiss towards the lit window before crawling into the backseat of the sedan beside Matthew.

I shut the door to the car and smile at Matthew before turning towards the driver, "Please take us to the airport."

I see a woman look up in the rearview mirror and realize it is the same driver that I had earlier tonight. I smile widely at her as she nods her head then wags her eyebrows at me with a little wink. I let out a laugh as I lean into Matthew.

He is on his phone booking tickets. He smiles down at me, "There is a flight leaving in an hour. If we hurry we can make it."

I smile up at him as I feel the driver hitting the gas pedal. I grin wickedly back at him, knowing in just a few hours we are going to be married. That nothing will come between us again. I lean up and kiss him again. I feel his hand grip the back of my head tightly as he holds his lips to mine.

I smile wider as I pull away and put my head on his shoulder. I can't believe I am doing this.

That is all I think about the entire ride to the airport. That is all I think about as we board our plane. That is all I think about when I wake up and we are landing in Vegas. That is all I think about when we step up to a line of taxis waiting to take us to our next destination.

That is all I am still thinking about as I watch the man I love lead me towards our future.

8

Apollo

Say That You Will - Sleep Token

I can't stop the smile that has been imprinted on my face for the last 6 hours. Hope is sitting beside me in a taxi as we are ushered to an all night chapel. I squeeze her hand in mine and she smiles widely back at me.

I can't believe we are doing this.

Lucy is going to kick my ass, but I don't care.

We pull up to the chapel and Hope giggles as she slides out of the seat beside me. I see her eyes as they roam over the building. Stepping around to the back of the car, I grab our luggage then move back to her side.

I look up at the building again before turning to her, "If you have changed your mind, I would understand. I won't be mad."

Hope turns and smiles widely at me again, "You're not getting out of this that easily sir."

I grin back at her as she picks up her suitcase in one hand then wraps the other around mine, dragging me towards the building.

As soon as the doors open, I can hear an old Elvis song playing on the speakers. I chuckle at the surroundings as I look down at her and she is laughing just as hard, if not harder.

A woman comes around a corner dressed like a go go dancer from a B-52's video, "Welcome Lovers! I hope you called ahead because we seem to be booked up for the night."

13

I sit my bag down and reach into my back pocket for my wallet, "I did. Wedding for Kirkland. I want everything you can offer, flowers, champagne, a fake grandmother crying in the background. The whole thing."

Hope laughs out around the room as she wraps her hands around my bicep, pulling herself closer to me. I smile from her back to the lady behind the podium. She grins back at us, "Okay, not a problem. I just need to see identification for both of you and we can get the ball rolling."

I hand her my passport as Hope hands over her own driver's license and social security card.

The woman takes down all of our information, "You will need to go to the county clerk's office and get a marriage license for this to be legal. You have 24 hours from the time of the ceremony to get that finalized. I see that you are here on a work visa which is fine. But if you plan on staying, there will be some hoops I am sure you are going to have to jump through."

I nod back at the woman when Hope leans forward, "He is only here for work. We will be moving back to London within a few months."

I turn, smiling down at her, "Are you sure?"

Hope smiles back at me, "Of course I am sure. That is your home, now it's my home. Plus, we know I love London so why not?"

The woman behind the podium hands us back our id's, "So, Hope, if you wouldn't mind coming with me. We are going to get you a veil and see if there are any flowers you may want. Matthew, I am going to ask you to walk through those double doors over there and stand up by Elvis."

I laugh out loud at the absurdity of what she just said but still make my way towards the doors. I watch Hope as she rounds a corner, smiling incredulously towards the woman. Once she is out of sight, I push the doors open and step through.

Elvis is waiting for me at the podium.

14

I try not to laugh at the insanity of seeing him for the first time. He curls his upper lip at me as he seems to readjust his body in the sequined jumpsuit he is wearing. I laugh to myself as I shake my head and move towards him.

I settle in, just taking in my surroundings for a few moments when I hear a non Elvis song start playing on the speakers above us. Instead, it sounds like an instrumental version of one of our older songs. I smile from the ceiling down to the doors as they open.

At some point, Hope has changed out of her t-shirt and skirt into a short yellow dress. She has a white veil coming off her head dragging behind her like a cloud.

The bouquet of white roses in her hands seems to be shining just as brightly as her. Her smile is radiating towards me, leaving me in awe of the vision that is her. She doesn't even seem a little bit nervous. Like she is just as excited as I am for this.

My heart seems to know at this moment, we are making the right decision. I have never seen any creature as beautiful as the one before me.

Yeah, I may have been begging for love from someone else for these last few years but Simone is not even a thought at this point. I truly feel that all of the pain I felt from her was just preparing me to recognize love when it finally found me.

Hope's smile only widens the closer she gets to me. The woman from the podium and some other guy are standing back by the doors watching her walk my way. She finally steps up to me and turns to me with a wink of her eye.

The music is lowered then the two witnesses have moved to be standing on either side of us. Hope grins as she turns and hands her flowers to the woman then turns back towards me. She seems to let go of a full body shiver as Elvis steps up.

In a horrible impersonation, he starts the ceremony.

We both stare at him, trying to understand the absurdity of what he is saying. It is not easy considering every sentence is followed with either a growl or a hey momma.

He finally turns towards me, "Matthew Kirkland, do you take this little momma to be your wife? From this day forward until you have no more?"

Smiling, I turn to her seeing her eyes welling up, "I do. Forever."

Elvis then turns to Hope and I watch her face as it slowly pulls back to him, "And do you Hope Russo take this man to be your husband? From this day forward until you have no more momma?"

She lets out an audible laugh as her eyes come back to mine, "I do, always."

We stand before Elvis and God, declaring our love eternally.

Elvis swivels his hips a bit causing us both to look at him like he is having a seizure or something, "Well then by the great state of Nevada, I now pronounce you husband and wife. Kiss her already."

I laugh at him as I turn and take her face in my hands before kissing her deeply. Her hands wrap around mine and a small moan escapes her mouth.

I breathe her in deep, still in complete astonishment of what we have just done. I open my eyes as I start to pull away, looking over her face intently. Making sure she doesn't regret it.

She opens her eyes and I watch a tear roll out of her eye. She smiles at me, "I love you so fucking much Matthew."

I pull her in close for another kiss as I dip her deep into my hip. She laughs around my lips as I pull away from her, "I love you more."

Hope shakes her head at me, "Never."

I laugh as I stand her back up and she reaches around and takes her bouquet back from the go go dancer. Taking her hand in mine, we start running back down the aisle towards the lobby.

As soon as we hit the doors, she turns to me and jumps into my arms, wrapping her own around me as her lips meet mine again.

The lady from before comes back out, smiling to us both, "Here is your luggage. And like you requested earlier, there is a car set to take you to your hotel I am assuming?"

I continue to smile at Hope, unable to take my eyes from her, "Yeah, we are staying at the Bellagio."

Hope's eyes go wide in shock and I smile at her again as I lean down and kiss her neck right below her ear. She lets out a giggle, "Matthew stop, people are looking."

I growl into her neck, "I don't give a fuck. Let them look."

Hope starts laughing again as she pulls away from me, thanking the woman and waving goodbye to Elvis. I grab her hand as a driver comes forward and helps me with the luggage. We slide into the backseat of the sedan and he starts the very quick drive to the hotel.

Everyone is smiling at us as we walk through the lobby. Obviously just married.

Hope laughs as she eyes a girl probably not much younger than her. She runs over and hands her the bouquet of roses before turning back towards me. I quickly get us checked in and we head up to our penthouse suite.

The door swings open and we both drop our jaws at the room surrounding us. I knew it was going to be extravagant but god damn. I smile at Hope as she takes it all in then she turns her head towards me and smiles back. I step up close to her, "Hello Mrs. Kirkland."

Hope wraps her arms around my waist and smiles back, sitting her chin on my chest as she looks up at me, "Hello Mr. Kirkland."

I cannot believe we did this. Lucy is going to fucking murder me but I still don't care.

I had to make a grand gesture.

I had to make sure Hope understood on every fucking level that I wanted her, only her. I have never truly felt loved before. I have never actually had anyone tell me that they loved me.

Grinning back down at her, I give her another quick kiss on top of her head. I reach down and sweep her up into my arms bridal style and step into the suite before us.

I laugh as I look around the room then back down into those adoring hazel eyes that I seem to get lost in repeatedly. I have never seen her glow like this before. She seems truly happy.

My heart starts to pick up as I realize she truly does love me. It is not just an infatuation. It is not just a passing moment. She truly does love me.

I sit her down on her feet as she giggles and spins around the room. She runs over to some of the cabinets before turning and leaning back onto them. She smiles widely at me again, "I cannot believe we are here."

I grin back at her, "Only the best for my wife."

I can hear her giggling as I pick up the bags then glance over my shoulder to see Hope moving around the room, opening doors and exploring everything. I continue on and sit everything down in front of the dresser. Kicking my shoes off, I then pull my shirt over my head.

I take a quick sniff of myself and nearly pass out. I laugh into the air around me before poking my head out of the bedroom door, "I am going to shower real quick."

Hope nods to me and continues on her exploration.

The bathroom is just as decadent as the rest of the room with a marble shower and gold fixtures. I reach into the open shower and turn the water on full blast to get heat running through the pipes. After undressing, I step into the shower and let the water run down my body.

We will be able to spend a few days here, just exploring the town and each other before we have to head to Orlando for the next show.

Hopefully, that will be enough time for us both to steel our nerves. Telling the band will be weird but telling Lucy scares the hell out of me. I just hope she still likes me afterwards.

In the morning, I am going to take Hope to Harry Winston and let her pick out any ring she wants in the entire store. Personally, I want to get her name tattooed around my ring finger. I am not big on jewelry but I still want to be able to say I am married while holding up my finger to people.

I quickly wash my hair and step back under the water to rinse the soap out. I turn my head towards the water pouring from the ceiling as I feel two hands come around my sides.

I lower my head and exhale an anticipated breath. I watch as her hands raise up to my chest then I feel her mold her tight little body into mine. Raising my hands up, I place them on top of hers as I feel her nails dig into my chest as she makes a fist with each hand.

Slowly, I turn to face her. Hope's eyes are closed as she turns her face upwards towards the falling water. She smiles into the air around us, "I missed you."

Gently, I put my lips to hers, whispering, "We have been together all day baby."

She smiles back widely, "I meant my entire life. Not just today."

I open my eyes and stare into her face, "Look at me."

Hope's eyes open and I see my entire life in them. My past, my future—everything.

I shake my head at her, "I have never felt this way before. It feels like my heart is going to explode every time I hold you, like it can't hold in everything I feel for you. I am obsessed with you Hope."

She goes up on her tip toes, bringing her mouth closer to mine, "Good. I want you to be obsessed. I want you to never even look at another woman but me. I want you begging for me every...single...day."

My hand runs up her back and grips her hair tight as I slam my mouth down into hers. I can feel the electricity run through my veins as I spin her and pin her back to the wall.

The citrus of her scent lingering in her taste as well. I turn her again, plastering her front to the glass wall dividing the shower from the rest of the bathroom.

I wrap my arm around her waist and lift her up before leaning in and running my tongue up her neck to her ear. I watch her hands as they glue themselves to the glass divider. She looks over her shoulder, panting at me.

Bringing my lips to her ear, my voice doesn't even sound like my own, "How do you want me to fuck you?" I see her eyes close as I shove myself into her. She leans her head back moaning into the room around us. I bite at her ear, "Like this? You want me like this?"

I continue to shove myself into her as she presses the side of her face to the cool glass in front of her, "You make me so wet it doesn't even feel real."

I brace my other hand on the wall in front of us as I continue to slam into her from behind. My eyes close as I feel her so tightly wrapped around my cock. I hear her let out another moan, "Fuck Matthew. Fuck me harder. Please."

I growl into her neck as I pummel her with my dick. I can feel her pushing back on me, trying to spear me deeper into her. I take a few steps back before turning her towards the built-in seat, "Lean onto the seat baby."

I watch her hands fall as her chest goes forward. She uses her arms to push herself into me as I grab both hips in my hands and thrust so deep into her that her entire body jerks forward. She screams again and I can feel her grip tightening on my dick.

I lean my head back onto my shoulders as I start to lose myself in her.

This is heaven.

This woman is everything I have ever dreamed about and more. I feel her starting to tremble around me. I grip her hips hard enough to leave bruises as I slam into her, feeling my balls slapping on her pussy.

Hope arches her back just enough for me to hit that rough patch inside of her that makes her feral every single time. She screams again as I feel her clamp down on my dick.

I wrap one arm around her, holding her body close to mine as I brace my arm on the wall above her. I lift her up higher, watching her hold her balance with her hands as I slam into her again. Her feet dangling barely off the ground.

I feel myself letting go, "Fuck Hope. I'm cumming." I hold her close to me as I feel myself pulsing inside of her.

She moans again into the air around us as I feel her finally releasing her grip on me. We are both spent messes holding onto each other. Hope smiles as I slide out of her then lower her feet back down to the shower floor.

Her smile lights up the air around me as I run my fingers down the side of her face. She leans her face into my hand and I feel my one insecurity melting away.

She actually loves me.

I can see it in her eyes.

Words are just words but I can actually see the adoration from just her looking at me. I have never really felt wanted. Not by someone I wanted at least. I smile back down at her before we wash each other clean and leave the shower.

We step into the bedroom, wrapped in nothing but towels. Hope grins back at me as she shrugs out of her towel then climbs into bed. She lets out a heavy sigh as she melts into the pillow. I climb in naked next to her, pulling her close to me as we fall asleep tangled up in each other.

I wake up sometime after the sun has already come up. I reach up and wipe the sleep from my eyes. I yawn loudly as I feel a small hand slide over my stomach. I look over to see Hope smiling at me, "Good morning sir."

I smile back at her, "Yes it is. How did you sleep?"

She nods her head back at me, "Okay. But I dreamed about you."

I push the hair away from her face, "Oh yeah? What was it about?"

She slides a leg over me before straddling me, "I think I should show you instead of telling you."

I lean my head back and moan into the room as she grips my dick with one hand before sliding down on me. I wrap my hands around her hips, pulling her down onto me further.

I look up and see Hope's head hung back between her shoulders. She rolls her neck then brings her eyes to meet mine. I shake my head at her, "You can't be real."

She smiles like the devil as she starts to speed up her movements, "This doesn't feel real to you?"

I wrap my hands around her waist as I grip her tight and bounce her up and down my cock. I feel myself starting to breathe heavier, "Oh it feels real. It most fucking definately feels real."

She smiles again as she leans down and bites my neck, hard. "Oh fuck Hope!" I am screaming into the room as I feel her slamming down onto me. Her hair cascades around us as her scent envelopes me again.

She pulls back and continues her motions. I watch as her eyes fly open wide and I feel her start to pulsate around my dick, try to pull me in further.

I wrap my arms around her and roll her underneath me. I bring both of her legs up over my shoulders and slam myself into her.

She screams my name as I continue to plunge deeper and deeper into her. I feel her pussy strangling my cock and I finally let myself go. I scream her name as I fill her completely with my release.

Her body finally relinquishes me from its hold and I smile as I roll onto my back beside her. I leave her panting into the air above us. Hope turns her face to me, smiling before she rolls towards me and runs her fingers up and down my chest.

Leaning in, I kiss her before pulling back, "We have some shopping to do before we have to hit the county clerk's office."

Hope nods her head at me then rolls to her back, stretching her arms high above her head. I run my fingers down her chest, grazing her nipple along the way.

She makes a small noise as I look back up into her face, "When do you have to go to the doctor or get a new prescription or whatever?"

She turns to me confused, "What are you talking about?"

I look back up into her eyes, "You said you wouldn't get pregnant. I just assumed you were like on the pill or have an IUD or something."

Her eyes gloss over a bit as she scoots herself up to lean against the headboard. She lets out a heavy sigh before pulling the blanket up and covering her tits with it.

Her eyes finally meet mine again but I can see a slight hesitation in her gaze, "I guess we should have talked about this before. It might be a deal breaker for you. I didn't even think about it though."

I sit up next to her, confused and shaking my head, "Think about what?"

She looks away from me for just a moment before turning back, "I can't have kids. I don't have any ovaries. I was born with a condition that caused them to be severely underdeveloped. I had them removed when I was 9."

I nod my head back at her. She is looking at me like she is waiting for me to break down or leave or something.

I give her a smile and a kiss, "I guess it is a good thing I never thought about having kids then isn't it?"

She pulls back, staring at me, "You mean it? You never thought about it?"

I shake my head back at her, "No not really. But if down the road it is something we decide we want to do, we can always adopt. We will just cross that bridge when and if we get to it."

She smiles widely at me with what looks like relief, "I fucking love you so much."

I grin back at her, "Not as much as I fucking love you."

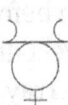

Watching her move from glass case to glass case, her eyes lighting up, that smile that she keeps shooting me, it is keeping me going right now. I always thought that marriage, spending your life with just one person for the rest of time, kinda sounded like a death sentence.

But Hope, her soul, her words, her mannerisms, they all keep me on my toes. I never seem to know exactly what she is thinking or what she is going to say or do.

It is exciting.

It is enticing.

Hope puts a finger up and starts calling me closer to her. Grinning widely, I step over and she points into the case.

She lightly taps on the glass with her fingernail, "What do you think of this one? It's pretty right?"

I follow her finger looking at the small diamond on just a basic solid white gold band.

I roll my eyes back up at her, "Really?"

She looks at me confused, "What? You don't like it?"

I laugh back at her, "I give you free fucking reign to pick anything in the entire store and you pick the smallest fucking diamond they carry?"

Her cheeks turn red and her eyes go back to the ring, "I don't need anything big and flashy Matthew. And I don't want you spending a small fortune on me either."

I stare her down then give her a small smile. I wave over one of the employees. He looks me up and down before rolling his eyes and stepping towards us.

I am used to that reaction honestly so it doesn't really bother me.

I glance in his direction before pointing to the ring she is interested in, "What is the largest diamond this style comes in?"

The employee pulls the tray of rings out then points to the one Hope has been looking at, "This one? This is currently a half carat. This style goes up to a 4 carat. But that is very expensive."

I slowly turn my head back towards the employee, not dropping the sarcastic smile on my face, "My wife does not want anything big and flashy. So please size her finger, we will take this ring with the matching diamond band in a 2 carat."

His eyes go wide as they jump quickly between us, "Are you sure sir? That will still be rather expensive."

I continue to stare him down, "Are you trying to tell me that my wife is not worth a 2 carat ring? I would be happy to take my money elsewhere if that is what you are implying."

The employee shakes his head quickly, putting his hands up in defense, "No sir. That is not what I am saying at all. I just wanted to make you aware that it would be more expensive than the one on display."

I let the smile drop a bit from my face as I roll my eyes back towards Hope, "Obviously. 2 carats will be fine. I don't care what the price is."

Hope's face keeps ping ponging between the both of us. She steps up putting her hand on my chest, "Baby. I don't want a stupid expensive ring. I don't care if you can afford it. I am fine with the smaller one."

I wrap my hand around hers, bringing her knuckles to my lips, "I know you don't want a stupid expensive one, that is why I am not getting the 4 carat. I am compromising and going with the 2 carat. That is what married couples do right? Compromise?"

She gives me a slight side grin, finally realizing what I am doing. I will guilt her into a beautiful ass ring, I have zero shame in it.

She watches my mouth as it grazes her knuckles and her eyes narrow in on me, "You are a sneaky bitch you know that?"

I laugh as I turn her and give her hand to the employee. I smile at him again, "Please size her finger."

The man looks between us, now smiling, "I would be happy too. Madam, please step right down here for me."

I grin back at her as he leads her down to the other end of the counter. Another employee steps up offering me a glass of champagne.

Thanking her, I grab two flutes off the tray. I casually stroll behind Hope then set her flute down on the glass beside her.

She gives me another smoldering glare as she reaches over with her free hand then grabs the flute raising it to her lips.

I sip mine at the same time, still giving her a victory smile. If she thought I wasn't going to get my way, she has a lot to learn about me.

She turns her eyes back towards the employee sizing her finger as I pull my phone out and take a quick picture of her.

I love this part of her.

The humble, unexpecting side of her.

She said she would just get a tattoo of my name which I am still fine with her doing, later. Right now she is going to wear a ring that could double as an anchor for a cruise ship.

I want people to see it and know she is married. That she is married to a man that has every intention of taking care of her for the rest of her life.

A half hour later, we are walking hand in hand back towards the car I have rented for our few days here. I open her door for her, watching her slide in.

As I shut the door, I watch her bring her hand up and shake her head at the wedding set on her finger. I smile as I run around the front of the car to drive us to the county clerks office.

She thinks I don't notice her looking at the ring over a dozen times on the short drive there but I know she is secretly in love with the set.

She just doesn't want to admit it.

I pull up in front of the clerk's office and Hope smiles back at me before she pulls the paperwork out of her bag.

She turns to me, still smiling but then looks down at the paperwork with a new expression on her face. She looks back at me, hesitantly, "Are you absolutely sure you want to do this as is? I know you told me no pre-nup but I really don't want you to think that I am just after your money."

I throw the car in park and turn it off before turning in my seat towards her, "Baby. I don't fucking care about the money. Is it nice? Fuck yeah it is. But this, what we have, it isn't contingent on who has what. We are in this together. I am not

127

going anywhere. Are you planning on running out on me the first chance you get?"

Her eyes blow wide as she shakes her head at me. I hear her make a little huffing noise, "Of course not. I was the one that said you were stuck with me. I just...people are going to talk don't you think? They are going to assume."

I take Hopes' face in my hands and kiss her softly on her lips. I pull back just enough for our lips to barely graze, "Fuck them. I love you. I don't give a shit what everyone else thinks."

Hope nods her head at me then leans in to give me another soft kiss. She pulls back from me staring into my eyes as she starts to shake her head at me.

I pinch my eyebrows together in confusion as to what she might be thinking.

She lets out a short breath, "I just. I never expected my life to go this way. I just...Matthew you give me purpose. You make me feel like I am enough.

"And I have never felt that before.

From anyone.

I am just afraid that this is all just a dream and I am going to wake up and none of it will be real."

My chest feels tight.

Like she reached in and squeezed my heart with her bare hand.

I reach up and touch her cheek, caressing her jaw with my fingers, "You are enough baby. You are more than that though. You are, you are everything.

"I just want to make you smile. I want to give you the fucking world because you deserve it. You are the kindest, most honest person I have ever known in my entire life. You don't love me for what I am. You love me for who I am. How could I ask for anything more?"

She gives me another small smile as I wipe the tear from her cheek.

I give her another soft kiss before pulling back and smiling wildly at her, "What say we go make this official? Yeah?" Hope nods her head at me as I finally pull back from her. We leave the clerk's office less than an hour later, as one.

9
Hope
I Told You Things - Gracie Abrams

Being this happy is honestly something I never even imagined
for myself. We spent 4 mesmerizing days in Vegas before getting
on this fucking plane to head to Orlando. Matthew has a show
tomorrow night so it is time for us to make an appearance back
in public.

Mom and Daija have both texted me a million times. I
told them I am alive and I will see them soon but that doesn't
stop them from trying to figure out where we have been.

Matthew is sleeping in the seat next to me. I keep
looking at his hand, seeing my name tattooed across his ring
finger.

I told him I will get his name as well but he didn't want
my first tattoo to be a super painful one that wraps around my
finger. So instead he took me to Harry Winston and bought me a
beautiful wedding set. It is an emerald cut 2 carat diamond with
matching band.

I still can't believe we are fucking married.

Leaning over I kiss him softly on the cheek before
whispering into his ear, "Babe, we landed. Time to wakey
wakey."

Matthew grunts before opening one eye and looking
around like he is either lost or pissed.

Or possibly pissed because he is lost.

When he sees me sitting here beside him though, he smiles and nuzzles into my neck, "Hey."

I grin back at him as I unbuckle my seatbelt then stretch my legs out in front of me. He nuzzles my neck for another moment before rolling back into his own seat and unbuckling himself. Matthew stands up in front of me, looking both ways down the aisle before smiling down at me, "You ready for this?"

Anxiously I let out a huff, "Not even a little bit."

Seriously...someone might get murdered. (Matthew)

Matthew laughs back at me as he steps over my legs and gets our carry on bags out of the overhead bin. I collect my book and phone before standing up and following him off the plane.

Quickly I pull my shades down before taking his hand and walking through the terminal. I feel like I may be marching towards my own execution. I check my shirt real quick to make sure this isn't a big red letter stitched onto me.

Luckily, Matthew had called the driver ahead of time so we don't have to wait for a taxi. Unluckily though, that means everyone now knows exactly when we will be arriving.

That means we are either going to be ignored completely or jumped immediately. And knowing my mother and sister, it was going to be the latter.

We pull up to the Grand Bohemian about a half hour later. Scanning the front of the hotel, I don't see anyone that I recognize. Fingers crossed that we will be able to skate past any prying eyes. But just as I suspected, as soon as we walk through the front doors my mother comes running up to me.

She smiles as she smacks Matthew in the arm then turns to me pulling her into a hug, "Where the hell have you two been? I have been worried sick!"

I hug her back, glancing at Daija over her shoulder. I watch her eyes as they scan us then settle on the rings on my finger.

A shocked expression rolls over her face as she points to my hand, "MOM! MOM! MOTHER!"

Finally mom pulls away from me and turns to Daija, "What Daija? Why are you yelling?"

Daija is still pointing at my hand with her eyes wide and mouth hanging open as I look past my mother to see where Matthew went. Begging for a little bit of support, I finally catch a glimpse of him standing over by the elevators talking to Gideon with a smile on his face.

I turn back to my mother just in time to see her jaw drop open and she pulls my hand up in between us. She looks from the rings to me, "Tell me you did not get married."

I grin at Daija then back to my mom, "I did not get married."

Mom drops my hand an puts her fists on her hips, "Are you fucking lying to me right now?"

Nervously, I shrug my shoulders at her before looking at the floor, "You didn't tell me not to lie."

I feel her hand under my chin as she raises my eyes back up to hers, "Did you and Matthew get married?"

I stare into her face, not really knowing if she is happy or completely pissed. Daija is still standing to the left of us, staring at me in complete confusion and possibly shock.

I turn back to my mom and give her a soft if not scared smile, "We did."

My mother makes a face that I have never really seen on her face before. It is a mix between murderous anger and deception. She turns on her heels and stomps straight over to the guys. I look at Daija out of fear and she is trying way too hard to hold back a laugh. Looking back at Matthew, I run to catch up with my mother as quickly as I can.

She steps up in front of him and grabs his hand to look at his ring finger. She sees my name freshly tattooed around his finger and then turns her glare to his face.

132

It takes everything in me not to laugh out loud when he smiles and says, "Looks like I get to start calling you mom after all."

Mom drops his hand and turns back towards me, "Are you both completely fucking insane?"

Matthew wraps his arm around me, pulling me in tight to his side, "Yes we are. But more than that, we love each other. And that is all that really fucking matters don't you think? When you love someone you give yourself to them, entirely."

Gideon has a shit eating grin over his face as he watches the whole conversation unfold in front of him. I give him a soft smile and he reaches out, pulling me into a hug, "Welcome to the family Hope. We are going to drive you crazy. Buckle up."

Laughing loudly, I hug him back then turn back around to see my mother in Matthews face pointing a finger at him, "You just run the fuck off with my child and got married? I wasn't even invited? The mother of the god damn bride had to find out what, days later?"

I step forward towards my mom touching her lightly on the shoulder, "We are going to have another ceremony mom. This was just about me and Matthew. We wanted it to just be us."

My mother is shaking her head at me as Daija moves closer towards us, "Please for the love of all that is holy, tell me you got married in Vegas by an Elvis impersonator."

Glancing at the floor I try to keep the smile on my face hidden just a bit. But Matthew just grins widely at Daija, showing as many teeth as possible. Daija throws her hands up in the air, screaming, "CALLED IT!"

I laugh back at her before turning back towards my mother. Seeing sadness in her eyes.

My gaze softens as I pull her in close to me, "It's okay mom. Everything is going to be fine. After the tour settles down, we are going to have another ceremony. Involving everyone. I promise. I will still wear the white dress and walk down the aisle. Okay?"

She nods her head as she pulls back from me. She looks from me to Matthew then back again, "Are you happy? This is really what you want?"

I nod my head back to her, "More than anything. Matthew completes me. He is my soul mate momma. I love him unconditionally. And he loves me just as much."

Mom nods back at me, wiping a stray tear from her eye. She turns back to Matthew, "You fucking owe me asshole."

Matthew smiles widely back at her, "Yes, mother."

I laugh louder when she reaches out and smacks him in the chest. Gideon turns to us again, handing Matthew a room key, "We are all on the 12th floor. Why don't you both go get settled and cleaned up. Maybe we can get a late dinner or something. We are heading to the arena around 4 tomorrow."

Matthew takes the key card from him before turning back to us, "What say we meet in the bar in an hour? Then we can see everyone and get all the questions out of the way at once, yeah?"

Gideon nods back at us as we head towards the elevators. Daija leans into me, "Mona is going to lose her shit."

I laugh back at her, "I am more worried about someone else's reaction. I don't think it is going to go nearly as well as mom's did."

Daija nods her head at me in agreement, "Yeah, I hear ya. That one might be a bit messier. But I got your back, okay?"

I turn to her, almost stopping in my tracks, "Why are you being so nice to me? What's in it for you?"

Daija looks at me quickly then back towards the floor as we continue towards the elevator, "I have kinda turned over a new leaf. It is something I definitely want us to sit down and talk about but for now, just take it for face value. Please."

Smiling at her, I squeeze her hand, happily accepting whatever this olive branch is that she is reaching out with, "Sounds good to me. Also, why did you say that about Mona? Are you two getting close or something?"

Daija smiles at me then looks shyly towards the floor, "Yeah, about that. We kinda already knew each other before all this. We met in New York after their last show. But I had no idea who she was, what she was. So now we are just kinda figuring it out as we go."

I grin widely back at her. Happy that she seems happy, "That is so fricken cute. Look at you blushing. I don't think I have ever seen you crushing like this before!"

She scoffs at me but still smiles like a loon as the elevator doors open. She winks at me, "At least we didn't run off and get married 2 days after meeting each other."

I laugh wildly at her, "Yeah. I got you beat there."

We all climb into the elevator and chat in nervous circles. When the doors open, we all spill out into the hallway before making our way to our rooms.

Once we are inside the safety of our hotel room, I turn towards Matthew, "I thought my mother was going to stab you or something."

He laughs as he sits our luggage down by the dresser then moves towards me, pulling me in close to him, "Same. But I think she is alright with it. Daija seemed okay as well. That's a good thing right?"

I nod as I lean into him, wrapping my arms around him, "Yeah, surprising thing but definitely a good thing. Now I am only worrying about one other person."

Matthew pulls back from me and kisses me softly on the lips, "Don't worry about her. If she tries to start any shit, I will end it right then and there."

I pull back from him and step over towards the window. Nervously, I look out onto the streets below us, "I don't want this

135

to come between the band. I really don't want to be the reason that you guys break up."

When I turn away from the window, I see that he is staring at me solemnly. I can tell he doesn't want it to come in between them all either. I put my hands in my pockets before looking back up at him, "Promise me. Promise me you won't leave the band because of this."

He moves closer to me, wrapping his arms around my waist and pulling me back in, "I promise. I won't just jump ship because of this. But if shit gets started, I am not saying I will not throw an ultimatum out there. I am not going to live in constant bullshit because somebody doesn't know how to let go."

Accepting it for what it is, I sigh into his chest, "Just don't make any rash decisions. That is all I am asking. Think it through before you do anything too crazy."

Matthew kisses the top of my head, "I do my best work when I am in crazy mode."

I chuckle back at him, "Yeah. Okay."

I pull away from him and move towards my suitcase. I know that Matthew loves me. I know that he only wants me. He has shown me that since the night at the chapel.

But there is still a heaviness in my chest. I don't know if it is just nerves or more like fear but it is there. I can only hope that it goes away sooner rather than later.

Shuffling through my clothes, I finally find something that is halfway clean and decent to wear to dinner, "I have to find somewhere to do laundry."

Matthew smiles as he heads towards the bathroom, "Just throw it all away and we will buy you new clothes."

I laugh at him as I change into a mid thigh skirt and tank top, "I will not. I like my clothes."

He peeks his head back around the bathroom door at me, "I prefer you with no clothes at all but whatever."

He laughs as I throw my dirty t-shirt at him then turn back to the suitcase to pull out a pair of chucks. He finishes up in the bathroom and walks back out, taking my hand in his. He gives me another kiss before pulling back, "Are you ready for this?"

Letting out another nervous exhale, "No. But let's do it anyway."

If looks could kill I would be 6 feet under right now.

Thankfully though, Simone has kept her mouth shut. At least to me and Matthew. I have seen her in some pretty heated discussions with everyone else though.

Mona screams when she sees the ring on my hand, "OH MY GOD! That ring is fucking beautiful! Where did you get it? Or did he surprise you with it? Oh please tell me it was romantic."

I laugh back at her, "We got it the day after at Harry Winston. And it was romantic in a sense. We got married at an all night chapel by an Elvis impersonator."

Daija is still cackling at the fact that she guessed it right away. Mona just shakes her head in Matthew's direction, "Are you fucking kidding me? That is the saddest thing I think I have ever heard."

Shaking my head, I grin back at her, "No. It was amazing. I had them play an instrumental version of Entangle. We were able to just focus on each other. No one there knew us. It was just us, together. It was perfect."

Daija pulls me in for a hug. Which is still fucking awkward as hell but I let her anyways, "I am happy for you sis."

Still reeling from whatever this alien version of my sister is, I smile back at her, "Thank you Daija. I am really happy that

137

you are okay with this. I didn't know how everyone was going to react. It just feels really good to have somebody in my corner."

She squeezes my hands, "We may not have always seen eye to eye but I will always be in your corner. No matter what."

The emotions running through me tonight are starting to become overwhelming. Everyone for the most part seems completely happy for us. I am still getting an evil side eye from Simone's direction but I don't care.

Majority rules.

Susie comes running up to me with Lily quick on her heels, "YEAH! You are part of the old married bitches club with us now! And you even beat me to it!"

I laugh at Susie as she yoinks me into a hug.

I see Lily over her shoulder and she has tears streaming down her face. She laughs at me as she wipes the tears away, "I am okay. I promise. I cried at a fucking Tide commercial on tv this morning. It is nothing personal I promise."

Laughing back at her, I open up an arm and pull her into the hug with Susie and I. Grinning contently, "Thank you. Both of you. This really means a lot to me. You have no idea."

Susie steps back from us, grinning from ear to ear, "So since you guys are going to have another ceremony for all of us to be at, does that mean I get to throw you a bachelorette party?"

I shake my head at her, making an indecisive face, "Yeah, no. That won't be necessary. But I will happily attend yours."

Susie groans at me then crosses her arms over her chest, pouting, "But I was gonna hire strippers."

Lily laughs at her, "Don't worry. We will still have strippers at your party."

At the same time Lily says this, Edge moves towards us with a questionable look on his face, "Why are we talking about strippers?"

Daija laughs as she and Mona move closer, hand in hand, "For Susie's bachelorette party. Strippers."

Edge's face turns hard as he looks back at Susie, "Two can play at this game woman. Remember that."

Susie leans over and gives him a quick kiss, before wiping the lipstick off his mouth, "I will behave. I promise. I will even leave Brian at home with you so you know I am not enjoying myself too much."

Turning confused to Lily, "Who is Brian? I don't think I have met him yet."

Lily laughs loudly before turning back towards Gideon, "Trust me, you don't want to know."

Confused, I let the comment slide and glance back around the room. I smile as I look over at Daija and Mona, obviously a lot closer than I expected them to be. Their little romance seems to be moving even faster than mine and Matthews.

I watch them with each other. Daija is running her hand up and down Mona's forearm while Mona lays her head on Daija's shoulder.

They are cute together.

Mom steps up beside me, "Apparently, your sister and Mona already knew each other. They met in New York last week."

I look from Daija back to my mother with an incredulous look on my face, "That is what Daija was telling me earlier. Seriously, what are the damn odds in that? Did Daija really not know who Mona was?"

Mom smiles as she shakes her head turning back towards me, "Nope. She had no clue until she showed up at the house the other night. They both just stood there staring at each other. It was awkward as hell until Mona smiled and said 'Surprise!'. I thought your sister was going to come unhinged."

Laughing loudly with my signature snort, I imagine Daija losing her shit over not only meeting her all time favorite band but finding out she had been in a relationship with one of them for over a week and having no idea.

139

I legitimately wish I could have seen it. It is not very often that someone catches her off guard.

I excuse myself and move towards the bar to order a drink. The bartender takes my cosmo order and then I am left standing there by myself. Allowing me a few moments of peace where I can just breathe and let the whole situation set in.

I glance around the room waiting for my drink when I see Matthew and Simone over to the side talking. He is standing a good 3 feet away from her but she keeps trying to inch her way closer.

Matthew is completely closed down to her though. I can't get upset over her reaction, but luckily knowing that he is completely uninterested helps me deal with the situation a bit better. I thank the bartender and take a sip of my drink.

Daija moves up beside me, eyeballing the Matthew and Simone situation with me, "How are you feeling about that?"

Following her stare for only a moment, I turn my back on them, "I trust Matthew. And I know it must be hard for Simone. I am going to just let them talk and air it all out. We can go from there."

Daija nods her head in my direction but her eyes are still across the room, "You are a better person than me. I would have ripped her head off by now."

I smile into my drink as I watch her eyes fly back towards Mona. A moment later Matthew's hand is on my lower back and he is nuzzling his mouth into my neck.

I smile as I lean into him then turn to face him. He reaches down and takes my drink from my hand, drinking it down quickly, "Okay, everyone knows. It's alone time now."

Laughing loudly again, I smack him in the chest, "We just got here. The least we can do is visit with everyone for a little bit longer."

He shakes his head at me, "Nope. They have had enough of us. Now it's our time." He leans down and picks me up, throwing me over his shoulder.

I squeal into the room while trying to hold my skirt down so my ass isn't out there for the whole world to see. I laugh wildly as he practically sprints us back to the elevators.

"Who the fuck is beating on the door this early?"

Matthew uncurls from me before rolling out of bed and throwing some shorts on. I barely have enough time to stretch out my body when I see a red head bounding around the corner.

Looking up I see Mona, Daija and Susie standing at the end of the bed. Susie jumps onto the bed, "Wake up girl! We are going shopping and you are coming with us!"

I look past her and watch Daija step over to my suitcase, "Is there even anything clean in here?"

I shoot Matthew a glare while he laughs at us, "I am sure you can find something clean ish in there. Please take her. Make her buy some more clothes."

Growling at him, I sit up in bed, pulling the sheet tighter around my naked body. I look around at them, all full of life and beautiful.

I pull the sheet up higher to cover my shoulders as well. Matthew is staring at me, I know he can read me like a fucking book.

Daija walks over and throws some clothes at me, "You have 5 minutes. Get your shit on. We will be in the hall waiting. Don't make me come back in here."

I nod at her and wait for them to leave the room before lowering the sheet and gathering up all the clothes she threw in my lap. I let out a heavy sigh as I grab some underwear and slide them on under the sheet, then do the same with a bra.

Matthew is leaned against the wall with his arms crossed over his chest, just watching me.

Glancing at him out of the corner of my eye, "What? What are you looking at?"

I slide into my jeans and shirt quickly before grabbing my chucks to put on as well. He drops his arms and steps up to me, "Do you know how beautiful you are?"

I shake my head at him, "I haven't been to the gym in over a week. I am going to ruin all the hard work I have put in. I just don't feel right, not at least running."

He nods at me before pulling me in close to his chest, "Go with the girls. Buy some nice things. Maybe buy some work out clothes too. We will start hitting the gym together at every hotel."

Gleefully, I smile up at him, "You mean it?"

He kisses me on the forehead, "Yes, baby I mean it. If it is important to you then it is important to me. Now go. Have fun. I love you. Just try to make it to the arena around 5. The show doesn't start until 7 but I don't want you to get lost in the shuffle."

I press my lips back into his for one last long kiss, "Okay. I love you too ya know." On my way to the door, I grab my purse before throwing him another smile over my shoulder.

The girls quickly swarm me when I step out into the hallway. I smile as I link arms with Susie, "So where are we going?"

Susie smiles back over her shoulder, "I have a few places in mind. We are going to go get you some new toys. For you and Matthew."

Feeling my neck turn crimson, I turn and look to Daija for some sort of help. Instead, she just laughs at me and pulls Mona down the hallway after us.

I immediately realize that I have been thrown to the wolves and no one is going to be able to save me.

After 5 hours of shopping, I finally make my way back to the hotel. I lug all of my bags in, before picking out some of the new items to wear to the concert tonight. I already have a mask so I don't have to worry about that.

I pull my hair up into a messy ponytail and do a light coating of make up. Just enough to make me feel like I might actually look pretty.

The shopping bags filled with my new sexy lingerie makes my heart flutter at the thought of what Matthew will do when he sees them on me. Grinning down at them, I start to filter through what I should wear tonight.

I put on a matching bra and panty set that are black lace and see through then settle on a red leather mini skirt and satin top. I even decide to wear heels

Which is something I never ever do.

But I want to look perfect for Matthew.

This is going to be the first time I see him perform live on stage. It is also going to be the first time the public sees us together.

I smile as I reach down and pull a bracelet out of a bag from one of the many sex boutiques that Susie forced me to go to.

I take out the wide leather bracelet and put it on my right wrist. Smiling devilishly, I run my fingers over it, knowing that with just one little buckle it opens up to become full wrist restraints.

I feel the goosebumps roll over my body as I think about what Matthew will do with them.

What he will do with me.

Glancing in the bag seeing all the other toys. Some honestly scare the hell out of me. But Susie said scarousal is a real thing and that I would love it.

I finally head out of our room, knocking on Susie's door 3 down from ours. The door flies open and Susie's eyes blow wide, "Matthew is going to fucking pass out. Hope, you look fucking amazing."

Blushing enough to heat a sauna, I run my hands down the front of my skirt, "Really? You think so?"

Susie steps out into the hall, gripping my hand, "I fucking know so. And I see you are wearing your new bracelet. Maybe you will get to try it out later. Maybe just maybe you can ask him for a hand necklace too."

I feel the shock roll over my face as I lean in closer to her, "Does Edge do that to you? The hand necklace thing?"

Susie laughs loudly as she grasps my hand in hers, "Oh you are going to be so much fun to teach. Yes, Edge and I both like to experiment with each other. Trust me, you will like it."

Nodding back at her, I follow her through the hotel and to the awaiting car. Being with Susie seems to raise my confidence somehow. It is like she just oozes so much of it that there is plenty for me to collect and keep for my own.

20 minutes later we pull up to the arena.

She had explained in great detail the fun and measured patience you have to have with a hand necklace. At one point, I felt like I should be taking notes or something. Maybe one of these days I will try it out, see if it really is as easy to get the timing down that she says is the most important part of it.

144

I watch Susie as she puts her mask on before sliding mine on as well.

I get it.

I feel like a completely different person with this mask covering my eyes.

We slip in through some back door and giggle as we head towards the dressing rooms.

I can't believe I am here.

I can't believe this is happening.

I truly cannot believe that this is my life now!

I watch Susie as she runs past the first door then jumps into Edge's waiting arms. I smile at them, excited that this is what my future gets to look like.

I round the corner into the dressing room to see Simone and Matthew standing very fucking close to each other. Stopping immediately I look him over.

He is not standing anything like he was last night.

Last night, I knew he didn't want her near him. Right now though, I am getting a completely different vibe from him entirely.

Simone steps up closer to him, neither of them seeing me in the open doorway, "If you don't want me then why did you let me into your room earlier?"

Matthew shakes his head back at her, "I am with Hope now. We are over Simone."

I watch her hands as they run down his chest to his waist.

Breathing has become something my body doesn't even know how to do anymore. Matthew just watches her but doesn't move to stop her hands.

Simone leans up into his mouth, "Then why did you kiss me again? If we are over?"

Matthew shakes his head as his hands go to her hips, "That was a mistake. It never should have happened. And it will never happen again. I mean it."

Simone just smiles back up at him as she moves her mouth closer to his. The soul crushing part is seeing him not move back from her.

I feel the blood drain from my face and anger build from deep within. I take my mask off and throw it onto the table inside the door.

The movement causes both of them to turn towards me. Matthew looks utterly terrified.

He takes a hesitant step towards me, "Hope?"

I take a step back from him. I look from him to Simone then smile widely at them both.

Shaking, I take my wedding rings off and sit them on the table right next to the mask.

I let out a heavy sigh before bringing my eyes back to his, "I thought you would have at least lasted a week. I guess it was all just a dream after all."

Matthew moves towards me in two steps, "Hope, baby wait. Let me explain."

I throw a hand up in between us, "Did you let her in our room? Did you kiss her?"

Matthew stops in his tracks as his head tilts to the side like he is searching for some sort of understanding from me.

I nod my head back at him before glancing over at a smug smiling Simone. My heart is thrumming so loud in my chest it is making my chest hurt, "Did you fuck her?"

He shakes his head at me, "No baby. I didn't fuck her. And she kissed me."

I look from Simone back to Matthew, "Did you kiss her back?"

The answer is written clearly all over his face.

My heart shatters into a million pieces onto the floor around me. My skin goes cold and my emotions somehow turn off, not even allowing one tear to fall.

I nod my head back at them both, "Have a good show you guys. I am sure you will do great."

As I turn to leave, I feel Matthew's hand grip my shoulder and spin me back around to face him. My hand immediately connects with his cheek. He does not get to touch me. Not after his hands have been on her.

He turns his eyes back to mine.

I know he is seeing a fire there that he has never really witnessed from me before, "DO NOT touch me. Ever fucking again. Go be with your fucking whore. She obviously means way more to you than we do."

Matthew's eyes scan my face.

His eyes are seeming to plead with mine.

I can see the shock and fear in them, "I made a mistake baby. I'm sorry."

Shaking my head back at him in anger and disappointment, "So am I. I'm sorry I ever let you in. You lied to me. You fucking cheated on me Matthew. With that smug fucking bitch that has been between us since the god damn beginning.

"The moment I fucking left you alone you couldn't not fucking be with her. What happened to me completing you? Huh? What happened to us being soulmates?"

He can't answer me.

He doesn't even fucking try.

I shake my head at him, voice still calm and steady, "We're done, Matthew. Don't call me. I will have my mother deliver the divorce papers. I never want to see you again."

Turning quickly, I walk through the door before moving towards where I saw Susie and Edge disappear earlier. I can hear Matthew still behind me, begging me to stop. Begging me to turn around. I round into the next room to see Susie painting Dionysus for the show.

147

Her eyes round to mine then she sees Matthew running into the room behind me. She drops the paintroller and turns back to me, "What happened?"

I shake my head at her, "Nothing I didn't expect. Maybe Matthew and Simone can tell you all about how much they enjoyed each other while we were shopping today. Thank you for everything Susie. I will keep in touch."

A curse leaves Dionysus' lips behind me as I turn around. Then there is a fist flying by my ear and hitting Matthew in the nose. He grabs his face immediately and I turn to see Susie, beet fucking red and panting. I place a hand on her shoulder, "He's not worth it Susie."

She turns her eyes back to me, softening them a bit as I see a tear roll down her cheek, "But you are."

I nod my head at her then kiss her cheek before turning back to the door. I stop in front of Simone, who still hasn't said a fucking word.

Smiling at her, I look over to Matthew who has blood running out of a nostril, "You two fucking deserve each other. You're both disgusting. No wonder you can't stay away from each other."

I turn and leave the room. Briskly walking back down the long hallway before climbing the steps up to the stage to find my mother and let her know I am leaving.

And that I want a restraining order.

Everything Changes - Staind

I am a complete fucking idiot. I never should have let her in earlier. Never should have let her kiss me.

And I sure as fuck never should have kissed her back.

I spent so many years just begging for her to want me the way she apparently does now. I just had to know what it felt like to kiss her knowing she actually wanted me.

But it didn't feel like I thought it would.

It tasted bitter.

It tasted like betrayal.

I made her leave immediately and I have been trying to come up with some way to explain it to Hope when I see her later.

Hera steps up closer to me, running her hands down my chest. Balling my hands into fists in my jeans pockets, I watch her mouth lean up closer to mine, "Then why did you kiss me again? If we are over?"

I shake my head at her, breathing heavily.

Putting my hands on her hips, I try to push her back from me a bit, "That was a mistake. It never should have happened. And it will never happen again. I mean it."

Hera's eyes fly over my shoulder and I turn to the side to see Hope standing inside the doorway.

She looks fucking stunning.

She obviously dressed for me.

My heart slams into my throat as I look from her eyes to the mask she just sat on the table. I take my hands from Hera's hips and step towards her, "Hope?"

Hope takes a step backwards and I realize she is wearing fucking high heels.

I have never seen her like this.

This version of her.

Barely able to breath, I take in her toned legs all the way back up to her abdomen then her face. I am a fucking idiot.

Thinking Simone could be half the woman Hope is.

Confusion falls over me when I see her smile widely back at me and Hera. Whatever emotion she is feeling right now, it is one I have never seen before.

I watch her slide her rings off and set them next to her mask before her eyes reconnect with mine, "I thought you would have at least lasted a week. I guess it was all just a dream after all. "

Quickly, I start to move towards her. I can feel my fear taking over and my heart breaking, "Hope, baby wait. Let me explain."

Hope puts a hand out, stopping me in my tracks immediately. I scour her face for any hint of love but there is none.

Her eyes are glued to mine as she lets out a heavy breath, "Did you let her in our room? Did you kiss her?"

I don't know what to say or do to make the situation any better. I don't know how to fix this.

I try to convey with my eyes how sorry I am but I am failing miserably.

Her eyes glance to Hera quickly then back to me, "Did you fuck her?"

Shaking my head at her, trying to take another step closer but I am afraid she is going to bolt on me if I do. I plead with her, "No baby. I didn't fuck her. And she kissed me."

I see her eyes go back to Hera shooting fucking daggers her way.

This is it. This is what we talked about earlier.

She made me promise to not let the band break up over us.

Over her.

Her eyes come back to mine, "Did you kiss her back?"

My shoulders fall heavy. I can't lie to her. I will not lie to her. She deserves better than that.

Her eyes go to the ceiling as she starts nodding her head.

She straightens her shoulders a bit before giving us both a forced smile, "Have a good show you guys. I am sure you will do great."

I watch Hope as she turns to leave the room. I move to her quickly, grabbing her by the shoulder and spinning her towards me.

I have to fix this.

I can't lose her.

I can't let her walk away from me. Not like this. Then I feel her hand as it connects with my cheek. The sting of it vibrates straight to my soul.

Slowly, I look back into her eyes, seeing all the shattered pieces of our relationship lying there.

All on fire.

She curls her upper lip at me, "DO NOT touch me. Ever fucking again. Go be with your fucking whore. She obviously means way more to you than we do."

I shake my head at her again, scanning her face for some hint of the girl I fell in love with. The girl that fell in love with me.

The quiet beautiful woman who learned to play the drums because of me. I feel myself starting to fall apart. She has to be able to hear the tremble in my voice, "I made a mistake baby. I'm sorry."

She lets out a small laugh as she shakes her head back at me in obvious disgust, "So am I. I'm sorry I ever let you in. You lied to me. You fucking cheated on me Matthew. With that smug fucking bitch that has been between us since the god damn beginning.

"The moment I fucking left you alone you couldn't not fucking be with her. What happened to me completing you? Huh? What happened to us being soulmates?"

I have no words. There is a lump in my throat and a heaviness on my chest, making it almost impossible to breathe.

I see the finality of us on her face before she even speaks the words, "We're done, Matthew. Don't call me. I will have my mother deliver the divorce papers. I never want to see you again."

Hope turns and quickly leaves the room, hanging a right into the hallway. I feel Hera pull on my shoulder but I shrug her off and run after Hope, "Please baby. Stop. Please talk to me. Don't leave. Hope. Don't fucking leave me!"

I follow her into Dionysus and Susie's room. She comes to an abrupt stop in front of me and I see Susie turn around with a smile on her face that instantly drops when she sees Hera behind me. I watch Dionysus turn his eyes on me as Susie drops the paint roller, "What happened?"

Hope's voice is cracking now, like she is barely holding it together. I look at the back of her head, the muscles in her neck that are constricting with every word she nearly whispers, "Nothing I didn't expect. Maybe Matthew and Simone can tell you all about how much they enjoyed each other while we were shopping today. Thank you for everything Susie. I will keep in touch."

Hope turns around and stops abruptly. Seeing me standing right behind her. I raise my hands to try to pull her close to me.

Maybe since I can't seem to find the words, maybe I can just hold her and she will feel what I am trying to say. I don't even see Susie's fist as she punches me square in the face.

I grab my nose with both hands with a grunt as I feel wetness on my hands. 80% sure that Susie just broke my fucking nose.

I stand back up to my full height and watch Hope as she turns to Susie, "He's not worth it Susie."

She is gone.

There is nothing that I am going to be able to do or say that is going to bring her back to me.

I look at Susie and see a tear slide down her cheek as she looks at Hope, "But you are."

Hope leans in and kisses Susie on the cheek before turning past me, not even looking in my direction. She moves back towards the door but stops in front of Hera.

Only then does she glance back at me, with so much pain on her face that it is literally destroying me.

She looks back to Hera, "You two fucking deserve each other. You're both disgusting. No wonder you can't stay away from each other."

Hope doesn't even bother to look at me again.

No goodbye.

Nothing.

She just walks past Hera and out the door. Hera turns back towards me and rushes up to me quickly, trying to look at my nose.

I push her back roughly, "Don't fucking touch me Hera. I am fucking serious. I just lost my fucking wife because of you and your fucking bullshit. Stay the fuck away from me."

I feel Dionysus as he is trying to pull me back deeper into the room. Hera steps up closer but then Susie steps in between us, blocking Hera from my view.

She stops abruptly as Susie leans in closer to her, "You have gone too fucking far this time *Simone*. How could you? You know he is married. You just can't handle not starting fucking drama can you?"

Hera stands up to her full height, squaring her shoulders, letting it register that we are all calling her by her real name, "How could I? Because I love him. I love him and I know he loves me. It should be us together. Not them!"

Before Susie can say anything, Dionysus is moving around me and steps up to Hera, "You don't fucking love him. You know you don't fucking love him. You are just fucking jealous that he moved the fuck on. You didn't give two shits about him or his feelings until you saw him interested in someone else.

"We all fucking saw it Simone. You have been pulling his fucking strings for years. That bullshit stops now. You just broke up his fucking marriage. How do you not get that? You and your selfishness just ruined the best thing that has ever happened to him!"

Simone looks from Dionysus to me, pointing in my direction, "He kissed me back. He wants me too!"

I wipe my throbbing nose with the back of my hand, "I don't fucking want you Simone. I kissed you back because I wanted to know what it felt like to be kissed by you when I thought you actually gave a shit about me. Newflash, it was no fucking different. Because you don't care about me! You only fucking care about yourself."

I turn back to Susie, "You have to help me stop Hope. We can't let her leave. Not like this. I just...I have to stop her, Susie."

Susie shakes her head at me, "You don't fucking deserve her Apollo. You fucked up. Too much."

I stomp towards the door before turning back on all of them, "How does it feel? Huh? To be so fucking perfect? Like neither of you have ever made a fucking mistake! If either of you

154

have ever given a shit about me or Hope, then you will try to fucking help me fix this! I fucked up. That doesn't mean I don't love her. I made a fucking mistake."

I watch Susie's face as her anger starts to transform into something different. Dionysus looks from Simone back to me, "Yeah. Okay. Let's find her. Try to figure something out at least." Susie looks to Dionysus but then nods her head at him.

She turns to Simone, "You stay the fuck away from the both of them. You have done enough fucking damage."

Simone stands silently, a tear running down one cheek. Silently, I look at her in disgust before turning and running out the door ahead of Susie and Dionysus.

I reach into my dressing room and grab her rings before heading back out into the hallway and running towards the steps to the stage.

It is the first place I can think of to check.

Is with Lucy.

Who is probably going to punch me as well but I don't give a fuck.

I deserve it.

I take the stairs two at a time, hearing Dionysus and Susie following close behind me. Cresting the top of the steps, I see Lucy holding Hope.

Her shoulders are shuddering and I know I have completely destroyed her.

How could I do this to her?

Perfect, quiet Hope.

I wish she never would have met me. I wish I had never heard her voice or looked into her beautiful kaleidoscope eyes.

Susie and Dionysus step out from around me as Lucy brings her eyes up to meet mine.

I can see the hatred blazing from her as well.

Good.

I deserve to have every fucking one hate me.

55

I just can't let her leave not knowing that I love her. Slowly, I take a step towards them, "I am so fucking sorry Hope. Things just got way out of hand. I never meant to hurt you."

Her eyes turn to mine and I see nothing but loathing behind them. She takes a few steps towards me, "Things got out of hand? Are you fucking kidding me *Apollo*? Tell me, what part do you think was out of hand? When you had your tongue down her throat or your hands on her tits? Or maybe you pinned her to the fucking wall and rubbed yourself into her. Was that what made it too out of hand?"

I shake my head at her, "I didn't do that. Any of that. I kissed her back for maybe one second then I pushed her away from me. I told her I wasn't going to hurt you like that. I couldn't hurt you like that."

She is trembling as she spits her words back at me, "Maybe you should have thought about that BEFORE you kissed her back. BEFORE you invited her into our room. OUR room!"

I can feel myself crumbling in front of her. She has to see it as well. Feeling a million eye on me, I know the entire fucking crew has stopped and is watching us now but I don't care.

I just want to fix this. I step closer to her and grab her by the shoulders to pull her closer to me.

Hope lets out a blood curdling scream as her knee comes up and connects with my dick. My eyes bulge as I lean into her from the pain shooting through my body. Then I feel her hands on my shoulders shoving me back away from her.

I stumble back, losing my footing completely and start tumbling backwards down the stairs. I hear a distinct crunch then a snap.

Landing at the bottom of the stairs in a heap, I still only feel the radiating pain from my dick. Hope is standing at the top of the stairs with her hands over her mouth, her eyes wide.

Dionysus is to me within a moment. Then Ares is pushing Hope out of the way to get around her.

156

He was on the other fucking side of the stage just a few seconds ago. How the fuck did he get over here so quick?

Hope is crying now. The first time since all of this has started. I try to get up to go to her but then I notice the pain that is shooting up my arm and into my shoulder.

I look down and see what looks like a bone sticking out of my skin. I roll onto my back, not really sure what part of my body to hold onto at this point, "FUCK!"

I look back up the stairs but Hope is backing away from me.

Away from us.

Leaning onto my good side, I try to stand, "No, Hope. Don't go. Don't leave. Please."

Her eyes move from my arm to my face then around everyone watching all of this unfold. I somehow know exactly what she is thinking.

Why she is so upset.

I shake my head at her, "Baby, it was an accident. I know you didn't mean to do this. Don't go. Please."

She is shaking so hard I can see the tremors in her shirt. She looks at Lucy then she turns and runs. I try to get to my feet but the pain is just too fucking much right now.

Falling back onto my side, I yell with all the energy I can muster up, "NO! HOPE! Someone get her back here. NOW! Do not let her fucking leave!"

Susie nods her head at me, then runs up the stairs in the direction that Hope just ran off in. Ares is on the phone with apparently 911. His eyes keep going from my arm to my face.

Dionysus is pacing behind us, "What the fuck are we gonna do? We are fucked! God DAMMIT!"

I watch him as he slams his hand into a wall a few times. "D, fucking stop. Don't fuck your hand up too. We will figure something out okay. Just fucking stop."

He turns to me, half painted for the show with his chest heaving, pointing towards where Hope was just standing, "She fucked us all over now. We are so screwed."

I sit up towards him, "Don't you fucking dare put this on her. This is my fucking fault. Don't bring her into this shit. I brought this on."

Dionysus's eyes go from me back to Ares but he is nodding at me.

He knows I am right.

He lets out another heavy sigh as he leans up against the wall. Ares puts the phone down, "They said not to move you. Paramedics will be here in a few minutes."

I nod back at him, "Find Hope. I am not going to the hospital until I talk to her. Find her now."

Ares nods back at me then slaps Dionysus in the shoulder, "You take the dressing rooms, I am going after Susie."

Dionysus looks at me but rolls his eyes and nods his head before running down the hallway.

A few moments later, Hestia is on the floor beside me with tears running down her face, "What the fuck happened Apollo?"

She moves forward and helps me lean against the wall behind me. I let out a heavy pain laced sigh, "Nothing I didn't fucking deserve."

I look beyond Hestia and see Simone leaning against the wall behind her.

I can't fucking stand her.

I can't even fucking look at her.

The thing is...it's all my fucking fault. I should have just shut her down when she knocked on the door. I don't know why I thought we could talk like fucking adults.

This is all on me. No matter how much I hate Simone.

158

I try to breath through the pulsating pain that is ricocheting up my arm but this fucking hurts. I have never broken a bone before.

Then it hits me, why Dionysus was so mad. My arm is obviously fucked. We still have 2 months left in the tour. I can't fucking play like this. And I sure as fuck can't play with just one arm.

My name isn't fucking Rick Allen.

I lean my head back into the wall as I see a gurney coming towards me. The medics swarm me and start checking me over for more serious injuries. One guy helps me stand then turns me to sit down on the gurney.

Looking up at him, "I am not leaving until I talk to my wife. They are looking for her right now."

He nods back at me, then looks at my arm, "We can wait a few minutes but we need to get you to the hospital and get that x-rayed. You may need surgery."

I grimace back at him but nod my head in agreement. Over his shoulder, I see Susie leading a distraught Hope beside her.

I sit up on the gurney, "Hope, baby come here."

She steps up closer to me, her eyes swollen from tears. I reach my good hand up and hold her cheek as her eyes go from my arm to my eyes, "It's okay Hope. It was just an accident. It doesn't change anything. I love you. I need you okay? Please."

She nods her head at me, still in shock, "I am so fucking sorry Matthew. I didn't think you would fall like that. I didn't mean to hurt you. Not like this."

I pull her in close to my uninjured side, "It's okay baby. I don't blame you. I promise okay. Just promise me you aren't going to leave while I am at the hospital. Please? Just don't leave me."

159

Her eyes are still glued to the bone sticking out of my arm and the blood covering the left side of my body, "Look at me baby. Please."

Her eyes slowly come up and connect with mine, "Matthew? I can't....I didn't mean....I'm sorry."

I pull her mouth to mine and kiss her hard. I can feel her still shuddering beneath me but she kisses me back. I feel a roll of relief run through my body when I feel her hands on my cheeks.

I pull back from her and put my forehead to hers, "It's you. Only you baby. I love you."

I can feel her nodding her head back at me but I know she is in shock. Pulling back just enough to raise her chin so her eyes meet mine, "Baby are you okay?"

Her eyes are completely vacant.

Like she isn't comprehending anything that is happening. I look over her shoulder and see Lucy on the phone still pacing at the top of the stairs. I know everyone is losing their shit right now.

I still haven't figured out how I haven't.

I look back to Hope, "I need you to do something for me baby."

Her eyes snap back to mine and she nods her head at me, "Anything Matthew. What do you need?"

Smiling softly at her and I pull her forehead back to mine, "I need you to stand in for me tonight. Can you do that for me baby?"

She yanks her body back from mine, shaking her head, "I can't fucking do that! Matthew? Fuck! I can do anything but not fucking that, okay?"

I shake my head back at her, "You have to baby. They are never going to find someone in time to cover for me. It has to be you."

She continues to shake her head at me as she starts to turn a putrid shade of green, "I don't even know the new music. I can't do it Matthew. Please don't ask me to."

Daija steps up beside her gripping her sister tight at the shoulders, turning Hope to face her completely, "Don't fucking lie to him. You know every god damn song by heart. You have to fucking do this Hope. He is laying there with a broken fucking arm because of you. So take some god damn accountability right fucking now!"

I spit in anger at Daija, "I am not fucking laying here because of her. I am lying here because of me. If I had been a better fucking husband to her, we wouldn't be in any of this shit right now. Don't fucking talk to her like that Daija. I swear to god!"

Daija turns to me with a smile before looking back over at her sister, "See, he still loves you. He defended you. He needs you right now. You have to take care of him, just like he is trying to take care of you."

Hope turns her face from sneaky Daija back to me.

She lets out a shaky and uncertain breath before nodding her head, "Yeah. Okay. I will do it."

I feel relief hit me in the chest as I lay back on the bed. Okay, at least we got one fire put out. Daija really is a sneaky little bitch. Instantly, I like her more.

I turn my face back to Hope's, "After the show, come back to the hotel. Don't leave okay. Please. We have to talk."

She nods her head at me then looks over to Ares, "I don't know what to do."

Ares gives her a small smile, "Kiss your husband goodbye because he is going to the hospital. Then trade shoes with your sister and get your ass on stage. We need to sound check you on drums. I will write out the set for you."

Ares turns to Daija, "Go find her mask. She needs it."

161

Keeping my eyes locked on Hope, I am trying to get a read on her emotions right now, "Her mask is on the table right inside the dressing room."

Daija nods at me then runs around Ares to go to the room.

Hope's eyes meet mine again, "You're gonna do great baby. I know you will. I wish I could be here to see it. But promise me you are going to come back to the room after. Okay?"

I watch her as she nods at me. She steps up to me and kisses me on the forehead then I feel myself being wheeled towards the back door.

I turn my head on the bed, "I love you Hope!" I don't hear a reply as the door is slammed open and I am loaded into the back of an ambulance.

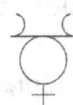

I wake up to Gideon and Lily sitting beside my hospital bed. Lily is asleep on Gideon's shoulder, snoring loudly. Letting out a groan, I try to push myself further up onto the bed, "How does she snore so loud for such a small person?"

Gideon and Lily are both now standing up beside the bed now. Lily looks me over then puts a hand on my shin, "How are you feeling?"

I smile back at her, "Like a pin cushion. Where is Hope?"

Lily looks to Gideon then back to me with a smile, "Susie took her back to the hotel after the show."

Nodding my head at her, I look at Gideon, "How did she do?"

Gideon smiles back at me, "She fucking killed it. She might even be better than you."

I laugh back at him as I readjust myself in the bed yet again, "I don't doubt it. Have they said how bad my arm is?"

Gideon crosses his arms on his chest, "You aren't going to like this but you are going to be in a cast for a couple months. They had to go in surgically and put in some pins.

"They said they will come out though when the cast comes off. Then something about physical therapy may be needed afterwards."

I let out another loud sigh, "Fuck. Okay. Well at least we have a few days to figure out a permanent replacement for me through the end of the tour. After that I should be good to go again."

I look back up at Gideon and his eyes won't meet mine. Turning my gaze to Lily, she is just staring up at Gideon.

I look between them both a few more times, "What? What is wrong?"

Gideon lets out a heavy sigh and leans into the railing on the bed beside me, "Simone quit."

Of course she fucking did.

Like she hadn't fucked us up enough.

I lay my head back on the pillow behind me, "Fuck."

Lily squeezes my leg and I look back down at her, "But at least we only have to worry about finding someone for bass."

I sit up again shaking my head, "What do you mean? We are down 2 right now. We are basically fucked and not in the fun way."

She smiles back at me, "Hope is going to stand in for you for the rest of the tour."

I feel something roll through me.

Pride? Happiness? Relief?

I look at Gideon, "Seriously?"

He nods back at me with a smile on his face. Maybe this means there is a chance for us after all. I mean if she completely hated me she wouldn't stick around right?

I look over the little room they have me in, "When can I leave? I need to see her."

Lily nods at me before moving to the end of the bed, "I will tell the doctor you are awake. They said after that they would get you some meds and send you home."

I let out a grateful moan into the room, "Thank god. There was no way in hell I was staying here all night."

Lily turns and hurries from the room. I look back to Gideon, "How pissed is Edge?"

Gideon chuckles back at me before sitting back down in his chair, "He actually seems relieved that Simone left. Mona is a little torn up but she will be fine.

"Simone didn't even fucking say goodbye. We got to the green room after the show and she just walked up and said she was out then turned and left. Like we all meant fucking nothing to her."

I laugh to myself, "That sounds like her. She is selfish as fuck."

Gideon tilts his head to the side, "I don't know if that is all it is. I think she also didn't want to see you and Hope together every day as well. I mean, none of us think she is actually in love with you but still it can't be easy to see someone you care about with another person."

I nod my head and look back up towards the ceiling.

He is right.

I need to just let this anger go.

It isn't going to help me fix shit between me and Hope. There is no reason to hang onto it.

I turn my head back towards Gideon, "Do you know where my clothes are? I wanna go ahead and get dressed so when they say I can leave we can just split."

Gideon stands up and pulls a bag up onto the bed, "We got you some clean clothes. Your others were covered in blood. Plus, they had to cut your shirt off you."

164

I let him help me get dressed since I am currently wearing a sling as well as a cast. He nods towards it, "You don't have to use that all the time but they said to try to use it as much as possible in the beginning."

I nod as I look down at my arm, "Yeah okay. Seriously though, how is Hope? Did she really do okay up there?"

Gideon smiles back at me, "She was nervous as fuck at first but by the time we were halfway through the set, I wouldn't have been able to tell the difference between the two of you. She did amazing. I am happy to replace you with her permanently."

Laughing loudly, I flip him off with my good hand.

The doctor rounds into the room and informs me that my arm indeed will need to be in a cast for a minimum of 2 months.

Then he lets me know what I can and can't do during those two months. He also gives me a pharmacy full of medications to take. Some for pain, some to prevent infection.

An hour later, we are exiting the elevator into the hallway of our hotel.

Gideon turns to me smiling, "We are here for a few days before heading to South Carolina. Thought I would give you a few more days to recover before we put you through that torture."

I nod back at him as I pull my room key out of my pocket and slide it into the lock, "Yeah okay. Talk to you both tomorrow?" They both nod back at me as I turn and push the door open.

The room is completely dark as I walk inside. I don't want to turn on a light and wake Hope up if she is sleeping but I really don't want to trip in the fucking dark and break my other arm. I fumble around on the wall trying to find the light switch when the light comes on over the bed.

Turning, I see Hope curled up under the blankets all the way to her chin. I drop my bag of drugs and dirty clothes before kicking off my shoes and making my way towards the bed. She won't even look at me.

I sit down at her feet and place my right hand on her leg. Seeing her visibly flinch at my touch, I move my hand away and prop myself up with it instead.

Sadly, I stare at the floor in front of me, "Are you okay?"

She rolls onto her back and looks at me, taking in the cast and sling on my arm, "I should be the one asking that since I am the one that broke your fucking arm."

She rolls back to her side so she doesn't have to look at me any longer than necessary. I let out another sigh as I glance around the room, "Do you want me to get another room? You can keep this one."

She looks over at me and shakes her head, "No. There is no need for that. I am going to be the one taking care of you until you can use your fucking arm again so we might as well be in the same room."

I laugh nervously at her, "You don't have to do that. I can take care of myself. I got myself into this shit show. It is only right that I deal with the aftermath."

She rolls over onto her back again staring at me, "Did you really mean everything you said? That you felt nothing when she kissed you?"

Turning towards her on the bed, "Of course I meant it. I wouldn't lie about that. I honestly was shocked at first that she was even kissing me, then my brain was like wait is it different now that she said she loves you? But it wasn't. It was even worse. Because my heart wasn't in it anymore. I immediately pushed her away. Because it wasn't you."

She nods at me then I see her eyes tear up a bit, "I can't find my rings. I went back to get them before the show but they were gone. I think someone might have stolen them."

I stand immediately reaching into my pocket, praying to god they are still there. I had put them in my pocket at the hospital but knowing my luck I fucking lost them.

I let out a relieved sigh as I wrap my hand around them and pull them out. Hope smiles at me when she sees them in my hand. But instead of reaching out for them she just stares.

I look from her to the rings then move over to sit them on her nightstand. Turning back towards her, "I really want to talk baby but I am exhausted. Would you hate me even more if I just took some pain meds and went to sleep?"

She looks up at me with a pained expression, "I don't hate you, Matthew. It would make life alot fucking easier if I did, but I don't.

"And yes, we can just talk tomorrow. I didn't realize how much of a fucking workout it is to play a full show. My muscles are screaming at me right now."

I laugh at her as I reach down and try to unzip my jeans with one hand. I fumble for a minute before I see her rolling onto her back again. I look up at her and she is smiling at me.

Shaking my head at her, "Not fucking cool. I am technically handicapped right now and you are laughing at me."

She shakes her head at me, "I am not laughing at you not being able to get undressed. I am laughing at what is going to happen next."

I look at her more confused than ever, "What do you mean what happens next?"

Hope smiles at me as she throws the blankets back and slides out of bed. She is wearing a pink bra and underwear set that are completely fucking see through.

As she turns and stands up, I notice that the underwear is a thong. I know my eyes are bugging out of my head at this point.

She laughs at me and points, "That. That is what I am laughing at."

I shake my head at her, "You are the devil. Legitimately you are the fucking antichrist aren't you?"

She smiles as she steps up to me, "No. I am not the devil. If anything, I am an angel because you are injured and I am not going to risk hurting you so you are not allowed to get handsy. But I am still giving you a show. So see, Angel."

I shake my head back at her, "Yeah, the angel of death maybe."

She laughs again and it sounds glorious. I watch her hands as they unbutton my jeans then slide them down my thighs. I use my good hand to balance myself on her shoulder as I pull my feet out of them. Luckily, Gideon had put me in a button up shirt at the hospital so I am able to shrug out of it pretty easily.

I watch Hope as she walks over to where I dropped my bag of stuff when I walked in the door. She reaches up and latches the door then bends at the hips and picks up the bag.

I let out a groan into the room watching her cute little ass in the air and there is literally nothing I can do about it. Even if she would let me, there are so many drugs in my system they are having an adverse affect on little Matthew.

Hope turns around with my medications in her hands and a smile on her face. She nods to my side of the bed, "Come on big guy. Let's get you comfy."

I stand and move to my side of the bed and slide down onto the pillow. Luckily, I broke my left arm so I don't have to worry about rolling onto it in the middle of the night or anything.

I watch Hope as she moves to the bathroom and runs some tap water into a glass then rounds the bed back over to my side. She sits the pill bottles and water down before reaching over me and grabbing a spare pillow from her side.

I moan again at the proximity of her almost naked body so close to my face. She laughs again as she pulls the pillow over and gently picks up my slinged arm and places the pillow under it.

She moves and gets my meds then she puts the pills in my mouth and helps me lean forward to swallow them down with some water.

Hope makes her way back to her side of the bed then slides in and turns the light off. I am staring at the ceiling when she rolls over to face me, "I don't forgive you for what you have done Matthew."

I nod my head towards the ceiling, "I don't expect you to."

I know she can hear the truth in my voice. I don't expect her forgiveness.

Not when I can't even forgive myself.

I turn my head and see her staring up at me. I look down and see that she has put her rings back on. A hint of optimism runs through my veins as I reach over and run my thumb over the rings.

Letting her know that I can see them on her finger.

Hope lets out another sigh, "I am not ready to forgive you. But I don't want to give up on us either. I think we just need to take it slow. Figure out where we are in the morning. Decide what to do from there."

Grinning at her in the darkness, "I only have one condition."

I hear her laugh beside me, "And what is that sir?"

I lay my good arm flat against the bed, "Come over here and lay with me. I just want to hold you. I want to know that this is real. That you are still here."

I feel the bed moving just a bit then her body is molding into mine. Letting out a relaxed breath, I feel her hand spread out on my abdomen and her cheek pressing against my chest.

I take a chance, "I love you Hope."

Her face molds into a smile on my chest, "I love you too Matthew."

The pills quickly start to kick in and I feel myself drifting off to sleep. But at least she is in my arms now. That gives me a reason to actually want to wake up in the morning.

Hope
touchin' me - Chandler Leighton

"Matthew, seriously! Stop trying to shove a fucking pencil down into your cast! You're going to get lead poisoning or something!"

I reach out, attempting for the 18th time to get the pencil away from him. He yet again twists away from me, letting out a moan as he apparently reaches the spot he has been trying to scratch.

I shake my head walking away from him and throwing my hands in the air in defeat, "If you fucking die from infection, nobody better fucking blame me. I tried!"

For the last 4 days, he has been shoving anything sharp he can find down into the cast. After the first night of uncomfortable sleeping, he has even refused to even use the sling the doctors told him to use.

He is not a good patient.

And I am an upset nurse at this point.

I watch him as he tosses the pencil onto the hotel desk and turns around with a satisfied grin on his face, shaking my head back at him and his antics.

Matthew sits down in the chair, leaning his chin onto his good arm, "I'm bored. Let's go do something." He sounds like a god damn toddler that has been stuck in the back of a station wagon for 800 miles.

I look over my shoulder at him as I continue to repack the clothes he insisted on packing for himself, with one hand.

Letting out a sigh, I turn back towards him, "What do you want to do? I heard there is a really cool beach just south of here that has a shit ton of sand dollars. Or maybe we could go to the Angel Oak? It is a tree that is like a bazillion years old or something."

He, of course, scrunches up his nose at every suggestion I come up with. I throw my hands out to the sides as I turn around to continue cleaning up yet another mess that he has left behind, "I don't know then. You are shooting down every idea I am coming up with."

I hear him moving around behind me. I glance over my shoulder again and watch him move towards the window.

He looks out for just a minute before turning back around and crossing his arms, or at least attempting to, across his chest, "I will make you a deal. I will go to this beach with you IF you agree to wear a thong bikini the entire time we are there."

I laugh at him as I roll my eyes and turn back towards the bed, "Creep."

He laughs as he moves up closer to me, "You have to give me something here Hope. You won't let me touch you. At least let me look at you."

I feel his good hand as he reaches up and puts a strand of hair behind my ear.

I am not holding out on him because I want to. I am also not holding out on him as some sort of punishment.

I am scared.

What if I open back up and Simone comes back? Or maybe someone else from his past? Or even someone new, he could always meet someone new. I just don't want to have my heart carved out again.

Right now, we have more of a friendship than a marriage. Yeah, it isn't easy but I don't know what else to do with it. I just don't know how to move past what happened.

Move forward with us.

I shake my head as I zip his suitcase back up and set it on the floor up against the wall. I turn and face him, "Maybe I am not ready for you to look at me like that yet."

He drops his hand back down and I see the anger roll over his face. I know he is going to hold back his words but honestly, I kinda wish he wouldn't.

I feel like if we just fucking screamed at each other for a minute we might actually feel better. At least, I know I would.

But I don't want to just start attacking him out of nowhere. I want to have a good reason to fight back.

Instead, he huffs at me and turns back towards the window, "Nevermind. We can just sit here."

I throw my head back and look at the ceiling.

Enough is fucking enough.

Throwing my hands back out at my sides, "Fine." I move past the bed to grab my purse and room key.

Hearing him moving behind me, his voice sounds scared, almost concerned, "Where are you going?"

I look over my shoulder quickly, "Anywhere you're not."

The door slams loudly behind me as I make my way down the hallway. I am fully expecting him to come barreling out of the room and down the hall after me. As I hit the down button for the elevator and wait. But he never comes out. The elevator doors open in front of me as I glance back down at the empty hallway again.

Fuck him.

I step inside and hit the button for the lobby. There is a whiskey coke calling my name in the bar. The doors shut and I check my purse making sure I at least have my wallet for cash and ID.

I look at my hand, seeing the rings still sitting there, though recently they feel like they weigh a thousand pounds. How can he not see that I am struggling too? That I am just trying to fix us but I can't do it alone.

The elevator stops at the lobby and I step out, making a bee line for the bar. I keep my head down as I move quickly and round into the restaurant.

I wave at the hostess, "Can I just sit at the bar please?"

The girl nods and leads me towards the far side of the bar. She sits a menu down in front of me and I throw my purse down as I climb into my seat.

A handsome bartender steps up and gives me a smouldering smile, "Hello there. What can I get for ya?"

The southern drawl in his voice is captivating. I haven't heard an accent that thick since I lived in Georgia. I smile back up at him, "Whiskey coke, on the rocks please."

He smiles as he leans into the bartop in front of me, "Do you want to order any food or anything?"

Shaking my head, I look down at the menu then push it to the side, "No thanks. Just the drink."

He knocks his knuckles on the bartop a few times before turning around to go mix my drink. I lean back in the seat letting out a heavy sigh as I push my hair back from my face.

I have to figure out what the fuck I am going to do. I can't keep pushing him away but he is giving me nothing to fucking work with here. We still haven't even really talked about what happened.

Every single time I try to bring it up, he closes off. Which I get but I deserve a fucking answer. I am the one that was destroyed that day.

I lean forward as the bartender sits down my drink. I smile a thanks to him before picking up the glass and taking a long sip. I see movement out of my periphery but don't even bother to look to see who it is.

"Hope? Hope Russo?" I turn and look up into a pair of shockingly blue eyes that I never imagined I would ever be seeing again. I sit back in my seat in surprise before smiling up at the man I left in my past almost 10 years ago, "Tyler? What the hell?"

He smiles as he steps up to me, "What are the fucking chances that I would run into you here, of all places?"

I laugh at him as he leans down and gives me a hug. I hug him back, noticing that his hand lingers a little longer than necessary on my back. I pull away from him, leaning back in my seat again, "What are you doing here?"

He sits down in the seat next to me, "I could ask you the same thing!"

I laugh at him, not really sure how to answer that question. He can't seem to take his eyes off of me. Which doesn't really make me uncomfortable and that should probably worry me.

Tyler leans back in the seat next to me before turning his attention to the bartender, "Can I get a vodka soda please?" The bartender looks between us then nods towards Tyler before turning around to make his drink.

Tyler turns his attention back towards me, "I thought you moved overseas?"

Nodding back at him, "I did. Me and Daija went to boarding school in London. We have been back for close to 2 years now."

Tyler leans forward putting his forearms on the bartop. I quickly take notice that there is no ring on his finger. I glance back up at him, he hasn't changed a bit.

Matured yes, changed no. He still has that crooked smile that hides his perfectly straight teeth. His eyes are still the color of the Caribbean. His voice is a bit deeper but he still has that southern drawl to his words.

His shoulders and build have definitely filled out though. He looks like he could be a linebacker for the NFL. He turns towards me, pushing some of his blonde locks out of his eyes, "Are you and Daija still close?"

I nod back at him, "Yeah. She is actually here too. She is probably up in her room with her girlfriend."

He smiles back at me, "Same old Daija then. What are you guys doing here? Are you on vacation? Is your mom here? I would love to see Lucy as well."

I pick up my drink and take a large swallow, realizing he is staring at the enormous ring on my finger. Good, he needs to know that I am off the market. He needs to be completely aware that just because we have run into each other that I now belong to someone else. Someone that didn't just walk away from me because it was too hard.

I sit my glass back down, "I am actually here on business. Kinda. My mom is a music manager. She is on tour right now so we kinda hijacked her for a bit."

His eyes are still on my rings as he reaches over to the vodka soda that was just sat down in front of him. He takes a slow drink before pointing to my hand, "I see you are married now?"

I smile at my hand then back up to him, "Yeah, just a little over a week now."

His eyes bug out of his head, "You are travelling with your mom instead of on your honeymoon? That is strange Hope, even for you."

I laugh back at him as I run my finger along the rim of my glass, "My husband Matthew is here too. He is up in our room. He had an accident a few days back and broke his arm so he is kinda laying low for a bit."

Tyler nods his head as he smiles back at me, "Damn, it is so good seeing you again. How long has it been? At least 10 years right?"

I widen my eyes and roll them towards my glass, "Almost yeah. I think the last time I saw you I was asking if you wanted to have a long distance relationship and you were shooting me down."

Reaching out with my ringed hand again, I bring my glass back up to my lips, shooting him a side eye. Let's see how he responds to that. Smiling at myself, I am getting way too good at making people uncomfortable. But for some reason, I like the thrill it gives me.

He laughs nervously as he picks up his own glass and takes a large drink from it.

He sits the glass back down, without even looking in my direction, "Yeah, I have been kicking my own ass over that for years. I will be doing it even more now that I see how fucking beautiful you are. You really grew into yourself didn't you?"

I feel my cheeks heating up but before I can say anything I hear, "Tyler fucking Weaver? Is that really you?"

We both look up to see Daija, Mona and Matthew walking down to our end of the bar.

Matthew looks pissed. No, not just pissed, livid.

I let out a sigh and roll my eyes, knowing this will be just one more thing to hang between us with words left un-fucking said.

Daija skips up to Tyler, wrapping him in a tight hug. Mona glances from Matthew then to me, giving me a sympathetic face. The soft smile I return to her says it all.

Matthew steps past Tyler to stand behind me.

No, more like lay claim on me.

Tyler sits back down with Daija and Mona on his far side. He turns his glance back to me and sees Matthew now standing behind me.

He stands up, eye to eye with Matthew and sticks out his hand, "Hey, you must be the husband she was just telling me about. My name is Tyler. We all went to grade school and junior high together."

Matthew reaches out with his good hand and gives Tyler a fake smile as he shakes his hand back, "Yeah, I am the husband. The name is Matthew."

Tyler smiles back at him, "Nice to meet you Matt. Hope here was just telling me about what all she has been up to for the last 10 years."

I can feel Matthews heavy breathing on the back of my neck. I finish my drink and sit a twenty down before turning sideways in my seat so I can watch both of them.

Matthew grins back at him and through gritted teeth says, "The name is Matthew. Not Matt."

I smile up at him while giving him a stop being an asshole stare, "I was just telling Tyler about how we have hijacked my mother and are following her around for a bit."

Matthew looks from me back to Tyler.

Tyler sits forward and takes another drink, "Yeah, it sucks that you hurt your arm and had to cut your honeymoon short. A girl like Hope definitely deserves to be pampered on a beach somewhere or something."

Matthew turns to me, obviously annoyed and done, "I am going back to the room babe. You coming up soon?"

I nod back at him and grab my purse, "I will go back with you now."

Turning back to Tyler, I smile at him, "It was really good seeing you again Tyler. I hope you have a nice visit in town."

I scoot between the two guys as they stare each other down. Tyler finally looks back at me, smiling again, "It was good seeing you too Hope. I will give my number to Daija. Maybe we can all meet up and have dinner one night. I am in town until Sunday. It would be great to catch up on lost times."

I politely smile back as I feel Matthews cast on my lower back as he tries to move me along, "Yeah we will see. You have a great night. Good bye!"

I glare at Matthew over my shoulder as I start to walk briskly back out of the bar. I can feel Matthew hot my tail as I make my way back over to the bank of elevators.

When he finally catches up to me, he leans into my neck, "What the fuck was that about?"

I glance over my shoulder at him, "He is an old friend from school. He saw me at the bar and came over to say hello. It was completely fucking harmless so I don't know why you are being such an asshole right now."

He laughs at me as the elevator doors open and we step inside. I hit the button for our floor and he turns on me as the doors shut, "That guy wants to fuck you."

I turn my face towards him, refusing to play this fucking game with him. He does not get to be jealous over every single fucking man I talk to.

Not after what he did.

I turn back towards the closed doors and stare at them in silence. When they finally open, I march out of them and down the hallway towards our room. I make it to the door and slide the key into the lock before flinging the door open and stomping inside.

Matthew is right behind me as I throw my purse on the table and turn around to face him, "Are you really fucking doing this right now?"

He shrugs his shoulders at me, playing like he is innocent, "What am I doing? I was just making an observation."

Nodding my head at him, I kick my shoes off and move towards the window. I turn back around to him as he is stepping closer to me, "Ya know. I am not the un-fucking trustworthy one in this relationship. You have no fucking reason or right to be acting the way that you are right now."

I see the hurt then anger roll across his face. He nods his head back at me, "Yeah I know. I am the piece of shit here. You have made that abundantly clear time and time again."

I move closer to him, my voice raising, "When? When have I made that abundantly clear? You won't even fucking talk to me about it so when would I have had the chance?"

He turns his back on me and moves towards the other side of the room. Frustrated, I throw my hands out to my sides again, "Of fucking course. Run away. I ask a question you don't fucking like and there you go. Running away like a fucking child again."

He turns back towards me, his face red from anger, "Are you fucking done?"

Disgusted, I look him up and down from head to toe, "Yeah, I am fucking done." I turn around and move closer to the window as I feel a tear run down my cheek. I reach up and angrily swipe it off my face.

I shake my head towards the window, "This isn't going to work. I am going to get my own room. We can just finish out the tour separately."

The warmth of his skin starts to radiate behind me and I know that he is just a step away now, "I don't want that."

I turn around and pin him with my stare, "Well, I don't really give a fuck what you want right now. I am not going to live the rest of my life with you punishing me for your mistakes. I am not the one that cheated just days after we got married.

"I am not the one that "wondered" what it would be like to make out with my ex. If I had, I would be downstairs with Tyler right fucking now."

Matthew's eyes fly back to mine and I realize I have said more than I intended. I cross my arms over my chest and try to stand as tall as I can. Hoping he didn't catch what I said when the whole situation would be obvious to fucking Helen Keller at this point.

He moves closer to me, "He is an ex?"

I let out an aggravated sigh, "Yes, he is an ex. I haven't seen him since I left for London. So since I was what? 14?"

Matthew turns around and starts pacing the room before turning back around on me, "Have you fucked him?"

I feel my own anger coursing through my veins now, "I am going to pretend like you didn't just fucking ask me that."

His eyes continue to dig into mine, "I think I have a fucking right to know. If you are having drinks with ex lovers. I am your fucking husband."

His words spit at me like I am the one that has been running around on him. I shake my head at him, moving closer, "Are you fucking kidding me? No! I haven't fucked him. Not now, not ever. But it is nice to know you think I was spreading my legs for anyone and everyone when I was barely a fucking teenager."

He throws his arms out to his sides, "How would I know? You have never fucking told me about your sex life. You could have been with half of the eastern seaboard for all I know."

I snicker back at him, "Well, that is how you like your women. Easy and after everyone else has had their turn."

He is fuming at me as he shakes his head, "Don't fucking bring her into this. It has nothing to do with her."

Rolling my eyes at him I move back over to my luggage. I start throwing things into it, not even caring where it lands.

He moves up beside me, "Your not fucking leaving. Not like this."

I turn and pin him with my stare, snarling at him, "Try and fucking stop me."

I step around him and move towards the bathroom. Matthew reaches out and grabs me by the arm before spinning me back towards him.

I try to pry his fingers off of me but his grip is too tight. His fingers are gripping me hard enough to leave bruises as I growl at him, "Let me go. You're hurting me."

He shakes his head back at me, "You are the violent one here, remember?" He raises his arm at me to show me his cast.

I feel the tears as they breach my eye lids.

Of course, he still fucking blames me.

Even after all the times he has told me it wasn't my fault. Streams of tears start running down my cheeks as I grit out between my clenched teeth, "Let. Me. Go."

He seems to see that he has pushed me to my limits. He lets go of me and I rub my arm, noticing the red handprint around it.

He shakes his head at me, "I'm sorry. I shouldn't have said that."

I nod my head angrily back at him, "Yeah, there are a lot of things you shouldn't have done. Fun part is the I am the only fucking one that pays the consequences for them."

I turn to head back towards the bathroom and he steps in front of me, "You don't think I am paying for my actions? You won't even fucking touch me Hope. Let alone look at me. You want absolutely fucking nothing to do with me. You don't think that is killing me?"

Good. Chuckling to myself, "I hope it is killing you. You fucking deserve it. You fucking deserve to feel some of the pain you forced on me. I didn't ask for this, remember? I was ready to walk the fuck away.

"You are the one that suggested Vegas. You are the one that asked me to marry you. You are the one that LIED to me when you told me she was your past and I was your future."

He steps up closer to me, "You are my future Hope. You are the only fucking future I want. I made a fucking mistake. I have apologized for it over and over again. But you won't even fucking look at me. It's not like I fucked her. I realized my mistake and I pushed her away. I told her no."

I laugh in his face, just inches away from mine now, "Yeah, after you had a little sample though. Just to see how it felt to make out with someone other than your fucking wife. How the fuck would you feel if I stood here and told you that I love you and that you are the only one that I want, then I go downstairs and kiss Tyler? How would that make you feel? Special? Loved? I fucking think not."

He steps up closer so that our noses are basically rubbing together now. His eyes are all over my face, "Is that what you want? To go make out with him? Would that let you love me again?"

I laugh in his face again, "That is the difference between me and you Matthew. I don't wonder what it would feel like. I wasn't sitting down there thinking about what his lips would feel like on mine. If there would be some kind of spark that wasn't there before. I wouldn't fucking do that to you."

Matthew nods his head back at me before turning around and screaming into the room, "I fucking messed up Hope. Don't you think I fucking know that? Don't you think I wish I was fucking strong enough to just walk the fuck away from you. I know you deserve so much fucking better than me. But I can't picture my life without you in it. I don't want to have a life if you aren't in it."

Crossing my arms over my heaving chest, I shake my head back at him, "So you are just going to hold me emotionally hostage for the rest of my fucking life? That's fair. That I have to pay for the mistake you made."

He turns back around, more angry than I have ever seen him. Eyes wide he screams back at me, "Fine, then just fucking leave me. Go. If you think that is what I am doing here. Just pack your shit and fucking leave."

I throw my hands out to my sides again, "Fine! I fucking will!"

I move towards my suitcase, barely even able to see it through all the tears in my eyes. I throw the top back open and Matthew spins me and presses his lips hard into mine.

I push back on his chest but he wont budge. He pushes himself into me harder until I feel the wall at my back. I continue to beat on his chest with my fists, trying to get my face away from his. He finally pulls back from me and I slap him hard across the face again.

How fucking dare he try to fucking take me like this?

Who the fuck does he think he is?

This isn't his choice to make. My heart is thrumming in my chest, hard. But it is abundantly clear that it is impossible for me to walk away from him. It is impossible for me to ignore the fact that I am burning alive for him. He stares back at me hard as I wrap my hands around his neck and slam his lips back into mine.

Matthew presses his body into mine against the wall and I can feel him hard already. I open my mouth and his tongue immediately invades mine, swirling around like he has never even kissed me before. His hand is reaching up under my shirt when I put my hands on his chest and push him off of me again.

He stares at me confused as I reach down and pull the shirt over my head. His lips slam back into mine as my hands go to his jeans. I unbutton them and slide the zipper down before undoing my own and kicking my pants and underwear off my legs and onto the floor. I push him back roughly and he lands on his back on the bed, bouncing just barely.

I lean down and pull his jeans and underwear down his legs, watching his cock spring out at me. I hear him moan as his eyes refuse to leave mine. Curling my lip up at him, "Shut up."

I climb on top of him and grab his arms pinning them above his head. He flinches at the force of my actions but I don't care. I hope I am hurting him.

I reach down between us and line him up with my entrance before slamming down onto him. His entire body buckles forward as he screams my name into the room around us. I continue to rise up and slam down on him, with zero regard to him or what pain I might be causing him.

I am showing him what he is pushing away. I will prove my fucking love for him one fucking thrust at a time if I have to.

He looks down watching me as I take him for everything that he has. His eyes come back to mine and I lean forward and kiss him hard as I continue to slam his cock into my pussy.

I feel myself already starting to tighten around his thick cock as I start slamming down onto him in short bursts. I pull my mouth from his, gasping in air as I start to moan into his neck. I feel his good hand come down and push on my lower back, adding pressure to me ramming him into me.

He leans his head back into the mattress, "Fuck me Hope. Fuck me harder."

I growl into his ear as I take his earring into my mouth and bite down hard on the lobe around it. His dick is twitching inside of me and I know he is fucking close. I stop moving completely and look into his face.

His eyes fly open wide, "Please Hope. Please baby."

I shake my head at him, honestly thinking about denying us both our releases. He shakes his head back at me as he starts to push into me from below, "Fuck me. Fuck me now Hope."

I stare into his face, "Why? Why should I?"

His eyes come back to mine as he stops thrusting into me, "Because you love me. And I love you."

I let my eyes jump back and forth between his before I lean forward and kiss him hard again. I start slamming myself back down onto him, feeling my release just barely holding back. I grind hard down into him, my clit rubbing on the patch of roughness above his shaft and I lose myself all around him.

I scream into his neck as I continue to thrust down onto him harder with no rhythm at all. He is slamming himself up into me when I feel him thicken inside of me then he is letting go.

His body curls up towards mine again, "Fuck Hope. Oh my god baby!"

He continues to push down on my back and I keep slamming down onto him. Taking every last fucking drop from him before I even think about slowing down. When I feel my climax finally starting to let go I lean back and look into his eyes.

Ashamed at myself for how I just behaved.

I pull myself off of him and roll over to the side of the bed. Pulling my knees tight to my chest.

I can feel him behind me, "Hope? Baby? Are you okay?"

Streams of tears are now running down my face, "We shouldn't have done that. I shouldn't have done that."

I feel his hand wrap around my waist as he tries to turn me back towards him, "Why not baby? We love each other. There is absolutely nothing wrong with angry make up sex."

I shake my head at him, "Is that even what that was? Make up sex? Cause it feels like it was just fucking rutting around on eachother. I don't feel very fucking loved right now."

I feel his grip tighten on me then he is pulling me down and pushing me into the bed. He rolls over until he is on top of me completely. He eyes scan my face before he lifts his hand up and wipes away the tears with the small amount of fingertips that are sticking out from the end of his cast.

I stare at him a moment longer then he reaches down between us and slides his dick back into me.

I look up at him as he slowly, gently slides in and out of me. His eyes never leave mine except when he leans in and kisses me gently on the lips.

I watch his face contort with pain when he shifts and puts all his weight on his bad arm. He reaches down in between us and starts circling my clit with his good hand.

I feel myself panting below him as he starts to push in and out of me faster but not punishing. Not like before. I feel him speed up his fingers and I fall over the edge again.

Tears running down my face as he forces me to take him deeper into me. He pushes in further and further until I feel him quiver above me and I know he is cumming as well.

He continues to slide in and out of me until mine passes then he seats himself fully inside of me. His dick is practically vibrating inside of me but the look on his face is pure adoration. It is almost painful to see. Because I don't know if it is real or not.

He looks at my lips, "You are the only person that I have ever loved Hope. You are the only person that I will ever love. Even if you leave me today, that will never change. I was born to be with you.

"I can't live without you baby. And I will pay for my mistakes every single day for the rest of my life. But please, don't walk away from this. Don't walk away from us."

I look up into his pleading eyes while he is begging for me to love him. I bring my hands up to his face and cup his cheeks as I bring my mouth gently back up to his.

I kiss him deeply before leaning back down onto the bed, "I love you too Matthew. And I am trying. I want this to work too. But I have to learn to trust you again. It is not easy. I want to but something inside me is just holding back."

Matthew smiles at me again as he runs a finger down my cheek, "We will figure it out. I will prove to you that you can trust me. That nothing like that will ever happen again. I swear to you, it is only you. You are my everything."

I grin back at him, kissing his good hand, "Look at you. Who knew you could be such a golden retriever?"

He smiles out a laugh back at me, "Not me. But baby for you, I would be anything I needed to be to keep a smile on your face."

12
Apollo
OMENS - The Pretty Wild

This is weird as shit watching everyone get set up for the show and knowing that I will not be the one up there on the drums. I know the band is in good hands with Hope but I feel lost right now.

I don't like it.

The stage is looking a little extra tonight as well since it is Halloween. We celebrate it back home as well but I have been told that it is a whole different beast over here in the US.

Apparently, I am to expect costumes and jump scares galore. Which I am fine with, I love me a little Art the Clown here and there.

Susie is also planning an over the top celebration later as well since yesterday was Edge's birthday. Something about cake, ice cream and possibly strippers. I mean...I am down but it just depends on how Hope feels after the show.

It is only about an hour before the doors open and I am chomping at the bit to rip this fucking cast off my arm. I just wanna be up there. But then I see Hope as she makes her way to the set.

She is painted all in black, almost every single inch of her because she is wearing a black halter and skimpy little black shorts. They have painted her to look like a skeleton over the top of the black body paint though.

From her fucking curb stompers up to her hair that is wrapped up in hat she is dripping with sex. I watch her as she sits down at the drums, twirling a stick in her fingers as she readjust the stool, making sure she can reach everything.

Smiling proudly, I watch her settle into herself. She seems so relaxed when she is behind the set. Like that is the only place she really feels comfortable.

Which makes me a bit sad because I want to see her comfortable all the time. Especially with me. But that is my own fucking fault.

I took that from her.

My head lowers back down and I wander backstage again. I don't know what to do with myself. It feels like a lifetime before the show actually starts.

I hear movement to my right and look up to see Hope coming back down the hall towards me. She smiles which is creepy as fuck since she is painted completely black so all I see is her pearl white teeth coming at me.

I smile back at her, "You ready for tonight?"

She nods her head back at me before pointing to the girl's dressing room door and walking towards it, "I think so yeah. My nerves are a lot worse than they were the last time. I feel like my skin is crawling and on fire.

"Not sure if I want to throw up or pass out. At least the other show was so last minute I didn't really have time to be too nervous. But tonight, I am freaking out a bit."

I watch her as she walks to the mini fridge and pulls a bottle of water out of it. She looks like she is in complete beast mode right now. All in black, hair concealed, she looks like a harbinger of death, and I can't lie....

It is sexy as fuck.

I smile as I step closer to her, "I wish I could step in for you. I tried to hold a stick earlier but it was a no go."

She turns back towards me, nodding her head before leaning back into the wall and letting out a heavy sigh, "More and more I wish I wouldn't have pushed you. Maybe we can try like duct taping a stick to your cast."

I laugh as I step up closer to her, running my hand across her waist line, "If it helps, I wish I hadn't given you a reason to push me."

Her eyes come back to mine but at least she is smiling now. Until this moment, she would just look at me with uncertainty, but now she looks like she might actually be starting to believe me.

I will take whatever I can get at this point.

I move my mouth closer to hers, "You know. I can help remedy some of the nerves for you."

Hope's eyes fly to mine before looking over my shoulder towards the door then back to me, "Matthew! The door is standing wide open and I really don't want to have to get repainted."

I chuckle into her lips just a bit, "Don't worry, no one will even know. And I promise you won't have to get repainted."

I pop open her tight leather shorts and pull the zipper down. Her eyes are back on mine. I slide my hand down the front of her lacy underwear, letting my finger roll over her clit.

Hope lets out a little moan as her eyes roll back in her head a bit. I smile as I watch her bite her lower lip and lay her head back on the wall behind us. Her clit is throbbing against my finger, like it was just waiting for me to step up and do my damn job. I slide my hand a bit deeper pushing my middle finger into her, feeling her already wet.

Probably from a mix of me and anxiety for the show. I know I have the same issues sometimes when my nerves are high.

I add another finger and push in and out of her as her hand comes back down on my wrist. She lets a moan leave her throat as I bring my thumb up over her clit as well.

Her face melts under my touch, "Is this helping baby? Is this taking your mind off of other things?"

I watch her nod her head with her eyes still closed. I pull my finger from inside of her and start circling her clit hard and fast.

She moans again then I hear Lily from behind me, "20 minutes Hope."

Hope's eyes fly open and her grip tightens on my wrist as I smile at her, still circling her clit viciously, "She will be there."

I don't even look over my shoulder to make sure everyone is gone. I lean into her ear, "Cum all over my hand baby."

She is nodding her head now, her eyes still closed, mouth hanging open.

She is so fucking close. I slide my fingers back down and start thrusting them into her, keeping my thumb locked onto her clit. I feel her tighten around my fingers and legs start to shake.

She reaches out and braces her hand on the mini fridge beside her. Her other hand comes up to my bad shoulder but I don't even care. She is falling apart just from my touch alone and that is all that matters to me.

I watch her face as she begins to loosen her grip and smile from her release. She rolls her head to the side and smiles widely at me, slowly opening her eyes, "I have a new reason for you to be here before every show."

I laugh at her as she watches me pull my fingers from her cunt and bring them straight to my mouth. Her eyes watch my fingers as I lick them clean.

I see her biting her lip again and I smile at her, "Just a little something to tie me over until later."

She laughs again as she leans forward and kisses me. She pulls back a moment later and buttons her shorts back up.

191

She tries to look herself over, "Am I still looking okay?"

I give her a soft kiss back, "Gorgeous."

Hope smiles back at me, "Thank you baby."

I watch her as she struts past me. I reach out and smack her ass before following her out of the room and back to the stage. She moves to the far side and I climb to stage left to watch the show with Lucy, Susie and Daija.

I have my balaclava that I had used from back in the day. Luckily it is rayon and not wool so I won't be sweating to death.

I settle in beside Susie, giving her a little hip bump, "How are you doing?"

She smiles and moves to my other side to hip bump me back without hitting my bad arm. I laugh as I throw an arm over her shoulders as we see everybody walking out on stage to take their marks.

For some reason, I am as giddy as a child right now. I have never watched us from this aspect.

I get it now.

When Susie and Lily would fangirl over us. I just assumed it was because of their attractions to Gideon and Edge but no. The whole band as a collective is mesmerizing from this side of things.

The lights drop and the crowd starts screaming. My heart is about to beat out of my chest as well. The lights come back on and Ares is across the stage in a flash.

I only ever see him from behind so to see him from the side like this, he is fucking entrancing. He seems to be everywhere at once.

I laugh as I see him dancing down the main runway that goes out into the crowd. I turn back and look at Dionysus who is currently jumping in circles but still shredding at the same time. He nods over to me and Susie as we start jumping with him.

I throw my bad arm up in the air, screaming into the rafters above us as Susie starts laughing at me. Three songs later I hear the beginning chords to Resist the Violence begin.

I smile turning to Susie, leaning into her ear yelling, "Hope fucking destroys this song!" Susie nods her head, turning her attention to Hope.

We watch Hope as she tilts her head back and just lays into it. She is so in the zone, she doesn't even have to look around for any ques.

She is fucking amazing.

She rolls across the set like she has been playing her entire life. She holds the beat perfectly. I feel the heat coming and turn to Susie, smiling widely again, "She is about to crash in!"

We both watch her in pure fucking amazement. They roll into Firestorm and I see Aphrodite on the big screen above Hope's head. I about shit myself when I see she has painted Hope on the drums.

Every other member standing around her. Watching her with their backs to the crowd. Everyone except for the stand in bassist, Micah. He is killing it but we aren't really ready to initiate him yet.

I think that maybe Gideon is thinking that Simone will come back but honestly, I fucking pray that she doesn't. I don't have the patience or energy to deal with her anymore.

I look back to the big screen and I see Lily throwing her final touches onto the portrait. It has become her trademark to basically make it look like blood has sprayed over the whole thing. I am pretty sure it is just watered down red paint but it gives it a vibrant touch that everyone seems to dig.

Hope plays a steady kick drum, rolling the cymbals before the song comes to an abrupt halt. Susie and I both scream out onto the stage.

Dionysus runs over and kisses Susie quickly before running back out onto stage to bow. Ares looks over at me and waves me over. I thought he might do this so I wore a hoodie just in case.

I pull the sleeve down over my cast and throw the hood up before walking out on stage. I know that people can tell from my stance that it is me, though they have never really seen me out of character before.

Hope comes down from the set and stands beside me. Bowing and waving at everyone. I reach my good arm around her and pull her close to me as we continue to wave towards the crowd.

Knowing there are already going to be rumors flying because I have missed another show and there is chick filling in for me I say fuck it and turn to her, smiling before I wrap both my arms around her and kiss her roughly.

She squeals and tries to get away for just a moment before settling into me and kissing me back. I finally pull back grinning again as I turn back around and wave a bit more.

We watch Ares and Dionysus lower Aphrodite onto the floor.

I don't like her doing that.

Not while she is pregnant.

Some kind of protective uncle mode comes over me and I decide to pull Gideon aside later at the hotel and tell him as such. Maybe Hope can hand out the canvases for the rest of the tour. She is going to be on stage anyways so why not.

Hope grips my hand tight and we all walk off stage. Micah is more talkative than I thought he was going to be. Ares makes a point to remind him that once we are in the green room it is mouth shut until everyone leaves. He nods back at us, keeping his mask down at least.

I look at Hope with a roll of my eyes. I don't know how long this guy is going to last.

194

But I have to be appreciative.

He is kinda saving our asses since Simone dropped us on them. We filter in the green room and I hold an arm out for Hope to sit in the chair next to Dionysus.

She gratefully falls back into it, stretching her legs out in front of her. Her skeleton painted body now looks more like a chalkboard that at one point had writing on it then someone opened a window during a rain storm.

All of the paint is just rolling together from sweat. It is still hot as fuck though. I move to the bar and pour us both a glass of Dalmore then walk back to the other side of the room.

No one has started to filter in yet so we at least have a few moments to breathe. Ares turns to me, "Hope fucking killed it again. You should worry about your job, old man."

Hope laughs loudly as she reaches up for her drink, "You do not have to worry. I am exhausted. This is only a temporary situation. Plus, I can learn anything, I just can't come up with my own for shit. That is all you baby."

I smile back at Ares, "Look there, job security."

He chuckles as he walks back over to sit down next to Aphrodite. I turn around the room seeing Susie laying over Dionysus. Her tattoo on full display for everyone to see, whether they know what it is or not. Daija has even worn a mask and is curled up in the same chair as Hestia.

I will admit though, it is weird seeing someone else in Hera's seat. She had filled that spot for almost a decade.

Now she is gone.

That is the only part of her that I miss.

The person she used to be.

I shake my head and move to walk around the back of the chair. Hope stands up quickly, "Where do you think you are going?"

I point behind her, "I am just gonna lean into the back of the chair. That is your spot now, until I come back at least."

195

She shakes her head at me and points towards the seat, "This is your throne sire. I am not overthrowing today. Sit your ass down."

I tilt my head at her, shaking it, "No, that was your show, you get the chair."

She stands up a bit taller, I see the left side of her lips raise up in a partial smile, "If you sit in the chair, I will give you a blow job later."

I choke on my Dalmore looking around, seeing everyone smiling and staring at Hope. Daija is the first one to whoop out, "Fuck yeah she will!"

I clear my throat again as I hear Dionysus, "Sit the fuck down dude. We do not turn down blow jobs in this band."

I laugh at him as I step back around the chair and sit down. Hope goes to move beside me and I grab her arm, "No you don't. You sit right here."

I pulled her down across my lap and she laughs into my neck.

I smile back at her.

I love this side of Hope.

The one where she is just her.

She isn't worried about anything. She isn't looking at herself in disgust. She isn't overthinking the past or the future. She is just living in the moment.

She readjusts in my lap and leans back into my good shoulder. Two minutes later, Lucy walks in, opening the doors and leaving them open for the charade to begin. We collectively let out a breath and get comfortable.

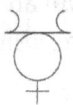

An hour later, my ass is officially asleep. My left cheek is tingling but at least I have had enough Dalmore that I shouldn't need any pain pills tonight.

I have been trying to not take them. I fucking hate pills. Everytime I have to take them, I think of my brother Joe.

He broke his leg in high school and before we even fucking knew it he was hooked on those bitches. It turned him into a completely different person.

And not a good one.

I plan to flush whatever I don't need after the next few days.

The pain itself isn't horribly bad anymore except when I settle in to go to sleep. Then it's like I can feel the bone fusing back together. It just pulsates and radiates with pain. The last of the people start to trickle out and Lucy shuts the doors.

She turns around with a heavy sigh, "Thank fuck for that."

We all laugh at her as Aphrodite sits forward in her chair, "Group meeting. We don't have to be in Raleigh until Friday. Nag's Head?"

Everyone except Micah who looks completely confused yells out their agreement with her.

I turn and lean over, "Hey Micah, I know we haven't really met yet. I am Matthew, er, Apollo. I really appreciate you stepping in and helping out on such short notice."

He grins back at me, "Are you fucking kidding me? This is all fucking amazing. I can't believe I got so lucky."

Hope laughs as she slides off my lap, "Don't worry. It will pass."

I smack her ass hard, Micah's eyes going between the two of us, "Hope is my wife. It's fine. Plus she owes me a blow job. I am allowed to get handsy."

Micah laughs loudly at me before leaning back in his chair, "How long have you two been married? I hadn't heard

197

about anyone in the band getting hitched besides Gideon and Lily. I mean, Ares and Aphrodite."

I nod back at him, putting a hand up, "As long as you don't slip in public we are good. Basic band rule is if the mask is on, we go by our god."

Micah nods back at me like he is taking a mental note of every single thing that I say. I look back over at Hope, "We have been married for 16 days. We did it in Vegas so no one really knows about it yet."

Micah smiles back at me, "That's awesome man. Congratulations. I haven't really had a chance to talk to her yet but she seems pretty cool. Also, it's kinda iconic that she can play the drums too."

I finish the last of my Dalmore before sliding to the edge of the seat, "Yeah, it's hard to believe that up until 19 days ago she didn't even know who I was. Now she is my fill in because of my fucking arm."

Micah turns back to me in shock, "Wait. 19 days? You guys got married like 72 hours after meeting?"

I stand up stretching my arms out above my head. Micah stands up beside me, still dumbfounded.

I come back down from my toes, "Yup. Sure did. I locked that shit down tight."

He laughs as he looks around me towards Ares, "So what did Aphrodite mean about Nag's Head? What's a Nag's Head?"

I reach over and pat him on the shoulder, "That is our secret bat cave. Where we can just chill and be free. Trust me, you will love it."

I turn back towards Lucy, "Hey Mom. You coming to Nag's Head too?"

Lucy flips me off. Daija and Hope are both cackling so she flips them off as well. She smiles as she turns back towards me, "Yeah. I may be a day or two behind you but I will be there. I ran into some old family friends earlier. I am going to visit with them for a day before I head up."

I nod at her then catch Hope's eye. She is staring at Lucy like she is shocked she is not going right away.

Lucy turns towards her, "I ran into Tyler Weaver at the hotel earlier. You remember him right? You two used to be inseparable as kids. Anyways his mom wants to see me. So I am going to go to Georgia for a day or two. Then I will head up to the beach house."

Hope slowly nods her head before turning towards me. Probably to judge how I am going to react. But I could give a shit less.

She is mine, not his.

I step up to her then smile at Lucy, "Well Mom, we would love to stay and chat but your daughter has promised me a blow job and I intend to cash that bitch in tonight."

Lucy's eyes blow wide as she slaps me in my bad arm. I instantly flinch and she moves towards me, "Oh fuck. I'm sorry. I didn't hurt you did I? Wait, no. After that comment I hope I did."

Smiling sarcastically back at her, "Thanks for the concern, mother. But I am fine."

She shakes her head back at me, "You have got to stop calling me that. It is weird as fuck."

I continue to grin as I grab Hope's hand and start to lead her towards the door, "Later losers. Text with travel details." I throw my arm up in the air, unable to make a peace sign right now so I just look like Judd Nelson from the Breakfast Club instead.

Susie yells in our general direction, "Hotel bar in 2 hours you guys. I don't care if you miss your blow job for it!"

Hope continues to giggle loudly as we make our way out of the room and down the long hallway to the back door. I glance over at her and see her smiling as she stares at her feet. I grin back at her before opening the back door and leading her towards one of the SUV's.

We climb in quickly and start to make our way back towards the hotel. I can tell she really is exhausted.

I roll my head across the seat to look at her, "You know. I will let you out of your blow job duties tonight. I can tell you are tired."

She rolls her head back to mine, smiling, "No chance. My word is my bond. I just need a shower and I will be good for a few more hours."

I chuckle back at her then look down to my cast. I let out a frustrated growl, "I wish I could help you with that, but it is one arm wrapped in plastic while bathing for the foreseeable future."

I look back over at her and she has that distant look in her eye. It is obvious what she is thinking about. And though I have told her a million times that I don't blame her, I can tell that she blames herself.

I reach a hand out, placing it on her thigh, "Hey. That was not a dig at you. Just an observation. You know I am not mad about this right?"

She looks at my arm that I have pulled up between us and nods her head, "I know you're not. But I still feel like you should be."

I lean in and give her a soft kiss, "Too bad. I'm not and I won't ever be. I had it coming and whether you want to admit it or not, it was deserved."

She shakes her head back at me as the SUV comes to a stop in front of the hotel. We slide out and make our way up to the room.

Hope walks in before me, instantly grabbing some clothes out of her suitcase and making her way to the bathroom. She yells over her shoulder, "Just give me 20 and I will be all yours."

I smile back at her as I make my way towards the other side of the room. Taking my hoodie and mask off, I throw them on the table. Sweat coats my hand as I run my good hand through my hair, feeling the cold air hit it after being covered in rayon for hours. I pull my shirt up and off of me as well, throwing it to the side.

I walk around to my side of the bed and fall back onto it. Quickly grabbing the remote off the night stand, I turn it on to some local channel. There is an old episode of the Simpsons playing so I just zone into it while I wait on Hope to finish getting cleaned up.

Half an hour later, Hope comes walking out of the bathroom wrapped up in a robe. Hair still curly from washing it. She steps up to her suitcase then looks over her shoulder at me with a devious smile.

I turn the tv off, placing the remote back on the night stand, "What was that grin about? I am not sure that I trust it."

Hope let out a giggle, "I was just thinking." I watch her as she moves around her suitcase, digging through it. Obviously looking for something.

Then a few moments later she drops the robe from her body, showing me that she is only wearing a tight black sheer corset with matching thong.

I instantly sit up to attention.

If she had high heels on right now I would literally pass out. I let my eyes roam from her legs all the way up to the back of her neck.

She looks over her shoulder again, still smiling, "It isn't fair that I haven't been punished for pushing you and causing all this drama."

Hope turns around to face me and has a leather paddle in her hands. I feel my eyes go wide and my jaw almost hits the floor. Standing, I move closer to her. My eyes devouring her every breath.

She grins back up at me as I approach her. I grin wildly as I reach out and take the small leather paddle from her hands. I turn it over in my own a few times, before smiling at her and running the flat surface of it down her chest.

It rolls over her tit then the plains of her abdomen. Hope closes her eyes and I smile as I watch the paddle slide down to her pussy. I pull back and tap it hard on her center.

Her eyes fly open and she smiles back at me. She steps around me, putting her back towards the bed.

Hope smiles innocently as she starts to unbuckle the leather bracelet on her wrist. I hadn't even noticed it until now. She opens it and moves something along the buckle before smiling at me. She puts her wrists together and moves them towards me. "You should probably buckle this back up, for your safety that is. You don't want me getting violent again. Right?"

I feel the growl grow in my chest when I realize this bracelet is made to turn into leather handcuffs. I lift the paddle towards her mouth, "Open."

I watch her pouty lips as they part and then put the paddle in between her teeth. I smile as she bites down on it then move to her wrists to bind them.

I can feel her pulse starting to quicken in her veins. I never would have imagined that Hope had this side to her. I am not complaining, just fucking suprised.

I finish tightening the buckle and smile at her as I take the paddle from her mouth. She grins back at me shyly. Leaning forward, I give her a soft kiss before moving to her ear and whispering, "Turn around and put your hands on the bed."

Her cheeks are now pink but she gives me a shy smile and does what she is told. I watch her as she bends over in front of me, the hesitation in her arms as she tries to plant her hands firmly on the bed.

I run my fingertips over her ass and I see the shivers roll up her shoulders and down her arms. Smiling at the sight of them, "So you think you should be punished for what you have done, do you?"

I continue lightly dragging my fingers over her ass as she looks over her shoulder at me, "Yes. I do."

A thrill runs down my spine as I place the paddle flat against her ass, "Yes, I do, what?"

Her breathing gets heavier, "Yes I do. Sir."

Well fuck.

This is a new one for me.

I didn't even know I had a fucking sub kink until this moment. I can feel my own breathing getting heavy, matching Hopes. I open the button of my jeans to relieve a bit of the pressure then pull the paddle back just a bit before slapping her asscheek with it.

She lets out a moan as she leans forward from the impact of it. I throw my head back onto my shoulders, feeling the anticipation from the paddle running down my own spine. Fuck this is amazing. The tension from the paddle radiates up my arm then straight down to my dick.

I look back down towards her, "Are you sorry for what you did?"

She doesn't raise her head this time but instead almost whispers, "Yes. Sir. I am sorry."

I raise the paddle again, smacking her ass a bit harder with it. This time instead of letting the impact push her forward she actually pushes her ass back into the direction of the paddle.

Wanting more.

I hear her let out another heavy moan and I am just about to burst out of my fucking jeans. She seems to be enjoying this more than either of us thought she would. 50 pounds says she is dripping wet right now.

I run my fingers over the light red marks that are starting to form on her ass. She moans again before looking over her shoulder at me, "I didn't mean to hurt you Matthew. Not like that."

I feel her words in my soul. I throw the paddle onto the floor by her feet, "Fuck this. Come here." I pull her up by her waist and spin her to face me. She stands up in front of me, slamming her mouth into mine. I grip her hair tightly in my hand as I shove my tongue into her mouth.

I can feel her bound hands at my zipper, trying to get my pants off of me. I reach down and finish unzipping them and then pull them and my boxers down off my legs. Before standing I reach up and grab her almost non existent underwear, sliding them down her legs as well.

Hope turns me and pushes me down onto the bed. She gets on her knees, stretching her bound hands up onto my chest as she leans forward and takes me deep into her throat.

I push my head back into the mattress and close my eyes as I moan into the room. The slick heat from her mouth is forming to every part of my dick, "Jesus Hope."

I feel her rolling her tongue around my head before taking me in deeper again. Her nails are digging into my chest as I reach my good hand down and put it on the back of her head, pushing her harder onto my cock.

I look down and watch her devouring me, "Yeah baby. Just like that. You're doing so good, baby. Don't stop."

My praise seems to cause a change in her somehow. I watch as her cheeks hollow out and she is taking me all the way to the base.

I can feel my cock hitting the back of her throat. I throw my head back again, not sure how long I am going to be able to hold out on her, "Fuck Hope!"

I look back down at her then move my hand under her arm, "Come here baby. Get on me."

She releases me from her mouth, letting my cock twitch on her lips while she smiles at me. She shuffles up further as I reach down and grip myself so she can slide down onto me.

She lets out a loud moan into the room as she takes me into her. Hope closes her eyes and smiles, "God dammit Matthew. I will never get enough of your cock."

I smile at her as I grip her hips and slam myself up into her. She screams into the room as I continue to pound into her from below. I hook one leg over hers and roll her under me seamlessly.

I grab her bound wrists and hold them tight above her head as I start thrusting harder into her.

Hope has her head thrown back, letting out little moans every time I slam into her. I watch her face as she starts to just melt with pleasure, "God baby you feel so good. I feel like god himself when I am inside you."

She smiles wider as she starts lifting her hips to meet my own. We slam into each other over and over until I can feel her starting to clench around my cock.

I look back at her face and I can see she is just begging for it to hit. I lean forward, biting her nipple through her corset. She screams above me and I feel her tighten around me harder.

I continue to slam into her with no rhythm at all. She pushes her arms up over my head so her bound wrists are behind my neck. I look into her eyes and she smiles at me, "I love you."

I can feel the truth behind her words. They are so powerful it pushes me right over the edge. I scream her name as I feel myself let go inside of her. She continues to slam her hips into mine until we are laying there completely spent.

I smile down at her, kissing her with all the passion my heart contains. Her lips curl into a smile as I pull back to look at her face.

She opens her eyes towards me, "I should be punished more often."

I chuckle back at her before kissing her again and sliding out of her. I roll over to my back as she throws her bound hands up over her head again.

Turning my face towards hers, "I love you so fucking much. I hope you know that."

She turns her head towards me, "I know you do. I never questioned if you loved me. I only worried about who you loved more."

I roll to my side, laying my casted arm over her stomach, "I never loved her. Not like that. I just, I think I just wished for so long that she would have any feeling other than indifference towards me that I just got lost in myself for a minute.

"I don't care if she ever has feelings for me. Not anymore. I honestly don't care if I never even see her again. I will miss the friendship that we had but nothing else. Nothing more."

Hope smiles widely at me before nodding her head, "I can live with that. What say we just call it what it is. The past. Let's just move forward. Just me and you. Happy, together."

I feel my heart about to burst out of my chest, "That is all I want baby. I just want you. I want to be the one to make you smile. The one to be your comfort. I want you to feel like my arms are home, because yours are to me."

Hope brings her hands down towards me, "Can you please undo these? I really want to fucking hug you right now."

I laugh as I sit up and turn towards her slightly to unbuckle the bracelet. As soon as her arms are free, she sits up and wraps them around my shoulders, pulling me closer to her, "I love you so fucking much Matthew, sometimes I feel like my chest is going to explode from the force of it. I can feel you everywhere. You are engraved in my soul at this point. I just want you. I want us."

I hold her tight to me, thanking the heavens that I am getting another chance with her. I can't imagine her not right here, in my arms where she is meant to be.

I kiss the side of her head then pull back just a bit, "We should probably head down to the party soon."

Hope lets out a heavy sigh then nods her head at me, "Yeah. But no lap dances unless they are from me."

I smile widely back at her, running my hand down her cheek, "Good thing I have plenty of ones then."

13
Hope
Do or Die - Natalie Jane

I need these few days at Nag's Head to recuperate from the one previous. It has been fucking insane, between me breaking Matthew's arm and Simone leaving us scrambling, everyone has been on high alert it seems.

Matthew is still snoring but I can't lay here anymore. I have to move. I haven't ran in a long time but honestly it's the ocean that is calling to me.

I immediately devise a plan to slip into town and buy a board. I quickly leave a note for Matthew and slip downstairs.

Lucky for me Lily is already down here as well. Smiling, I step up to the island, "Good morning Lily!"

Lily beams over her shoulder at me, "Good morning Hope. You seem chipper this morning."

I nod my head at her, "Yeah I guess. Hey, I have a weird question for you."

Lily turns to me smiling as she continues to stir her cup of coffee, "I love weird questions. What ya got?"

There is a stool beside me so I climb up on it, setting my forearms on the counter, "If I was to say, buy a surfboard today. Would there be anywhere I could store it? I really want to surf but I don't want to rent a board. That is like wearing someone else's bowling shoes. It's just gross."

Lily laughs loudly at me, "Of course. There is a little yard barn thingy under the deck. It should be big enough for a board.

I would check first but it should work. The only thing I really keep in there is the stuff for the pool and hot tub. It should be at least half empty."

I pump my arm in the air as I jump off the stool. I smile at her again, "And you don't mind me leaving it here, for when we are here between shows?"

Lily shakes her head at me, "Hope. We are family. This house may have my name on it but this place is for everyone. If you want to claim a room and paint polka dots on the wall I would be fine with it. I want you to be comfortable here."

Quickly, I move around the island and pull her into a hug, "You are literally the best. I don't think you are told that enough."

Lily giggles back at me, "You're kinda great as well."

I smile as I pull back from her, "I am going to call an uber and run into town then. Matthew is still sleeping so hopefully I will be back before he wakes up."

Lily nods her head at me, then points towards the back door, "Micah said something about wanting to run into town as well. He may have already ordered an uber if you wanna share."

I look towards the back door, "Sweet. Thank you Lily!"

I run towards the back deck, pushing the door open as I look around the side of it. Micah is sitting under the umbrella drinking what looks like a cup of coffee, "Yo Micah?"

He turns his head towards me then smiles and raises his mug, "What's up Peach?"

Laughing loudly back at him, "Peach is Susie. I am Hope."

Micah laughs as he stands up, "I knew it didn't feel right as soon as I said it. Do you have a nickname or stage name?"

I shake my head back at him, "Not that I have been made aware of yet. Hey, Lily said something about you maybe running into town. Did you already order an uber or maybe want to share one? I need to run into the surf shop."

He smiles widely back at me, "You surf? So do I! Yeah I have already ordered one. I was actually going to try to find a

209

funboard. I don't think the surf is stout enough for a shortboard here."

I look out over the ocean, nodding at it, "Yeah, I have to agree with you there. I am going to pick up a long board though. Lily said I could store it in the yard barn under the deck. I will see if there is enough room for a funboard too."

I shut the backdoor behind me and make my way down the steps. I turn to the left, seeing the shed. Immediately I remember the night that Matthew pinned me to it and proposed.

I can't believe I didn't realize that was the yard barn she was talking about. I smile at the memory of that night before I step up to it and open the door, noticing quickly that there is plenty of room for two boards.

Still grinning, I shut the door and run back up the stairs, "There is so much space in there. We should be set. How long till the uber gets here?"

Micah checks his phone then stands up, "He should literally be here any second. Let's go."

Micah and I make our way through the house, making sure everyone knows where we are going then step out onto the porch. The car pulls up immediately and I thank the lucky stars that it is an SUV. I run down the steps and knock on the passenger window. The driver rolls it down, "Sup?"

Grinning back at him, "Good Morning! We were gonna pick up a couple boards in town. You got straps or do I need to bring some." By the looks of him, I think I can pretty much guess the answer but I have to ask just in case.

Bruh smiles back, "Of course I do, baby girl. I know a killer shop too. Jump in, we'll head straight over."

I smile as I move to the back and slide in, leaving the door open for Micah. We get settled in as the car starts to move from the house, "How far is it?"

Bruh nods his head as he looks both ways before turning onto the road, "Not far. Maybe 10 minutes tops."

I nod my head back at him, "Sweet."

Turning in my seat a bit, I look at Micah, "So, Micah. How long have you been playing?"

He looks at the driver then back towards me, "I would say about 12 years or so. How about you?"

I shake my head, making a more skeptical face, "I have only been playing for maybe 4 or 5 years tops."

Micah turns his face to me, jaw hanging open, "No fucking way? You are a fucking beast up there. There is no way you have only been playing for 4 years."

I laugh back at him, turning in the seat a bit, "No seriously. I never touched a set before that. I guess I kinda hyperfixated on learning. I wanted to have something to make me feel closer to the band. Not knowing that I would ever actually meet them."

Micah laughs as he points at my finger, "Or marry one of them."

I nod back at him looking at my finger. He is right, I never imagined this in a million years. I smile back up at him as I turn to look out the window at the ocean flying by.

Bruh looks in the rearview, "What are you guys talking about? What do you play?"

I look at Micah and smile with a wink, "We are in a jazz band. Indigo Jones. Have you heard of us?"

Bruh shakes his head as I hear Micah beside me chuckling under his breath.

I smile back at Bruh, "You should look us up. We are really getting big. You might like us."

Bruh shakes his head again, "Yeah, not really my kind of music. I am more of a Bad Omens or Carnal Decay fan."

I shoot Micah a quick smile, "Yeah, I haven't heard of either of those bands. I will have to look them up when we get back to the house."

A few minutes later, we pull up to the surf shop. I jump out of the SUV turning back to Bruh, "Are you okay with waiting for a few minutes? Keep the meter running. We shouldn't be long."

Bruh opens the door, "What are you talking about baby girl? I am going in too."

Nodding a smile at him, I turn back towards the shop and head inside. Bruh was right, this shop is killer. They have fucking everything here. I check out a few different boards before settling on one that just speaks to me. I also grab a 10" Quicksilver fin and then a leash. Deciding there is no real need for a bag or wetsuit.

Micah is still checking out boards so I spend a few minutes looking at the wax as well. I get some banana scented and throw it up on the counter as well.

I smile as Bruh offers to take my new Panda Repeater out to the car and strap it for me. I grab my bag full of goodies and look towards Micah, "You good Micah? I am going to head back out."

He throws a hand up over his shoulder, "Give me 3 and I will be right behind you!"

I nod back in his general direction before stepping back out front. Taking in the sunshine and salty air, I tilt my head towards the sky.

It is fucking beautiful out today. Not too humid yet but there isn't a cloud in the sky. I stand there for another moment just letting the sun soak into my skin when Bruh steps up to me, "You seriously surf longboard?"

Covering my eyes with my hand I bring my gaze back down to him, "Yeah. I love it. I am from Malibu so it is kinda in my veins."

He smiles and nods back at me before turning towards the car. I go to take a step as well when he turns back around, running his hand down the back of his neck, "And dude said you were married?"

I smile back at him as I raise my hand, wiggling my fingers at him. He sees the Harry Winston on my finger and his eyes go as round as half dollars, "Fuck yeah you are. God damn baby girl who did you marry? A Rockefeller?"

I laugh back at him as Micah comes out with his funboard. I watch them strap it down then we all climb back in the car to head back to the house.

I was smart enough to go ahead and put my bathing suit on under my clothes so once we are back all I have to do is attach the fin and wax the board.

The thrill of the thought of being on the water runs through me. It has been months since I have been on a board. Hopefully I don't fall on my ass straight away.

We pull back up to the house and the guys get the boards down. Bruh hands me mine and I smile back at him, "We are gonna be right behind the house if you wanna join later. I don't know about Micah but I will probably be out there awhile."

Bruh smiles at me as he pulls his blonde hair out of his eyes, "Sweet. Yeah I might show up if the rides are slow."

I nod back at him and angle my board to walk around the side of the house and down to the beach. Micah pays Bruh then he is right behind me. I yell over my shoulder, "Just let me know what half was and I will cash app you."

Micah trots up beside me, "No worries. I am just glad I didn't have to go alone."

I smile over at him the step around the back of the house. I move about halfway down the beach and sit down all my stuff. Remembering that I saw a tool box in the shed, I run quickly scouring the toolbox until I find a screwdriver.

"Bitch that board is twice your size!" I look up and see Lily looking at the board I laid on the beach. I look at it then smile back up at her on the patio, smiling and shielding my eyes from the sun, "It's supposed to be. It's a longboard."

Lily laughs at me and pulls a chair up to the railing, "I have to see this. I have never watched someone I actually know surfing before."

Throwing her a quick salute, I move back into the shed to find the elusive screwdriver. I quickly attach my fin then set to waxing the board. Micah finished way before me so he is already out in the water. I smile as I watch him out there shredding the small waves.

This is what I needed. I was right to make the decision to drop a couple grand this morning. I finish waxing my board and strip down to my bikini. After attaching my leash, I run out into the water to join Micah.

I easily fall back into my rhythm, paddling out just far enough to barely ride in before standing on the board. I use my arms to balance myself as I walk the board. Feeling my toes curl around the front of the board until it starts to dip into water then walking backwards back down the board to give it a bit more lift in the front to carry me forward.

I get to the end of the run and lower myself back down to the board. Hearing a deep chuckle, I look over to see Micah laughing as he manuevers up beside me, "Hope, that was fucking beautiful. It has been forever since I saw someone longboard that actually knew what the hell they were doing."

I smile back at him as I reach over and high five him. We both lay down and paddle back out further for another run. It feels fucking amazing to be out here.

To me, surfing is a lot like drumming. I feel at complete ease. Nothing can bother me when I am out here. I just ride the waves and let them settle any uneasiness in me.

Just like when I play, I zone out and forget about whatever insanity is going on after I sit the sticks down. It may be a bit unhealthy though.

Mentally that is.

I have caught myself trying to brush a lot of my feelings under the rug recently. It's not good for me or for my relationship with Matthew.

I am glad we were actually able to see eye to eye the other night though. I whole heartedly believed him when he told me he loved me and only me. And now that Simone is gone, I can see him for who he really is.

How could she not want that?

He is funny and smart.

Of course he is fucking gorgeous.

But his heart. His heart gets me every single time. I don't see as much pity as I did before. Maybe it was never actual pity at all. Maybe it was empathy.

Just thinking about what she missed out on makes me smile wider. Her loss has definitely been my gain. I never in a million years would have imagined that I would have married someone after just meeting them. But from the first moment his eyes met mine, when he shook my hand, I just felt it.

I belonged to him at that moment.

I smile as I ride another wave then wait for Micah to finish his run as well. We sit in the water just paddling our feet. There isn't even a reason to speak. We can just be.

A quick glance at the patio shows me Daija and Mona are both out as well now. I watch them, walking around in their bikinis and I can't help but compare myself to them. I look down, still seeing nothing but skin and bones.

I haven't really tried to calm the voice in my head but instead I have just been ignoring it. The only problem with that is by ignoring it, it only makes it louder.

I take a deep breath and decide to go back to the land for a bit. I smile as I see Matthew up on the deck talking to Daija. I quickly paddle inland and drag the board out of the water.

Feeling the sand as it curls under my toes, I walk the board out and drop it on the beach, "I thought you were going to sleep the day away old man."

Matthew laughs back at me as he watches me remove the leash from my ankle. He moves down the steps to the sand, "It is 10 in the fucking morning. Sue me."

I laugh loudly at him as I drop the leash and then move closer towards him. I look up seeing Daija still on the porch watching us, "What did she have to say?"

My eyes come back down to Matthews as he rolls his eyes glancing at the deck quickly before back to me, "Nothing that didn't need shut down."

I chuckle to myself, nodding my head, "That sounds about right."

I turn around to watch Micah out on the water and I feel Matthew move up beside me. I love how comfortable we are now. We can just stand here, completely content and talk about surfing and the band. The future and the choices being made. And for once I am not worried about what I look like. Or who is watching me. At least, for a few moments that is.

From behind me I hear the deep rasp of Edge's voice, "You been out playing?"

Pointing to the board on the beach in front of us, "Just got that beautiful lady this morning."

Edge and Susie briskly walk past us and straight to the board. Susie turns around with that megawatt smile she always possesses somehow, "Hey do you mind if we look your board over? I have never really seen one up close."

I smile and nod back at her, "Yeah that's fine. There is a bar of wax over with my clothes if you wanna coat it. Get a real feel for it."

I watch Susie as she barrels over to my stuff quickly finding the bar of wax. She smiles as she races back to the board, dropping onto her knees beside it and Edge.

Matthew and I continue to converse about random topics again until he pulls me in close to him. I love the feel of his body molding into mine.

It is the only time I really feel complete.

I continue to slowly breathe in and out just packing this moment away in the good memories folder I keep in the back of my mind.

For some wild reason, Matthew has brought up the topic of self defense. I have no idea what has brought this on but I smile at him, "I have taken some self defense classes before. I also did karate for a few years. I am not completely defenseless. I didn't want to be alone in London and not be able to take care of myself, just in case."

He holds onto me tightly as I turn back around in his arms to watch Susie and Edge still trying to get a feel for the board. They are each taking turns standing on it.

Edge looking like a complete ass each time.

I hear Matthew let out a sigh behind me, "Makes sense. Maybe you will have to teach the girls some stuff. Just to give them some piece of mind too. Maybe you and Susie could spar together. Not gonna lie, that would be kinda hot."

I laugh loudly and unexpectedly. Loud enough that everyone turns to me either wide eyed or laughing at the snort that Matthew and I both knew would be following.

Edge raises an eyebrow at me, "Did you just snort?"

Rolling my eyes hard at all them, trying to not let my cheeks turn any redder than they already are, "Yes. Yes....the new girl snorts. Sometimes! Not all the time."

Susie stands back up before going back to the board. She looks at me hesitantly, "Hope, do you care if I stand on the board? I always wondered what it would feel like. Just for funsies."

I nod at her as I start to step away from Matthew. I give him a quick smile over my shoulder before moving towards the board, "Sure, I will show you the right stance, how to keep your balance."

Susie starts pumping her arms and hopping from foot to foot like she has been given the absolute best Christmas present ever. Holding her hand, I have her step on the board. I show her how to keep her arms out at her sides, slightly bent to give her more control. I make sure she understands the physics of the board itself. Bracing her hips with my hands, I jump up onto the board behind her. Teaching her slowly how to baby step your walks.

You have to step with purpose on this thing, too far one way or the other and your ass is in the water with a rouge board flying through the air. She laughs back at me as I patiently go over the correct placement of your feet. Explaining why you have to be quick about it.

Why you have to walk it. She just grins the whole time before turning and pulling me into a hug, "Thank you Hope. I can't wait to actually try it one of these days." She squeezes me one last time before turning and running back towards Edge.

I watch her skipping back towards the guys and decide I am going to do a few more runs before calling it quits for now. I quickly retether the leash and move back towards the water. I paddle out a few hundred feet before turning around and watching everyone mulling around in the sand.

Matthew walking out onto the beach with Edge and Susie not far behind. I smile as I wave to them. Susie in turn waves madly back at me, watching me like she has never seen a girl on a surfboard before.

Susie is a fucking trip.

You would never believe that she had been through the most tragic last few months of her life. From stalkers trying to kidnap her to losing a child. She is seriously the strongest woman I have ever met in my life.

Plus, her energy is fucking contagious.

218

She is always smiling it seems. The way she looks at Edge, with this passion and heat. I have never seen two people more in love. Unless we are talking about Gideon and Lily. Those two seem to rival Edge and Susie on that aspect.

Susie is sitting on my towel watching me. She was super stoked when she asked if I could really teach her how to surf and I said yes. I want to be closer with her, with everyone really. It would be nice to have someone to confide in again. I haven't had that in a long fucking time.

I swim me and my board out until I find that sweet spot that will hopefully bring me some small breaks. I meant it when I said this place is beautiful. Even from out here, seeing how close the neighbors actually are, how many people are nearby on the beach the house itself is just fucking perfect.

I scan the beach again and see Matthew standing there watching me. Like he is expecting me to perform some sort of magic trick or something.

Grinning to myself, I feel the swell starting to move in. My stomach does that little nervous flop it does everytime I get excited and I drop to my stomach to paddle along the break.

I am on my feet just a few seconds later. Nothing but me and the board. All of my worries, all of my fears just drop away.

Again, I am one with the ocean.

It is allowing me this single moment of complete contentment. I quickly walk the board, keeping my balance with my hands before slowly retreating to the back of the board to give it leverage again.

You can't linger on the front of a longboard. Your weight will drag it down. You have to move back, stealthily to kickstart it into movement again. I like to think of it as like doing a wheelie without the wheels. It jets you up and forward, giving you more time to ride the break.

It finally starts to slow down and I sit back down, straddling the board again. I slowly turn and start to paddle

224

back. I can see basically everyone out on the beach now. But for the life of me I cannot figure out what the hell they are doing.

Mona, Daija, mom, Lily and Susie are all striking poses in their bikinis. All of them except for mom and Lily and those two have their tank tops and shorts pulled up. Like they are all fucking auditioning for Sports Illustrated or something.

Matthew looks over his shoulder at me then leans over to Edge saying something. The guys all drop their phones as the girls go back to laying out or whatever they were doing before.

I am not sure what they are up to but watching all the guys taking pictures of the girls makes me want to put on a parka. I do not want anyone taking pictures of me in this bikini.

I know that I am enough to make Matthew happy but I want to be happy too. I want to feel comfortable in my own skin. I look at my stick legs, just once I want to see myself healthy.

I have been sickly for so long. I just want to be content. And I know the dysmorphia isn't just in my head. I know where it stems from but that isn't something I like or want to talk about.

I will eventually tell Matthew but I just fucking hate the look that people get on their faces when you use that word.

The one that instantly causes pity.

Cancer.

14
Apollo
Euclid - Sleep Token

This bed is so fucking comfortable, I wake up not even knowing what day it is. I blink a couple dozen times trying to figure out why it is so quiet. Then I remember, we are at the beach house.

I smile as I reach over and run my hands over the sheets feeling them cold. She has been gone for a while. Sitting up, I wipe the sleep from my eyes then glance to the other side of the room. I smile when I see her suitcase is still laying there. Completely scavenged through but still here.

That is all that matters.

I grab some shorts and throw a shirt on before grabbing my smokes to head downstairs to find some coffee. Lily is standing in the kitchen, apparently in a cooking mood because there is a whole buffet laid out on the island. Bacon, sausage, biscuits, even a platter of scrambled eggs.

I smile at her, "What's up Betty Crocker?"

She laughs back at me, "I just wanted to cook everyone a good meal at least once this week. I am so tired of fast food and take out. The baby needed real sustenance."

I laugh back at her as I pour myself a cup of coffee, "I am sure everyone will devour it soon. Have you seen Hope yet this morning?"

She smiles back and looks up at me, "Oh you mean your orgasm buddy. Seriously, I am going to have to sound proof your room. For somebody so soft spoken her lungs work really fucking well!"

Smiling, I rub the back of my neck, thinking about last night. Those leather cuffs and a few other new toys she introduced me to. I feel the heat starting to rise in my neck and try to cut the thought process by looking around the island.

Nervously, I laugh out loud again as I grab a few pieces of crispy bacon, "Yeah, my bad. I will see if she is into like gags or something."

Lily laughs back before nudging her chin towards the back door, still stirring the batter for something in her hands, "Her and Micah went into town earlier and bought some boards. Last I saw her she was out on the water. Micah too."

"Awesome. The house smells fucking phenomenal by the way. Thank you for cooking." Lily grins back then nods her head while continuing to stir whatever is in the bowl in front of her. I grab another piece of bacon and my mug of coffee. Quickly, I step outside and over to the far side of the deck. Scanning the beach quickly, I only see a towel with a few discarded items of clothing. Carefully, I sit my mug down on the railing then light a cigarette before looking out over the water.

My heart nearly stops in my chest.

Hope is out there in a bikini surfing like she is on the pro fucking tour. I have never seen somebody move the way that she is right now. Her lean ass legs just running up and down the board. Her bikini clinging to all of her curves. If I was an obsessive man I would demand her to put on more clothes, but honestly I am just glad she felt comfortable enough to wear so little.

The waves are not huge at all but she is out there on a longboard just slicing through them like a hot knife through butter. The board she bought looks like it is twice as long as her entire body. She was sitting on it until a small swell came in, then she turned and paddled along it before climbing to her feet and leaning back into the board a bit.

A few moments later, she is taking small little steps forward, using her arms for balance.

I watch her feet as they dance along the board then her toes almost curl around the front of the board for a moment. Then just seconds later she is walking backwards down it until it runs out of wave left to ride.

I continue to smoke my cigarette watching her sit on the board out in the ocean. Hearing the door open behind me, I turn to see Daija walking out with two cups of coffee.

She sits one down on the table before walking towards me, "Can I have one of those?"

She points to my cigarettes so I hand her the pack before going back to watching Hope in her zone. She seems so at peace out there. Like there is nothing else in the world bothering her in this one particular moment.

Daija hands the pack back after lighting her cigarette, "Don't tell Hope I was smoking. She will fucking murder me." I am instantly confused because she has never said anything to me about my chimney habits.

Daija lets out a long smoke filled exhale, "Should have known she would be out there showing off."

I turn to look at Daija, already not liking her attitude.

I am not the one.

She does not want to try this sibling rivalry bullshit with me again. I have 5 brothers and sisters and no fucks to give. I will end this bitch if she even tries.

Before I can even say anything though she exhales again, "I have tried to surf with her probably a million times. But she is just too fucking good. I swim like a rock. Always have, but her, she is like a ballerina out there on a board. She can just twinkle toe her way back and forth without a care in the world. I am jealous to be honest."

223

Smiling back at her, I happily accept her jealousy for what it is. I turn back to Hope, catching her attention and waving at her. I can see her smile back as she throws one finger in the air.

Turning back towards Daija I eyeball her for a second, "How are you and Mona doing?"

She blows some smoke out in front of us before taking a large drink of coffee. She looks around, probably making sure no one else can hear, "I am infatuated. But her, I think she might be getting tired of me already."

Laughing loudly I turn my body towards her, "Yeah, that is fucking doubtful. She has been talking about you non stop for weeks now. If anything, we are all getting tired of hearing about you."

She smiles but her cheeks turn a soft shade of pink. She shakes her head at me then looks back out at Hope, "Yeah, I don't know about that. I kinda just feel like she might be in a different place than I am. I really want to be with someone exclusively. I don't know if that is what she is looking for or not."

Walking over, I stub out my cigarette out in the ashtray on the table, "Then fucking ask her. It's not that hard. What's the worst that could happen? She would say no then you two could just fuck around until she is ready. And who's to say her answer wouldn't be yes?"

Daija takes another hit of her smoke, exhaling while watching Hope, "I don't know that I have the balls to ask honestly. I really fucking like her. I don't want her to be upset that I want more. Or worse, she tells me she doesn't want more. That would blow."

I nod at her then look back out at Hope, "You and your sister are a lot more alike then Hope let on. She has the same types of insecurities."

She looks at me in complete shock, "Miss Can't Do Wrong? Insecurities? I don't fucking think so."

I look back at her sternly, "She has a lot more going on in her head than you know. And from the way it sounds, a lot of it was caused by you. So you might want to tone down this jealous sibling bullshit and start seeing her for the grown ass woman that she is. I bet it would do you both some fucking good to be in each other's life a bit more."

Daija looks startled by my words as I push off the railing and move to go down the stairs. Mona steps out the back door smiling at me. I give her a quick wave before running down the steps and across the sand to meet Hope at the edge of the water. She smiles as she pulls the board alongside her, "I thought you were going to sleep the day away old man."

I laugh back at her, "It is 10 in the fucking morning. Sue me."

She laughs again as she lays the board down and unhooks the teether from her ankle. She nods back up towards the deck, "What did she have to say?"

I shake my head then look back into her eyes, "Nothing that didn't need to be shut down."

She nods her head and rolls her eyes, "Yeah I am sure." Hope turns around and looks back at the water. Micah is still out on the water looking like he is having the time of his life.

Nodding towards the water, "You got a new bestie?"

Hope laughs as she turns back towards me, "I don't know about bestie but he seems like he is a pretty cool guy. We get along well. I think he would be a nice addition to the band."

I roll my head on my shoulders a bit, "That is still yet to be seen. I mean he can play, we just have to make sure he is a good fit for the long haul. I don't know how many more years of this we have in us but hopefully it's a long fucking time."

Hope looks over my shoulder smiling. I turn around and see Susie and Edge walking towards us. Edge smiles as he looks towards the water, "You been out playing?"

Hope laughs as she points to her board, "Just got that beautiful lady this morning."

Edge and Susie walk over looking at her long board. Susie turns back halfway, nearly bouncing out of her own skin, "Hey do you mind if we look your board over? I have never really seen one up close."

Hope doesn't even lift her head, "Yeah that's fine. There is a bar of wax over with my clothes if you wanna coat it. Get a real feel for it."

Susie turns and runs over to the clothes before coming back with a small square. They both bend down and take turns coating the length of the board.

I smile at them, "Is that why you smell like bananas right now? The wax?"

She smiles and turns her face to me, leaning back a bit, "Yeah. It smells delicious doesn't it."

I pull her in close to me, turning her around so her back is to my front. Nuzzling my face into her neck, I inhale deeply taking in the scent of bananas and citrus. I pepper her neck with a few small kisses before staring out over the water then glance towards Susie. I squeeze Hope just a bit. If I could keep her in my arms all day every day I think I could actually feel like she is safe. That she is taken care of and looked after.

I don't know how Edge does it.

With everything that happened. How he isn't tethered to Susie 24/7.

A chill runs down my spine as I think about something like that ever happening to Hope. As if she can sense something is going on she turns her head up towards my face a bit, "Are you okay back there?"

Smiling, I kiss her temple, "Yeah, I am okay. Just thinking. I was thinking of asking Susie if she would teach you some self defense moves. With everything that happened with her, I am just worried. Probably over nothing. But if I am not with you, I want you to be able to defend yourself. People do stupid shit to get close to us sometimes. I want you to feel safe."

Hope turns in my arms a bit, "I have taken some self defense classes before. I also did karate for a few years. I am not completely defenseless. I didn't want to be alone in London and not be able to take care of myself, just in case."

We both turn and start towards her board, "Makes sense. Maybe you will have to teach the girls some stuff. Just to give them some piece of mind too. Maybe you and Susie could spar together. Not gonna lie, that would be kinda hot."

She laughs out loud with another snort as she slaps me on the chest. Both Susie and Edge look up.

Edge looking confused as hell and Susie holding her stomach from her own laughter, "Did you just snort!?"

Hope rolls her eyes at us all, "Yes. Yes....the new girl snorts. Sometimes! Not all the time."

Susie laughs as she stands up and points to the board, "Hope, do you care if I stand on the board? I always wondered what it would feel like. Just for funsies."

Hope nods before taking a few steps towards Susie, "Sure, I will show you the right stance, how to keep your balance."

Susie starts jumping from one foot to the other in pure excitement. It is good to see her smiling again. It has been about a rough go of it for Susie since everything went down.

She acts like it doesn't bother her, but I know that it does. She hasn't been actively showing everyone her emotions but at the same time she has kept her distance from us as well.

Edge seems to notice the immediate change in her as well. He smiles as he walks up to my side, "Looks like our girls are gonna be best friends after all."

I nod my head, watching Hope as she holds onto Susie's waist. She grabs Susie's arms and puts them out to her side like they are on the Titanic. She slowly walks through the sand up the side of the board as Susie mimics her actions. Before long though she is up on the board with Susie, showing her how to position her feet.

Seeing them together, it really sinks in that they are truly friends, "Yeah, she is fitting in perfectly. I am just glad we got past all the other shit."

Edge looks over his shoulder at the patio, "What do you think of the twin? I haven't really had a chance to get a feel for her yet."

I follow his eyes before turning back around to Hope, "That is still to be determined. I hope it isn't something that is going to be rift between them but I have a feeling Daija is going to hate me before it is said and done. I won't put up with her being a bitch to Hope."

He laughs as he turns back to look at his girl, "Yeah, true. I guess it is what it is. I am just happy to see you smiling. That is something you haven't done a lot of in a long time."

He is right.

I know he is right.

I pretended for the longest time that everything was fine. But now that I am actually happy I can see it for what it was. I was just making due with the scraps that were being thrown my way. I thought it was happiness. Only because I had never actually experienced the real thing for myself.

I smile, turning to Edge, "So, I need you to do me a favor. And it is going to sound fucking weird. Honestly, it is gonna sound like I am trying to make some kind of weird ass porn but I'm not. I just need help with something."

Edge turns to me, confused and honestly a bit worried, "What because the threesome is off the board for you, Lily and Gideon you think you can squeeze in over here?"

I punch him in the arm as he tries to pull away, "No. You fucking monster. I just..." How am I supposed to ask my friends to do this?

Without it sounding fucking creepy as shit?

228

I sigh again turning to him, "Okay, so Hope has something called body dysmorphia."

Edge shakes his head confused at me, looking from Hope to me, "What the fuck is that?"

I look over my shoulder quickly, to make sure she can't hear me, "So when she looks at herself, she doesn't see what's really there. She sees this twisted version of herself. I think its from fucking years of being treated like shit by her sister. But I am sure there have been other people that have contributed to it.

"Anyways, she sees herself as basically anorexic or something. She described herself as looking like a meth addict to me. Which is fucking insane considering she looks like she could crush walnuts with her ass cheeks."

Edge lets out a laugh as he looks over at her. I can see him really looking at her now, from head to toe, shaking his head before turning back to me, "That is honestly the most ridiculous description of her that I have ever heard. She looks like a fucking hot yoga instructor."

I laugh at him, "You're not wrong. Anyways. What I was thinking, and only if Susie is cool with it. But could you send me pictures of her? Not of her face, and nothing perverse. Just like a random shot of like her collarbone, maybe her abs. Fuck I don't know, her ankle? Just places you guys think a girl would be self conscious of herself.

"I am going to ask Gideon and Lily to do the same. Maybe even ask Mona too as well. Then I am going to take pictures of her. I am going to basically lay them all out for her. Her not knowing who is who. Maybe she will be able to see what we see then. Before she knows she is looking at herself."

Edge nods his head at me before looking back towards Hope, "Yeah that could work. I will talk to Susie about it. I will explain it to Lily too, so that way you don't have to try and find a chill time to talk to her. We could all just keep them on our phones and lay them out for her to see side by side. I am not going to complain about having more hot pictures of Peach on my phone."

I knew he would understand. Grinning back at him, "Thanks man. I just, I think this might help her. I mean it can't hurt right? And let Susie know if she says no I am completely fine with that too. I don't want her to feel like she has too."

Edge smiles as his eyes run over Susie again, "She has no issues showing her body off. Trust me."

I smile back at him before turning back to my girl. This was either going to go over really fucking well or she was going to stab me.

Either could be hot honestly, but I am a slow healer so I am hoping for the first.

Susie jumps off the board and runs back over to us like an excited toddler, "Hope said she will teach me how to surf!"

I watch Edge as he opens his arms smiling at her, "That's awesome babe. Maybe it will help with your clumsiness. We are spending all my paychecks on bandaids."

Susie laughs as she slaps Edge in the arm but still leaning back into him. Edge looks at me, giving me a wink before leaning down into Susie's ear. Probably asking about my favor. I look back out over the water watching Hope skimming the waves again.

She looks like an angel out there. She moves like she is weightless back and forth across the board. I still can't believe she is mine.

I can't believe I almost lost her.

My heart literally feels like it is going to explode in my chest at the thought of her leaving and never coming back.

I can't be without her.

Ever.

I don't think I would last a day honestly.

I turn when I see movement as Susie starts running around the beach talking to the girls. Edge smiles at me and

230

gives me a thumbs up letting me know my plan is officially in motion.

I smile and nod as I look back out at Hope. I just pray she doesn't kill me for this. But I truly think it will help.

Hopefully.

"If you don't stop taking pictures of me I am going to break your phone in half. I swear to Christ, Matthew!" He just laughs at me as he takes another picture on his phone. I turn towards him and start to full sprint towards him.

Matthew laughs loudly again before stuffing his phone into his pocket, "There I put it away! Truce!"

I stop running but still flip him off, "Why the hell were you taking pictures of me anyways?"

Matthew smiles as he walks back towards me, wrapping his hand around my neck pulling my mouth to his. His lips feather across mine as he whispers, "I needed some fuel for the spank bank. Ya know, for when you are on stage or sleeping."

I laugh at him again as I grab his sides, tickling him. He immediately bends to the right and tries to back away.

But now I know one of his secrets and I will not let this die, "You are ticklish? Is it just your sides? What about your feet? Behind the knees? Oh this is going to be too much fun!"

Matthew is walking backwards, with his casted arm out in front of him, "I knew you were the angel of death. I fucking called it!"

I laugh at him again before turning around to go pick up my board and stuff. Grabbing everything, I move towards the shed, "Can you open that door for me please?"

Matthew swings the door open and stack my board inside over Micah's funboard. I throw my wax and leash beside it before backing back out and shutting the door.

Pointing at the closed shed, "We need to find out if she has a lock for this thing. I really don't want a $1500 board getting stolen after we leave."

Matthews eyes go wide, "$1500 for that? Are you shitting me? Fuck, yeah I will make sure we get a lock for it if she doesn't have one."

I nod back at him before taking his good hand in mine and start to make our way back up to the patio. My stomach growls loudly and I groan just a bit, "I am starving. I hope there is some leftover bacon from breakfast."

Matthew leans over and kisses my temple, "I had Lily put you a plate of bacon and hashbrowns in the microwave. I figured you would be hungry after playing in the water all day."

I look at him, amazed again. He continues to think of me at every turn.

Like it is nothing.

But he doesn't understand, no one thinks of me like that. Except maybe mom. And that isn't all the time. But he seems to be tuned into Hope radio 24/7.

I open the back door and we both step through still hand in hand. Obviously something is going on because everyone scatters like we busted up some important conversation.

Suspiciously, I look over my shoulder at Matthew, "What the fuck is going on?"

He just shrugs his shoulders at me, "Who fucking knows with these guys."

I let it go, because he isn't wrong. I step over to the microwave, making sure my plate is indeed inside. I turn it on for about 10 seconds then grab a fork and toss it in between my lips as I wait to dig in. The microwave beeps and I grab my food and turn around to lean against the counter and eat.

233

Susie out of nowhere shows up beside me, she leans across the counter after looking quickly over her shoulder, "So do you think you could teach me how to surf like maybe on our next hiatus?"

I shove an entire piece of bacon into my mouth while nodding my head, "Yeah. That would be fun actually. It would be nice to have another female to ride with too. Don't get me wrong, Micah is great but he is also a dude."

Susie chuckles as I shove half a hashbrown into my mouth next. She looks over her shoulder again then back towards me, "Are you doing okay after everything that has happened?"

I eyeball her closely.

Something is up.

She is being weird and I don't like it.

I turn to look behind me and she jumps up again, grabbing my attention, "You don't have to answer me, I am sorry I said anything."

I look her dead in the eye, "What the fuck are you doing? You are being weird as shit."

She looks over her shoulder smiling then turns around spreading her arm out towards the island for me to look at something.

Matthew has everyone's phones laid out on the counter. All of the cases are off of them and thrown into a pile so they are all basically identical at this point.

Hesitantly, I step up beside him, looking at the island, "What are you doing? What is all this?"

He smiles as he puts a strand of my hair behind my ear, "I talked with your mom and we wanted to try something. Think of it like visual therapy. We want you to see yourself how we see you. So on the phones are pictures of body parts."

My eyes go wide as they fly across the devices that are not lit up yet. I look up and see Edge smiling at me, "Don't worry. He wouldn't let us take an dick pics."

I cackle out a snort then cover my mouth as I roll my eyes, Jesus I really need to work on that.

Mom laughs at me as she steps up to the counter, "Don't get mad at Matthew. This is actually a really good idea and I wish we had thought of it a lot sooner."

I look from her back to Matthew and he looks just god damn hopeful. I smile at him then fan my hand out towards the island, "Okay. I will play along."

Matthew steps up to the phones and taps each screen to turn them on. He quickly pulls up the camera roll on all 6 phones then stands back. I am looking at stomachs.

All toned, some tanned, some not. I look at him, still confused as he wraps an arm around my waist, "These are pictures of Mona, Lucy, Lily, Susie, Daija and you."

My eyes fly to his quickly before leaning back over the devices trying to determine who is who. I sit my plate down and move closer to the phones. I shake my head at him, not really recognizing any of them.

He steps up and starts swiping each one. Next there are pictures of clavicles. I scan them again and smile when I recognize a set of them.

I point to the next to last phone, "Those are Daija. She has a birthmark on her right shoulder."

Daija smiles and steps up to the phone on the other side of the island, "I told you she would guess me right away. We are fucking twins after all."

Matthew laughs as he leans over and swipes the phones again, Daija's included. Next, all I see are legs. All toned. I shake my head at them and look to Matthew, "Okay I don't understand. What is the game?"

He smiles at me as he pulls me into his side, "Which one is you?"

I turn back to the phones and study them all, sweeping through the photos again. I can't tell. I have it narrowed down to 3 but none of them are what I see when I look in the mirror. I feel my eyes tearing up again as I shake my head at them.

I turn back to Matthew, "None of them are me. I would have noticed if you were taking close ups of my body."

He shakes his head back at me as my mother steps up, "One of these is definitely you. I swear it, baby."

I look from my mother back down to the phones.

Susie steps around my mom and stands in front of a phone. She swipes the screen again and I see her standing on the beach smiling at the camera. It looks like they just zoomed in and screenshot different parts of her body for the other photos.

Next Lily steps up and does the same. She is followed quickly by my mother, then Mona. That leaves one phone left. I look down at it, afraid to touch the screen and bring the images back to life. Matthew reaches down, tapping the screen. He smiles at me as I stare at the legs on the screen.

I shake my head as I scroll back through the photos. There is no way this is my body. This is someone who obviously takes care of themselves a lot better than me.

Matthew swipes back to the left until all I see is a picture of me standing on the beach with Susie. Matthew must have taken this when I was teaching Susie how to keep her balance on the board. I can't believe what I am looking at. It is me but it feels like I am looking at a different version of me.

I smile up at my mom then back to Matthew, "This is me? But how?"

He pulls me in close to him, "This is what you have always looked like. This is why I asked if you were delusional. You are fucking stunning. I don't know why you see what you do when you look in the mirror but your eyes, your brain, they are lying to you."

My eyes scan the pictures again before I look around the room at all these people that stepped up to help Matthew.

To help me.

I feel this rush of gratitude come over me and it feels like the room starts to spin. I smile as I turn back into Matthew, leaning into him as I wrap my arms around him.

He holds me for a long time as I hear people moving around behind us. When I finally pull back, I see that everyone has grabbed their phones and cases. Matthew reaches over and grabs his phone and slides his case back on before tucking it into his back pocket.

He smiles as he takes my hand then kisses me on the temple before pulling me through the kitchen and up the stairs to our room. I smile at him as he shuts the door. His eyes jut over to the dresser and he sees the towel I have draped over the mirror earlier when I was getting dressed.

He tilts his head to the side and gives me a soft smile before walking over and pulling the towel down. He throws it into the hamper before turning to me, "No more hiding. We are going to get through this together. I will steal a million candids of you if I have to. We are going to break this cycle."

Nodding and letting out a heavy sigh I watch as he turns and starts to undress. My mouth starts to go dry watching him peel out of his clothes. I am never going to get used to seeing this man naked. This walking perfection. I start to peel out of my clothes as well, throwing them onto my suitcase leaving me standing here staring at him in nothing but my swimsuit.

Matthew turns around, completely naked and smiling. He moves closer to me and reaches around behind me and unsnaps my bikini top with his one good hand. He pulls my top off then kisses me as he slides his fingers into the sides of my bottoms and pulls them down my thighs, letting them drop to the floor on their own.

He turns from me and moves towards the door. I hear it lock behind me as I step towards the bed to crawl under the blankets. Matthew steps up behind me before I can climb in and I feel him pull all my hair to one side of my neck then his lips are on my shoulder. My heart starts to flutter as he kisses his way up my neck slowly.

He slowly turns me back around and walks with me towards the mirror. I can see my naked image in front of me, him standing just behind me looking at my reflection over the top of my head.

I look at myself, shaking my head, "I still don't see it. I mean I know what I saw downstairs but right now, I don't see what you see. I don't understand this."

I watch Matthew's hand in the reflection. In my head, I can feel his fingers as they roll across each rib, but in the reflection his hands are just moving slowly down my sides. His fingers are not moving in waves against my ribs like my brain is saying they are.

He rests his hands on my hips, fingers pressing into my skin enough to cause little white spots. But in my head it seems like there isn't any flesh there at all, just bone on skin.

I shake my head back at his reflection again, "This is just weird as hell. My brain is telling me one thing but with my eyes I am seeing something completely different."

Matthew's eyes reach mine in the reflection before turning me back towards him. He wraps his good hand around my jaw, pulling my face up towards his. He smiles back down at me, "We will figure this out baby. Even if it takes forever. I will continue to show you what is real. I won't let that feral little brain of yours drive you crazy. Well, crazier than you already are."

Laughing loudly at him, he brings his lips down to mine. I feel his hand as it grazes across my shoulder then slowly down my back. Matthew slowly turns us while still kissing me so my back is now towards the bed. He pulls his lips from mine then grins like the devil himself as he turns my body to face the bed.

I smile as I spread my legs about shoulder width apart then lean over the bed. I push myself into him, feeling him hard and ready behind me. His hands continue to caress my sides when I feel his lips on my spine.

A shudder runs over my body and arch my back a bit more, lifting my hips up and back into him further. I grin as I wiggle my ass at him, "Maybe we should come up with some kind of punishment again. Maybe when I am down on myself or my brain is playing tricks on me, maybe you should show me some sort of discipline."

He chuckles behind me as I feel him stand up, still running his hands over my sides and back, "What kind of discipline do you think you need this time?"

I look over my shoulders and meet his eyes with mine, "Spank me. With your hand."

His eyes go wide and I feel his dick flinch against my ass. I can hear my voice dropping a bit, becoming a bit huskier, needy even, "Maybe that is what I need. It could just be the way for me to discipline my brain to make it stop tricking me. So if you spank me then possibly I can see things differently."

He smiles at me as he rubs my bare ass with his good hand. I hesitate for just a moment. I have let him use the paddle on me before, but never just his bare hand.

He seems to notice the hesitance then his hand connects with my ass. I let out a little yelp as I feel the sting burn into my skin. Smiling into the blanket, I push my ass further into him, "Again Matthew. Please."

I hear him shuddering a breath as he slaps my ass harder the second time. I grip the blanket tight in both hands as I feel

239

heat rise up in my center. I arch my back again but before I can beg for more he slaps the other side of my ass.

I squeal a bit then I feel his hand gripping the base of my hair, pulling my head back roughly. His breath is hot in my ear, "Is that what you wanted, Hope? Does that make you fucking wet for me?"

I feel his hand run down my ass to my center, knowing he is finding me positively dripping. I can feel it on my inner thighs already. Smiling again as he pulls on my hair a bit harder, "Yes Matthew. Only for you."

I hear a noise come from him that I have never heard before. Next I feel the head of his cock as it slides over my clit. I close my eyes and moan into the blankets again. He slaps my ass again then slams into me from behind.

I scream out at his intrusion into my pussy. I feel him grip my hips tight as he starts pulling me onto him as he slams into me from behind.

Panting for him already, I find myself pushing back on him just as hard as he is pulling me towards him.

I look over my shoulder and he is watching himself slam into me. I am a bit jealous because it is something I would love to see as well. Maybe next time I can get him to video it for me.

I smile at the savage thoughts running through my head.

I try to lift up onto my hands a bit then I feel him grabbing each wrist. He pulls them behind me, holding them in place in the center of my back with his casted hand while he grips my hip tight with the other and starts to slam into me harder.

My pussy starts to quiver and I know I am not going to last long. He growls into the room around us and I know he can feel me about to lose it. I start whimpering with every slam into me.

Matthew pulls himself from me and pulls me up by my arms. He turns me to him then picks me up by the back of my

240

thighs before he backs me into the wall by the door. I wrap my legs around him as he slams back into me again.

Crying out into the room again, I move my lips to his neck. He grunts as he fills me, "I want to hear you make those little noises again. The ones you make when I slam my dick into you hard and fast." He immediately starts pushing into me harder.

I let out another scream as I start to dig my nails into his back. He is going so deep into me. I am not going to be able to hold on much longer.

I start to whimper into his ear again. I reach down with my tongue and pull his earlobe into my mouth then nibble on it. Panting, I whisper in his ear, "Your dick fills me so full baby. I can feel you everywhere."

Matthew starts to slam into me harder. Hard enough that a picture falls off the wall. I smile as my mouth moves down his throat. I can feel him thickening inside of me. I pant heavily into his neck before sucking down on the spot where his shoulder meets his neck.

He slams into me again and I bite down on him as my pussy grips his cock tight, pulling him into me. Trying to lock him inside of me. I barely even recognize the moan that comes from my body when he starts to release in me.

He yells into the room around us, "Fuck baby. Fuck me." I smile as he loses himself in me. He continues to slam into me as my eyes roll up in my head. I lean back and pin myself to the wall, feeling him hitting me everywhere inside. My face contorts as I feel myself clamp down onto him harder.

He swings us around and lays me down on the bed. He puts a leg up over each of his shoulders as he grabs my hips and slams himself so deeply into me that it feels like I am never going to come down.

I grab his biceps as I scream his name into the room around us. He throws his head back and roars into the ceiling

241

above us. I can feel him filling me completely. Matthew is slowly sliding in and out of me now as I watch beads of sweat roll down the side of his face. I smile as we both start to come down around each other.

He kisses the inside of my knee as he lets my legs fall down around us. He reluctantly steps back, pulling himself from me. I open my eyes and see him staring down at me.

I sit up then he pulls me up into his arms again. He kisses me fiercely before walking us back around the side of the bed and laying me back against the pillows.

He curls up next to me, running his fingers up and down my side. He smiles at me, "Do you really see what I see now? Or were you just saying all of that to make me feel better?"

I look up into his eyes.

He is truly worried about this.

Which is strange, considering I always thought I would be ridiculed for the tricks my brain likes to play on me. I look back down at myself then back to him, "I don't see it when I look at myself. I still see me how I feel I look. But I can't deny the pictures that you took. When you were touching me, my brain was telling me one thing but my eyes were seeing something completely different. I think it is a mind over matter situation at this point. If I just continue to look at myself through your eyes, maybe eventually it will clear up for me."

Matthew nods his head at me, "Do you know what caused it to begin with? Like I know you said your sister liked to torture you as a child, but was there other people that maybe put you down or made you see yourself differently?"

I feel my heart start to quicken. This is not something I want to talk about.

With anyone.

Not even my mother.

But he deserves to know the truth. I just don't want him to pity me. I don't pity myself. I just see it for what it is. I was sick and now I am not.

I let out a heavy sigh as I roll onto my back, looking at the ceiling, "I didn't really tell you the whole truth before. I gave you a fractured version of some shit that has happened."

I feel the bed shift a bit as he raises himself up to look at me, "What do you mean? Daija wasn't a holy terror growing up?"

Smiling over at him a bit, I roll back to face him again, "No, she was definitely that. I just didn't give you the full story. Or at least not the entire truth of it."

I know he can see how nervous I am.

I can feel it radiating off of me just trying to talk to him. He puts his hand back on my hip, bringing my eyes back to his, "You can tell me anything Hope. I won't think any differently of you. I will still love you."

Nodding my head at him, I look back towards the bed, "No. I know that. I know you will still love me. I am just afraid that you are going to see me as weak. Or even fragile maybe."

I feel him squeeze my hip and I let out another frustrated sigh. I roll back onto my back, letting his hand fall on my abdomen.

Closing my eyes tight, I make a silent wish for the best, "So when I said that I was born with underdeveloped ovaries that wasn't completely the truth. That is just the story that I give people. So I don't get the make a wish stare, that I am sure you are giving me right now."

I feel him move a bit closer to me, "I don't know what a make a wish stare is supposed to be, but I can assure you I am looking at you like I am confused. Maybe, a little worried."

I chuckle at him just a bit, still not opening my eyes, "I was diagnosed with pediatric endometrial cancer when I was 8 years old. I went through all the chemo and radiation that I could handle but I ended up having a full hysterectomy when I was 9. It is not something that they like to do to someone that young. I had to go through a lot of treatments.

"And by a lot I mean A LOT of treatments. There was hormone therapy as well. I also started seeing a therapist that year because my body was thrown into full hormonal chaos and I didn't really know how to mentally or emotionally deal with it.

"Then when I was 12, they found some more precancerous cells on my bladder. Those cells were removed as well, I didn't have to go through chemo or radiation but the stress of it all didn't help calm my mind at all.

"I think from all of that, mixed with my home life. That is what has caused all this in my head. I still see myself sick. I see myself broken, barely holding it together. I can't make it go away, no matter how hard I try.

"No matter how hard I work out and take care of myself. I just see myself sick and dying again. And I hate it. I just want it to stop. I just want to be healthy again. I want my brain to stop fucking torturing me."

I feel Matthew's hand come up and touch my face. Wiping away a tear I didn't even know was falling. I let out a heavy emotional sigh as I turn to look at him again. He is smiling at me. That was definitely not what I was expecting.

He smiles wider when he sees the confusion on my face, "I can tell by the look you are giving me that you are not expecting the reaction I am giving you."

I shake my head at him, still confused. I assumed he was going to give the pitiful "oh no" look that I have become accustomed too. Anytime I had to tell anyone that is the face I would always fucking get and I hate it. I hate it more than the dysmorphia.

Matthew chuckles at me again, before booping me on the nose, "I am smiling because you kicked its ass. Like I imagine you would. Hope, you are one of the strongest people I have ever met. You take everything that is thrown at you and you either wear it as armor or you let it simmer in your soul. Most people just take the bullshit and fixate on it. Or ignore it completely.

"You don't tell people about your issues. You settle them within yourself. Is that the healthiest? Probably not. But you deal with them the best way you can. And you hate to inconvenience people with your thoughts, your feelings. I am happy that you trust me enough to share this with me.

"I am proud of you for winning this fucking battle. Now though you don't have to worry about facing anything alone. Ever again. I will be right beside, in the trenches, dealing with the shit show like a good husband should."

I laugh at him, feeling more tears rolling down my face, "I fucking love you. You know that right?"

He smiles back as he gives me a gentle kiss before pulling back, "I had heard a rumor that you did."

16
Apollo
The Summoning - Sleep Token

Raleigh, check. Baltimore, double check. Philadelphia, triple
check. Next and final stop on this tour, New York City. I am
excited as hell, still hoping they will let me hit the rage room
even with a cast though.

We have two shows back to back then we are done. That
also means that I only have 3 more weeks with this fucking cast
on. I am more than ready for it to come off.

It will be interesting to see what my arm looks like. More
though I want to ensure I can still play the fucking drums. I
never in a million years would have imagined that I would miss
playing as much as I do.

Hope rolls over, stretching her body out then draping her
leg over mine, "Good Morning babe."

I lean over, kissing her on top of the head, "Morning. Are
you ready for tonight?"

She cracks one eye looking up at me, "I am ready for next
Tuesday."

Smiling, I pull back a bit so I can look at her, "Why next
Tuesday?"

She rolls over onto her back, stretching her arms above
her head with a yawn, "Because we will be back home. I am so
fucking ready for London. I would literally shank somebody for a
halloumi salad from The Hayden."

I roll towards her, probably more awkward than necessary, "You are really wanting to go back straight away? There isn't anywhere here in the states you wanna go first? Maybe Malibu?"

She shakes her head at me as she sits up, pulling her arms one at a time across her chest, "Nope. I wanna just go home. I wanna meet the family. I want to get comfortable. I want to see your house. Well, I guess our house. Wait, you have a house don't you? Maybe it's an apartment. Hell I am even fine with a townhouse at this point but I just want to..."

I lean forward and cover her mouth with mine. I feel her smile into my lips as her arms come around the back of my head. I kiss her a few more times before pulling back, "Your mouth had the zoomies again."

Hope grins at me as I pull back and lay down on my side of the bed again. "And yes, I have a house. It isn't far from where my parents live actually. Most of us kids are scattered around London. Except for Lera, that's my youngest sister, she is in Scotland. She moved there not long after graduating secondaries."

Hope rolls over and smiles at me, "Do you think they will like me? Even after they find out what I did?"

Laughing, I roll back towards her, "They all already know about it. And yes they will still like you. They do like you. They, of all people, understand how my mouth sometimes writes checks that my ass has to cash. They know we were arguing. They know I tried to force you to hug me when you were not comfortable with it. They know you pushed me off. They understand that I lost my balance. All of that is the truth. I was called a dumbass by the majority of my family over it. The others called me a daft fool. They were all right on all accounts though."

Hope grins back at me. I watch her eyes go past me focusing on something behind me. She is losing herself in her own mind again.

247

Reaching out, I take her chin and turn her gaze back towards me, "Hey, eyes over here baby. It is fine. They are going to love you. I promise."

Her eyes smile towards me as I pull her in close to my chest, "What are you wanting to do today?"

I feel her shake her head into my chest, "Nothing. Absolutely nothing."

I laugh back at her, remembering what Susie had said the night before on the flight here, "I thought Susie was going to kidnap you today to go shopping."

Hope groans into my chest and as if she knew she was being summoned there is a knock on the door.

Hope groans again, "NOOOOOO."

I laugh as I throw the blankets back and find some pants to throw on real quick. I glance over my shoulder and see Hope start rolling herself up in the blankets like a hand rolled smoke.

Susie is bouncing on the other side of the door, "Where is my girl? We have adventures waiting!"

I point towards the bed, "Hibernating."

Susie laughs as she runs around me then I see a pile of blankets being drug off the end of the bed and into the floor. I laugh as I see hands and feet splayed out around us as Susie yells, "Get up bitch. We have stuff to do!"

Susie turns towards me with a wink, "I am going to steal your husband for a minute out in the hallway. Get your ass ready, we are leaving in 5 minutes. And brush your teeth, I know where your mouth has been."

I shake my head at Susie as she walks towards me, wrapping her hand around my bicep, "Come with me."

We wander out into the hallway and I step out to lean against the wall. Susie has put the barlock on the door so it stays open just a bit. I can hear Hope moving around in the bedroom as I turn towards Susie, "What's up?"

Susie checks the crack in the door before bringing her face back to mine, "The last time we went shopping together you got up to some serious fuckery Matthew. I just want to make myself abundantly clear, if you do anything...ANYTHING... fucking stupid today I swear on christ I will definitely break your fucking nose this time."

I smile as I nod back at her, putting my hands up in defense, "I promise Susie. I will be on my best fucking behavior. I would never do anything like that to her again. I swear."

Susie takes a step back, crossing her arms over her chest, "No one thought you would have done it the first time either."

I flinch at the jab, but it was deserved.

She is right.

I know my actions caught everyone off guard. But I also know that my actions almost cost me my marriage. I am not going to do anything to jeopardize that again.

Nodding my head, I look towards the carpet lining the hallway, "I know. But you have my word this time. It is only Hope. No one else."

Susie nods her head at me while giving me a mom glare. I cross my arms over my chest as well, just staring her back down when the door opens beside me. I watch Hope as she steps out into the hallway in a pair of cut off shorts and a Carnal Decay tshirt. I smile at her attempt at being girly with her hair in a messy bun and what looks like an attempt to wear comfy slip on shoes.

Looking down at her feet, "Where are your chucks?"

Hope looks down at her feet as well then back to me, "This bitch made me try on so much stuff last time. I don't want to spend 5 hours of my day re-tieing my shoes."

Hope leans forward giving me a kiss and smile, "I love you babe. I will be back soon."

I nod my head at her as I head back into the hotel room, shutting the door behind me. Slowly walking towards the bed, I think about Susie's concerns with me. It seems that everyone is basically waiting for me to fuck up again.

It will be funny to see the looks on their faces when they realize I am a good boy now. I am not going to hurt Hope.

Not like that.

Never again.

I step up to the window and let out a sigh. I look out over the city, wondering what kind of trouble I can get into that won't lead to a divorce.

Looking down at my arms then over towards the desk, I reach over, grabbing my phone and then hit Edge's number. Two rings later he answers to me asking only one question, "Tattoos?"

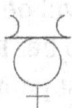

"Hope! Are you almost ready? We have to head to the venue! The show is in like 2 hours babe!" Seriously, she has been in that bathroom for almost an hour. What in the hell could possibly be taking her so long?

I stand up from the end of the bed and step to my bag, pulling out my hoodie and balaclava. I can still feel the pull of the bandage covering the fresh ink on my side saying 'Addicted to the Pain'.

I let my head fall back on my shoulders, my voice echoing around the room, "BABE! SERIOUSLY!"

I don't even hear the door open to the bathroom when I hear her voice behind me, "There is no need to yell. I am right here."

I turn towards her and almost fall completely over. She is standing in front of me in a leather corset and a pair of leather booty shorts that are laced up the front and showing half of her ass. She has on this pink necklace that is a leather strap going around the back of her neck but 3 chains hanging down towards her tits.

Her hair is pulled up into a pony tail with braids coming out of it. Her makeup is simple with a light gray eye shadow and no blush but with bright cherry red lips. She smiles at me, "You gonna pick your tongue up off the floor or do you need me to call for help?"

Taking a step towards her, it feels like my heart is going to jump out of my chest, "Jesus fuck Hope. You have got to quit dressing like this. You are going to give me a fucking heart attack."

She smiles as she wraps her arms around my neck, "Enjoy it while you can, they will be painting me up soon."

I let my hand roll down her lower back and onto her exposed ass cheek, "Don't. Just paint the face, maybe down to the corset. Let them all see the rest of you. Let them all see what is mine and they will never be able to touch."

Hope giggles but then nods her head at me, "Okay."

She turns and walks ahead of me as I try to calm down the blood pumping hard through my veins now. This woman continues to shock me at every fucking turn. I cannot believe I almost missed this.

We all arrive at the venue not 20 minutes later. Susie takes Hope into the girls dressing room to paint her up. I in turn decide to go up on the stage and watch them getting everything set up. Looking out over the empty floor that in just a few hours will be packed, it truly hits me how much I miss being up on this stage.

God, I can't wait to play again.

It's not much longer now.

Then we will have like 8 months in between tours. I can practice and jam with Hope. We can settle into our lives together. We can be there for the birth of our little niece or nephew since Lily only has about 5 months left.

She has already declared she will go on the next tour but she most likely will not be painting. But she said she will skip only one tour. Then the next one she will be more than prepared for. It is going to be interesting to see how they make life on the road with a baby work. But if anyone can pull it off it is Gideon and Lily.

They are serious relationship goals.

I look up to see Lucy pacing up towards the front of the stage. Stepping up to her, clocking her nerves immediately, "What's up Lucy?"

She turns, smiling at me, "Nothing much. Just trying to get everything lined up for the off tour time. We have a few podcast interviews that are wanting to be set up. With voice emulators of course. Also, I have some news for all of you. So meet me down in the girls dressing room. Go grab Ares and Dionysus as well. They are on the other side of the stage."

I look over my shoulder as she points to the guys on the other side of the stage. I turn back to ask her what she is talking about but she is already half way down the stairs. Now I am just standing here with my arms out to the side like a child lost at the zoo.

Quickly, I move to the other side of the stage, "Hey boys! Lucy needs us apparently. She has some sort of "announcement" to make. She wants us in the girls room."

Ares and Dionysus nod at me then start following towards the stairs. I feel Ares' hand on my shoulder, "Any clue what it's about?"

I shake my head as I make my way down the steps, "No fucking clue actually."

Dionysus sighs loudly behind me, "Hopefully, she isn't fucking quitting too."

Chuckling over my shoulder at him, "Dude, she wouldn't fucking do that right before a show. And I am pretty sure Hope would have dropped that bomb on me before now if that was happening."

We round our way into the girls dressing room just as Susie finishes up the paint on Hope. Fuck, she looks gorgeous.

I smile as I cross the room and wrap my arm around her, "Hey love." I give her a soft kiss on the lips as she giggles back at me. I turn towards Lucy who is now standing in the center of the room, all eyes on her.

She moves towards the door and shuts it quietly. You can hear all of us mentally freaking out. Something has definitely happened, I just can't tell if it is good or bad yet. Instantly, I think Simone has conjured up some next tier level of hell for us though.

I watch her shoulders heave as she turns back around at us, smiling from ear to ear, hands out in front of her, "You have been asked to perform at the Billboard Music Awards this year."

We all jump basically out of our skins.

I turn wide eyed at Ares and smile bigger than I think I have ever smiled in my life. The air around the room has somehow stilled and you can hear everyone trying to heave in oxygen. Apparently, it is not only me that is trying not to pass out.

A fear runs through my veins as I turn back towards Lucy, "When? When are the awards?"

She smiles back at me as Daija lets her out of a hug, "They are in two months. So your cast will be off."

Pure excitement stirs in my chest when I hear Hope behind me, "Thank fuck for that!"

I laugh again as I turn around and give her a bigger kiss. She is squeezing me tighter than I ever imagined she would. She is just as excited as I am. I pull back grinning at her as she wipes my bottom lip with her thumb to get the red lipstick off.

Lucy steps up, "There is more. There is a reason they want you to perform. Firestorm is up for heavy metal album of the year."

I feel my head as it slowly turns back to look at Lucy. All the excitement seems to drain from the room immediately.

She has to be lying to us.

There is no fucking way.

I look at Dionysus and he is just shaking his head back and forth like he is in shock as well. Taking a small step forward, still holding onto Hope's hand, "You aren't fucking with us, right?"

Lucy smiles widely back at me, "No Apollo. I am not fucking with you. This is huge guys. I think....I think it's finally happening."

I let go of Hopes' hand and run to pick up Lucy. I hold her up high as I spin her around the room while she screams at me to put her down. Finally, I release her and run to Ares, pulling him into a hug.

Dionysus and Hestia step over joining us in a big circle. I look over at Hope and she is beaming at me. She has her hand on Micah's arm as she jumps up and down in excitement.

Susie is still standing beside her stock still, jaw hanging open with a weeping Aphrodite in her arms. The scene looks like a mix between shock, tragedy and euphoria.

I turn back around and look at Ares.

His eyes are on Micah as well.

He looks around every member of the band, getting a nod from each of us. We all know exactly what he is thinking and couldn't agree more.

He steps around me and towards Micah, "You better get to picking a god. You have 2 months until you are officially announced as our new permanent bassist. That is if you want it."

Micah's jaw about hits the floor as Hope starts jumping up and down clapping her hands while squealing. I laugh at her, being a girlie girl while dressed like a wet dream.

Micah seems to be shaking from head to toe. He has probably blinked a dozen times in 30 seconds. Laughing, I step up to him, "Dude. Chill. This is a good thing."

Micah smiles back at me, smiling widely. He turns back to Ares, "It would be a fucking honor Ares. Thank you. Thanks to all of you. I can't fucking believe this honestly."

Ares puts his hand on Micah's shoulder, "Welcome to the family. We have been impressed with you or we wouldn't even have made it this far. You deserve to be here just as much as the rest of us. You saved our asses. We will never be able to repay you for that."

Everyone runs up and starts hugging Micah, tussling his hair, or trying to shake him senseless. I look at Hope and it looks like she is going to start crying at any moment. I knew they were pretty close already but seeing her so happy for him makes me feel like we definitely made the right decision.

The fact that I know she is exhausted and more than ready to be done with this tour but yet she still shows her excitement and happiness says something about her as a person. The gods definitely blessed me when they had us meet that day.

Susie steps up beside me, "You really shouldn't be looking at your woman like that. Not right now."

Smiling devilishly, I wrap my casted arm around her back, "Oh yeah. Then when is an acceptable time to do that?"

Susie smiles as she leans down towards my ear, "After the show, when you are on stage, grab one of those chains on her necklace and pull. Hard. You will get a nice little surprise."

My eyes roam over her necklace, wondering what kind of surprise could be in store for me. The door to the dressing room opens and one of the stage hands lets us know it is 15 minutes to lights down. We all move to take our places, more energized than we have ever been.

I stand beside Susie, just like I have done at every show since I got injured but tonight. Tonight, though, it just feels more complete. It feels like we are finally beginning to make a real mark. Don't get me wrong, we have a huge fan base already but the fact that we are being recognized in any capacity.

It should be overwhelming but honestly, I feel nothing but pride. We have worked our asses off to get to this point. Through personal and professional struggles. We have turned our torment, our trauma into something healing for so many people.

We receive hundreds if not thousands of dm's a day saying that exact thing.

That we have saved them. That we have pulled them back from the brink of some sort of finality.

But what they all don't seem to understand is that they have saved us.

They have believed in us.

They have fueled the fire that is Carnal Decay. Without every last one of them, we would have never made it here.

They are also the reason we continue.

Sure there are the ones that want to uncover us. Those that try to break us down at almost every turn. But they are easy to push to the back of our brains. They are only trying to catch their own 15 seconds.

Fuck them.

They can't take this from us.

I hear Firestorm start up and everyone seems to play with a new sense of vigor. I smile at Hope on the drums then look up onto the overhead to see Lily has painted us all on a stage, with a sea of people in front of us. We are standing in a prayer stance with our heads bowed. My chest tightens at the sight of it. Hope, Susie, Daija, even Micah is there.

This family that we have constructed is the strongest relationship I have ever had the honor of being a part of. I still can't believe that any of this is actually real. To go from nearly secondary school drop out to performing at the Billboards.

It seems like a dream.

I watch everybody line up and I pull my sleeves down on my hoodie and pop the hood up. I jog out onto the stage and step up beside Dionysus. He looks over at me then kisses me hard on the cheek.

Laughing at him, I feel Hope step up beside me. She just made her way back on stage after delivering Lily's art of the night. I bow to the crowd before looking at my goddess standing beside me.

My eyes go to the necklace around her neck and I hear Susie's words in my head. 'Pull on one of the chains. Hard.'

Turning, I catch Hope's gaze. Her eyes watch my hand as it raises up and I grip one of the chains, pulling down hard on it.

The chain is yanked through some heart shaped hoops on either side of the leather strap and it instantly turns into a leash in my hand. The anxious flutter in my chest turns into a low growl that only she can hear.

Hope smiles widely at me as I step up to her and slam my mouth into hers. I kiss her with zero abandon while everyone continues to give their thanks around us.

Pulling back from her lips is almost impossible but I finally grab the bottom of the chain and I lead her off the stage with me. I can hear her laughing behind me but laughing is far from what I want to be doing. Though something with my mouth involved does come to mind.

She laughs the entire way towards the green room. As we step inside I turn on her, grinning back at her, "So it's safe to say you are wanting to try something new?"

257

Hope stops laughing as her hooded eyes meet my own. She smiles coyly as she nods her head up and down slowly. I run my finger down the center of her chest, in between her breasts. Her breathing picks up as I lean forward, "Use your words Hope."

The smile drops from her lips. Her tongue darts out, making them moist before she pulls her bottom lip into her teeth. She finally lets out a breathy moan, "Yes sir." I feel myself let out a groan as I pull the chain bringing her mouth closer to mine.

I kiss her hard and fast as I feel her arms go around my neck. Breathing heavy into her face, I pull back smiling at her. I grab her hand and pull her towards the chairs. Everyone else starts to trickle in as I wrap my arm around her waist and pull her down onto my lap.

She looks over her shoulder at me, smiling because I know she can feel me hard below her. She shifts just enough to cause another groan to leave my body before she settles in.

She has her hand under the back of her thigh, gripping my dick for almost the entirety of the next hour. By the time the room is cleared, I am sweating and in a frenzy for her.

We decide to split up between the SUVs and make our way back to the hotel. Agreeing to meet up in the hotel restaurant for lunch the next day. Micah still seems nervous as fuck but as soon it finally settles in that this is real, maybe he will calm down a bit.

I must say though he is really starting to grow on me. He is tall and lanky and just weird as hell. Which really actually kind of rounds us out.

We have Gideon the serious one.

Edge the batshit crazy one.

Mona is of course the firecracker.

Me, the nice guy.

And now Micah. I am really pretty interested in which god he is going to choose.

As soon as we step into the hotel room, Hope makes a straight line for her suitcase. But then she looks over her shoulder smiling at me and tells me to close my eyes. Normally, this would mean something amazing is about to happen.

I smile as I close my eyes but still hear her moving around the room. A few minutes later I hear the bathroom door shut. I turn around, opening my eyes when I hear the shower come on.

Laughing, I kick off my boots and pull my shirt over my head. I decide to beat her to the punch this time though and I go ahead and strip down naked before crawling up on the bed.

I swear I have watched more TV since I broke my arm than I have in my entire life. I can almost guess the next scene on just about any show I watch. The tv immediately gets turned off when I hear the water turn off in the shower. I let out a short yawn when I hear the bathroom door open and what sounds like high heels clicking.

That immediately peaks my interest.

Here I am just leaning forward in the bed, waiting for Hope to come around the corner. And when she does I almost fall over myself. I instantly get hard again. She is standing before me in absolutely nothing besides black nylons and leather high heels.

I know my eyes are bugging out of my head as I drink her in. Her mouth curls up at me like an invitation, "I thought we would try something new tonight."

My eyes follow her curves from top to bottom and back again, "I don't know why. This is working out wonderful for me as it is."

She laughs as she steps forward towards the bed and sits down a powder blue dildo that looks like it has wings on it. I move forward a bit, trying to figure out exactly what this thing does when she throws something into my lap.

259

I look down to see a matching blue remote control. I pick it up, giving her a devious smile before hitting a few buttons and watching the new toy dance and vibrate.

I grin back up at her wildly, "Oh this is going to be fun."

She grins deviously back at me, "Yeah but it can't all just be fun for me." Confusion sets in as I give her a questionable side eye. She throws something else down on the bed in front of me. I look down seeing a bottle of extra slick lube laying there.

My eyes instantly fly back to hers, "Is this....I mean....does this mean I can. I mean, fuck, are we thinking the same thing?"

I see her cheeks start to turn pink as she bites her bottom lip and nods her head in agreement. I smile back at her, moving the lube to the other side of me, then patting the bed to the right of me, "Come here baby. Lay down."

She does as she is told and lays down beside me as I climb out of the bed. Already harder than I ever dreamed possible. I watch her eyes as they roam my body. Kneeling in front of her, I wrap my arms around the back of her knees, bringing her down towards the edge of the bed.

I look up into her face and see she is watching me. My lips curl into a smile as I lean forward pushing her knees wider. I taste her from entrance to clit and back again. She tastes like an orchard exploding on my tongue. She lets out a moan and arches her back towards the ceiling. I continue to devour her for a few more moments until she is positively dripping in front of me.

I reach over and grab her new toy, positioning it so I can watch her face as I slip it inside of her. She brings her eyes down to mine just as I hit the on button.

Her eyes fly wide as her mouth forms a perfect circle. I continue to watch her reactions while I try out a few of the other settings on the device. The last one I hit starts making the dildo vibrate but the little wings start to massage around her clit as well.

She lets out another moan into the room as I stand up in front of her. I reach down, sitting down the remote for just a moment as I grab her by the waist and flip her over to her stomach. She lets out another loud moan around the room as she goes up on all fours and starts to push her ass back towards me.

Now frantic again, I reach over and grab the lube. Watching it glide down her center, I am breathing heavy in anticipation. I slowly coat and stroke my dick watching her writhe beneath me. Grabbing the remote, I am hoping I will be able to still use it with my injured arm. Leaning into her slowly, I take my time as I slide into her ass a small amount at a time. I don't want to hurt her.

But it seems the more restraint I try to have, the more feral she becomes. I lean my head back into my shoulders as I grip the remote in my now slick hand and hit the button to speed up the vibrations inside of her. She lets out a small scream into the room and I can feel the vibrations inside her as I continue to push deeper into her.

She is now trying to throw herself back on me so I hit the button to max out the vibrations on her little butterfly. Her arms get shaky and she leans forward just a bit so she can push back onto me entirely. I let out a satisfied moan around the room as I feel myself seated inside of her entirely.

Hope looks over her shoulder at me, smiling, "Fuck me Apollo."

My eyes go wide again as I throw the remote down and grip her hips. Letting out a deep breath, I pull back then slam into her. Hope screams into the bed in front of us but she is still trying to push back on me. I bring my hands down and squeeze her ass cheeks together tight as I start to slam in and out of her ass.

My heart is racing so fast but I can't stop, "Fuck Hope. I am not going to last long."

266

I know I won't. This is all so overwhelming. I just want to explode. I watch her as she looks over her shoulder at me, "Harder baby. Fuck me harder."

I grit my teeth as I start slamming into her again. She is now screaming with each intrusion. I reach down between us and grab the base of the butterfly and start moving it quickly from left to right while it is still inside of her. Stimulating her in a new way with each thrust.

Just a few moments later, Hope is now slamming herself back down on me erratically. She lifts her head and through a broken breath cries, "I'm gonna cum baby. I'm gonna cum."

I let go of the toy then slam into her from behind. I feel my release ripping through my body with no warning and I scream at the ceiling. She is gripping me tight as she screams into the comforter in front of her. My veins feel like they are pulsating just under my skin. I keep slamming into her, "God dammit Hope. I am still cumming."

I have never had an orgasm last this long. She is still going as well as she pushes back on me. I watch her reach down and pull the butterfly out, throwing it over the side. Then her fingers are right back to her clit, extending her own release as she circles her clit in tight little circles.

She goes completely still and I can feel her entire body trembling. She is finally hitting her peak as I feel my own release starting to give in. I lean over top of her, laying her down underneath me as I continue to push in and out of her. I see her face pressed into the bed as she smiles, "Jesus fucking Christ Matthew."

I smile as I slide out of her one last time and roll to the left of her spent body. She doesn't even turn her head towards me as I hear her let out a sigh, "I am completely boneless now."

I laugh towards the ceiling, hearing myself still panting. I look over at her beautiful body in front of me and I lightly tap her bare ass, "Stay there. I will clean you up."

She nods her head at me as I go and get a moist towel to clean her up and then myself. I throw the toy and lube over on the table then roll her over so her naked form is laid out in front of me. I take each foot and slide a heel off then the nylons, until there is nothing but bare Hope in front of me.

Climbing up beside her, I start to roll her towards me, "Come on baby, let's scoot up onto the pillows." She nods her head at me without even opening her eyes.

I get her settled into the bed and smile at her, "If I would have known that fucking you into submission was an option I would have been making different decisions concerning your mouth zoomies."

She laughs at me as she swats me in the chest with her hand, "I love you. You fucking freak."

I smile back at her shaking my head, "No I think that title definitely belongs to you. I love you baby. Good night."

17
Hope
Specter - Bad Omens

If I was forced to describe a cookie cutter family, it would be Matthews'. His mom looks and acts just like someone from an old 50's sitcom. She is even wearing a swing dress with an apron over top of it. His dad loves to watch football (let's be honest it's soccer) as much as humanly possible.

His 3 sisters and 2 brothers freaking adore him. And what is completely fucking insane, they have no idea that he is Apollo. One of his brothers has heard of the band but none of them know that he is actually in it. Apparently, after secondaries he told them all he was going to just backpack wherever the winds took him.

And they believed that shit!

Now they think he has some kind of corporate IT job and just travels all the damn time. That is apparently how he can afford his own place and why he is never home.

My mother would have released the Spanish inquisition on me if I tried some shit like that. I cannot fathom the amount of either gullibility or trust that is happening on his parents side.

He wasn't wrong though. They all welcomed me with open arms. They also all called him an idiot to his face. I can't help but smile at the support they are showing me. Even if it is more just to give him hell than to defend me. A win is a win in my book.

I lean over his mother's kitchen table, "Are you sure there is nothing I can help with Claire? I hate just sitting here and letting you do all the work."

Claire glances over her shoulder at me, smiling, "It is refreshing that one of you kids is actually offering to help. But no thank you Hope. I appreciate the offer but I am almost done here then we will have Don put these burgers on the grill."

I nod a smile back at her as I lean back in my seat. The house already smells phenomenal from all the side dishes she has prepared. There is even an apple pie sitting on the counter that I fully intend on making my bitch before the day is through.

I would be content sitting here for a lifetime.

Looking out the sliding doors, I can see Matthew sitting around a patio table talking to his dad and brothers. They seem to be deep into some kind of hilarious conversation as I watch Matthew laugh and give his brother a high five.

I smile at him before turning back to Claire, "Has everyone always been this close? It seems like everyone really gets along well."

Claire nods her head at me, "For the most part, yes. There have been a few tiffs over the years though. Matthew was a definite problem child through secondaries. I swear that boy is the cause of 90% of my grey hair."

I laugh loudly at her before standing and walking beside her, "I definitely believe that. He is a bit of a wild one sometimes. Which is so strange because on the surface he seems so reserved. Almost shy sometimes."

Claire throws her head back in laughter as she points out the door towards Matthew, "Shy? That one? Never. He may keep some of his thoughts to himself sometimes but if you make him mad or offend him, he will definitely tell you how he feels about you. Or the situation."

I nod back at her as I watch her start to pat out hamburger into patties, "That I have definitely noticed. Tell me more about him. What was he like when he was younger? Like as a child?"

Claire gives me a quick side glance and a grin, "He was, well. He was athletic. He always had a basketball or a baseball in his hand. He also loved music. I think that is why him, Gideon and Edge got along so well all through secondaries."

She turns to me with a questioning smile, "Have you met them yet? I am sure they all still keep in touch. They were inseparable."

I nod back at her, feeling my cheeks turn red because I am a horrible liar, "Yes. I have met them. They do all seem very close."

Claire continues to prepare the meat for the grill, "So how did you two meet? What is love at first sight? I love a good love at first sight story. That is how it was with me and Don. We met in school and I fell instantly. I knew he was the one."

I laugh then look out the patio door again at Matthew. He glances over and catches me staring at him. He smiles and winks at me before I turn back to Claire, "We met through a mutual friend. We just happened to be visiting her at the same time and met then. And yes, I think it was love at first sight. At least, it was for me. I guess I could say the same for him since we were married 3 days later."

Claire laughs then looks at me solemnly, "You seem like a very sweet young lady. I am happy that he is happy. I am even more happy that he makes you happy. Shows me I did something right in raising him."

She lets out a sigh as she looks out the back door, smiling proudly, "I don't think I have seen him smile this much since he was a child."

Watching him with his family, just solidifies within me that staying with him, working through all the shit was the right decision. Before I let out a steady breath I turn to her, "He makes me very happy. We have had a few bumps in the road but just

266

seeing him here with his family, it does something to me. He is like this with my mother and my sister as well. Everyone just meshes so well. I couldn't have asked for anything more from a man. Truly."

Claire looks at me like she might start crying at any moment before smiling out the window at her boys, "That makes me happier than you will ever know, Hope. Honestly."

I nod at her, watching her finish up the last patty then wash her hands. She grabs the tray smiling, "Let's go outside, give these to Don."

I slowly follow her out the sliding doors, looking around the table at everyone sitting before me. A loud conversation starts wafting its way through the house and I turn to see 3 chatting females walking towards us. By the bickering, I would say these are definitely his sisters. Matthew jumps up and runs past me and through the doors, slapping my ass quickly as he goes.

His arms instantly go around all three of them. The youngest one pulling back and looking at his arm in concern.

I feel myself getting nervous, maybe they aren't all okay with what happened. I sit down in the chair that Matthew vacated and look around the table at the 3 sets of eyes now staring back at me.

I hate having eyes on me.

Matthew knows I hate having eyes on me.

I feel like I am being judged for every single little flaw. As I try not to pass out from the pressure, Don leans up on the table, "You really married that clown?"

I laugh immediately feeling a bit of a release in the tension around the table. Nodding back at him, "I did. Voluntarily even."

One of his brothers leans forward towards me, "No offense but he is reaching. You are way out of his league. Like seriously, gorgeous."

267

I feel my cheeks turning red as I look back towards the table, "Thank you. I uh, I think we just even each other out. We are each our own signature brand of crazy but they seem to mesh well."

I look back up and see Matthew pointing towards us on the patio. I take a deep breath before standing up to greet his sisters as they step out through the door.

The two older ones, Mary and Taron seem super nice. But I have been getting an evil glare from Lera since the get go.

I smile at them as Matthew walks around the table to put his arm around me. He smiles at the girls, "Mary, Taron, Lera, this is Hope."

I wave meekly back at them as Mary and Taron smile widely at me. Welcoming me to the family.

Lera on the other hand looks at Matthew, "Isn't she a bit young for you?"

I feel my jaw drop open, literally no one has given a shit about my age before now. I feel Matthew tense his arm around my waist, "She is 23. You are 21 and engaged. I don't see the difference."

She just gives me a mocking smile then looks at Matthew, "And Gregory is 23. Not 29. I just don't want you getting swept away in someone's daddy issues."

I flinch like someone has slapped me.

I turn to Matthew, seeing his face in complete shock as well. I plaster a fake smile on my face before turning back to Lera, "My father died before I was born so I never had a daddy to know what those issues might be."

Turning quickly back towards Matthew, "Excuse me. I am going to go somewhere less volatile."

I feel him grip my waist but I turn back towards him. His eyes staring at me in concern, "Please, let me go."

He loosens his grip as I turn back and walk past the girls. Hearing Matthew behind me, "What the fuck is your deal Lera?"

Then the same shit bubbles back up, like it always seems to do when I hear Lera say, "She isn't Simone. Simone just seemed more stable."

I turn around catching his eyes in mine as I shake my head. He told me that no one knew about the band. Looks like there was another lie brewing this entire time.

I walk through the house quickly pulling out my phone to order an uber. I text the app, dropping my location.

Less than 5 minutes later, I am climbing into a stranger's car, Matthew none the wiser.

Immediately, I call Susie, "Hey. Where are you guys? I need somewhere to lie low for a bit."

She lets out a heavy sigh, "What did he do now?"

I let out a matching sigh, "I will tell you when I get there, just please send me your address. And if he calls, tell him you haven't heard from me."

Susie groans through the phone at me, "Are you running away again?"

I look out the window at the scenery flying by, "Not running away, just removing myself from a shit situation. Just give me your address and if he calls tell him I will be home after she is gone. He will know what I mean. I will explain when I get there."

Susie agrees and immediately texts me her address. 28 minutes later the car is pulling up to a beautiful two story Victorian style home on the outskirts of London.

I stand in the front yard just staring at the house after paying the driver and watching him pull away. This place is fucking amazing.

No wonder she wants to get married here.

I am still ogling over the home when I see the front door open and Susie steps out on the porch.

She leans into the railing, "He will be picking you up after dinner with the family is over."

269

I nod my head at her then drop my gaze towards the ground in front of me as I slowly make my way towards the porch. I move up the steps slowly before leaning against a wooden spindle pillar, "He lied to me. I know he did it to protect me though. I thought none of his family knew about the band. But apparently his little sister does.

"And she is also a super fan of Simone. I overheard her tell Matthew that basically I don't even compare to Simone. I just didn't want to be there anymore. I don't need that shit in my head."

Susie nods her head at me then steps over putting her arm around my shoulders, "Let's go get fucked up."

Smiling, I lean into her shoulder and let her guide me inside. Thank god Susie is....well Susie. Her don't give a shit attitude is kinda what I need right now. Edge is sitting in the living room, obviously afraid to say anything to me. I smile at him and wave, seeing him instantly loosen up.

I follow Susie through the house and back to the kitchen. Pulling out a chair at the table, I slump into it and wait for her to pour me a drink. I see her pull a bottle of Dalmore out of the cabinet and I smile, "Make it a double."

She chuckles as she pours me an extremely large glass. I just continue to wring my fingers together, not really knowing what to say. Or how to feel.

She sits the drink down in front of me, pulling out the chair opposite of me with her own glass in hand. I take a large drink, clearing about half the glass in one go then look at her, "I am never gonna be free of her am I? I will always be compared to her, no matter where we go or what we do."

Susie shakes her head at me as she sits her own glass back down on the table, "Just because other people are comparing you, doesn't mean that Matthew is."

I nod back at her, knowing she is right. The words didn't come from him so there is no good reason for me to be upset with him.

And I'm not, even though technically he lied.

Again.

I take another large drink then let out a sigh, "I get why he lied. I think. I mean I am guessing he did it so I wouldn't sit back and worry about what everyone was thinking about me. Comparing me to her.

"Or maybe he just didn't want me to know that they were closer than what I knew about. I don't know. I just know that Lera is kind of a bitch. That is not going to make for an easy relationship."

Susie grins over at me, "I would bet money that if they are friends, Simone ran to her telling her version of what happened. Not the truth in its entirety. Just her side. I would be happy to set that record clear for you."

Shaking my head, I smile softly at her, "Thank you but no. This is my battle. I will fight it on my own. I am just fucking exhausted. Just mentally and emotionally spent. I feel like I have spent more time fighting for our relationship than I have been enjoying our relationship."

Susie nods as she watches me swallowing down the last of the extremely large glass of whisky.

She tilts her head to the side a bit, "Do you realize how many people out there wish that they had a love worth fighting for though? That they cared enough about someone so deeply that they *would* fight for them."

I smirk back at her, knowing she is right. I let out a huff and stand up, moving towards the sink to look out the window, "I am not saying I am not grateful for our relationship. Because I am. I was lost before Matthew. He centers me.

"He makes me feel seen and loved in a way I have never experienced before. I just don't understand why it has to be so hard for everyone else to just accept us for what we are."

I watch the tall grass swaying in the breeze in the back yard. It looks like Edge hasn't hired a landscaper yet. I feel like how that tall grass looks. Like I am just being pushed around by a force more powerful than myself. With no say at all in where I go.

"Fuck them. And fuck Lera." Matthew is standing in the doorway to the kitchen.

I feel a smile start to creep over my face as I continue to look out the window, "Why are you here already? You should be having dinner with your family."

I turn around and lean up against the sink.

Matthew is still standing in the doorway, shaking his head as he walks towards me, "Like I said. Fuck them. I let everyone know exactly why I was leaving. And whenever, if ever, they all accepted us then I would be back. But I was not going to force my wife to be in an uncomfortable situation. That when they decide they can be civil then we MIGHT think about coming back for a visit."

I shake my head back at him as I cross my arms over my chest, "It wasn't everyone. It was just Lera. I really like your mom actually. Claire is a sweetheart."

Matthew starts to take a few more steps towards me, "Well when I say I let everyone know, it was mainly Lera. I told her that if she can't accept you then she doesn't accept me and my choices. That when she is ready to be my sister again, to call me."

I let out another heavy sigh as my head falls back into my shoulders, "I don't want to come between you and your family Matthew. That is not what I was going for here."

He is right in front of me now, bringing his hand up to my neck, rubbing his thumb down my jawline, "I know but you are

272

my family now. I love Lera, I do. But you are my wife. You are my everything. And if she can't accept you, then there is no place for her in our life, together."

I look back down into his eyes, smiling back at him, "I love you. You know that?"

Matthew leans forward and kisses me, "I know. I love you too."

Susie jumps up and claps her hands together loudly, "Well since you are both here and everything is well in the world again. Who wants to see where the ceremony is happening?"

"No, I completely agree with you Peach. This is the perfect place for the wedding." I continue to look out over the part of the back yard they have partitioned off for the ceremony itself.

Carefully stepping around where she has pointed the dancing area would be, shaking my head, "I still can't believe it is only a week away."

Susie smiles back at me as she pretends to walk down the aisle, "You and me both, Hope. You and me both."

I laugh at her, "Are you excited? Is Edge getting nervous at all? Cold feet?"

Susie laughs as she turns back around, "We would have been married months ago if it would have been up to him. This was my decision, to wait until we were back home. I loved Gideon and Lily's wedding but I didn't want some big production. We see enough of that on tour. I just wanted this to be about me and Gavin."

I feel my eyes blow wide, "Wait, is that his real name? I just assumed his parents were weird as hell and named him Edge."

Susie nearly falls over in hysterics, "That would have been hilarious but no. His full name is Gavin Edgewood. I guess they started calling him Edge in secondaries or something."

Nodding my head, immediately feeling a bit of anxiety run through me. Secondaries is where the band really started to form. I hate that Simone left the way she did. It didn't just hurt the band as a whole, it hurt every single person in a different way.

I am sure that Edge on some level misses her. I think Matthew might even miss her a bit as well.

Walking back towards Susie, I stretch my arms out over my head, going up to my tip toes then feeling a twinge in my lower back. I instantly throw my hand on my lower back like I am expecting the pressure to take care of a pulled muscle, "OW, shit that hurts." Laughing a bit, I come back down off of tip toes.

Susie turns around, concern in her eyes, "What? What did you do?"

I shake my head back at her, laughing a bit at myself, "I freaking tweaked my back stretching. I can't be falling apart already. I am only 23."

Susie laughs back at me as she walks towards me, linking her arm in mine, "We are about to be old married bitches together. When you hit that level, anything can happen."

I laugh along with her as we make our way back towards the house. I can hear the boys before we even make it in the back door. Edge is playing guitar and from the sound of it, Matthew is sitting at the drums, mainly hitting the bass pedal.

I stand in the doorway smiling at them as Matthew turns to look at me, "2 more days. 2 more days and you are free from your radial prison."

Matthew smiles back at me before looking back down at his arm, "The next 48 hours is going to take a month to pass."

I walk towards him, rubbing his shoulders trying to release some of the tension I know he has felt building up for months, "I know babe. But it will all be over soon. And I promise to never break another one of your bones. As long as I live."

Matthew stands wrapping his arms around me, "I will take that promise. And I appreciate that promise. This has been the longest 2 months of my life."

I go up on my tip toes giving him a light kiss, "I know babe. But it's almost over. And to think, you get the cast off just in time for Edge's bachelor party."

Matthew smiles over his shoulder towards Edge and Susie before turning back to me, "Honestly, I am more looking forward to playing. I mean I will show up for the party but I have a feeling I will be thinking about my set the whole night."

Grinning wildly at him I whisper, "Don't worry then. I will enjoy enough strippers for the both of us."

He throws his head back groaning, "Now I wanna go to the bachelorette party instead."

I laugh at him, "Not happening. No boys allowed. Unless they are strippers."

His eyes come back to mine, with a darkness in them, "I will happily be the stripper if you would let me."

I pull back from him, shaking my head, "I don't fucking think so sir. Not in this life."

Matthew chuckles as he pulls me closer into him. Wrapping his arms around me and holding me tight as I let the stress of the day resolve around me.

I put my cheek on his chest and smile towards Susie. Everything is turning out just the way it was supposed to.

18
Apollo
Like a God - Lia Marie Johnson

Nervous air filters around me. It is like there is something in the room that knows I am scared to death to attempt to play. The cast has been off less than 24 hours and here I am, sitting behind my set.

I look down at my left arm, seeing it white and withered. It looks smaller than my right, and I hope to fuck it doesn't take much to get it toned again.

I pick up the sticks, looking across the room at Hope as she smiles and raises her chin at me.

Pushing me on.

I give her a hesitant smile back as I take a deep breath and start to play a roll. Just like I prayed for, my muscle memory takes over. I am all over the place. I smile across the room again as I start to roll into Firestorm.

I see Hope out of the corner of my eye, jump up from the couch in my music room and start dancing around the space in front of me.

Laughing back at her, I finish up Firestorm then move onto Resist the Violence. Hope starts jumping around the room again, obviously excited for me.

She cups her hands around her mouth, "APOLLO! YOU'RE AMAZING!!"

I laugh at her as I bring the sticks back down to a halt. She quickly runs around the set, wrapping her arms around me.

Then she is kissing me, everywhere.

She peppers my face and neck with so much love it is almost overwhelming.

I turn on the stool, pulling her closer until she is straddling me. I kiss her as I turn back towards the drums and continue to play, while she invades my senses with her mouth.

She finally pulls back, smiling at me, "You are a god. You know that?"

I smile as I set the sticks down behind her and wrap both of my arms around her. Feeling her against me like this, like it's the first time I held her.

She squeezes me back then kisses me again before getting up and moving over to the side.

She tilts her head at me, "You, play. I am going to go read my book. I only have about 100 pages left and you sir, have some practice to get down to."

I laugh at her as I give her a salute and watch her walk from the room.

Everything is finally falling into place.

Edge and Susie are getting married. Gideon and Lily are about to close on a house. Daija and Mona seem happier than ever. Hope and I have found our easy medium.

Even Micah is starting to find his place in the band. It is almost like Simone was never here to begin with.

As the songs continue to pour out of me, I practice until it feels like my shoulders are starting to burn. Looking at the clock I realize I have been sitting here for almost 2 hours. I sit the sticks down on the snare and stand up stretching my arms across my chest one at a time.

We have about 5 weeks before the awards show. I will definitely be able to play that night.

Thank fuck.

I move around the set and make my way out into the hallway. Glancing into the living room, I see Hope laid out on the couch completely asleep.

I smile as I walk over and sit down on the cushion next to her. I push some hair back out of her face and she turns her head towards me with a soft smile on her face, "Are you done already?"

I laugh at her, "I have been playing for 2 hours."

She opens her eyes wider, looking around the room like she is lost, "Really? I feel like I just laid down."

I lean forward and kiss her again, "Welcome to tour drain babe. You are going to be a zombie for at least a few more weeks. It happens to all of us."

She nods as she starts to pull herself up.

She makes a wincing face and I smile at her, "The couch isn't comfortable is it? That is why we have a king size bed just one room over. That is super comfy and calling our names right now." I smile then wink at her as I move in for a kiss.

Hope laughs back at me, putting her hand on my chest halting me in place, "Excuse me sir but I am starving. I need sustenance. Like 5 minutes ago."

I stand up, reaching a hand down for her, "Well then it is a good thing we have plans with everyone in about an hour. Go get changed and we will head out to dinner. The last group get together before the wedding, remember?"

She smiles at me, taking my hand to stand up, "Where are we going? I want to dress appropriately."

I give her another wide smile as I start to follow her to the bedroom to get changed myself, "The Hayden."

She turns around wide eyed and grinning from ear to ear, "Halloumi salad?"

I nod back at her, "Halloumi salad."

Hope runs down the hallway to the master bedroom, holding onto the door frame as she propels herself into the room.

I laugh at her as I follow close behind.

278

It doesn't take me more than 5 minutes to get ready. A black button up shirt and some trousers and I am ready for dinner.

Of course though, I am waiting on Hope.

This has become a bit of a ritual for us. I get ready in record time then I wait a lifetime for her. I lean back onto the bed, excited that I don't feel any pressure in my left forearm, "Hope! We gotta go babe!"

I hear a clicking noise on the tile, immediately excited again knowing that she is wearing heels. My eyes are quickly filled with the sight of Hope rounding her way out of the master bath wearing a silk gold dress, with a deep v neck. The hem of it dancing just above her knees.

She has pulled her hair up into a loose bun with little pieces hanging down randomly. I follow the lines of her body all the way down to the leather heels I knew she was going to be wearing. I let out another groan, wishing immediately we didn't have plans.

Hope laughs as she walks towards me, picking up her clutch off the bed, "It'll be okay little guy. We can have fun time later."

I look back up at her, picking her up and spinning her back to the wall quickly, "Who are you calling little guy?"

I see the smile that rolls over her face when she feels me pushing myself into her. The fire that burns in her eyes, I know has never burned this brightly for anyone else before.

She gives me a quick kiss before wiping the lip gloss off my mouth, "Sorry, I meant big man. We can have fun time later, big man."

I laugh as I nod my head at her, letting her go, "That's better."

Taking her hand, I lead her out of the house. We make our way to the street and climb in the car to head to the restaurant.

279

I cast a few glances at Hope, sitting next to me stoically. She is so beautiful. Not just on the surface either. The heart that this woman has. I have never met someone like her before. She doesn't give up on people. No matter how much they hurt her, sometimes even destroy her.

She just seems to hold them tighter. Like she knows that without her, they will diminish. They will no longer matter, to anyone or anything.

I am thankful every single moment of every single day that she has given me the chance to prove myself to her. Though I will never stop proving myself, even if she ever says she forgives me.

We arrive at the restaurant a few minutes later. Smiling, we join hands and make our way into the building. The hostess takes us back to a private room, already half filled with our family. The only ones missing are Micah, Gideon and Lily.

Hope runs around the table and pulls Susie into a deep hug. They smile and giggle to each other.

I in turn step up to Edge, patting him on the shoulder smiling, "Shots?"

Edge turns back to me smiling, "Hell yes!"

We head to the bar and make sure the bartender knows that we are going to be needing copious amounts of alcohol tonight. He just smiles at us and makes sure to have another server brought in.

A few moments later, we see Gideon and Lily walk through the front door. I wave at them, "Hey, we are in that back room over there." I point down the hallway when I hear Edge beside me, "What the fuck?"

I turn and follow his gaze as he watches a server heading to the back room with a tray full of shots. I look at him questionably, "What?"

Edge looks like a mix between scared and pissed. He turns to me, fuming, "That's the fucking groupie."

I look back at the girl, not really recognizing her without all the leather I remember seeing her wearing last time. I shake my head, "No way. That can't be her. Are you sure?"

Edge is nodding his head as he tilts his head towards Gideon in a greeting, "Yeah, I am fucking sure. Hopefully, she doesn't recognize Peach."

I turn to him, "Well, if she doesn't recognize her she is definitely going to recognize Daija."

Edges eyes go wide, "FUCK! I forgot they are friends. Come on. Let's get back in there. We have to keep this shit chill."

I nod my head at him, following quickly back in the backroom. When I enter the room, I see Susie standing off in a corner with Hope. I move to them quickly, watching Edge go over to Daija while trying to avoid the groupies' eyes the entire time.

I move up quickly to the girls, "Peach. We have a possible problem."

She looks past me and then brings her eyes back down, "What now? This is supposed to be a drama free night. What the fuck has happened now?"

Hope looks around me, but the groupie situation was before her, she wouldn't recognize her either way.

I lean into Susie's ear, "The groupie is here. Apparently, she works here. Edge is talking to Daija right now. We are just gonna play this shit off as best we can. Do not do anything that will make her put two and two together."

Pulling back, I see her eyes wide as she scans the room. When they land on the groupie she huffs, "You have got to be fucking kidding me?"

I shake my head back at her, pulling Hope closer into my side, "I wish I was. She is only bringing the booze back. She isn't our actual server. So just get through the few awkward moments and we are solid okay?"

I watch Susie as she nods her head back towards me. Then her eyes go wide and she looks to the far side of the room.

As I turn to see what she is looking at I hear the groupie, "OH MY GOD Daija! I didn't know you were back in town!"

Daija smiles as she walks towards her friend. We are all fucking clenched right now, not really knowing how this is going to go.

Hope leans into me, "Why is everyone staring at Willow?"

Susie and I both turn to Hope immediately.

She looks back at us both shocked, "What?"

Susie lowers her voice, narrowing her eyes across the room, "Her name is Willow? Like the tree? What kind of fucking name is that? No nevermind. How the fuck do you know her?"

Hope looks back towards Willow then turns back to us, "We went to school with her at Queenswood. I have known her for like almost 10 years or something. Her and Daija are really close. Have been for years. Why?"

Susie let's her head fall back between her shoulders, "Of course you all would be fucking friends with her."

Susie brings her face back down to mine, chuckling to herself, "Why am I fucking cursed Matthew? What did I do to piss the gods off this much?"

I laugh back at her, "She doesn't know who we are. Just be cool."

Hope leans in closer, "What are you talking about? What is happening right now?"

I lean into Hope's ear, "I will tell you about it later. Just for now, if you have to talk to Willow, just keep her away from Susie. It will all make sense later I promise. Just trust me."

I pull back, seeing understanding in Hope's eyes. She nods at me, "Of course. Not a problem. I trust you."

She looks back over the room as I continue to stare at her. I don't think she understands how much those three little words mean to me.

She trusts me again.

I want to pull her close to me but instead I just put my hand on her lower back and lead her to the other side of the room to say hello to her friend.

We step up to Daija and Mona who both look sheet white right now. Hope smiles at them, "Hi Willow! I didn't know you worked here!"

Willow turns around, her eyes going wide as she sees Hope standing behind her.

She smiles widely as she reaches out for a hug, "Hope! This is fucking great! I haven't seen you in so long! Yeah, I have worked here for a few years now. I had to get some kind of job so daddy wouldn't cut me off. I only do maybe two shifts a week though. It is so good to see you!"

Willow's eyes come to me and she looks me up and down, and not in a friendly way. She obviously has more than friendly thoughts going through her head right now. Obviously, a pulse is all she seems to need to get excited.

She gives me a little half grin, sticking her chest out a bit further, "Who is your friend here?"

Hope stands a bit straighter and leans into my side, "This is my husband. Matthew."

Willow's eyes go wide as she looks me over again. I hold up my ring finger, letting her see the word HOPE wrapping around it. Hope in turns lifts her finger showing off her rings as well. Willow sputters at the site of the Harry Winston set on her hand.

She grabs Hope's hand bringing it closer to her, "Fucking Hell Hope! Who the fuck did you marry?"

Hope just smiles at her before glancing at me, "My soulmate."

I watch Willow drop her hand then look over my shoulder in Susie's direction. She looks at her like she is trying to place where she might know her from.

I nervously step in her line of sight and open my mouth to change the subject when I hear from the doorway, someone yell "PEACH!"

We all turn to see Micah standing there with his arms open for a hug. Willow turns and looks back towards Susie as I grab a few shots off the tray, "Micah hey! Yeah this is the peach vodka. You have to try it. Come over here."

I move towards Susie to block her from Willow's view. Micah walks over to me confused as fuck but doesn't say anything else as he takes the shot glass from me, "What are you talking about? I was just saying hi to Susie."

Quickly, I lean into him, "Just don't pay any attention to Susie right now. I will explain everything in a minute, but right now, just chill with me. Have a drink."

Micah shakes his head at me like I have completely lost my mind but does what I say. He and I take the shot then gravitate back towards Hope and the other girls.

Daija is giving Willow a hug, "Yeah, I will totally call you. I think we are good on drinks right now, but if I don't see you again tonight I will definitely reach out in the next few days. I have some plans but I will make space."

Willow smiles back at her before giving Hope a hug, "It was really great to see you again Hope. Hey guess who I ran into the other day? Alan! Of all people! He is living over on the east side somewhere. But I will let you guys get back to your party."

Willow turns back to me, waving before looking at Micah and blushing a bit.

Her eyes meet mine again, "It was really nice to meet you Matthew. I am sure I will run into you again sometime!"

We all breathe a sigh of relief when she finally leaves the party room. Micah, Daija and Hope continue to look around the room like everyone has gone completely insane.

Edge runs over to the door to make sure Willow is actually gone before turning around and grabbing a shot glass.

He downs it fast before turning to Susie, "Do you wanna fill them in or should I?"

The rest of the night went off without any more drama thankfully. Daija had no clue about everything Willow had done.

And when she found out, she told us all she would not be reaching out like she had promised. I believe her words were 'bros before hoes'.

Everyone decided to call it an early night after dinner since we would all be seeing each other the next afternoon at the wedding. Hope and I were silent the majority of the way home, other than pleasantries.

But there is a question that feels like a lead balloon weighing on my brain. And I know I have no business even asking it, and it is probably going to cause a fucking fight.

Still, I turn to her after shutting and locking the front door, "So. Who is Alan?"

Hope snorts a laugh before turning back to me smiling, "That was literally killing you wasn't it? You just couldn't not ask?"

I smile back at her, feeling my cheeks heating up.

I throw my arms out to the sides, "I'm sorry! It has been literally eating away at me since Willow said what she did. Is he like a friend or...?"

Hope continues smiling as she reaches down and takes her heels off. She carries them on her fingertips towards the bedroom with me right fucking behind her the entire time.

"You are killing me right now, Hope. I have been bursting for two hours over here. Please don't make me suffer any longer."

I watch her as she walks over towards the closet and sets her shoes down inside. She turns around reaching behind her back to unzip her dress. She smiles at me as she slides it off over her shoulders, now standing in nothing but her white lace underwear.

She smiles at me and all I can think is, maybe I don't need to know who he is. But my intrusive thoughts win out, per normal.

I take my shoes off, walking beside her to put them in the closet as well. I unbutton my shirt, slowly watching her as she struts half naked to the other side of the room to take off her earrings and necklace.

I take my shirt off, wading it up to toss it in the hamper as she puts her jewelry away in a box she has put on the dresser.

She turns back around walking back towards me with that sexy ass grin on her face as I take my slacks and socks off, throwing them into the hamper as well.

She steps up close to me and wraps her arms around my neck. I put my hands on her waist then nuzzle my nose into her neck, "You are literally killing me here. I don't know if I want to strangle you or fuck you."

Hope pulls back, smiling at me, "Why not both?"

I let a growl out into the room then I am kissing her.

Hard.

She lets me possess her space with my own until we are nudging up against the bed.

I pull back smiling at her, "Don't think this is getting you out of answering my question."

She smiles as she reaches her thumbs down and slowly pulls her panties down her hips, letting them fall to the floor. I lick my lips then kiss her as I feel her hands at my waistline next.

She slowly pulls my boxer briefs down as well. I kick them off then pick her up, turning so when I sit down on the bed she is now straddling me.

Her beautiful full tits are right at mouth level so I lean forward, taking her nipple into my mouth and nibbling on the peak. I can hear her moaning above me and I pull back to look at her face.

She smiles down at me before leaning in and kissing me harder. I can feel the heat radiating off her center. I would put money on she is slick with need already.

She moves her body to the side, rolling onto the bed below us while pulling me on top of her. She grins up at me as I lean into her to kiss her again.

I pull back, "You are still gonna answer my question."

Then I push myself into her tight little cunt, making her moan into the air around us.

She brings her eyes back to mine before giving me a side smile, "Do you really want me to talk about other men while you are fucking me? Because if so, how do you feel about Henry Cavill?"

She laughs a bit harder until I slam into her again, shutting her up real fast.

I push in and out her faster and faster, keeping her from being able to utter another word about Alan or Cavill.

I smile down at her as she arches her chest up towards me, "Not in this house young lady. The only dick you get to think about is mine."

She smiles at me again as her eyes meet mine, "I saw an interview once where Cavill hinted that fucking is the only cardio he does."

I growl at her as I slam into her faster and harder, "Maybe we should be working out more often then. If you want me to look like him and all."

She leans her head back into the pillows and moans loudly around the room again. She brings her hand up, placing it on my newly uncasted arm.

Then she pulls my hand until it is up and wrapped around her neck.

287

She smirks as she lets her hand drop, "Let's see how much strength you still have in this arm."

I tighten my hand around her throat, not enough to cut off her air supply but enough that her eyes and mouth both go wide. I start slamming into her harder before looking down in between us so I can watch myself destroying her cunt.

I feel her starting to pulsate around me so I squeeze a little bit harder and continue to thrust into her. She moans loudly again, arching her chest towards me. I lean down and take a nipple in my mouth and bite down at the same time I tighten my grip again.

Her hands are on my biceps now, nails scraping down my skin. I pull back and smile at her as I close my eyes and chase my own release.

When I feel it starting to build fast, I open my eyes and look back down at her. She is grinning wider as she puts her hand over mine and squeezes tight. I know she must not be getting much air this way.

I thrust into her harder and deeper feeling myself about to fall over the side of the cliff with her. I grunt as I slam into her again then release her throat completely. As soon as I hear her gasp in air, I feel her clamp down on my dick.

"God dammit Hope!" I push myself into her harder than before, as I feel her pulsate in hard waves around my cock. Her eyes are closed but her mouth is open in a delicious O making me think all kinds of devious thoughts.

"That's right baby. Let that tight little cunt strangle my cock. God baby you are taking me so well." I watch as her mouth closes and her eyes fly open.

Her hands are instantly on my shoulders, fingernails digging in as she starts screaming, "I'm cumming again baby. Fuck me. Hard!"

I slam into her over and over until I am also screaming into the room around us, cumming harder than I think I have ever in my entire life. It feels like I am still going minutes after as I continue to slam into her greedy pussy.

She finally starts to come down, slowly letting her body relax. I feel her starting to release me but I am not done yet. I continue to slam into her, trying to prolong this as long as humanly possible. She smiles up at me as she runs her fingers down my arms.

I grab her, rolling her on top of me and start thrusting into her from below. I can feel my release already running out of her with every thrust but I feel like I am at the edge of blowing again. She braces her hands on my chest and starts slamming down onto me.

I growl into the room then wrap my hands around the back of her neck, "Come here. Give me your mouth." She leans down onto me, kissing me hard as she continues to slam onto me in short bursts.

I pull back with a hiss, "Faster Hope. I am going to cum again baby. Fuck me."

I can't even open my eyes but I feel her speed up, sliding up and down my cock fast enough to start a wildfire. One last slam of her hips and I feel her tighten around me again.

I roar into the room as I feel myself let go again. I grab her by the hips and hold her body tight to mine, with me pushed up inside of her as deep as I can go.

We both shake and quiver with our release. Breathing heavily with our sweat and cum mixing together to become one. I feel my body continue to release into her and finally I can breathe normally again.

Hope rolls off of me and falls into a heap beside me on the bed. I smile as I look towards her, "Okay, you can tell me about Alan later. You win."

She laughs as she continues to gasp for air.

I turn my head towards her, smiling, "All I need to know is, did you ever fuck him like that?"

Hopes eyes come back to mine and she smiles back, "Baby, I have never fucked anyone but you like that."

I grin back before looking at the ceiling again, "That's all I need to know then."

19

Hope
Crazy in Love - Sofia Karlberg

The sun coming through the curtains is what wakes me up. I smile as I turn my head to the left seeing Matthew still sleeping soundly. I look him over, sleeping peacefully, not a care in the world.

Everything is about to get crazy with the band. Especially if they win. I look back towards the ceiling, laughing at what my life has become.

6 months ago I had zero purpose.

I was just wandering around aimlessly trying to help out when and where I could.

Now I am married to the drummer of one of the biggest bands in the states. They are well known in the UK as well but people are seriously losing their shit over them back home. I constantly wonder how it is all going to play out.

I let out a sigh as I roll off of my side of the bed and make my way towards the bathroom. I check the clock on the way, noticing we have about 4 hours before the wedding. I smile down at Matthew deciding to let him sleep a bit longer.

I move into the bathroom, starting the shower then sitting down to pee. When I pull the toilet paper out, out of habit just checking is when I see it is streaked with blood. Not a lot, but enough that my heart starts to kick up a few beats faster. I flush the toilet then step into the shower.

I stand under the rain shower letting the water roll down my skin. Only now, in this moment will I let the fear take over.

Not when Matthew can see it.

I will never let him see that.

I have known for a bit that something is going on. I know my body. I've known that it wasn't just a pulled muscle at Susie's.

Turning my face up into the water falling from the ceiling, I let the tears mingle with it.

Immediately, I start to strategize a plan in my head. I am not going to worry him with any of this before I even know what is going on.

And definitely not before the awards.

I breathe heavily into the shower. I will talk to mom today after the wedding. She will help me devise a plan.

She will keep this secret.

If it is even a secret that needs to be kept.

It could be nothing. But my heart squeezes tight every time I think that.

I clean up quickly then turn the shower off. I step out, wrapping a towel tight around my body then stepping towards the vanity. Looking into the mirror, I see that gangly girl again.

The one that is sick.

The one that is knocking on death's door.

And just for a split second, I wonder if that is how I really look to others. But I know I don't, someone would have said something.

Matthew would have said something.

I just pray he doesn't ever have to see me through my own eyes.

It would destroy him.

I towel dry my hair then pull out my hair dryer. I blow dry it, styling it into long beach waves. I watch my hands move as I style it, hoping I don't lose it again. I don't want to start over again.

It took me so long to grow it back out.

I shake my head trying to dislodge these thoughts from my head. I can't just jump straight to the end. There is no reason to worry.

So I won't until I know I need to.

I move back into the bedroom and lean over to give Matthew a kiss. I feel his lips grin into mine. He wraps his arms around me and rolls me down onto the bed with him.

I laugh at his insanity but my heart is still thrumming hard in my chest. He opens those honey brown eyes and smiles at me, "Good morning love."

I lean forward and kiss him, feeling tears trying to breech. I pull back slowly, trying to keep them contained, "I love you."

Matthew looks at me a little closer, "Are you okay? What's wrong? Why are you about to cry?"

I wave my hand at him, laughing, "I am a female. We are supposed to cry and get weepy when it comes to weddings."

Matthew smiles at me, kissing me again.

He leans back on his pillow then turns his head back to me, "How about after the awards we have our ceremony? We can renew our vows in front of everyone."

I nod my head in agreement, though my brain is telling me I may not be able to. I give him my best smile and roll off my side of the bed to start getting ready.

I can hear him behind me as he says he is going to take a shower. I just nod at his reflection in the mirror in front of me.

As he steps away, I look into my own reflection in the mirror, "Get yourself together Hope."

Somehow, I am able to keep myself distracted through the ceremony. And just like I knew I would, I cry like an infant. From the moment that Susie started walking down the aisle with Lily giving her away. To the moment that Edge spoke his written vows, swearing his undying love for her, in this life and the next.

I am pretty sure that Matthew bought stock in kleenex because he has handed me at least a box full already.

With me sheepishly apologizing each time.

He just chuckles at me then goes back to watching the nuptials take place.

When the ceremony is over and everything is official, Susie is beaming like the sun itself. She grins at everyone before grabbing Edge's hand and running back down the aisle towards the house. I follow them with my eyes, watching as they embrace each other.

I turn to look at Matthew, feeling this overwhelming moment of sadness grip my heart. He is smiling at them, seeing them so happy and in love.

It scares me to death that if something is wrong with me that he may be left alone. Thankfully, he has already seen me crying so he has no real idea what these new tears are really for.

The entire group starts to trickle over to the large white tent they have set up for the reception to begin. I see my mom walking about 10 feet ahead of me.

Subtly I lean into Matthew, "I will catch up with you in a minute. I am going to go talk to my mom. Save me some cake!"

Matthew chuckles and nods at me as I make my way over towards my mother. Her eyes connect with mine and she gives me a soft smile as she pulls me into a hug, "Ah, my poor baby girl. I knew you were going to cry. Just ask your sister. I called it 2 hours ago."

I pull back from her, no longer smiling, but tears still rolling down my cheeks, "Can we talk? Privately? Just for a few minutes."

Concern rolls over her face as she looks over my shoulder, most likely at Matthew then back to me, "Of course. Are you two fighting?"

I shake my head at her, "No, nothing like that. Just step over here to the side with me. Please."

I see her face falling even more as she takes my hand then guides me out of the tent and further out into the yard where no one will be able to overhear us.

She turns around immediately pulling me into a tight hug, "What is it baby? What has you so upset?"

I pull back from her, seeing the concern in her eyes. I hate that we are back here.

Back in this place again.

I thought we were good.

I thought it was all past me.

I let out another shuddered breath as I try to square up my shoulders and at least pretend to be strong, for her, "I have been feeling off for the past couple of weeks. I have had this stabbing pain on my right side, like my lower back. At first, I thought maybe I just tweaked a muscle but it never really went away.

"It has been progressively getting worse too. I thought maybe a kidney infection or maybe even a UTI but nothing over the counter has worked. And this morning there was a small streak of blood when I peed. I am kinda starting to worry. I know my body, something is off."

Watching my mothers face as the fear of my words start to roll over her is going to replay in my nightmares for the rest of my life.

Then she shakes her head, like she is trying to clear cobwebs from her mind, "Let's not get too worried yet. They sell uti tests at the pharmacy. Let's start there. We will just think small until we are given a reason to worry that it is anymore than it is. No reason to get worked up yet, it could very well be nothing."

I hear her words, hopeful as they are, but her eyes are telling me a completely different story. But she is right, I can worry in my brain all I want but there is no reason to get worked up over any of this until we have a reason to be upset.

She pulls me back into another hug, "Have you said anything to Matthew yet?"

I shake my head, pulling back from her, "No. And you can't either. Not until we know what is happening. And definitely not before the awards. If this is what I am afraid it is, I don't want him jeopardizing anything for me. And if I have to get treatment, I don't want him to see me like that."

Mom reaches up, placing her hand on my cheek. I lean into her palm, feeling her love coming through with just the simplest of touches.

She gives me a soft smile, "I will keep it quiet for now, but if it is more serious, you have to tell him. Or at least let him know where you are going to be if you need treatment."

I nod back at her again before pulling her closer to me. I am scared.

I know she can feel it.

I also know she is probably terrified as well.

But this is not the first time we have been scared. And it probably won't be the last. I just wish the universe wasn't trying to destroy me at every turn.

We return to the reception hand in hand. Somehow, though nothing has even really changed, I feel better. Just putting the words out there into the world has made me feel better.

I try to push the screaming voices to the back of my mind. I just want to focus on today. On celebrating my friends, my family.

Matthew steps up to me, grinning deviously, "I think you owe me a dance." He puts his hand out for me to take.

Smiling back at him, I take his hand and let him lead me to the floor. There is some slow instrumental playing so I just wrap my hands around his neck and push myself up close to him.

I feel his arms tighten around my waist then I hear him scream, "HIT IT!"

I jump, startled from his scream.

Instantly the song Dancing Queen comes on overhead and everyone starts running to the floor. Matthew keeps my hands in his as he starts spinning us in a circle.

This is legit something out of a fucking movie.

I start laughing at his insane dance moves.

He takes my hand and spins me in circles before him. I finally stop, laughing harder than I have in a very, very long time.

Susie and Lily come up close to me, both singing the words loudly. I turn to them, singing right back as we all start dancing and jumping around the dance floor. Daija and Mona are off to the side pretending to be Travolta.

I keep dancing and spinning.

Laughing and living.

This is different.

When I was younger, I didn't really know what I was fighting for because I didn't know what life really held for me. I was just a child.

But this moment, with all my family and friends around me. This moment in time is what I lived for.

This moment is what will help me continue on.

Because who is to say there won't be another moment like this again soon.

One that pushes the voices aside. One that captures me, entirely, body and soul.

I want that.

I want to experience this feeling as much as humanly possible.

I will fight for that.

297

I have to fight for that.

I look over at Matthew and he is locked arm in arm with Edge and Gideon. They are all singing loudly as well. Of all things a fucking bubble machine is going off behind them, making them look like some fairy godfather situation from a fucking Disney movie.

The song finally ends and I run up to Matthew. Kissing him deeply before grabbing his hand and pulling him towards the open bar.

I finally turn around smiling at him, "You scared the shit out of me when you screamed in my ear." I smack him on the chest and he just starts laughing at me.

Matthew wraps his arms around me, pulling me close to him, "I felt it was the perfect time to get this party officially started."

He turns looking out on the dance floor at Susie and Edge. I look right along with him, smiling at them.

Letting out a deep sigh, I confess, "They are so fucking perfect for eachother."

I can see Matthew nodding his head out of my periphery, "Exactly why we had to keep that Willow chick at bay. I really didn't want Susie going to jail right before the wedding."

I laugh as I turn back to him, "Yeah, that would have sucked. But all is good, Willow is on the no fly list and the wedding went off perfectly. All is well in the world."

He cups my cheek in his palm, his eyes looking deeply into mine, "Is it? All well in the world?"

I smile and nod at him, "Matthew you have proven yourself time and time again. We are good. I trust you. I love you. And more than that, I forgive you. I can't expect perfection from you when I myself can't even live up to that hype."

His eyes go wide when he hears me tell him that I forgive him. I honestly think he believed it would never happen. He kisses me again before turning me around to watch the crowd.

He pulls me in tight to him, "Our renewal is going to be even better than this. I am thinking of hiring maybe a traveling gypsy band. Or, hey, what do you think about sloths? We could have sloths!"

I laugh at him as I slap his arm, "Sloths are cool but a bit handsy. Let's just get through today then we can talk about our ceremony tomorrow."

I feel his lips as they press into my temple. It is like the air around us isn't even heavy anymore. I never imagined that 3 little words could fix us.

But that is what it feels like.

It feels like everything is going to be okay. Maybe it is just my acceptance but a part of me wants to believe that it is an omen.

"I cannot believe it is almost time to head to Vegas. Like seriously, we are leaving in 2 days babe. In a way, I kinda wish Lucy hadn't told us about the nomination. My nerves have been in a fucking riot for weeks." Matthew acts as if I haven't been here, watching him pace for the last month.

I smile at him, "Calm down babe. You guys are going to fucking destroy it and you know this. I know you are excited, I know you are anxious but it will be okay. Just try to keep yourself as level as you can. Last thing we need is you having a fucking stroke over this."

Matthew struts over to me, picking me up off my comfy spot on the couch and pulls me onto his lap as he plops down beside where I was.

I giggle at him, wrapping my arms around his neck, "So what, you are just gonna hold me hostage until the plane takes off on Thursday?"

His eyes narrow on mine, "I think if I just keep my cock buried in you for the next 48 hours, I *should* stay calm enough to survive this."

I laugh at him, pulling his mouth close to mine. I kiss him fervently. I kiss him thoroughly. I kiss him with enough passion and love to cover up the fact that I am going to make his world shatter, possibly just hours after everything goes so right for him.

How I have been able to keep my condition under wraps until now, I have no idea. He doesn't know that I will be leaving for treatment the day after the awards. He won't know until after I am already gone.

My mother has promised to keep him away from me, for as long as it takes. Until I can at least get a few weeks worth of treatments in.

To see if they even make a difference.

But until then, I will continue to hold him close.

Closer than close.

I will love him like every breath is my last and pray to god that it isn't.

20
Apollo
Take Me Back to Eden - Sleep Token

To say that I am nervous would be a gross understatement of how I am actually feeling. I am tense, queasy, and at times even possibly delusional.

Thinking all this can't be real.

That everything can't finally be falling into place. Something will go wrong because it must. It always does. I just don't know what it will be.

But it's inevitable.

We are back at the Bellagio. They are going to think I am taking up permanent residence here before too long. The awards are tomorrow but all of us are too nervous to even leave our rooms not in full gear. The amount of people in this town right now is debilitating.

I roll over, looking at Hope sleeping beside me, though it is only 4 in the afternoon. I smile as I take a strand of hair and gently tuck it behind her ear.

She is my constant.

She is my muse.

Without her, I never would have found true happiness. I would never have learned what it felt to love someone, truly. And be loved in return.

The ringing of my phone is the only thing that can pull me out of the trance I fall into while looking at her.

I reach over grabbing my phone, sitting up on the bed, "Yeah?"

Gideon's deep voice is on the other end of the line, "We are going to go to dinner in about an hour. Do you guys want to come along?"

I look over at Hope, knowing she will be hungry, "Yeah, Hope is asleep right now but I will wake her up. She will be starving at 2 am if I don't."

Gideon chuckles, "Yeah. Okay, I will call Edge too. You want to reach out to Mona and Micah? Oh and apparently, Micah has decided on his god. He said his mask will be delivered later tonight. Lucy had it specially made for him."

I nod as I stand up, walking towards the window, "Nice, who did he pick?"

Gideon laughs again, "He won't fucking say. Says he wants it to be a surprise. I bet we can get it out of him at dinner though."

I laugh back at him, "Fuck yeah. Alright I will give them a call. Lobby in an hour?"

Gideon agrees and we hang up. The first phone call I make is to Mona.

After 3 rings the raspy deep tone of Daija answers, "Mona's sex pistol. How can I help you?"

I laugh, probably louder than necessary, "Well thank you for that introduction. What are you two up to in like an hour?"

I hear Daija moving around on the other end of the phone, whispering, "Mona says nothing. What's up?"

Nodding, I move towards my suitcase to find some clean clothes to wear tonight, "We are meeting in the lobby in an hour to go get dinner. You in?"

There is more whispering on the other end, followed by laughter, "Yeah we are in. Hey, what is Hope doing right now? Ask her what she is wearing so I am not grossly over or under dressed."

I look over my shoulder back towards the bed, "She is asleep right now. But I can have her call you after I wake her up."

I hear a sigh on the other end of the phone.

It grabs my attention, "What? What is that heavy sigh about?"

Daija is trying not to trip over her own words it seems. Maybe it is the twin telepathy thing or whatever but she seems more chill when she says, "She has been tired a lot recently. I think I have seen her more asleep than awake."

I turn around looking at Hope laid out on the bed.

I feel something roll through my chest, "Yeah. I guess. I guess I just wasn't paying that close of attention."

There is another heavy breath through the phone, "I am sure everything is fine. Just have her call me when you wake her up."

I nod my head while still staring at Hope curled up under the blankets, whispering back, "Yeah, okay."

I lower the phone from my ear and continue staring at her. She has seemed more tired than normal. Maybe it is still her recovering from the tour. Or maybe she has like seasonal allergies or something.

Yeah that must be it.

I look back down at my phone, dialing Micah's number. He agrees to meet us in the lobby as well so I shoot Gideon a text letting him know everyone is down. I step over towards the bed, shaking Hope gently on the hip.

Her body moves but her eyes never open.

I move closer to her, sinking down onto the bed beside her, "Hey, baby. Time to wake up. We are going to dinner."

She doesn't even flinch. My heart instantly goes to my throat. She is so still. Too still.

Why isn't she waking up?

303

Panicking, I start shaking her harder, "Hope? Baby? Wake up!" My voice is shaky as I feel this intense fear roll down my spine.

Two seconds later, her eyes flutter open and she yawns loudly. I let out a held breath, still scared but at least able to breath now.

She looks around the room before settling her eyes on me, "How long was I asleep? I didn't even know I was tired."

I reach down, tucking more hair behind her ear, "You were out for about 2 hours. Hey, you feel warm. Are you coming down with something? Have you felt a cold coming on?" I put my hand on her forehead and she playfully bats it away.

I watch her as she scoots up into a sitting position, "I was tucked into a comforter for two hours, yeah I am toasty and cozy. That's probably why I slept so good."

I nod back at her, that makes sense.

I try to let my fears roll out one breath at a time but now that they are there, they don't seem to want to leave.

Reaching out, I put my hand on her thigh, "We are supposed to meet everyone in the lobby in about 45 minutes. We are going to dinner. And Daija wants you to call her so she knows what to wear."

Hope nods at me again, letting out a big yawn before throwing the blankets back, "Okay. Let's get this going then."

I watch her as she moves around the room, finding what dress she wants to wear. She calls Daija, laughing and joking for about 5 minutes before she hangs up and starts to get ready herself.

Once she is in the bathroom, I start to get changed into dinner clothes as well.

There is something going on.

I can't tell what it is but something is there. Something that wasn't before. I slowly get dressed trying to come up with

304

some kind of idea of what could be going on behind the curtain, but I come up empty at every turn.

40 minutes later Hope steps back out of the bathroom wearing a mid thigh floral tight as fuck dress. I smile as I look at her feet and see her wearing heels.

I step up to her smiling back at me, "We are wearing our masks tonight right?"

I nod back down at her, "Yeah, no paint because we are covered in clothes anyways. The guys and Mona all have nylon balaclavas. You, Susie, and Lily have your half masks. We should be good. Just don't wanna be picked off as soon as we open the door to the hallway."

Hope smiles at me before leaning in and giving me a kiss, "Sounds good. Let's do the damn thing."

I watch her as she slides her mask down. I give her one more kiss before I pull mine down as well.

"Are you ready? It's just like we rehearsed. Everything is just like normal. Just keep to your marks. It's just another performance." I am not sure who Ares is trying to convince but it sounds more like a pep talk he would give a mirror.

I continue to bounce back and forth from one leg to another.

Just another show.
Just another show.
That is televised to millions of people.
Just another show.
We can do this.

I roll my shoulders again before catching a glimpse of someone tall and lanky stepping up to us. If it wasn't for the blonde hair, I probably wouldn't have recognized him at all.

I reach out and tap Ares on the shoulder. He turns, his eyes following mine.

Micah steps up to us. His mask is a dark charcoal grey with the faces of three dogs on it. One on each cheek and another on his forehead. All with glowing eyes.

I smile at him, "So who are we introducing tonight?"

He steps up closer to me, putting his hands behind his back. He smiles at me, "The name is Hades. Ruler of the underworld. These are my hell hounds whom I lovingly call Apollo, Ares and Dionysus. Though only when it's just us. I am pretty sure the dog's name was Cerberus."

I nod my head back at him, "Hades. I love it. It's perfect. It suits you."

He grins back wider, "Thank god cause I was drawing blanks for weeks."

I laugh at him when Lucy comes running up to us, "Alright everybody. Time to get on stage. The lights are about to go out, you know where your marks are illuminated. Don't fuck up, make it count!"

I smile at her, pulling her into a tight hug, "Thank you. For sticking this out, for helping us get here. We owe you more than you know."

Lucy laughs as she pushes me off of her, "Don't get mushy on me now kid. Get out there. Kick some ass."

Turning myself towards the stage, I let Apollo take over.

He will get me through this.

He always does.

And knowing that Hope is out there somewhere watching me, means I can't fuck up. Because she will never let me live it down.

We all turn in a circle, facing each other. Ares, Dionysus, Hestia, Hades, Apollo. We stare each other down, nodding our heads at eachother. When we hear our que, we all turn and silently make our way onto the stage.

I climb up to my set, getting comfortable and settled. Quickly making sure everything is where it should be. Then I look out into the darkened crowd.

The lights are down in the entire building but there are hundreds, no thousands of people out there. A lot of them are in the same industry as us.

A lot of them are just fans, maybe not necessarily fans of us, but fans of music as a whole. And that is what fuels me right now.

In this moment, knowing that we are about to reach out further than we ever thought possible. That our word, our sound is about to be shared by millions.

I get the que that it is 5 seconds before we are announced. Inhaling deeply, I roll my neck on my shoulders again. I hear us being introduced by whatever Hollywood star is the most popular this week. Before the crowd can even finish clapping, I am rolling into the opening for Firestorm.

I try to keep myself focused on the set in front of me. But when those lights come up, I can see the sea of people watching us. Either enthralled or waiting for us to fuck up.

It is fucking overwhelming.

But I continue to breathe and roll through my licks. The solo is about halfway through the song and it is fucking epic.

I carve my path through the song, letting the moment take control of my body. I finally get a chance to breathe again and I see Ares and Dionysus as they are both running around the stage. Hades is standing stoically but swaying almost mechanically. Every few moments he will take a few steps left or right.

Hestia is continuing to do her thing behind the keyboards. You would not believe the amount of techno we actually put into the background of our songs.

My eye catches one of the big screens that is pointing out for the crowd to see. Lucy has put together a sort of slide show of every single one of the paintings that Aphrodite has done on stage. They have been rolling on a loop so it's almost as if she is up here on stage with us.

We finish out the song strong.

No one fucked up.

I watch Ares as he bows then the lights go off on the stage again. Curtains instantly pull closed and I basically slide off the stool onto the floor in a puddle.

I let out a heavy sigh, "We fucking did it."

Swiftly, I make my way off to the side stage, so they can break down our equipment and get it loaded back up. Lucy is waiting for us, giving each and every one of us a hug.

She pulls me in tight, "You all have about a half hour before your category is up. Get something to drink and get out there to sit with the girls."

I nod at her when Ares steps up beside me, "Lucy, hey. I don't want to jinx it or anything but if by some fucking miracle we win. I want you up there with us. Thanking everyone for us."

"The girls, the fans, the gods, you. Thank fucking everyone. Because even if we could talk, I think in that moment none of us will be able to say a fucking word."

She nods back at him, smiling widely, "It would be my honor."

We all make our way backstage and through the corridors. It is hard not to hear all the whispers as we are seen walking to our seats while they are announcing some other award.

I can feel the eyes on us.

I am not used to being on this side of things. Becoming one of the few out in the crowd.

I am used to being up there.

I follow Ares closely as he makes a hard left up an aisle. Immediately, I see Hope standing to hug me. I smile as I pull her close, giving her a kiss.

She leans in close to my ear, "You were fucking amazing babe. Seriously."

I smile as I wrap my hand around hers and take a seat next to her. All the girls, Daija included, are wearing the same long black silk dress. Each of them wears a mask that represents either their mates colors or in Lily's case, Aphrodite.

Hope eyes are shining brightly behind her hunter green mask. She squeezes my hand, putting her head on my shoulder.

Finally, I can fucking breath.

I don't feel like there is an anvil on my chest anymore.

We have already accomplished more than we ever dreamed fucking possible. If we walk away with an award, that is only going to fuel the fire we have already lit under our own asses. It will open doors for so many more opportunities. I can barely wrap my head around them all.

As soon as I finally get comfortable being around all these strangers, I see two new people walking out on the stage. The one guy I recognize from the Avengers movies. The girl seems vaguely familiar, maybe a pop singer.

I am not too sure.

She steps up to the microphone, holding an envelope. She smiles widely to the crowd, "This next award is for the Best Heavy Metal Album of the Year. The four bands that are nominated have risen to the top and have shown great vigor in their performance."

She turns and looks at Captain America beside her.

He nods his head at her, "That is right Mia. These four bands have proven time and time again that they are at the top of their game. The nominees are Spirit Box, Metallica, Carnal Decay and Bad Omens."

I feel Hope's hand tighten around mine when our name is said. I look at Ares, seeing him sitting staring directly in front of him. Probably not even breathing at this point.

I turn back to the stage and close my eyes.

I see the last decade of my life pass behind my eye lids.

The ups and the fucking downs.

There have been struggles right alongside the achievements. And they have all led us here. We are exactly where we need to be. Where we are meant to be. Even if we don't win, this is happening.

This is just the beginning.

I keep my eyes closed as the girl on the stage announces, "And the Best Metal Album of the Year goes to..."

There is a short pause before together they announce, "Carnal Decay."

I keep my eyes closed.

No fucking way.

This is not fucking happening.

I feel my arm being jerked around and I open my eyes to see Hope standing beside me, smiling as wide as her lips will allow. I stand in complete awe.

We fucking won.

Hope pulls me close and gives me a kiss before leaning back in her seat so I can walk past her. I am still in a fucking daze. Peach and Daija both reach out and hug me as I try to figure out how the fuck this is actually happening.

I go to step by Aphrodite, realizing she is not with Ares. I smile and shake my head at her, grabbing her hand and dragging her with me.

She is part of this band.

We would not be where we are without her. She smiles at me and follows beside me to the stage.

Ares turns and sees her. He smiles as he runs back to her, taking her hand and helping her up onto the stage. She is very obviously pregnant. I smile at Hades and Hestia before I turn and see Lucy close behind me. I grab her hand and walk up on stage with her.

Captain America hands the award to Ares.

I move over close to him, taking the envelope from the girl's hand. Grinning, I pull a trembling Hestia tight into my side with my arm wrapped around her shoulders.

She is shaking so hard you would think we were standing in a freezer. I squeeze her a bit tighter and she wraps her arm around my back.

Lucy steps up to the microphone, "Thank you everyone. We are blessed to be here tonight to be able to accept this award. On behalf of Ares, Hestia, Apollo, Dionysus, Hades and Aphrodite, I have a few people we would like to thank. First off, I have to thank myself."

She fans herself with her hand, making the crowd laugh, "As the manager of this crew. I have been with them from the very beginning and we are honored to be going down this road. We would like to thank the other nominees. Without you being on the top of your game, we would have never strode to be at the top of ours.

"To the fans, you are all insane, and we love and adore every single one of you. To Hope, Daija, and Peach. You are the world, not just to your mates but to all of us. You have completed our family, making us all whole again. We want to thank our families, for having the patience to put up with our shenanigans for as long as you have.

"And lastly we want to thank all you struggling garage bands out there. The ones playing their music too loud and obnoxiously. The ones that are getting the cops called on them for noise complaints. That was us. This could be you. Never give up. Continue to create, fight and prove yourselves. Maybe one day we can all be up here together. Thank you again!"

The crowd stands and starts clapping wildly again. We are turned and escorted off the stage by the two announcers. As soon as we are behind the wall, I am hugging Ares.

He pulls back smiling as I break character, "We fucking did it. I can't believe we fucking did it."

I pull back seeing everyone is basically crying and losing their fucking minds.

Captain America steps up to us, turning to Ares, "Congrats man. I love you guys."

Ares nods his head at him then turns back to me grinning, "An avenger is a fan. Of ours. What the fuck is happening right now?"

I laugh back at him, slapping him in the shoulder. Lucy makes sure to let us all know that we will all have our own rewards delivered in the next 30 days.

Which I am completely fine with, I have no desire to take this away from Ares. He is our frontman after all. Without his voice, his words, we would not be here right now.

We make our way back out to our seats. Shaking hands as we go. I don't even know who half of these people are but I don't care. I make it back to Hope and give her another long kiss before sitting down and finishing out the show with her hand in mine.

Two hours later, we are back in our hotel room. I smile at Hope as she slides out of her heels, massaging each foot before putting them down on the ground. I pull off my mask and then shirt.

I smile over at her, "I am going to take a shower. Wanna join me?"

Hope grins over her shoulder, "How could I possibly say no to a Billboard Music Award winner?"

I laugh at her as I step around her, smacking her ass hard as I pass by. I move into the bathroom, turning on the water to let it warm up before we step inside. Hope steps up behind me, kissing me on the shoulder.

Turning, I look down at her. Seeing her already completely undressed. She steps around me into the shower.

As she makes her way in, she points her face towards the water coming from the ceiling. I grin as I continue to take the rest of my clothes off then follow her under the water.

She reaches out with a wet rag, removing all the lingering body paint from my hands, face and neck. I watch her as she cleans me.

Her eyes come back to mine and I smile down at her, "I think you are my lucky charm. Ever since you have come into my life, everything that I have ever dreamed about is happening. I met and married my soul mate. The band is finally reaping the benefits of the fucking struggles we have put in. I couldn't be any happier than I am right now."

I see a shadow fall over her eyes but she smiles at me, "I am the lucky one. That I have been able to be a part of your life. Of this world. I never imagined that I would ever love somebody as much as I love you. It scares the hell out of me, but it's a good kind of scared I think."

I smile back at her as I lean in kissing her deeply. I hear her drop the rag and then her arms are up and around my neck. As if to unheard music our tongues dance together.

Hope pushes her slick body into mine, pulling a moan from my chest. But tonight, I don't want any paddles. I don't want any toys. I just want Hope.

My Hope.

I lift her up by the back of her thighs and step forward until the wall meets her back. She continues to kiss me ferociously until I slide into her. Then her mouth is open and she is leaning her head back against the stone behind her.

313

I slowly push in and out of her, taking my time. Making sure she understands with each and every thrust that I am hers.

There will never be another. We will be sharing a nursing home room.

I can never be without her.

I can hear her whimpering in front of me so I speed up just a bit. Just enough to make her fingernails dig into my shoulders as she holds on. I bring my lips back to hers now shoving myself into her harder than before.

When I feel her clench around me, I swear it looks like she is crying. I kiss her harder as I continue to slam into her. I feel my release sneaking up as well. And just a few moments later I am following her straight over the side of the cliff.

Free falling into the nothing.

I wake up to the sun coming in through the curtains. Smiling, I roll over reaching out for Hope but she's not there.

And the sheets are cold as well.

She has been up for a while.

I sit up, yawning loudly as I stretch my arms up over my head.

I glance towards the table in the middle of the room seeing an envelope propped up on it. I throw the blankets back and make my way to the note, seeing the name Matthew written on it.

I smile as I open the envelope and pull the note out.

"Matthew, first off I want you to know how much I love you. You are my everything. I want you to understand that fully. I want you to remember that as you continue to read this letter.

You have to understand. I was put in an impossible situation. I couldn't tell you what was really going on. Not with the show, not with the awards looming over you."

My heart starts to clench again as I continue to read her words, "I didn't think it would ever come to this. I didn't think I would ever be back in this position again. But I am.

I have left. By the time you read this, I will be halfway across the country. I am not leaving you. I am just taking a step back. I have to be honest with you, no matter how bad it hurts. And trust me baby, it fucking does.

The cancer has come back. I was checked by a doctor in London 3 weeks ago. There is a tumor on my right kidney. I was given the option of surgery to just remove the kidney or to try chemo and radiation treatments. I could not bring myself to lose another piece of me. This fucking disease has already taken away my ability to be a mother. I don't want to live the rest of my life knowing I only have one functioning fucking kidney as well.

I hate myself for keeping this from you. And I will call you soon. I just need to get settled in with my doctor. I need to get treatment started. And I can't do that if I am being a distraction to you. I need you to keep taking care of yourself. Keep taking care of our family.

And I know you are pissed at me right now but you have to understand, I already see myself as sick. I don't want you to see me through my own eyes. I don't want you worrying about every single breath I take. And I know that you will if you are with me. I just need you to know that I love you. And you have to let me get this going. As soon as treatments have started and I have some of my results coming back in, I will let you know when I will be able to come home.

But until then, just remember me happy and in your arms. That is where I will be imagining myself until all of this is finally over.

And if for some reason this all goes south. I will make sure you are aware. I wouldn't leave without saying goodbye. And the funny thing is, I am not scared of dying. Not really. I am only scared of what you will do if I am gone. But that is a bridge to cross on another day.

I love you Matthew. More than you will ever fucking understand. You are my Apollo. You are my god. I promise I will call as soon as I know more. Until then, I love you baby.

       -Always, Hope"

21
Hope
Only Love Can Hurt Like This - Paloma Faith slowed down version

Yet again, I am a coward.

I couldn't tell Matthew to his face.

I couldn't destroy him like that.

Though I know that it still destroyed him. My mother let me know that. Daija let me know that. Susie and Lily both let me know that. But I can't let him see me this weak.

Yeah, physically I am not that weak, yet. But I have felt it for weeks.

Fuck, months.

I am getting weaker each fucking minute of each fucking day. I can't let him watch me fade away.

From vomiting.

From fatigue.

From the inability to even eat.

I don't want him to look at me and see nothing but bruises because I barely grazed something.

I don't want him to see my face sunken in, my fingers looking like a skeletons. I don't want him to feel like he is afraid to touch me.

I can't handle that.

I would literally rather die than put him through that. And if that is selfish then so fucking be it. But I am not going to do that to him.

He can hate me if he wants to.

He can scream and yell.

Throw things and fuck even ignore me.

I deserve all of that and more. But one day, if the gods allow it, he will realize that I did this to shelter him from the chaos that is this disease.

I should have won my own award. I have been an Emmy deserving actress for the last few weeks. With the help of my mother, we were able to keep all of this under wraps.

Every single day, I was sleeping more. Walking less. Unable to do normal day to day things.

Mom even lied for me and told Matthew that she wanted to start going to the gym with me in the mornings. For some mother daughter time.

But every morning, I was laying asleep with my head in her lap as I draped across her bed. Thankfully, he had so much going on, he never really noticed how weak I was becoming.

A vibration rumbles through my bones as I feel my phone go off again.

I look away from the airplane window to the phone laying in my lap. It is him again. I refuse to block him, but I can't answer his call.

If I hear his voice, I will give in. I will let him know where I am going and what is going to happen.

Though it nearly kills me, I silence my phone and look back out the window. He has sent me dozens of texts, begging me to call him. Begging me to let him know where I am. I feel the tears roll down my cheeks as the captain announces we are about to land. I make sure my seatbelt is secure before looking back out the window.

Augusta is coming into view through the clouds. It has been literally years since I have been here. As the plane finally comes back down to earth, I turn my phone on again, ignoring the texts from Matthew to make sure that Diane and Tyler know that my plane is landing on schedule.

I am staying with Diane, Tyler has his own home in downtown Augusta. He offered me his spare bedroom. And even though it is closer to the hospital, I can't do that to Matthew.

He is already going to be worried about me because of my health. I don't want him to have anything else to stress over.

A half hour later, I am walking through the doors leading to the terminal. Diane rushes me as soon as I come into view. Smiling, I let her hold me.

She caresses my head, "Hope, baby girl. You are going to be fine. We are going to get through this together, me and you. Your mom said she should be here next week, granted everything goes to plan. But until she can get here, I will be your momma."

I hold her back tightly, remembering how much comfort she always provided. I breathe her in smiling at the hint of mint on her. She always did like her juleps.

Squeezing her back, "Thank you so much Diane. I really appreciate you letting me stay with you while I am going through treatment. I really didn't want to try to get through this from a hotel room."

Diane pulls back from me, leaving her hands on my shoulders so she can stare straight into my eyes, "My home has been open to you since you were 6 years old. You don't even need to ask. You could show up at 3 am with purple hair and tattoos for eyebrows and I would let you in."

I laugh as I turn to move around her to go to the return to get my luggage. When I look up, I see Tyler standing about 10 feet away. I feel my face fall as he looks at me with concern.

He opens his arms wide and I walk straight into his chest. Pressing my face into him as he wraps his arms around me tight. He lets out a held breath then sits his chin on the top of my head.

Neither of us even need to say a word.

The unspoken is loud enough for us to understand what this hug is about.

We make our way to the luggage return, Tyler grabbing my suitcase for me. He then reaches over and takes my carry on from me and slugs it over his shoulder as well.

Normally, I would complain but right now, I will take all the help I can get. I am just so tired. So weak.

All the time.

Diane holds my hand as we make our way towards the parking lot. She goes on and on about everything I have missed since I have been gone. Tyler's dad passed away a few years back. Mom had told me about it but I didn't know if it was appropriate for me to reach out to him or not. I will definitely apologize to Diane though.

The 45 minute drive to Diane's house seems like it takes 5 months. I had 2 missed calls and 3 texts in that short amount of time.

All from Matthew.

I just want to get the first week of sessions behind me. Then after my first scans, if it looks like it is working I will let him know where I am.

That I am safe.

That it is working.

I can't call him now without having some kind of answer. Good or bad. I have to have something to give him.

The landscape flies by as I watch the scenery go from trees and rural homes to overly expensive and luxurious houses. It seems like a lifetime ago that I was riding my bike down these side streets. Running from Daija. Running towards Tyler. I exhale looking at him up in the passenger seat.

I truly thought that we were going to be together forever. He was my teenage world. Everything I did revolved around him and his thoughts, his plans. He could have told me to jump off a cliff and I would have done it.

320

But after meeting Matthew, I have learned there is a hard line between infatuation and love.

Love is transcendent.

Love is raw and powerful.

Love is diligent and at times painful.

Love doesn't slip away like infatuation does. It digs its claws into your heart, refusing to ever let go.

Patriot's Park finally comes into view then I feel the car turning to the right. Everything is just like I remember. Some updates have been done to the park but for the most part, everything is the same as it was more than 10 years ago when I left.

I sit up, looking out the window at our old house as we pass by it. "A really nice family lives in your old house now. A young couple with a few small children. I see them at the store every now and again." I turn my eyes to the rearview mirror to see Diane watching me. I smile back at her as I lean back in the seat again.

Her house looks exactly like the last time I saw it. The memory of sitting under the weeping willow in the back yard asking Tyler why he didn't want to be with me anymore runs through my head.

I glance at him quickly before gathering my stuff from the seat beside me. The car comes to a halt in the driveway as I quickly grab the last of my things.

By the time I make it out of the car, Tyler has already retrieved my luggage out of the trunk. Diane moves back to help me out of the car but I swipe her hand away laughing, "I am not completely invalid. Not yet at least."

She shakes her head at me but still shuts the car door behind me after I climb out. She turns to walk towards the front door, pulling her house keys out of her purse, "I am putting you in the guest room on the first floor. I don't want you hurting

321

yourself on the stairs. And I know that once the treatments start they are going to be rough on you."

I continue to look at the ground in front of me, nodding my head. I feel a hand on my back and look to my right seeing Tyler smiling at me again.

I give him a soft smile back then turn back to Diane, "Thank you for that. That is very thoughtful of you. If it is anything like last time, it will be rough from the beginning to the very damn end."

Diane turns around just staring at me. I see a sadness fall over her eyes as she blinks heavily a few times then turns around to move up the steps and unlock the house for us.

Tyler shoulders my luggage as he leads me to my room. My phone is buzzing in my pocket again. He sits my suitcase and carry on down on the bench at the end of the bed before turning towards me, "You gonna answer that?"

I look from him to my luggage, shaking my head no.

He lets out a heavy sigh, bringing my gaze back towards him, "You can't just shut him out you know that right? He is your husband. He is worried. He is probably scared shitless right now."

I move towards the window, crossing my arms over my chest as I look out over the pond in the back yard.

I look over at the weeping willow before turning back around, "I don't want him to watch me waste away. And if this doesn't go how I hope it will. I don't want him to ruin his future just to spend a little bit of time with me."

Tyler shakes his head at me, "What kind of future would he be ruining? I am sure wherever he works, they would allow him time off to be with his wife. Especially with her going through radiotherapy."

I turn back towards the window, "He has too much to focus on right now. He needs to focus on his career. I can't be the reason that anything falls behind or gets pushed to the side. You don't understand. Things are really starting to happen for him. I can't let him put that on the back burner for me. He has worked too fucking hard to be where he is."

Tyler lets out another sigh as he nods at me, "Do you want me to help you unpack or anything? Do you want something to eat?"

Softly smiling back at him, "No. I am okay. I will unpack in a bit. I think I might just go sit in the living room and visit with your mom for a bit. Let her know what my therapy sessions look like for the week."

Tyler turns, sweeping his arm out for me to walk past him. I move slowly as he says, "I will be taking you to your sessions this week. Mom will be taking you the second week until Lucy gets here."

I turn around quickly, losing my balance. Tyler reaches out grabbing me just as I am about to fall. I am breathing heavily with my hands on his forearms as he helps me get steady.

Slowly, I bring my eyes up to his, "I don't want you to go out of your way. I don't want this to affect your life too."

Tyler smiles as I get my balance back and brace myself on the door frame as I step into the hallway. "Don't worry about me. I have plenty of time to spare. Especially for you. I am taking you and that is that."

I snicker back at him as I round into the living room. I move towards the couch getting comfortable. I kick my chucks off under the coffee table and pull my legs up under me.

Sluggishly, I pull the blanket off the back of the couch and cover myself up. Tyler sits on the other end of the couch just staring at me.

We continue to just stare at each other, not saying a word until Diane steps into the living room.

She smiles at us both, "I am going to start us some supper. Hope, I know your appetite is probably shit right now so I was thinking maybe like a corn chowder or something?"

323

I grin back at her, "That sounds wonderful Diane. Thank you so much."

She waves her hand back at me, shooing me again. I laugh at her as she rounds back down the hallway.

Tyler picks up the remote, "You mind if I watch some tv? I missed the awards last night."

I chuckle at the thought of him watching a re-run of a moment in time that I was there for.

I grin back at him, "Yeah, that's fine. I am just gonna rest for a bit."

He nods at me as he turns the tv on low. I feel my phone buzz in my pocket again. I close my eyes but pull my phone out anyway. I see the most recent text is from my mom.

She has already talked to Diane but she just wanted to check in on me as well. I smile as I respond to her, letting her know I am safe and okay.

I respond to Daija and Lily as well. My heart immediately goes heavy when I see that I have over 70 messages from Matthew. Cautiously, I let out a haggard breath as I open the messages.

My eyes scroll through pleadings, admissions of love, acceptance of fears. The last one just said, 'Please don't leave me baby'.

I close my eyes hard, feeling the tears rolling down my cheeks. I wish he could be here. And I know if I called him he would be as soon as he possibly could. But I have come too far now.

I have to stick to my plan.

I look up at Tyler as he points the remote at the tv then turns to me in confusion. I tilt my head towards him, "What?"

He points the remote towards the tv further and I look at the screen, feeling the blood drain from my face as he asks, "Why is your mom giving an acceptance speech for Carnal Decay?"

I feel the lump form instantly in my throat. None of us even thought to make her wear a mask. She is the fucking manager.

She is trusted implicitly.

I turn back towards Tyler, lowering my gaze, "I told you she was a music manager."

Tyler sits up further, "Yeah, but not for fucking Carnal Decay! Have you met them?"

I laugh at him, fan girling over the band. I nod my head back at him, "Yes. I have met them."

He shakes his head back at me, smiling wide, "Lucky bitch."

I laugh louder as I throw one of the couch pillows at him. He laughs back as he tucks it under his arm and goes back to watching the awards from the night before.

I smile as I turn towards the screen, my heart clenching tighter seeing Apollo on stage with his arm wrapped around Hestia.

They are all just beaming from ear to ear.

My mother continues her speech, "To Hope, Daija, and Peach. You are the world, not just to your mates but to all of us. You have completed our family, making us all whole again."

I watch Tyler as he pauses the show again, turning to me with his jaw hanging low. He paused it right when the cameras panned out to the crowd. Showing me, Daija and Susie sitting in our seats, waiting for them to come down off stage.

I know he knows it is me. I shake my head at him, "I didn't expect you to find out. At all, let alone this way."

He throws the remote on the couch between us, "She said mate. Is Matthew someone in the band?"

I let out another heavy breath, "If I tell you, you have to swear that you won't tell a soul. You have to promise me. A dying woman. That you will never speak a word of it to anyone."

325

He throws his hands up in front of him, "That is a bit much but yes. I promise. And your not fucking dying. I don't want to hear you say that again."

I shake my head at him, my gaze turning back towards the screen, "Apollo. Apollo is Matthew. Daija is dating Hestia."

Tyler grabs the remote quickly, unpausing the screen. It pans back to the stage as mom finishes her speech. He pauses it again before standing and running towards the tv.

He points his finger at Apollo, "This is Matthew? The guy I met at the bar?"

I laugh at him, "Yes. That is Matthew."

He moves back to the couch, plopping back down on the end before turning back towards me with a smile, "I get it now. Why you didn't want him here for this. Why you didn't want him pushing shit aside. I am sure their lives are fucking hectic right now after winning last night."

I nod my head back at him, "Yeah, mom said they have photoshoots and interviews lined up for the next few weeks. Someone even said they might be on the cover of Rolling Stone soon."

Tyler laughs again, "This is fucking wild. Good on you, Hope. I am glad you found your other half. You seem like you really love him."

I nod at him before looking back at the tv, tears rolling down my cheeks as I look at him standing on stage, "I do. I love him with every breath I have."

The next morning I dress in comfortable and loose clothing, knowing that today is the first day of treatments. I have already done my consultation and the records were sent to my primary oncologist. His team was working all last week to nail down a game plan on my treatment.

I roll my head across the headrest of the seat, looking out the window and letting out a heavy sigh.

326

I feel Tyler's hand cover mine and I smile as I roll my head to look at him, "Thank you. For doing this. For being here with me."

He continues to look straight ahead but a smile covers his face, "Hope, no matter our past. We were friends first. We will be friends until we are old and gray. There is nowhere else I would rather be than right here, helping you through this."

I smile at him again as I roll my head to look out the window. I feel my phone vibrating in my pocket and I close my eyes tightly.

I know it is Matthew.

I don't even have to check the phone. He has been calling or texting every hour on the hour. I don't think he is sleeping much at all. I release another heavy sigh as we pull into the hospital parking garage.

The first few days of treatment aren't as bad as my brain imagined they were going to be. Though I am still getting weaker and weaker by the day.

But by the time day 3 rolls around, I can't even keep water down. I can feel my muscles constricting like they are being pushed to their max with just me walking from my bed to the hallway.

Luckily I won't lose my hair but I am getting a nice little radioactive burn on my back and abdomen. It is like a localized sunburn times a thousand.

The doctor prescribed me some cream for it and some pain meds as well. But I don't want those.

I will use the ointment but I want to be lucid for this. And I know being on those pain pills I won't be in full control of myself.

Or my actions.

I would give in and call Matthew. I would beg for him to come to me. I only have to make it 6 more days until Monday when they do my first scan.

I can make a real decision then.

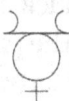

"I will have my first scan today. I know it is really soon but the doctor said that halfway through is the perfect time to do it. He said that if it is starting to shrink at all then that is a good sign. But he also warned me there might not be a change at all. I am just keeping my fingers crossed. I am hoping that the tumor is at least getting a bit smaller. If it is and I only have another week or two of treatments then I will call Matthew. I miss him so much mom. I have been dreaming of him every single night." Rivers are running from my eyes at just the mention of his name. Even just thinking about him sends me into hysterics.

I feel like a junkie that is trying to quit cold turkey. I never imagined it would be this empty without him.

Everything, my heart, my thoughts, I am just lost without him.

I hear my mom sigh on the other end of the phone, "Well, let me know as soon as possible. I am going to fly out in the morning regardless. But if he is coming with me I need to get another ticket. I haven't told him anymore than you have asked so he doesn't even know that you have a scan this week.

"He is just a shell of a man right now, Hope. He has been distant. Not eating. Smoking like a chimney. I am pretty sure I have seen him high more often than not. I think that is the only thing keeping him sane right now. You are going to have to reach out to him soon, either way. Good or bad. He is in pain, baby."

The tears fall a bit harder at her words.

I nod as I look out the window.

I take a deep shuddered breath, "Okay. I will. Today. Either way. I love you mom. It should only take a few hours and I will call you back."

Mom wishes me good luck and love before hanging up the phone. Tyler pulls us into the parking garage before turning the car off. He looks at me concerned, "You wanna call him?"

I shake my head at him, "No. I am going to text him then turn my phone off. Or maybe give it to you or something. If I call him right now, I will miss my appointment."

Tyler nods at me before pointing at my phone, "Get to it then." He steps out of the car to give me some privacy. I see him walk around and lean on the back passenger door.

I look back at my phone, nervously pulling up Matthew. I see a teardrop fall on the phone screen, "I love you baby. I miss you so much. I am getting my first scan today. I will call you later, no matter the outcome. Don't get mad if I don't reply right away, I am walking into the hospital now. I really hope you don't hate me right now."

I send the text quickly before I can delete it. Immediately, I turn my phone off and slide it into my purse. Pulling the visor down, I look at myself in the mirror. I have dark circles under my eyes and my cheeks look so sunken in.

I haven't really been able to eat for the last 6 days.

I let out a heavy sigh before I reach up and pull the handle to open the door. Tyler is there instantly. He opens the door then takes both my hands in his to help me out. I try to pull myself up but I am just so fucking weak.

Between the treatments and the vomiting, I feel like I have lost 20 lbs of pure muscle.

I know I look like I always thought I did. And that pisses me off more than I thought it would.

I let out a sigh and shake my head out of frustration. Tyler leans into the car, wrapping his arm around my waist and helping me to my feet that way. He shuts the door quickly before wrapping his arm back around me and leading me towards the hospital doors.

It only takes about 20 minutes for them to do the scan but I swear the doctor is taking his sweet fucking time reading them. I have been nervously spinning my wedding rings around my fingers waiting for him to come back in. When the door finally opens, I am too afraid to look up.

Tyler quickly stands beside me, putting his hand on my back. He rubs small circles on my spine, "How is it looking doc?"

The doctor sits my file down on the counter then sits down on his rolling stool.

He rolls it towards me, demanding my eyes on him, "Hope. The treatments look to be working. We are seeing a substantial difference in the size of the tumor."

I feel all the air rush out of my chest as tears start to stream down my face. Tyler grabs my hand, kissing the backs of my fingers. I look to him to see him crying as well.

I smile widely then look back towards the doctor, "Really?"

The doctor nods his head, "Yes. Now, the treatments you have already received will continue to keep working for quite some time, but I still want to push through and finish another 6 sessions.

"So maybe another week, to a week and a half. After that we will do another scan. If the changes continue to go well, then no more radiotherapy. We will just do scans every few weeks to monitor the continuing effects.

"From there if things continue to go well, I would say we are out of the woods. You are reacting much better than anticipated to the treatments. I would say right now it looks to only be about a 3% shrink but any at all is a good sign.

"So I want to see you back here first thing tomorrow morning. Try to get some food in you. But continue to ask for help if you need it. We can even get you a wheelchair if it will help with transport if needed."

I shake my head back at him, "No. No wheel chair. I can do this. Thank you so much Doctor McGraw. You have been amazing."

He smiles as he rubs a hand on my leg, "We have beat this once before Hope, we will beat it again. Are you needing any more pain pills?"

I shake my head back at him, "No. I am okay. I think I will be much better now."

Doctor McGraw narrows his eyes at me, "This next week of treatments is going to continue to be hard on you, Hope. You are already extremely weakened. I am going to give you another script anyways. And you are going to take a wheelchair with you. Just in case." I moan at him, but accept that he is probably right.

He looks to Tyler, "Just pull up to the side entrance. I will have a nurse meet you with a chair for you to take home."

He turns back to me smiling with a wink, "No one will even miss it."

I laugh as he grabs my file and stands to leave the room. He leaves the door open as I turn to look at Tyler. He grins widely back at me before kissing me on top of the head. He turns around grabbing my purse then reaches in and grabs my phone. I smile as he throws it to me, "Call your mother. Right fucking now."

I laugh at him as I take the phone and pull her up in my phone. It barely even rings once before she is answering, "Hope? How....How did it go?"

I let out a strangled cry and I can hear her breathe shudder on the other end of the line, "Momma. It's working.

Doctor McGraw says another week of treatments and then scans every few weeks to make sure it continues to shrink. But it sounds like, I mean he made it sound like I am going to be okay."

My mother starts weeping loudly on the other end of the phone. I smile at Tyler, both of us crying as well, "Mom? Are you there?"

I don't hear anything for a long moment.

Just when I am beginning to think she lost signal or hung up when I hear a deep voice come through, "Hope?"

My voice catches in my throat.

Matthew.

Matthew is with her right now.

I start weeping, loudly. I can hear him almost frantic on the other end of the phone, "Baby? Hope is that you? Please baby fucking say something?"

I try to talk through shuddered cries, "Ma...Matthew?"

I hear a relieved sigh from his end of the phone. Then my phone is beeping, letting me know he is trying to turn it into a video call. I look up at Tyler and he smiles as he steps out of the room to give me some privacy.

I hit accept and there he is. Right on the other side of the screen. I smile widely, knowing I look like complete shit. His eyes are wide, like he is still in shock that it is me, "Baby?"

I nod my head back at him, "Hi."

I see him look over beside him at something before turning back towards the screen, "Baby, tell me what is happening. Lucy can't stop crying. What happened? Was it the scan?"

I nod back at him, smiling, "The...the treatment is working. The doctor said....he thinks I am going to be okay. He said I am responding better than expected to the treatments."

I watch him on the phone and the room starts to spin around him. The next thing I know I see that he is on the ground, on his knees.

332

I start crying harder, "Will you come here? Will you and mom come here? Please?"

He nods his head quickly, "Yes. I will fucking run there if I have too. Where are you baby?"

I let out another heavy sigh. I know he will move heaven and earth to get to me.

I smile softly at the phone, "Augusta. I am staying at an old family friend's house. Diane."

He nods his head at me again before looking to the side, "Your mom is already grabbing my suitcase baby."

His eyes come back to me, tears still rolling down his cheeks, "I love you Hope. I will be there as soon as I can, baby."

I nod my head back at him, "I love you too Matthew."

22
Apollo
Missing Limbs - Sleep Token

It has been 9 days and 13 hours since I last spoke to her.

Since I told her good night and that I loved her. If I would have known what I was going to wake up to that next morning, I would have held her all night long.

But I didn't.

I just rolled over and fell asleep.

I was lost in a daze after reading her letter. I ran to Lucy's room immediately, but she wouldn't tell me where she went. No matter what kind of threat I threw out there. So I spent the next 48 hours texting and calling as much as humanly possible.

I knew she was talking to everyone but me. It pissed me right the fuck off.

Until I talked to Daija.

Until she explained to me what the treatment was doing to Hope. What she is physically going through. When Daija told me that Hope couldn't let me see her like that, I understood.

That is when I closed off, from everyone.

Everyone except Hope.

I still sent dozens of texts a day.

As many calls as I could possibly make.

I didn't even know if she was listening to them. So I just sat in my room, first in Vegas, then New York. We have been doing interviews, photo shoots, meetings with producers. But my head has not been here.

Not at all.

Thankfully Gideon made sure that Lucy would fill in whatever gaps I was leaving. Letting her know that I would be fine with whatever decision she made for me. Only because I was not capable of making my own decisions at all.

Mona and Daija were the ones forcing me to eat. Edge was making sure I wasn't too high to function. Gideon made sure to keep alcohol away from me.

But I just wanted to lay in bed.

I wanted to be left alone.

I could barely sleep, afraid that I would miss a text or a call from her.

I hear a knock on my hotel door but I don't even bother to answer it. A few moments later, the knocking is louder, then I hear Lucy through the door, "Open the fucking door Matthew. We need to talk."

Frantically, I throw the blankets back and grab some pants. I practically run to the door. She must have talked to Hope.

I fling the door open and Lucy is standing before me, visibly worried. She gives me a fake smile as she walks past me into the room.

Shutting the door, I turn towards her as I shove my hands into my jeans pockets. She turns around as she lets out a heavy sigh and sits down in the chair across from the bed.

I nervously step towards her, sitting on the end of the bed, "What is it? What has happened?"

She looks at me then her phone before sitting it down on the table, "I talked to Hope a little over an hour ago."

I nod my head at her, pulling my hands from my pockets and rubbing my sweaty palms on my jeans, "Is she okay? What did she say?"

335

She shakes her head at me, then leans it back against the chair, "I wasn't going to come here until I heard back from her. But it just didn't feel right. Not letting you know what is going on. Has she sent you anything today?"

Nearly jumping out of my skin, I run around to the night stand. My phone had died last night because I forgot to charge it while I was looking through photos of her on my reels.

I turn it on, seeing a text message from her pop up. I click on it quickly, this is the first time in over a week that she has reached out to me.

I open the message and read it quickly.

Then read it again, "I love you baby. I miss you so much. I am getting my first scan today. I will call you later, no matter the outcome. Don't get mad if I don't reply right away, I am walking into the hospital now. I really hope you don't hate me right now."

I feel my breathing getting heavier. I look up at Lucy, "Have you heard from her since she sent this? How did the scan go?"

She shakes her head at me before meeting my eyes, "She hasn't called back to let me know. I wasn't going to come in here until I had some kind of news for you. But I didn't know if you were freaking out too. I figured if you were then we could just freak out together."

I stand, re reading the text again before sliding my phone in my pocket. I ball my fists up, shoving them into my jeans as well, "How long do we think it will be before she calls back?"

Lucy shrugs her shoulders, "I have no idea. I wouldn't think it would take them too long. Unless it isn't good news."

I nod back at her then reach up and wipe the tears from my face. Nervously, I move towards the table and grab my cigarettes and lighter. As soon as I pull one from the pack, Lucy's phone rings.

I immediately drop them on the table and watch her as she pulls the phone to her ear, "Hope? How....How did it go?"

Her eyes immediately come up to meet my own. I have no idea what is being said but rivers immediately start pouring from Lucy's eyes.

I watch her try to stand but her legs are failing underneath her. I move quickly, grabbing her under her arms to make her sit back down.

She is utterly weeping.

She takes the phone from her ear and hands it to me.

I am looking at the phone like it is a bomb with a countdown ticking away.

I take a solid breath before bringing the phone to my ear, "Hope?"

I immediately hear crying on the other end of the phone.

It is her.

I would know that raspy whisper anywhere.

My heart clenches in my chest. I feel like I want to pass out or maybe vomit, possibly both, "Baby? Hope is that you? Please baby fucking say something?"

She is still crying but then I hear her voice cracking. Like she can't believe it is really me on the other end of the line, "Ma...Matthew?"

Hearing her voice sends me spinning.

My heart screams at me and I have to see her.

She has to prove to me that it is really her.

That my head isn't playing tricks on me.

I immediately hit the button, turning the phone call into a video call. I watch the screen as it connects and Hope is there on the screen.

She looks so fucking tired. She has dark circles under her eyes. She smiles widely and it looks like her skin is pulling so tight like it is going to crack. She has lost so much weight. It has only been 9 days.

I continue to stare at her, "Baby?"

She grins wider, still crying uncontrollably, "Hi."

I let out a laugh, feeling the tears rolling down my face. I look over at Lucy in the chair. She is sitting with her hands in prayer with her forehead pressed to her fists.

I turn back to the screen, "Baby, tell me what is happening. Lucy can't stop crying. What happened? Was it the scan?"

She continues to smile, reaching up with a very bony hand to wipe away her tears, "The...the treatment is working. The doctor said....he thinks I am going to be okay. He said I am responding better than expected to the treatments."

I immediately feel my legs give out from underneath me. I have never been so scared one second then completely relieved the next. I land on the floor hard, still gripping the phone in my hand. I didn't think it was possible but now I am crying even harder.

I look at the screen as she stops smiling, almost looking worried, "Will you come here? Will you and mom come here? Please?"

Relief floods through me.

I watch Lucy as she jumps up and starts grabbing all of my shit, throwing it into my suitcase. Like she was just waiting for the words to fall from Hope's mouth.

I nod my head back at the camera, "Yes. I will fucking run there if I have too. Where are you baby?"

Her eyes drop to the floor in front of her, her voice going low as well. She seems hesitant for a minute before looking back at me, giving me a soft smile, "Augusta. I am staying at an old family friend's house. Diane."

I smile widely back at her. I know where she is. Nothing will be stopping me now. "Your mom is already grabbing my suitcase baby. I love you Hope. I will be there as soon as I can, baby."

Hope nods back at me, "I love you too Matthew." I smile widely at her. Just hearing those words coming from her mouth, I feel like I have been blessed by the goddess herself. But I can't bring myself to end the call. Hope must sense it because she blows me a kiss then the screen goes dark.

I stand, turning back towards Lucy, "When can we leave?"

She turns back towards me, looking wildly around the room, "I have a flight leaving first thing in the morning. I can get you a seat as well."

Shaking my head back at her, "No. Not soon enough. Call now, get it moved up. Rent a fucking private jet if you have to. I will be holding my wife. Tonight."

Lucy laughs at me then rips her phone from my hand. She points towards my suitcase, "Pack your shit. I am going to go tell Daija. Be ready."

I nod my head back at her as I watch her leave the room. As soon as the door shuts behind her, I am back on my knees.

I put my face in my hands as I sob uncontrollably. She is going to be okay.

My Hope.

She is going to be alright.

I pull my face back then look to the ceiling. I don't know who is listening but I thank them all the same. Slowly, I get back to my feet and grab a shirt from the mound of shit Lucy has piled onto my suitcase. As soon as it is over my head, I hear a knock at the door.

Jesus fuck that was fast.

I laugh as I run to the door and swing it open. But instead of Lucy, I see Gideon and Simone standing outside my door. I look from her face to Gideon's.

He steps around her, "Are you okay? Have you been crying?"

I look past him, at Simone, "What the fuck is she doing here?"

Gideon looks over his shoulder at her then back towards me, "Can we come in?"

I let out a sigh, "Yeah but make it quick. I am about to leave."

They both step inside as I go back towards my suitcase, shoving everything in as best I can. I move around the room grabbing my wallet and chargers. I look back towards Gideon, "Talk."

Simone steps up, looking around the room then back towards me, "Where is Hope?"

I stop in my tracks, turning a fiery glare at her, "Don't say her fucking name. You fucking hear me?"

Gideon steps up between us with his hands out in defense, "She doesn't know. Don't just attack her. No one has told her anything."

Simone looks between the two of us, "Told me what? What is going on?"

I look at Gideon with a hard stare before turning around to my suitcase. I take deep breaths as I hear him explain the situation to Simone. I hear a noise and turn around to see actual concern on her face.

She turns her face towards mine, a tear running down her cheek, "I am so fucking sorry Matthew. I didn't know."

I nod at her as I grab some socks and shoes. I slide them on, "What the fuck is going on? I am about to catch a flight."

Gideon's head whips towards mine, "You talked to her? How is she?"

Smiling, I stand and turn towards him, "The treatments are working. They think she is going to be okay. I am going to Augusta today. I will be with her through the rest of this and through her recovery."

I feel my eyes get heavy thinking about what she looked like on the other end of the phone.

340

Gideon steps up, "Yeah, I get it. As soon as we get the all clear we will all come down. You just get to her. I am sure she needs you."

I nod at him as I look over towards Simone, "Why is she here?"

I turn my glare to Simone as she steps forward, "I came back to apologize. And to ask if I could come back."

I laugh loudly.

Pointing between the two of them, "Are you fucking kidding me right now? Simone, you left us. Not even with a fucking goodbye."

She nods as she looks at the carpet at my feet, "I know. And I am sorry. I just didn't want to see you two together. I thought it would be too hard."

I snicker at her, "But now that everything is going good for the band you want to come back."

Her eyes come up to mine, proving to me that I am right. She is only here because she saw the awards.

I shake my head at her, "No. No. Gideon, if you let her back in then I am out. She is fucking toxic. I won't allow her near me or Hope. Ever again."

Simone flinches like she has been slapped.

Did she honestly think that we were just going to welcome her back with open arms?

Gideon nods his head at me then turns towards Simone, "Majority rules. Me, Mona and Matthew all agree that you can't come back. No reason to even ask Edge. You have already been replaced anyways. Micah is part of us now. I am not just going to kick him out. Fuck, who knows how long you would even stick around anyways."

Simone flinches hard at his words before she starts to crumble in front of us. The sad part is I only half believe it.

She shakes her head at Gideon, "But I have been here. From the beginning. I was one of you."

341

Gideon shakes his head, "And now you're not. I am sorry Simone but we can't. And remember you signed a fucking NDA. You speak a word about us to anyone and I will sue your ass so fast your grandkids will owe me money."

She looks at me and I just smile widely at her, "I told you that you were a disease."

She nods her head as she wipes a stray tear from her face, "Understood." I smile at Gideon then turn to finish packing. I feel a hand on my shoulder and I turn around to Gideon pulling me into a hug.

He slaps my back hard, "Call me as soon as you know more. We want to see her. As soon as we can. It won't be long and Lily won't be able to fly anymore. And tell her that we love her and miss her too."

I nod my head at him, pulling back slowly, "Of course. As soon as I get a read on the situation, I will let you know."

Gideon nods back at me and I continue to gather my stuff until I get the text from Lucy stating that we are leaving in an hour. Sometime within the next 5 hours I will be back with Hope.

Where I belong.

To say that I am upset to find out that Hope has been allowing Tyler fucking Weaver to help her but not me is an understatement. Lucy is currently staring me down, but I am just trying to count to 10 so I don't explode on her.

She pats my hand, "The only reason he has been helping is because Diane is his mom. Also, he and Hope have known each other for years. He saw her go through all of this before. She was trying to protect you from seeing her that way."

I roll my eyes at her, "I am a grown ass man. I can handle seeing people sick."

She nods back at me, "I get that. And I am sure she gets that too. I think it is because she loves you so much she didn't want to see you hurting, knowing there would be nothing you could do to help fix the situation. This really wasn't a selfish decision on her part. She was trying to ensure that you wouldn't be upset."

I can't argue with her on that.

Rolling my eyes, I look back out the window, "I know but I should have been with her from the beginning of this. I wish she wouldn't have shut me out."

Lucy reaches back out, grabbing my hand again, "She didn't shut you out. She protected you during an extremely important moment in your life. She didn't want the focus on her. She wanted you to be able to focus on you. You have all worked your asses off to get to where you are."

I continue looking out the window as I nod my head in agreement. Even if I am hurt by her decision, I can't be mad at her over it. And I won't make her feel like shit over it either.

Do I still hate that Tyler has been there for her this whole time?

Yes.

But a part of me is smiling because she cared enough to not let me see her like this but she didn't think of him that way. He has literally just been a friend, a body to help her.

I turn my head back towards Lucy, "So what can I expect when we get there? I don't want to seem surprised by anything."

Lucy lets out a heavy sigh, buckling her seatbelt as the captain announces our approach on Augusta.

She turns to me with sympathetic eyes, which worries the hell out of me, "She hasn't really been able to keep much food down. The treatment has made her very weak and very nauseous.

343

"Luckily though, because it is radiotherapy it has been focused on her kidney by itself. So she has not lost her hair. But she is probably going to be pretty sore and tender around the site of the therapy.

"Also, Diane told me that they sent her home with a wheelchair today but she is stubborn and doesn't want to use it. Though Diane has said she definitely needs it. She is so weak she can barely hold herself up. Also, don't worry if you see a ton of bruises on her. That is normal as well."

I stare at her, completely mortified.

That is the moment that I truly notice the effect all of this has had on Lucy. She looks like she hasn't slept in awhile. There are dark circles under her eyes. And when she speaks to me, I can see deep groves around her mouth and chin. Lines that were not there just a week ago.

I feel my breathing picking up again as I try to keep my cool but this is a fucking lot. The tears are welling up again but I push them to the back of my mind. It is time for me to be strong enough for the both of us now.

Fuck for all 3 of us.

They need me.

And I refuse to fail them.

Not gonna lie, this town is beautiful. Lucy booked us a rental car so once we got it we were on our way. I can easily see why Hope thought that the street fair was so exciting. That is the kind of atmosphere she was raised in obviously.

We don't have towns like this in the UK. Sure we have the history but the atmosphere here is unlike anything I have experienced before. Apparently southern hospitality isn't just something they say.

The house we pull up to looks like an old farm plantation house. But obviously newer. I release a heavy sigh, trying to relieve the tension in my shoulders.

344

Hope is in this house.

She is just a few hundred feet away from me right now. Lucy turns the car off and looks at me, "Are you ready for this?"

I shake my head at her, "I am scared shitless honestly."

She grabs my hand giving it another squeeze, "We will get through this together. As a family. You are one of us now. I am always here if you need me."

I smile gratefully back at her before climbing out of the car. You can smell winter in the air. So much so, I wonder if it is going to snow soon. But apparently, the seasons here are just as bipolar as it is back home so who the hell actually knows what it is going to do.

I grab our luggage out of the boot and turn to walk towards the porch. Diane and Tyler are both standing on the top step with a smile on their faces.

I really hate him.

But I am also indebted to him, for taking care of Hope while she was trying to take care of me. I follow Lucy up the steps then sit down the suitcases on the porch.

Immediately, I reach a hand out to Tyler. He looks at it then back up to me as he takes my hand and shakes it, "Welcome Matthew. Hope is so fucking happy that you are both are here. She is lying down right now but told me to tell you to wake her up when you got here."

I nod my head back at him, "How is she?"

He gives me a sympathetic smile before looking over at Lucy, "She has been getting weaker each day but overall her spirits are still very high. She is, of course, refusing to use the wheel chair. She is also refusing to take any pain meds. She is still a stubborn asshole like she has always been."

Lucy smiles as she steps up to Tyler and hugs him tightly.

I grin as I turn back towards who I am assuming is Diane, "Hello. My name is Matthew. Thank you so much for allowing Hope to recover here. I owe you so much for this."

Diane shakes her head at me as she pulls me in for a hug as well, "We all love her. She's family. I wasn't going to let her go through this alone, no matter how badly she wanted to."

I hug her back gently. Understanding all too well what her words mean. Hope has kept me in the dark for weeks now. Months even.

Diane turns back towards the house, "Lucy, you know where your room is. Matthew, follow me. I will take you to Hope. She has instructed me that you are to sleep with her and if you try to take over the couch I am supposed to threaten you with fire."

I laugh loudly at her, "Yeah, that sounds like Hope."

As I follow Diane through the house, I really take in just how beautiful it is here. But not so beautiful that it doesn't feel lived in. There is no plastic on the furniture. Yeah everything is clean and tidy but I have yet to see anything that doesn't look like it is strictly for viewing purposes only. This is the kind of home anyone would be grateful to grow up in.

Diane takes me down a hallway until we get to the end.

She stops in front of the door before turning towards me, "In total she has only lost about 12 pounds. But she was so tiny before that she just looks really sickly now. Which she is, but I just wanted to prepare you. And she still has 6 more sessions to go so she is more than likely going to lose more before it is all said and done."

I nod back at her as she turns and opens the door. As I step into the room, I instantly notice that she has the curtains pulled open wide.

There are some weeping willows and a large pond in the back yard.

I smile at Diane as I sit my luggage down, "Thank you Diane. Truly."

She smiles and puts her hand on my shoulder before looking back towards the small lump in the bed. She gives me another apathetic smile as she turns and shuts the door behind her.

I move slowly around the bed, watching Hope as she comes into view from under the covers. She has her hair pulled back in a loose pony tail and she is completely still. If I didn't know any better I would say she is dead.

The skin on her face is pulled tightly over her cheekbones. I let out a shuddered breath looking at her small broken body laying before me. I quietly slide my shoes off then lay down next to her as softly as I can. She doesn't even budge.

I take my fingers and run them down the side of her face to her cheek before cupping it, "Hope?"

I watch her eyes as they flutter but stay shut.

Her mouth starts to form into a smile though, "Please tell me this isn't a dream. Please tell me you are really here."

I smile back down at her, a tear rolling down my cheek, "I am here baby."

I lean forward and give her extremely chapped lips a kiss. Her mouth forms into a smile against mine.

I pull back looking back down at her, "I am here now. Everything will be okay. And when you are better, I am kicking your ass."

Hope lets out a little giggle followed by a small snort. I smile back down at her, at the woman I feel in love with.

Even as she is laying here literally fighting for her life, she is laughing.

Her spirit, her soul is so fucking strong.

I have underestimated her at every single turn, but never again. She opens her eyes and looks up towards me, "I have missed you so much Matthew. I hope you don't hate me. For what I did."

I shake my head at her while running my hand up and down her thin arm, "No baby. I am not mad. I understand why you did what you did. But now it is my turn to worry about you. I don't want to talk about anything else besides you getting better."

Hope reaches out her small fragile hand, "Will you hold me? Please?"

I smile at her, "Forever baby. I will never let you go." I gently wrap my arms around her, feeling her melt into my chest. Her hand wraps around my side then starts sliding up and down my back. With a heavy sigh, I release all the tension I have been holding within myself.

I feel her shudder against my chest and I pull back to look down at her, "Baby, are you okay? Am I hurting you?"

She moves her hand under my shirt and she then pinches my side, hard. I laugh and squirm a bit from the tickling.

She laughs at me, "I am just happy that you are here. And if you start treating me like a porcelain doll I am going to murder you in your sleep. I am weak. I am not broken."

I continue to stare down at the top of her head, holding my breath. Slowly, she lifts her head and opens those beautiful hazel eyes to look at me. I feel the tears rolling down my face again.

Her hand comes up and wipes a tear away, "I am sorry Matthew. I was scared. I didn't want you to skip out on the band. They needed you too. You have all worked so hard for all of this. I didn't want you to walk away from it. And we both know you would have. I couldn't let you do that."

I nod back at her, scooting down on the bed so we are eye level with each other, "I get it baby. I was lost. I was pissed. But I get it. And I am not mad at you. I don't hate you. So please stop thinking that I do."

She smiles and nods her head back at me again before closing her eyes, "I am just so fucking tired. I want to see my mom but I don't think I can keep my eyes open."

Leaning forward, I place my forehead against hers. I hear the bedroom door open and I smile at her, "I think she just walked in. I will give you some time with her."

She smiles at me, "Don't go far. Please."

I give her another kiss before lightly rolling off the side of the bed. Standing to my feet, I turn to see Lucy walking in, eyeing the small figure covered up in bed. I smile towards her, "She is awake, barely. She wants to see you."

Lucy nods her head at me as she wipes more tears from her face. I move to step past her, "I am going to step outside and call Gideon. Give you two some privacy. I won't be far, I promise."

Lucy nods at me as she grips my forearm tight. I watch her as she moves to where I was just lying. She crawls up on the bed and pulls Hope close to her chest. Cradling her and rocking back and forth like Hope is still a child. But to her she is. She will always be.

I slip my shoes back on and step out into the hallway. I can hear people talking down back towards the front of the house. Instead of following the noise, I turn and go down a long hallway.

Taking a left, I realize I am at the back door. I open it and step out onto the back porch. Before me is a huge yard, full of trees and slowly dying flowers. Beyond that is the pond and willows I was able to see from the bedroom window.

It is so peaceful here. I get why she had the curtains pushed wide open. I look back towards the house, seeing the room she is lying in. Slowly, I turn back towards the pond and start weeping again.

Out of fear.

Out of anger.

Out of frustration.

I feel myself growl into the air around me, holding back the scream I want to let out into the world.

349

My blood has started to run cold in my veins. I knew she was going to be weak. I knew she was going to look bad but she is just a weak and tired soul trying to wear her smile like it is armor. I sit down on my ass hard, knees bent just staring at the pond in front of me.

Finally, I pull out my phone and hit Gideon's number. He answers after just a couple rings, "Hey Matthew. How is she?"

I let out a heavy sigh as I feel more tears slipping down my face, "She...she isn't great. But she will be. It is just going to take some time."

He lets out a heavy sigh, "I was afraid of that. Was she awake at all? Does she even know you are there?"

I laugh as I look over my shoulder back towards the house before turning back towards the pond, "She woke up when I got here. She is still a hellcat if that is what you are wondering. She is just...she is just so fucking weak. They said she has only lost about 12 pounds but I swear she looks like. She looks like what she told me she always saw when she looked in the mirror.

"I am sure I could count her ribs right now. Her cheeks are all sunken in. I feel like she has lost half of her muscle mass. They have a wheelchair for her, for fucks sake. I just. I knew it was going to be bad. I knew it was going to be hard. But this is just fucking tragic seeing her like this."

Gideon lets out a long breath, "That is why she didn't tell you. She knew what was coming. She didn't want you to watch her slipping away. But we have to focus on the fact that she is going to be better soon. She has what like another week or two of treatments? Then it is full recovery mode. She will get better. This is just a small hurdle to get past."

I nod into the open air around me, "I know. It is just rough seeing her like this. I think if you guys want to see her, sooner is better than later. She is only going to get weaker the longer this week goes.

"She has 6 more treatments then we can start working on her getting better. Getting her home. I think for right now I am just going to focus on getting some food in her. She hasn't been able to keep anything down since last Wednesday."

I hear an intake of breath, "Jesus. That is crazy. Like she hasn't tried or she just can't keep anything down?"

I stand and dust my jeans off, before turning back towards the house, "I think at first she just couldn't keep anything down. But now, I think she just isn't even trying because she knows it will make her sick. Also she is refusing to take any pain pills so I am sure that is not helping."

I start walking back towards the house slowly, "I talked to my mom on the way here. She told me to try like peppermint tea or lemon water. That is supposed to help with nausea. I am just going to try to help her keep as much down as she can.

"I am also going to carry her around like a rag doll. She is so frail but I think maybe getting her outside into the sun might help too. In short bursts of course. It is getting cold as hell here."

Gideon lets out a chuckle, "I am sure. It's the south. I will call Lucy here in a bit. Try to get a place for us that is close by. We are going to head back to London next week. Finish getting the house ready for the baby. But Lily will murder me if I don't bring her to see Hope first. I think Daija already said her and Mona have tickets set for a few days from now."

I stop at the bottom of the porch steps, looking up at the door, "Yeah. That sounds good. Just try to warn everyone so they aren't shocked when they see her. She is literally skin and bones. I don't want her to be any more self conscious than I know she is already going to be."

Gideon quickly agrees with me, "Yeah, that's not a problem. Also, I thought you would get a kick out of this, but Micah is subletting our apartment. So he will be in London as well when you get back. He is actually pretty excited for the move. But we can talk more about it when we get there. I will text you with the travel plans as soon as they are nailed down."

I thank him again for everything before hanging up my phone and sliding it into my pocket. Looking back up on the back steps, I see Tyler standing inside the back door watching me. I let out another sigh as I start to make my way up the steps.

Tyler walks out the door, crossing his arms over his chest, "How are you holding up?"

I give him a small smile as I reach the top step, stuffing my hands in my pockets, "Still scared as hell but grateful to be here with her now."

He nods at me before looking out over the pond, "I am grateful you are here too. Now maybe she will stop talking about you incessantly."

I laugh as I stand tall and turn towards him, "She talked about me?"

He grins as he nods towards me, "She talked about nothing but you. And also, before you freak out, I may have learned about your little secret. Not because she told me but because I guessed. I watched the awards the day she got here. She is a horrible liar by the way. I could read her like a book."

I laugh out loud again, "Yeah, not her strongest quality. That is probably why she ran from me as fast as she could."

Tyler turns towards me fully, "She ran because she loves you. You are literally her world. You are her air. She ran because she knows she is the same to you. She couldn't handle seeing you hurting because she is hurting."

I stand wide eyed staring at the man before me. Maybe I do like him after all.

I nod my head back at him, "Thank you for that. I really do appreciate it. And I truly appreciate you helping her this week. I guess you're not such a bad guy after all."

He laughs as he pats me on the shoulder and we turn towards the house, "I just want to see her happy and healthy. I think she can only be both of those things with you. So I am handing off the baby sitting torch. It is your turn. You and Lucy can take her to her appointments from here on out. You need to hear the truth from the doctors as much as she needed to hear it."

I follow Tyler in through the back door and slowly make my way back towards our bedroom. He stops at the open door smiling inside, "Look at that, someone is awake and sitting up like a big girl."

Grinning, I round the corner and see her leaning against the headboard, smiling and flipping Tyler off. Her eyes connect with mine and I see them starting to tear up again.

I smile as I move past Tyler and back towards the bed. Lucy on one side, me on the other we smile back at her.

Lucy gives me a small smile before patting the bed, "I am going to go help Diane get some dinner started. Is there anything you think you might be able to eat, baby?"

I turn and watch Hope as she scrunches up her face, "Not really no. But I will try something. I promise."

Lucy gives her another soft smile before standing and moving across the room. Her and Tyler both give us a soft smile before disappearing behind the closing door.

I turn back to Hope, just smiling that I am here. That she is here. That we are back together, where we are supposed to be. She gives me a small smile back and I decide it is the perfect time to give her the gift I have been holding onto.

I stand and move to my suitcase quickly. I glance back at her, watching her trying to see over the end of the bed to see what I am doing.

I stand back up smiling with the antique necklace in my hand, "I bought this for you the day that you ran away from me. I have held onto it all this time just waiting for the right time to surprise you with it. I think now is that time."

Her confused eyes go wide with recognition when she sees the antique styled necklace dangle from my fingertips. She

353

smiles softly at me, tearing up just a bit, "Is that from the street fair?"

I nod at her as I walk back to her and sit down softly beside her. Her eyes watch my face as I reach behind her neck and clasp it onto her, "Yes. I bought this when you and Mona went to have your talk. I knew how much you loved it. Even then I knew how much I loved you. I just wanted to do something to make you smile."

I let my stare linger on her welling eyes. Lightly, I run my thumb over her cheek, "I thought I was losing you baby. I was so fucking scared. I still am. I can't live without you. I can't even breathe thinking about it. I feel like I have an anvil on my chest."

The tears roll out of her eyes and down her boney cheeks. She shakes her head at me, "I never meant to scare you. I just didn't want you to throw away your future."

I raise her chin gently back up, bringing her eyes to me, "You are my future, Hope. You are the only future that matters to me. I love you baby."

Hope lifts up her arms slightly and I lean myself forward and wrap my arms around her. Holding her as tight as I feel is safe. I hold her until I hear her breathing finally going back to normal.

Pulling back slightly, "Let's go get something to eat. Yeah?"

Hope nods her head back at me before allowing me to pick her up and carry her through the house and to the dining room.

We all sat around the dinner table, telling stories new and old. Hope doesn't say much but that is okay. She is here. She is alive. She is getting better. And that is all that really fucking matters, isn't it?

PRAY TO ME - DeathbyRomy, Palaye Royale

"I love you Matthew but I swear to baby Jesus in the manger I will end you if you don't stop shoving potatoes in my face."

I stare him down so he can see the daggers getting thrown his way. There may be a smile on my face, but I am deadly fucking serious right now.

He just smiles back at me, raising a spoon full of mashed potatoes. He starts to push it towards me and I smack the spoon on the bottom, sending potatoes flying into a sickening splat into the center of his forehead.

I hear roaring laughter behind me as my mother tries to hold her shit together. I smile at him as well as he takes his fingers and drags them across his forehead before smacking the glob of potatoes back onto the plate in front of him.

I grin widely at him, "You were warned sir."

The spoon falls on the plate making a clanging noise as I watch him pick up a napkin and wipe his forehead clean.

He looks back at me with a half grin, "I am just trying to make sure you get something in you. You have barely eaten anything all day. At least let me make you some more peppermint tea."

I roll my eyes at him again before letting out a huff, "Babe. I know you are just trying to help. And I love you for it. I really, really do but you have to stop. You have made me so much peppermint tea I feel like I am going to piss a candy cane."

He sits his hand down in front of him, obviously defeated.

I reach over and take his hand in mine, "I love you. I love that you are helping me. I love that you are here. But you have to slow down.

"Rome wasn't built in a day. This is going to take some time. Just because I only have a few treatments left, that doesn't mean that I am back to full meal capacity by any means."

He nods his head at me, "Yeah, I know you are right. I just worry. I just want you to feel better. Apparently, I am more impatient than I thought."

I grin back at him softly again, rubbing my hand over his, "We got this. We are good. We just have to baby step it."

He places his hand over mine when we hear the doorbell ring. I look over my shoulder and watch my mom leave the dining room to head to the front door.

Just a few moments later I hear whispers, and a lot of them. I try not to cry as I see my friends round the corner into the dining room.

Gideon and Lily lead the way. Lily looks like she has gained 20 lbs in the last 2 weeks. Smiling, I turn in my seat and try to stand to move towards her.

But my arms wobble under the weight of me trying to pull myself up. Matthew is to me within a second. I let out a frustrated sigh as I let him help me stand.

He leaves his arm out so once I am standing I can use it to balance myself and move towards them. I huff as I look up at him but he just grins down at me like he is just happy I am allowing him to help in some capacity.

I still refuse to use the fucking wheelchair though.

I watch my feet as I slowly make my way the few steps to Lily. I look up into her face as I get close enough to hug her and she is balling her eyes out, looking me up and down.

I give a half smile, "Have you been watching Tide commercials again?"

She laughs loudly around her tears as she gently wraps her arms around me and pulls me close to her swollen belly for a hug. I hold her back as tightly as I can before slowly pulling back and putting my hands on her belly.

Smiling widely from her then to Gideon, "How is my little niece or nephew doing?"

Lily lets out another laugh as she sits down in the chair my mother was just in, "They are heavy is what they are. I swear, this child feels like the size of the titanic floating around in here."

I laugh as I turn to see Susie, Edge, Daija, Mona and Micah all standing in the doorway watching me like I am going to keel over at any moment.

My eyes lock on Daija and I watch a tear roll down her cheek. I motion my hand at her and she comes running to me wrapping me in a hug only we would understand. Her hands rest on my forearms as she puts her forehead to mine and starts wiggling her head back and forth.

I laugh at her, "You haven't given me a twins united hug since we were kids."

She smiles as she pulls her forehead away from mine, "It has been too long. I thought maybe some twin telepathy could help the healing process for you."

I bring my small hand up and put it on her cheek, to which she instantly leans into and closes her eyes while smiling.

I grin back at her, "I love you sis."

Her eyes open, sparkling with tears, "I love you too Hope."

Mona steps up beside her, "How are you feeling? Is today a good day for us to visit? We can totally come back another day if not."

Slowly, I turn towards her, feeling still a bit off center.

Daija puts an arm out for me to balance on, "Thank you Dai. No, Mona I am good. Matthew has been force feeding me baby food for 3 days now. I only have 3 more treatments then

357

this friggin nausea should start going away within a few weeks hopefully."

Mona nods her head at me then looks over at Matthew with an empathetic look in her eyes. I look between the two of them before looking back towards the doorway to see Susie obviously struggling to hold her emotions back. I give her a soft smile as I turn to move towards her next.

As soon as I feel myself try to take a step, I quickly realize I don't know that I will be able to.

My legs try to give out on me and before I know what is happening Matthew is behind me with his hands on my waist and Gideon has reached out to grab my forearms.

I feel Matthew put his head to the back of mine, "Will you please just sit down and let them come to you?"

I shake my head at him forcefully.

I am adamant about this.

I will walk to my friends.

I will show them that I am stronger than I look.

Matthew heaves out another sigh as I start to take small steps forward. It is obvious to me though that Susie is not going to just stand there and wait for me.

She rushes me, wrapping her arms around my waist. I can feel her crying into my shoulder so I bring my hands up and start to stroke the back of her head.

I feel tears in my own eyes again, "It's okay, Peach. I am gonna be okay. It is just going to take some time is all. But I promise I will be fine." I feel her nod her head into my shoulder but I can feel just how torn up she is by all of this.

I look past her to see Edge and Micah both standing awkwardly in the doorway, obviously not knowing what to do with themselves.

I feel Susie letting go of me and starting to pull back and I look towards Matthew, "Will you help me into the living room? Then we can all just sit and visit."

Matthew nods his head back at me before putting an arm out for me to grab ahold of. I smile back at him, "You win this round. I will let you carry me."

He grins widely back at me, "Thank fuck for that, it would have taken a month to get in there otherwise."

He wraps his arms around me and picks me up bridal style before carrying me into the living room. He settles me into the far end of the couch so I can watch everybody filtering in.

Everybody except Micah takes a seat somewhere near me. I look up to see him hovering in the door, seeming like he is not comfortable.

I smile at him, "Hey Micah. I have a favor. When you guys get to Nags will you make sure my board stays coated? I don't want it to rot from not being used."

He smiles at me, visibly loosening up, "Yeah, I would be happy to. But you will be back out there with me before you know it. This time I will show you up though."

I laugh at him, nodding my head as I watch him move closer to us, finally settling in with the group. I continue to watch him out of the corner of my eye though. Making sure that he stays in the conversation, where he belongs.

It has been 3 days since everyone left to scatter off to their own little corners of the world. Lily has only about 6 or 7 weeks left before she gives birth and I am NOT missing it.

I don't care what I have to do but I will be in London to greet my little niece or nephew. Secretly, though we all know I am pulling for a girl.

As I lay here on this cold table just waiting for them to tell me it is time to roll over, I think about everything that has lead to this moment. Now just one last little laser beam shot to the back and I will be done.

I hate this part of the treatment.

It doesn't really hurt, just irritates the skin a bit.

No, the only reason I hate it the most is because I am alone. Just me in an empty room with strangers on the other side of a glass partition.

I have gotten so used to Matthew being with me every single moment that I now miss him more in the few minutes we are apart than I did for the 9 days I went MIA.

I hear the deep voice of the wizard behind the curtain tell me to roll over onto my stomach. I slowly make my way to my other side but smile because I know this is it.

This is the last flip.

The last 2 weeks have felt like 2 years.

Finally, the lights come on and I can let out the breath I feel like I have been holding for months. Now the real work begins. I can start to maybe keep some god damn food down. I can get back to walking, eventually running. I have to get my strength back because I refuse to miss out on the birth.

I refuse to not have our ceremony.

I refuse to not live life to the fullest.

The nurse meets me with a wheel chair and for once I accept it. But only because Matthew isn't here.

I am still too stubborn to use it at his advice.

She helps me into the chair then starts to wheel me out the door and down to the doctors office for him to tell me how my scan has turned out.

I know that I am going to be sitting here twiddling my thumbs for at least a half an hour but I don't care. I don't want him to tell me over the phone. I want to see his lips moving when he tells me I can go home, finally.

The nurse opens the door to his office area and Matthew is instantly on his feet. He looks worried as he sees me coming through the door in a wheelchair.

But when it stops and I slowly rise up out of the chair on my own he starts to smile at me, "How are you? How was it? How are you feeling?"

I smile as I put my hands in his, "Calm down man. I am good. It is over. That was it. I am finally done. Thank God!"

As I let out a heavy sigh, he wraps his arms around me. I let my hands linger on his back a bit before squeezing him back with everything that I have.

He hasn't really held me since the night of the awards. Which I understand why, I am not thinking too deep into it. But I hope he will see me as I get stronger. Not just keep seeing me weak like I am now.

I finally pull back and point my face up to his, "Kiss me. I need some celebratory smooches."

He grins widely back down at me before kissing me just like I asked. Though he pulls away too quickly for my liking. We get settled into the two open chairs in the room as Matthew grabs a magazine from the table beside him.

I lean my head into his shoulder and listen to him going on and on about a new Masterworks set he is thinking about getting from Pearl. I gently slide my pendant back and forth on its chain as I listen to his ramblings.

A sort of peace, calm falls over me.

Like whatever the outcome, this part of it all is over.

I smile into the room just listening to him go on and on about what kind of setup he is looking for. He places his cheek on top of my head, "We need to get you your own set as well."

Pulling back gently, I look up at him, "We don't have to do that. This needs to be about you."

He shakes his head back down at me, "No, this is about us. We are going to have a big enough jam space that we can both

361

play together. I don't care if we have to add onto the house or sell it and find something bigger. It is happening."

I smile and go to reply but then the door swings open and Dr. McGraw comes walking in with a wide smile on his face.

I am instantly relieved.

I have been to him so many times over the years I feel like I have a pretty good read on him. But from the look on Matthew's face he isn't nearly as sure as I am.

Dr. McGraw sits down and spins on his little stool as he scoots up closer to me. He reaches out and takes my hands before looking up into my eyes again, "So, by the looks of things, the treatments are definitely heading in the right direction. It has shrunk another 5% to 6%. I think it is safe to say you are going to be in the clear very soon. Maybe even within a month or so."

I shake my head at him in disbelief.

How could it be shrinking so fast?

I assumed it would take the treatments months to get that kind of effect.

He smiles back at me, "I know, you are reacting a lot better than I could have ever hoped for. Here let me show you both on the scans."

He turns and grabs the folder containing my life in it. I feel Matthews hand as it gently squeezes my knee. I look over at him and he is staring down the doctor like he is about to get the worst news of his life. I put my hand on top of his watching his eyes nervously dart from me to the doctor.

Dr. McGraw turns around, opening the folder and pointing, "Here are your scans that were done almost a month ago. The start of the tumor was almost 7 cm. Close enough that we rounded up actually."

I watch Matthews face when I see a tear roll down it. I know this is hard on him. Actually seeing what was going on inside of me. I reach my hand up and wipe the tear away as his eyes come to mine.

I give him a small nod before turning back to the folder as Dr. McGraw turns the page to show us the next scan. The tumor is smaller in this next photo. Even Matthew leans in looking at it like his eyes are playing tricks on him.

Smiling wider as I look at the scans, he wasn't lying.

It is definitely shrinking.

I gaze up in the doctor's face and I see nothing but pure relief and happiness in his expression.

He points back down to the scan, "As you can probably see here, this is what I meant. It is noticeably smaller than it was. Way smaller than we had originally anticipated.

"It was like something in your body this time just accepted the treatment. I was really hoping that we would not have to have more intense treatments like before and it seems I was right to hope for that."

I wrap my fingers Matthews as we mirror smiles at each other, "It's going to be gone soon."

He nods his head at me as he leans in and gives me another kiss. I kiss him back with as much passion as I can muster up in the moment.

Reluctantly pulling away, I look back at the doctor and smile, "So what is next? What do I need to do?"

He shuts the folder and lays it on the examination table before turning back to us, "Nothing. You are going to do nothing but get stronger. Get better. No more scans for at least 2 weeks. No more treatments ever. You hear me. Ever. I love you, Hope, but I never want to see you in this office again."

I smile widely back at him as I try to push myself up to my feet. Matthew gives me his arm to balance on and I lean forward, wrapping my arms around Dr. McGraw, "Thank you so much. You have made this whole experience bearable somehow. I will forever be indebted to you."

Dr. McGraw pulls back from our hug shaking his head at me, "Just live Hope. Live and be happy and healthy. That is the only way I want you to pay back this debt to me. Just live."

I pull back away from him while crying, wiping the snot from my face. Matthew hands me a tissue then leans forward to shake the doctor's hand.

In what seems like a last minute decision though, Matthew pulls him in close and hugs him as well.

I can hear him whispering to the doctor, "Thank you. She is my everything. Thank you."

I put my hand on the small of his back as he turns back to me, wrapping an arm around me.

I finally feel like it is going to be okay.

I am going to be okay.

The sun is shining through the window onto the woman laying next to me in bed. It took about 2 weeks before she started to get her color back.

Another week for her to be able to walk stabally on her own. Then yet another week before she was back to eating normally.

Reaching out, I push a strand of hair behind her ear and I see her smile up at me, eyes still closed, "Good Morning baby."

I smile back down at her, "Good Morning. How did you sleep, love?"

I run my fingers down her back as she rolls towards me smiling, "I had a dream about you."

"Really? What was it about?" I continue to run my fingers up and down her side as she starts to creep in closer to me.

She opens her eyes smiling widely back at me, "I feel like I should show you instead of tell you."

I feel her hand as it starts to run up and down my dick. My eyes fly wide as I look back at her.

I shake my head firmly at her, "Baby, I love you but no. I don't want to hurt you. I think it would be too soon."

She slowly pulls her hand back and her face falls a bit. I see the expression that comes over her face as she nods her head then rolls to her other side putting her back to me.

As I reach out to touch her she sits up, throwing the blankets back. She slowly walks around the front of the bed then makes her way to the bathroom, not even giving me a second glance.

I look up at the ceiling. Not really knowing what to do with this situation.

Of course I fucking want her.

But I don't want to hurt her.

I don't want it to be too soon. But now I am worried that I have hurt her in an entirely different way. I don't want her to think I don't need her. That I don't feel the desire to lay her down bare and just annihilate her.

I sit up on the edge of the bed, leaning forward while resting my elbows on my knees. When the bathroom door opens back up, I watch her as she walks past me not saying a word and moves deeper into the house. I let out another long breath as I stand to go use the bathroom myself.

Looking into my reflection in the mirror, I can see the worry etched into the lines on my face.

I am scared.

I know she knows her own body.

I know she knows what she can and can't handle but I don't want to rush into the physical part of our relationship. I want us to both be ready and I am just not.

Even if she is, I am not.

I step out of the bathroom and she is on the far side of the bed again digging through the dresser.

She turns towards me, eyes wide and frantic, "Get dressed, we have to go!"

I move towards her, "Why? What has happened?"

She smiles as she pulls some jeans up over her legs, "Lily is having the baby. We have to go to the hospital like now!"

I smile widely back at her as I run to her side of the room and grab some clothes for myself, "Like is she having the baby right now?"

She grabs her hair wrapping it up in a rubber band from her wrist, "Apparently yeah. Susie has called me a dozen times. I had my phone charging in the living room last night."

I nod back at her as I hop around putting socks on, "Okay let me get my shoes on and we will go."

She runs past me grabbing her shoes and sliding them on as well. She looks around the room like she is lost and looking for something.

I reach out for her but she pulls away from me, refusing to meet my eyes, "Don't. Let's just go. Please."

I let my heart and my hand fall, "Yeah. Okay."

We rush into the hospital arriving no more than a half hour later. Hope doesn't say one word to me the entire drive.

Instead she just looks out the window, staring at the neighborhood as we fly through it.

Edge, Micah, Mona, Daija and Lucy are already sitting in the waiting room. I watch Hope as she runs by me and straight to her mother.

Marching towards Edge and Micah, I lower my head as I shrug off towards them.

I look over my shoulder one last time before turning back to Edge, "What do we know?"

Edge looks me up and down, "She should be pushing the kid out any time. What's wrong with you?"

I bring my eyes to his, "What do you mean? Nothing's wrong with me."

Micah turns to me, crossing his arms over his chest, "Dude. I just got here and I can tell something is up."

I roll my eyes at him, "Shut up, nothing is wrong."

I look at Edge and see him looking over my shoulder towards Hope. It takes every single fiber of my strength not to follow his eyes and stare at her myself. I stuff my hands into my pockets as I look down at the floor.

Edge clears his throat a bit, "So, how is Hope doing? Now that you guys are home."

I nod my head towards the floor before looking up towards the empty hallway leading to the delivery room, "She is doing better. A bit stronger each day actually. She has started doing light cardio in the mornings as well. Trying to get her stamina back."

Micah sits down in the chair beside him, "And how are you doing? Now with you both being back home? You falling back into the old routine?"

I glance at him quickly before turning back towards the hallway, "Yeah. I mean I am practicing as much as I can. I am still keeping a pretty close eye on her but all in all I think I am falling back in place."

Edge moves just enough to draw my attention back to him, "Why are you watching her so close? I thought the cancer was shrinking, like alot."

I nod my head back at him, finally getting the nerves to steal a glance at her before turning back towards him, "Yeah it is. Her scan this week showed another 10% of it was gone. I just...I didn't see it coming last time either. I just kinda feel like I have to keep watch 24/7. I don't want either of us to get blindsided again."

Micah shifts around in his seat as he looks past me towards Hope, "Aren't the doctors confident that it is all going to be gone though? Gideon told me something about it."

I nod again, "Yeah they are. I guess...I guess I am just scared it will come back is all."

368

Edge sits down next to Micah, "So then why are you so distant from her? This isn't how you were the last time I saw you two."

I shake my head as I let out a frustrated sigh, "Can you just fucking drop it? Just stop fucking hounding me about it okay? We are fucking good, just let it die alright?"

I can feel the anger rolling down my spine out of nowhere.

I don't know why I am getting so pissed at him.

He is just concerned about us.

I watch as his hands fly up defensively in front of him. Then something catches my attention out of the corner of my eye.

Gideon comes walking down the hall, grinning from ear to ear. Everyone jumps up and runs closer to us as he looks around the room, "7 lbs 6 oz 19 inches long. We just got to meet our daughter, Nicole Susanna Taylor."

Every little minute piece of anger instantly melts away from me. I grin proudly at my best friend standing in front of me, now a father.

I am the first to make it to him, hugging him tight, "Congratulations man. How is Lily? Is she doing okay?"

Gideon pulls back getting hugs and slaps on the arm from everyone, "Lily is doing fine. She pushed through like a pro. Though I think the meds helped the most."

He smiles as he turns towards Edge, nodding to him as well, "Peach is fine too. She held her own in there. She is very excited to be an aunt right now."

I look over at Edge seeing the relief fall over his face as he grins back to Gideon.

I instantly feel like an asshole.

I didn't even think about what Susie must be going through right now. Their own child not making it. And not

369

getting pregnant yet. I should have read the room before I started bitching about my own shit.

I look to my left as I see Hope and Mona step up, "When can we see her?"

Gideon smiles back as he reaches down and hugs Hope, "Soon. As soon as they are done with Lily she said we can start letting people in."

Hope smiles back at him before wiping a tear from her face. Then it hits me again. Just how big of an asshole I truly am.

Just because she can't have children doesn't mean that she isn't upset that this will never be her. I watch the tears as they roll down her cheeks and I know they are happy tears but a small part of me wonders if some of those tears are out of sadness as well.

I reach out for her but she glances at me quickly before turning back to her sister and hugging her. I slowly let my hand fall as I turn back towards Micah. He wraps a hand around my shoulder as we step back towards the chairs and sit down.

I stare at the floor in front of me when I hear Micah as he leans in closer to me, "What is going on with you and Hope? Obviously it is something."

I let out a defeated breath as I look up at her back quickly before turning to face Micah, "She wanted to have sex this morning and I told her no."

Micah chuckles just a bit, instantly pissing me off. He shakes his head at me, "How long has it been?"

I stare past him at the wall, "Almost 2 months. The night of the awards actually."

His eyes go wide, "Why? Why did you say no?"

I roll my eyes at the situation, before crossing my feet out in front of me and laying my head back into the chair, "Because look at her. She is still so fragile. I don't want to hurt her. I couldn't live with myself if I did."

I can feel his eyes boring into the side of my head. I turn to see him shaking his head at me before looking back up at Hope.

I turn my eyes following his stare when he says, "Did you ever stop to think that saying no to her maybe made her feel like you are not attracted to her anymore? That maybe you are seeing her the way she has always seen herself and that you are disgusted by her?"

I shake my head towards her before turning back to Micah, "That's not it at all. I still want her. I have been walking around half hard for a month now. It has to be obvious that I still want her."

Micah brings his eyes back to mine, "Have you told her that? In those words? That you still find her attractive? That you still want her?"

The realization of what I haven't said hits me hard in the chest.

I haven't told her those things.

What if she does think that I see her like she always saw herself?

There are a million thoughts running through my head at once when Gideon steps back out into the hall, "Hope, Matthew, Edge? She is cool with you three first."

I stand up as I watch Hope rush past me and down the hall. I smile into the floor as I turn and walk side by side with Gideon. I continue to pat him on the back as we turn and make our way into the room after the others.

I look up in time to see a smiling Peach handing the baby over to Hope. She is smiling down into her face, running her fingertip along her brow and down her cheek.

She smiles widely as she lightly bounces the baby and looks towards Lily, "She is beautiful you guys. Absolutely perfect."

I stand watching her and realize she is not as broken as I think she is.

She is not weak.

She is recovering.

She is stronger than I will ever be and it's about fucking time that I show her how I feel. I am not going to let her think that I don't love her, I don't want her.

3 hours later we are walking back into the house. Hope hasn't said 5 words to me all day.

That ends now.

I follow close behind her as she makes her way towards the kitchen. She opens the refrigerator and pulls out a bottle of water, opening it and drinking it half down.

I lean my hip against the counter just staring at her and smiling. Her eyes meet mine as she gives me a forced smile and starts to screw the cap back on the water bottle. She goes to step around me and I move to block her path.

She looks up at me, almost in a pissed tone, "Excuse you."

I smile as I bring a hand up, cupping the side of her neck, "Excuse you what?"

Her eyes come back to mine and a small hint of a smile falls on her lips, "Excuse you sir. Get the fuck out of my way."

I smile at her as I jerk her chin towards me.

Not forcefully but enough to make her eyes go wide. I lean down into her and kiss her passionately.

I feel her arms as she tries to sit the water bottle down on the counter missing it by a good 3 inches. I laugh into her lips when I hear the bottle hitting the floor.

I continue to kiss her harder as I turn her with her back towards the counter. Pulling back just enough to whisper into her mouth, "I hope you know that this morning, I was a fucking idiot."

I feel her lips go into a smile as well and then her fingers are dancing across my lower back before gripping my shirt tight.

She kisses me back fiercely as I push my hard dick into her abdomen. She leans her head back just enough to let out a soft moan.

Swiftly moving my lips to her ear, "I have been wanting to fuck you for weeks. You are so fucking sexy walking around this house half naked every god damn day. You have been teasing me haven't you?"

I hear her breathing becoming more labored as I pull back and look down into her hooded eyes, "I haven't meant too. I just thought you didn't want me anymore. Or yet, maybe."

I shake my head back at her, "I want you just as much as I always have. Actually more. Because now...now we have seen each other at our worst. And we survived. Together."

She grins up at me as I start to pull her shirt up over her head. I feel her hands at my jeans as I throw her shirt behind her towards the kitchen table.

I move my hands to her jeans as my lips crash into hers. We are both moving like inexperienced teenagers but I don't care.

I am prepared to show her exactly what she does to me.

As gently as I fucking can that is.

I tug on the sides of her jeans, lowering them and her underwear at the same time. I notice the small patch of healing skin on her abdomen but don't allow my eyes to linger there.

Instead, I let her step out of her pants then look back up to watch her unhook her bra and throw it behind me.

I stand up in front of her then pick her up behind her thighs. I walk us over to the kitchen table, scooting chairs to the side before sitting her down on the edge.

I stare at her lips as I take off my own jeans and shirt. Her eyes roam my body like she has never seen me naked before.

I step up close to her again, "Tell me if this is too much. Okay?"

Her eyes come back to mine and she nods her head. I shake mine back at her, "Fucking use your words baby."

She smiles back up at me as her hands slide down my hips, "Yes sir."

I growl at her as I crash my lips into hers then wrap my arm around her to pull her closer to me. I use my other hand and line myself up with her. I push into her slowly so as not to hurt her but before I can even get fully inside she is already moving her hips towards me.

I smile as I nibble on her bottom lip then watch her as her chest arches towards the ceiling. I look down watching her slam herself into me.

I start to move my hips in unison with her as she lays back flat on the table. I grip her hips a bit tighter as I lift her ass off the table and start to push myself into her faster.

I watch her as she bites her lip then digs her fingernails into my forearm.

I stop fully seated inside of her, "I love you baby."

Her eyes come down and meet mine, "I love you too."

I lean over her, bracing my hands on the table on either side of her hips as I start to push into her harder. I watch her go from wanting, to needing, to panting.

I feel her hands cover mine as she starts to quiver around me. I lift her up then sit down in the dining room chair behind me.

She smiles as she sits on top of me, sliding up and down my cock. I lean my head back as I put my hands on her hips, helping her slam into me.

374

I hear her panting getting heavier and I look up to see her watching where we are joined. I look down with her then pull her lips to mine.

Hope starts to move her hips frantically. I can feel her about to fall apart around me. I pull my lips back just enough to grunt out, "Fuck me baby. Fuck me harder."

She lets out a moan loudly into the room as she starts slamming herself onto me. When I feel her start to pulsate, I hold her hips tight as I slam myself up into her repeatedly. We both scream our release at the same time.

I feel her pussy clamp down on my dick and I am instantly transported to heaven. "Hope, fuck yeah. Ride me baby."

I feel her hands tighten around the back of my neck as she thrusts me into her deeper until I feel her start to break around me again.

She starts crying while smiling towards the ceiling. I sit and watch her as she finally starts to come down from her high.

She brings her eyes back down to meet mine, "I told you I was fine."

I nod back at her, smiling as well, "I will never doubt you again. I have been in a frenzy for you for weeks now. I was just afraid that I wasn't going to hold back, that I was going to hurt you somehow."

She leans down and gives me a soft kiss before pulling back smiling, "If you ever think about withholding this dick from me ever again, I swear to god I will make your life a living breathing hell."

I laugh as I watch the shift in her eyes go from loving to feral.

At that moment, I know that this was all worth it.

The pain, the struggle.

It was all leading up to this moment.

We have finally accepted each other fully.

375

She leans down and kisses me roughly again before I stand and move us back towards the bedroom.

And that is where we stay for the next 48 hours, happily entwined in each other.

A Sneak Peek
Of
The next installment

Perfectly Misaligned

I
Hestia
The Subway - Chappell Roan

She is so fucking beautiful. I can't believe she actually likes me. I mean, I guess I get it. I am a catch but laying here watching her staring back at me with those crystal clear blue eyes it just kinda hits me.

She actually really likes me.

Not just for the sex.

Not just for what I can give her.

She doesn't know about the band so that can't be it either.

Daija has laid in this bed with me for two days now. We have only broken apart from each other just enough to eat. Other than that we have been completely entangled in each other. Talking about everything and nothing all at the same time.

I lightly reach out and start running my finger up and down her forearm, "I hate that I have to leave so soon."

Daija smiles as she narrows her eyes at me devilishly, "Then don't. Stay here with me, wrapped up in this bed. We can just roll ourselves up like a double decker taco and never leave."

I laugh loudly at her as I shake my head, "Some of us work for a living, baby. I have to go back to work. I would have a lot of people pissed off at me if I didn't."

Daija rolls her eyes at me before scooting a few inches closer to me, "What is that you possibly do that is so earth shattering that you can't just take some time for yourself? Are you out solving world hunger or global warming?"

I giggle back at her as I wrap my arms around her, pulling my chest to hers, "No. Nothing like that. But I do have commitments to meet. I can't just walk away from the guys. What we do is important. Just not on a world domination level."

Daija gives me a soft nod, "Yeah okay. But when will I be able to see you again? I hate that I just found you and I feel like I am losing you already."

I smile back down at her, "Well, you have me for another night. I don't have to leave until tomorrow morning. Then I have an appointment on Friday that I can't miss. After that I should be free again for another week. Maybe we can meet up somewhere. Like a halfway point between where you are and where I am. Are you staying in New York?"

She rolls onto her back, letting my hand fall to her bare abdomen, "No. I am going to Georgia. A couple of friends of mine that I grew up with are getting married so I am going down for their wedding. I would just say fuck it and stalk you but I cannot bring myself to miss out on a lesbian wedding in the center of the fucking bible belt. Nothing says drama like a liberal function in the conservative backwoods of red neck country."

I laugh loudly at her before rolling onto my stomach and propping myself up on my fist, "What day is the wedding? Maybe we can meet up after. I don't want to pull you away from your shenanigans. But also, I am going to need pictures. Actually, video...video is better."

Daija turns her head back to me smiling wider, "The wedding is Saturday. So maybe Sunday or Monday? We can just play it by ear. I don't want to get in the way of your work. Whatever the fuck it is."

I lean over, giving her a light kiss with a smile. I feel her hand as it comes around the back of my head then she lets it roll down to the back of my neck. Holding my lips to hers. When she finally pulls back she gives me a half grin, "So, since it is our last night in New York, should we just stay here in bed or do you want to go do something?"

I roll back towards her, "I would love to go out and do something. Maybe go clubbing. Or hit a bar. I don't really care, as long as I am with you I know I will have a good time."

She grins wickedly at me again before rolling over and checking the clock, "It is 8. If we start getting ready now we can get some dinner somewhere then I think I know of a few spots we can hit."

I nod at her as I stretch my legs and toes out towards the foot of the bed, "Sounds good. Let's do this."

Daija rolls back towards me again as she lets her hand roam down my bare back and across my ass. I look up into her eyes and see that same heat that I have seen for two days. She gives me a small side grin before slapping my ass then rolling off her side of the bed.

I watch her move from the bed to her clothes that she has just thrown over to the side. She is fucking stunning. I watch the muscles in her back moving as they make the black and grey gothic pin up model on her back dance and sway with her movements.

She throws her clothes to the side then turns back to me, "Do you have anything I can borrow? I have worn the same clothes for 3 days."

I sit up, letting the sheet pool around my waist, then point towards my suitcase, "You have been naked for two days but sure babe. Grab whatever you want."

She nods at me then turns and struts her fine ass towards my suitcase. She is different and this is weird as shit.

I don't get clingy.

I don't get fixated.

But the fact that I never seem to know what she is going to do or say, it keeps me on my toes. I am used to just hooking

380

up, getting my fix then moving on. But Daija has found a way to kinda creep under my skin.

In a good way, I think.

I swing my legs over the side of the bed and start to make my way towards her. I slowly come to a halt though when she turns around holding Hestia in her hand.

Her eyes start running over my face then she starts to smile, "Someone is a pretty die hard fan don't you think?"

I laugh nervously as I make my way to her, grabbing the aged cherub faced mask from her hand, "Yeah. I guess I am."

Daija smiles again as she shakes her head and turns back to the suitcase. She finds a pair of jeans and a tshirt, quickly pulling them both on. I rifle through and find some clothes as well, tucking the mask deep into my suitcase below everything else.

That was fucking close.

A half hour later we are walking hand in hand to a nearby Italian restaurant. Daija grins widely at the hostess like it is her own fucking restaurant. The hostess greets us like we are regulars, smiling widely back at us as we are quickly seated and order some drinks and food.

I look nervously back up at her, "So. We haven't really talked about much of anything deeper than what our hobbies are. What do you do for a living?"

Daija takes a large drink of her long island, "Currently nothing. I am just kinda bumming around. Ever since I finished school, all I have really wanted to do is just travel. Which I have done. Extensively. But I am kinda getting to the point where I don't like to travel by myself.

"Don't get me wrong, I love meeting new people. Obviously. But re-introducing myself at every single place I go is getting really old really fucking fast."

I nod back at her then look towards my hands on the table, "So what are you going to do after you are done traveling? Is there something you are wanting to do with your time?"

She tilts her head slightly, like she is trying to figure something out, "I don't know. I know it is something I probably should have thought about long before now but I just haven't. I am more of a day by day kinda girl I guess."

I smile at her as I take a drink of my rum and coke, "Yeah, I could basically guess that about you."

She laughs as she flips me off then leans onto the table a bit towards me, "I mean. I could maybe be convinced to slow down my travels. If there was someone wanting to spend more time with me."

I smile back at her, surprised to be feeling the heat that is running up the sides of my neck.

I am not used to being the one that is shy but she does this to me. Every single look she gives me makes me want to run away with her.

I take another sip of my drink, eyeing her the entire time over the rim of my glass.

A moment later our food is sat down in front of us and we begin to eat.

I push some pasta around on my plate, "Well, most of my work appointments are on Friday and Saturday. So you said earlier that we could meet up on Sunday or Monday and that sounds perfect."

She grins as she takes a small bite of her chicken, "I like the sound of that. Where are you going to be? What would be halfway for us?"

I sit my fork down, wiping my mouth with a napkin, "North Carolina. Actually my appointment is in Virginia but I will be staying in North Carolina with my family."

Daija raises an eyebrow at me, "You have family here in the states?"

382

I nod my head back at her, "Yeah. I work with more of a family business. So we spend a lot of time together. Too much time in some aspects."

She laughs back at me, nodding her head, "I get that. I shared a room with my sister when we were in boarding school. Don't get me wrong, I love my sister. But it was a lot. We aren't really into the same things and we didn't really get along the greatest when we were younger so it wasn't the easiest sometimes. Spending all my time with her. Do you have any brothers or sisters?"

I shake my head back at her, taking another bite of food, "No. I mean, maybe. I am not sure. I was adopted by a couple from London when I was an infant. They came to Shanghai and adopted me just a few days after I was born. I don't really know anything about my birth parents so who knows...maybe there are more Mona's running around out there."

Daija laughs, "I don't know if the world could really handle that if we are being honest."

I laugh with her as I continue to eat my pasta. We continue to talk for what feels like forever when the check is brought and dropped off to us. I reach for it and she instantly slaps my hand away.

I laugh loudly as I reach for it again, "Let me get this one. You can get the next."

She shakes her head roughly at me before snatching the ticket from my hand, "Nope. I asked you out. This is on me. Don't even try."

I reach for it again but she moves the ticket far away from me before leaning back in her seat and yelling for the server to come grab her card. I laugh as I huff back in my seat.

I cross my arms over my chest and shake my head at her, "You are going to pay for that."

She smiles innocently back at me before pointing to our now empty dinner plates, "No. I am paying for that."

I roll my eyes at her as I continue to laugh at her insanity. The server brings her card back and she slides it into her wallet then into her back pocket.

She leans forward onto the table, "Are you ready to go or do you want to sit and sulk a bit longer?"

I belt out a laugh as I flip her off yet again. She grins wildly as she stands up and reaches her hand out to me. I take it and let her lead me back out onto the street.

Turning to her, "Hey. Where are we going now?"

She continues to pull me towards the street before throwing her hand up to hail a cab, "Just my favorite place in the entire city!"

I silently let the thought of that run through my head. This could either be very fun or very scary.

She has both sides to her personality so I am a little bit nervous as to how this may go. We climb into the cab that has just stopped in front of us and Daija rattles out an address.

I lean back in the seat as her hand comes to my thigh and she starts to slowly rub small circles with her thumb while she looks out the window at the city flying by. I smile at her hand then lean my head over onto her shoulder.

A few moments later I can feel her lips pressing a kiss onto the top of my head. I smile at the back of the cabbie's head in front of me.

What is this girl doing to me?

I am normally the sarcastic one. I am usually the one making the first move.

But since the day we locked eyes in that pizza place, she has been the alpha in this relationship.

She asked me out.

She gave me her number.

She initiated the sex.

She is the one that has begged for more.

I didn't think that I was a swooner but this woman, she has me rethinking all kinds of stuff about myself.

The cab finally comes to a stop and Daija quickly pays then slides out to the sidewalk. I follow right behind her letting my eyes drift up to a sign that says Henrietta Hudson.

I blink towards her as she turns her face to look at me again, "Where are we?"

She smiles widely as she grasps my hand tightly and starts to pull me towards the front door. As soon as we step inside, I immediately know I am going to love it here.

Between the music, the people, the brick wall that spells 'Built By Dykes' then the wide array of drink choices...I instantly feel at home.

Daija seems to notice the amazement over my face as she puts her mouth close to my ear, "I knew you would love it here."

I nod around the room, taking everything in, "I do. This place is amazing."

I turn and look into her ice blue eyes and she seems ecstatic that I am ecstatic.

I am so fucking screwed.

I thought this was just going to be a fling. Like my normal. I thought that we were going to flirt a little bit, maybe hook up then that be that. But I don't want to stop spending time with this woman.

I want to know everything about her. I want her to know everything about me.

But she can't.

Because of her friend.

The groupie would cause so many different levels of trouble for the band. I feel this heaviness sink into the center of my chest as I realize that this, these few days. This is all we are ever going to be able to have.

I try to shake the thoughts from my head though. I don't want to focus on the negative right now. I just want to enjoy my time with her here and now. I squeeze her hand then start to make my way towards the bar.

A super hot masc bartender leans towards us smiling, "Hey Daija! Who is your friend?"

I feel her dark eyes roam down my body as Daija pulls me in tight to her side, "This is Mona. Mona is mine. Stay away from Mona."

I laugh at the possession she thinks she has over me already. I turn back towards the bartender, "Not sure if you caught it or not but my name is Mona. Nice to meet you."

The bartender laughs back loudly, "Hey Mona. I'm Lina. What can I get you two to drink?"

Daija leans over the bar, "Two rum and cokes."

Lina starts moving around making our drinks as I turn towards Daija, "So, you are on a first name basis around here huh?"

Daija smiles as she moves her lips closer to mine, "Why? Are you jealous?"

I grin widely back at her before pushing my lips into hers. I feel her wrap her arms around my waist as she holds me close to her chest.

This is a very dangerous game I am playing. But I just can't stop myself.

She is amazing.

It would be a lot fucking easier if she wasn't.

Lina taps the bar letting us know our drinks are done. Daija reluctantly pulls her mouth away from mine as I smile then turn to pick up my drink. I nod my head at Lina before taking a deep drink, letting the alcohol take over my inhibitions.

We sit our drinks down at the bar, Lina pulling them towards her to keep prying hands off them. I start to pull Daija towards me as I back out onto the dance floor. I smile as a Chappell Roan song comes over the speakers.

Daija grabs my hand and spins me in a twirl before her then pulls me close, swaying with me to the music.

I watch her eyes finally settle on mine then they turn towards my lips, "I don't want you to go."

I feel a flutter go through my chest as I look her face over before her eyes fall back on mine, "I know. But I have to. It's my job."

Daija nods her head at me, "But that is going to mean I won't see you for at least 4 days. Maybe longer. I know we just met and all but I think...I think I am going to miss you more than you will miss me."

I can see the hesitance and insecurity in her eyes as they bounce back and forth between my own.

That is unexpected.

Which makes me wonder, is she feeling as strongly for me as I am for her? "Daija. I can guarantee you that I will miss you the same if not more. I have really, really enjoyed our time together. You are kinda my jam."

Daija smiles widely, seemingly shocked, "Really?"

I nod back to her, "Really." I push my lips back into hers as her hands come around the back of my head and we just continue to sway to the music.

www.ingramcontent.com/pod-product-compliance
Lightning Source LLC
Chambersburg PA
CBHW010522100726
47903CB00011B/2862